APPLIED BALLARDIANISM

SIMON SELLARS

APPLIED BALLARDIANISM

MEMOIR FROM A PARALLEL UNIVERSE

URBANOMIC

Published in 2018 by

URBANOMIC MEDIA LTD.
THE OLD LEMONADE FACTORY
WINDSOR QUARRY
FALMOUTH TR11 3EX
UNITED KINGDOM

BRITISH LIBRARY CATALOGUING-IN-PUBLICATION DATA

A full catalogue record of this book is available from the British Library

ISBN 978-0-9954550-7-8

This is a work of non-fiction based on unreal events.

Printed and bound in the UK by
TJ International, Padstow

K-Pulp: New Adventures in Theory-Fiction

www.urbanomic.com

For Sarah, Hazel and Marlo

There is no way to tell his story without telling my own. And if his story is really a confession, then so is mine.

— Willard, *Apocalypse Now*

PART I
MACHINES

1

PSYCHIC COMBAT

I can trace my decline. That is one of the bittersweet benefits of survival. I can locate the exact moment in time when I joined the theatre of the unwell. I was a high school dropout, pinballing between dead-end jobs. Once a bright student, I'd squandered my ambition, melting like a fuse under excessive voltage. No one knew why, let alone me. I turned inwards but nothing held my stare. The void was too deep.

I lost sight of myself within an interminable fever dream.

I awoke inside an anomalous world.

Something was waiting, oddly familiar.

Another version of me.

A clone, threatening me with erasure.

I was left with no choice but to spark an internal war. The mission: take out the clone. But the fight would expose me to interdimensional radiation. I became sick with time, unable to distinguish between the past, present and future. What's more, I was unskilled in psychic combat, asking the wrong questions and opening the wrong doors.

The dark matter burned me from inside.

SACRIFICIAL WEAPON

It was the early 90s, the zenith of cyberculture, an incandescent moment when the embryonic internet went nova. The net was wild and untamed, a frontier zone occupied by hackers, digital pirates and online insurgents—a cadre of undesirables romanticised in glossy cyberphile magazines. But in the land of the terminally unhip, it was a different story. Distinguished TV personalities made fools of themselves live on air, asking 'What is internet, anyway?' and struggling to pronounce the '@' symbol. The divide was clear. You were either a fearless cybertrooper storming the gilded gates of tomorrow or a clueless rube snowblind from pixel blizzards.

The net was hyped as a step change in human evolution. One day, thundered the cyberprophets, consciousness would be uploaded to computer mainframes, ditching the body like a booster rocket. The body was dead weight, so much 'meat', and cyber fads like body modification displayed contempt for physical limitations. Swept up in the fervour, I pierced my nose in three places and my tongue in two, but instead of ascension to an enlightened state, all I received was a nasty sinus infection and a speech impediment that lasted for months.

A gaggle of Californian cyberhippies had come to dominate cyberculture, peddling snake oil about digital utopias and the net as 'the new home of mind', but their dull rhetoric, forged from white-male privilege, left me cold. Where was the danger, the excitement, the diversity? My discontent drew me to cyberpunk, the nihilistic science fiction genre that would expunge forever the hippy communes transplanted from the desert to the net. It was a stark corrective to cyberutopianism. In cyberpunk, virtual reality is the new normal. Alienated loners log onto cyberspace via neural interface, their minds conjoined, their bodies lifeless and slack, but when things go bad the nervous system is destroyed and the mind is warped. Sometimes, death is the consequence. It was a worldview I could buy into.

Cyberpunk was a more accurate summation of the era, predicting startling research that exposed a sickness at the heart of our culture. In the wake of the cyberprophets, the global news agency Reuters had released a provocative report on information overload that was beginning to unnerve even the staunchest adherents. It detailed how the sum total of all available information was doubling in increasingly shorter amounts of time—a tsunami of data swamping the mind, streaming uncontrollably from the new overlapping technologies of faxes, mobile phones, modems, internet and online conferencing. Meanwhile, the human cost of assimilating and processing this material was increasing exponentially. The result was 'Information Fatigue Syndrome', a peculiarly 90s phenomenon that atrophied attention spans, shut down the mind and depleted the body. Symptoms included 'hyper-aroused psychological condition', 'paralysis of analytical capacity', 'anxiety and self-doubt', and a capacity for 'foolish decisions and flawed conclusions'. These matched my own situation, for I was nothing if not indolent, and I made an appointment with the doctor to complain about my malaise, which now had a name.

The so-called medical practitioner regarded me with barely concealed contempt as I shrouded my condition in pseudointellectual babble, quoting the Reuters report in a pathetic attempt to make my situation appear more significant than what it was: the torpor of a degenerate slacker. Information Fatigue Syndrome seemed heroic, an unavoidable consequence of serving in the Info War, of sustained immersion within the new cyber dawn of virtual reality and wraparound technology.

'I'm a cyberwarrior,' I told him. 'And my mind is going.'

The doctor rose wearily from his seat and walked to the medicine cabinet. On his desk was a set of golden blades. I supposed they were scalpels of some kind, but in any case medical scenes always made me nervous and paranoid, and the implements induced a rising panic. The blades were alarming, their geometry mystifying. One of the handles resembled a human knuckle, attached to a point so sharp it seemed to disappear into thin air, and I shuddered at the thought of the atrocities that could be committed with this sacrificial weapon.

He returned with an unmarked box of pills. He explained their purpose and gave me instructions for taking them, but the details failed to register, since I was distracted by an attractive middle-aged nurse who'd been observing our interaction. I felt a deep stirring of the loins. She seemed completely *present* in some recondite way, as if I'd always known her.

I left the clinic carrying the box, remembering nothing of the doctor's instructions. I opened it. A small, shiny disc fell into my hand.

It was mauve in colour, engraved with the crude outline of a dove.

3

STILL WORLD

The pills generated monstrous side effects. After ingesting them, I'd fail to remember thoughts I'd had moments before. Sometimes, I'd lose contact with critical childhood memories, even my own name and age, as if entire swathes of my brain had been wiped. This freefall within mindspace would always be accompanied by chaotic spatial disorientation. Walls would fall away, exposing an inky blackness. Floors would vanish, plunging me into a bottomless chasm.

In the precious moments between these apocalyptic hallucinations, I managed to hold down a part-time job in a warehouse on the outskirts of town. The warehouse belonged to a wholesale distributor, which supplied stationery and magazines to a chain of newsagents. My job was to heat-seal ballpoint pens into plastic blister packs. At the rear of the building was a storeroom for remaindered stock. One day, during a tea break, I scavenged it looking for something to read. Tempted by a cache of soft-porn periodicals, my eye was drawn to one cover above all. It featured a seductive young woman, her face flushed by a lurid red filter. Sporting devil horns and a saucy grin, she extended her tongue and winked at the camera. It wasn't a porno rag but an edition of *i-D* magazine, the popular fashion chronicle from the 80s, titled 'The Fear Issue'.

On the cover, arranged around the woman in the largest font, blared the headline for an interview with trash-metal musician Zodiac Mindwarp. Progressively smaller fonts advertised other attractions: an interview with legendary gonzo writer Hunter S. Thompson and a heading that simply screamed 'UFOS!'. Tantalised by this vivid mishmash of faded heroes and hypercurrent fads, I scanned the contents, only to discover an essential field guide to the *future*: an interview with cult author J.G. Ballard, nestled among the back pages.

In the 60s, Ballard had made his name as a science fiction writer, but he was on an elliptical orbit far distant from planets Asimov, Heinlein and Clarke. As a boy, I devoured science fiction but I never read him. He was too far underground. I knew of him through blurbs for his work tucked away in the end-papers of less esoteric novels. I was a simple lad keen on Doc Smith's *Lensmen* series, the sappiest of 'Boy's Own' space operas. What was I to make of works described by shell-shocked copy-writers as 'chill splinters of unreality' and 'the source of a bleak new evil'?

Clearly, for the *i-D* crowd, Ballard was not a drawcard like Mindwarp, for he was nowhere to be found on the cover—rejected by the devil-babe. Admittedly it was weird to find him there at all, this peripheral figure from my youthful forays into science fiction, mixing it with *i-D*'s bleeding-edge cast of 'Greboes, Waifs, Wannabes, Heavy Metal Christians, Sloane Rebels and Nocturnal Vampettes'. Yet he was more punk, more post-punk, more cyberpunk than any of them.

The interview was incendiary, showcasing his deadly ability to pinpoint the moment when technology strafes the uncanny valley. He predicted the exact form social media would assume when it came to be invented twenty years into the future, including the psychological fallout from heavy use.

'Deregulation of the airwaves,' he said, 'will lead to a deregulation of the imagination. People will start screening themselves. They will become their own TV programs.'

He reframed television as a cyborg extension of the mind's eye.

'The TV tube is like a flagging piece of nervous tissue—you need a bigger and bigger charge to get a kick out of it.'

As a bonus, he explained the theme of suburban breakdown that defines his work.

'Suburban life is a big strain. To maintain this fabric of absolute normality requires powerful repressive forces.'

Perversely, the suburbs animated him. He was fascinated by their existential stasis. For Ballard, dystopia is a world where everyone is completely sane, where deviance is factored out of the architecture, bleached from the landscape, siphoned off from human behaviour—the very terms and conditions of suburbia. In the suburbs, he reckons, time is empty. There is no past, no future, just enervation, an eternal present where nothing ever changes, a desert of the soul where memories are replaced by the fictional overlays of consumer goods and the future is always out of reach.

'The future is going to be boring,' he announced. 'The suburbanisation of the planet will continue, and the suburbanisation of the soul will follow soon after.'

But he also identified a radical counterpoint, a mutant strain. Perhaps a node of resistance. The tedium of the suburbs 'forces the imagination into new areas. I mean, one's got to get up in the morning thinking of a deviant act, merely to make certain of one's freedom.'

'It needn't be much,' he clarified. Nothing so dramatic as, say, bombing the local video store or beating up homeless immigrants, although characters in his later works would do just that.

'Kicking the dog will do.'

Accompanying the interview, a monochrome photo portrait enhanced the casual brutality of Ballard's truth bomb. The grain of the photo was large, gritty—as if it might scuff the surrounding pages.

Ballard wears a black shirt. He gazes off camera. Framing his left eye with his thumb and forefinger, he pulls the cheek down to reveal a wide, opaque pupil.

I was struck by that visual cryptogram and tried to crack its code. What exactly *was* he signalling? I never knew until years later, when, reading the local newspaper, the answer came at last, surfacing from a random connection before announcing its presence with alien electricity, like an unpredictable spark jagging from a Tesla coil. On the front page, there was a lurid account of a brawl at Sydney Airport between rival biker gangs who'd found themselves on the same flight. Neither was happy about being cooped up in a claustrophobic tube with sworn enemies, and when the plane landed a brutal skirmish erupted. One biker was sacrificed, his head caved in by a metal crowd-control bollard, wielded like an axe by his assailant, as desperate parents shielded their children's eyes from his brains splattered across the sleek terminal floor. How would these hapless holidaymakers cope with the savage event that shattered the unreality of their jet-lagged state?

According to a witness, the simmering tension aboard the plane was ignited when a biker sent a bizarre message to a rival: he 'put his hand to his face and with his finger pulled down his cheek to reveal the pink of his eye'. When I read that detail, it hit me like a captive bolt to a cow's head, for suddenly I *knew*. In the photo portrait, Ballard sends the exact same signal, an arcane intimation that his fictional experiments were aiming for an identical result: the awakening, by any means possible, of complacent suburban stiffs from their dreamlike existence.

However, at the time I encountered *i-D* I was yet to receive that insight. It would not be revealed to me until a far-future time, when events had taken their full course and I was in thrall to a black force beyond reason.

For the moment, all I could do was read and re-read the interview, staring into Ballard's open eye, inadvertently setting the wheels in motion, willing the Ballardian signal to overpower the broadcast feed that had colonised my brain, as if he were a pirate of the airwaves splicing pornographic material into prime-time television.

4

KICK THE DOG

When my shift ended, I commenced the long walk home from the warehouse. The weather was hot and dusty, and the deadly rays from the high sun reflected off the vicious concrete expanses that passed for public space. The intense glare, blotting out all life and colour, was like an atomic flash, and I half-expected my shadow to be seared onto the bleak pavement. I passed unpeopled industrial areas, hissing power substations and cavernous breaker yards. I negotiated the back streets that surrounded an infestation of dun-coloured brick factoryettes, each small and foreboding, with iron-bar windows, like private torture dens rented out to the highest bidder to do whatever they liked behind closed doors. On the road I discovered a slaughtered chicken, spattered with blood and innards. Its belly had been ripped open, presumably by a large knife, and someone had drawn a chalk circle around the miserable carcass. The bird's feathers were stuck to the chalk with blood and appeared to be deliberately arranged to form inscrutable symbols—a satanic suburban crop circle.

I passed three battered baby carriages discarded on a nature strip. The wheels and handles were missing and the hoods were in shreds, as if the demented prams had been chewed up and spat out. While people worldwide pondered the modern-day mystery of why sneakers were being suspended by the laces over suburban power lines, here these occult prams materialised instead, their origin and purpose unknown. Indeed, that trio of unholy carriages was not the first I'd discovered (they always appeared in threes), and I wondered whether their former occupants had been herded behind the heavy steel doors of those evil factoryettes to suffer the fate of the miserable chicken.

I reached my house. I knew that I was utterly trapped, that I would suffer the slow burn of suburban death if I didn't take swift action. I opened the front door. The fuses had blown and the power was off. The hallway was pitch black, the darkness hemming me in with the coordinates of madness, as if I was suffering another spatial hallucination from the damned pills. Ballard's peircing eye probed my mind, beckoning me into the mirror world.

I crossed the threshold.

With my senses reeling from the satanic breadcrumbs I'd

followed to find my way home, I decided to risk all and 'kick the dog'. I decided to read *Crash*, Ballard's most notorious novel. After all, those were the days when consuming dangerous literature could be a liberating act. And *Crash* was certainly in the danger zone, a work so depraved it was originally rejected by the publisher's reader, who could only issue a desperate plea: 'This author is beyond psychiatric help. Do not publish.'

With a come-on like that, I was unable to resist.

I became a Ballardian.

5

TECHNOLUST

Crash changed my life by torching everything that came before. It reversed the negativity that engulfed me, channelling it into something new, radical and sensuous. The narrator of this seditious work is called 'James Ballard'. He's a rough copy of the real Ballard, a flawed clone, who infiltrates a group of urban professionals bored with their jobs and their marriages—bored with themselves. They pledge allegiance to Vaughan, a 'hoodlum scientist' who nurtures their darkest desires, promising to recalibrate their android lives in 'a nightmare marriage of sex and technology'.

Vaughan has a master plan. He wants to induce global 'autogeddon', a primitive singularity uniting man and machine 'in a terminal congress of spurting loins and engine coolant'. Tuned in to police radio, his damaged crew descend like vultures upon car accidents and even cause and stage their own, inhaling the atmosphere of trauma like perfume, bearing the scars of numerous accidents as they fuck each other's crash wounds or pleasure themselves while watching crash-test dummies pulverised to oblivion.

When they admit crash-induced pain into their flesh, a hybrid lifeform bursts from its cocoon. The body is indelibly altered and the resultant scars become conduits to a new and more intense sexuality, accelerated by the logic of the car crash and its intimate reshaping of the human form. There can be no return, an insight revealed to 'Ballard' when he takes LSD and drives across the motorway system that defines his world. As the acid trip peaks, he hallucinates that he has become one with the machine, the bones in his arms 'forming a solid coupling with the shift of the steering column', the vibrations from the gears shooting down his legs and spine as if he were 'lying in the transmission tunnel'.

I knew that on some level *Crash*'s cyborg metaphor warned against the outsourcing of bodily functions to technology, but still it turned me on. I couldn't help it. At heart I remained a cyberfetishist, despite my injurious prior flirtation with body modification. I became obsessed with Gabrielle, one of Vaughan's initiates, a disabled woman clad in leg braces. Her physical frame has been reconfigured by her willing participation in numerous crashes, and she proudly displays the unique contours of her scarred hands and deformed knees, radiating a humid fetishistic charge. Ballard's prose isolates her jagged body parts, placing them in geometric conjunctions with leather car seats, disability-enhanced steering wheels and the chromium trim of vehicles. Her movements form a cryptogram of prosthetics, flesh and metal, obliterating the boundaries between woman and machine. Naturally, her callipers and wounds are worshipped by 'Ballard', his hypnotic obsession with them leading ineluctably to the moment when the couple fulfil their technolust. He strokes Gabrielle's leg irons as if admiring the finish on a new car, then fucks the vaginal, crash-borne scar on her thigh, 'irrigating' it with his semen.

In *i-D*, *Crash* is described as 'technoporn', a trashy, gleaming portmanteau word that reflected my soul back to me. When the novel was first published in the 70s, Ballard said it had 'a small intense following—a few psychopaths and amputees—sending me their porno photos'. It was as if it could warp the mind to become attracted to what was once considered repugnant.

Desperate to break free of my inexplicable stupor, I succumbed to *Crash*'s spell. Gabrielle's machinic curves continued to beguile, merging with my ongoing fantasy of the middle-aged nurse, who, having first materialised in the doctor's surgery, had taken up residency in my imagination.

The thought of Gabrielle's shimmering chromium callipers, offset by the blinding white of the nurse's uniform, cleaved my mind in two.

I never recovered.

It was, I suppose, a response to a sort of spiritual affliction—the sickness of no-time.

6

THE SIGN

One night, I drove while under the influence of the pills. I wanted to use them to my advantage for once, hoping their altered reality would replicate *Crash*'s LSD insights. But instead of a rapturous vision of my own union with technology, I experienced only a crippling loss of self. I should've known mass-produced pharmaceuticals would never do. Only an artisanal synthesised high, like the narrator's, could marry me with the machine.

After an hour of reckless driving, I pulled over into a slip road, convinced I would meet my doom if I remained mobile. I could see myself driving off an overpass in a moment of heightened panic and bursting into flames below, or hallucinating a phantom truck surging headlong towards me, forcing me to swerve onto the oncoming lane and into the path of an actual vehicle.

Through the shatterproof glass of the windscreen, I saw a sign scarred with an index of trauma.

Road Deaths in Victoria

1990: 601
1991: 876
1992: 548
1993: ?

I tried to decode this numerical mystery. Why had the stars aligned so catastrophically in 1991? What would 1993's tally be? The sign instilled heavy dread.

Why?

I lived in Melbourne, a blighted place, one of the world's largest exurban conglomerates, machine calibrated for vehicles to move rapidly across long distances. From a young age, I was forced to bathe in that metallic glow, developing a subliminal awareness of the status symbols and hidden meanings embedded in car culture. As a child, I lived in a suburb in the foothills of the Dandenong Ranges. The area was crosshatched by endless freeways perpetually crawling with heavy-duty industrial road trains, military-grade enforcement vehicles and juiced-up, high-speed muscle cars. Service roads scarred the landscape, lined with tyre outlets, truck mechanics and car showrooms. The stench of oil, petrol and rubber coated the air like industrial perfume.

There was a pub wedged into the intersection between the two major freeways, isolated like a remote Pacific island. Beer flowed like water there. There were no footpaths leading to the pub.

The only way to reach it was by car. The only way to leave it was by car. The quickest way to die was by car, drunk at the wheel. On the surrounding roads, there were no pedestrian refuge islands, nowhere walkers could gain respite. Walking? Unheard of. No one walks anywhere in outer-suburban Melbourne, not in an environment designed to wipe us all from the face of the earth.

Staring at the sign, I felt a chill sense of cosmic entrapment, as if I'd imagined parking in that remote slip road many years ago, drawing my body closer to the location until finally it was inhabiting the prediction. Clearly, my childhood had delivered me there, but as soon as I'd formed that thought I'd forgotten it. The realisation that I was once again adrift in mental space was the last straw for my battered psyche and I steeled myself for a return of the terrifying hallucinations, defeated by the medical terror pulsing relentlessly through my bloodstream. Nonetheless, I knew I had to wait it out, to let the horror wash over me in whatever form it might take, no matter the risk to my sanity, so that I might be cleansed as I emerged from the other side.

The sign continued to interrogate my soul.

7

ROADKILL

Growing up in Melbourne, I was subjected to an endless stream of roadkill public safety announcements. We all were. Made by the Transport Accident Commission, these horrific productions warned of the nightmare on our roads and were filled with scenes of carnage, yet I was ashamed to discover that their primal jolt thrilled me to the bone. The TAC staged their cautionary accidents with machine-gun editing, speed-cranked action and hyperfluid camerawork, all trademarks of the film *Mad*

Max, which fourteen years earlier had reinvented the cinematic car crash.

The film's tortured anti-hero is Max Rockatansky, a burnt-out, speed-addicted cop in a decaying, pre-apocalyptic society, where hotted-up cars sanction the murderous impulses of the dehumanised psychos behind the wheel. *Max* captures precisely the seductive, split-second cyborg rhythm of high-octane driving, but what was the TAC's real intent? To manipulate the viewer to climax with state-sanctioned illicit thrills? There can be no other conclusion. The *Max* aesthetic is triggered at the point of impact, the precise moment when we're supposed to solemnly condemn the terror of the roads, to feel the fullest revulsion at the casual violence underpinning our lives. Just as the hyperstylised *Max* implicates us in the total horror of the road crash, seducing us with the undeniable pleasures of speed, so the TAC embraces the total aesthetic experience of the film crash. They are two versions of reality, separated by ideology.

Doubtless the Transport Accident Commission films were designed to evoke the iconic role *Max* plays in the Australian psyche, mimicking the film's stylistic tropes, drawing upon its cultural resonance as a storied symbol of our predilection for vehicular carnage. Yet placed within their shocking, 'naturalistic' context, the *Max*-style impulses generated by the TAC productions are unnaturally disavowed.

Crash sutures the duelling ideologies. The novel embeds Ballard's concept of 'inner space', an alternative mindscape generated when his characters react against totalising systems of control so that 'dream and reality become fused together, each retaining its own distinctive quality and yet in some way assuming the role of its opposite'. He frames this paradox in the simplest terms: 'By an undeniable logic black simultaneously becomes white.'

Inner space is the engine of ambivalence that powers *Crash*, since for all the novel's radical sexuality its side effects are queasy and disturbing, revealing the flipside of Ballard's subversive dream logic. One particular sequence, riven with existential dread, forced me to plot my uneasy childhood, with its normalised backdrop of violence, onto new coordinates.

For many years, the narrator had been 'bludgeoned by billboard harangues and television films of imaginary accidents', the British equivalent of the TAC ads, bequeathing him a 'vague sense of unease that the gruesome climax of my life was being rehearsed years in advance'. He even has a premonition of how he will die: filmed unwittingly for one of these televised psychodramas on a secret road, its location known only by the filmmakers.

One day, he crashes into another car on the motorway and admits his fate: 'After being bombarded endlessly by road-safety propaganda, it was almost a relief to find myself in an actual accident.'

Although I was dimly aware that his rendezvous was a symptom of the inexorable logic driving Vaughan's program of posthumanism, that night I understood only this: white had become black. Under the watch of the ominous sign, the slip road where I'd parked had become the mysterious road upon which 'Ballard' would meet his doom, and I was marked for death simply by having viewed the TAC ads, thrilling guiltily to their superbly crafted *Max* aesthetic, my attraction to technique absorbing me into a hyper-simulated world where there was no escape from the vectors of speed and trauma.

For the historian Graeme Davison, 'the apocalyptic violence of *Mad Max* recalls a moment when Melbourne's roads were truly killing fields'. The sign, with its confronting statistics, begged a return to form. It sent a message: the killing fields had re-opened for business. The sign's single question mark, bolded in a blood-red font, press-ganged us all into a drive towards death, coercing us to beat the record, as if we were powerless to halt the carnage.

Davison is a sober writer, not prone to hyperbole. In fact, *Max*'s director, George Miller, developed the film's script after experiencing two threshold moments. During the global oil crisis of the mid-70s, he read in the paper about frustrated motorists who'd turned feral at a Melbourne petrol station, attacking each other for the last drops of fuel. Later, working as a doctor in Melbourne, he treated numerous road-accident victims and was struck by the nightmarish intensity and frequency of the crashes. For Miller, these events were interconnected, as if the city had been possessed by a malevolent force. In the 70s, drink-driving was horrifyingly common in Melbourne, frequently accompanied by savage aggression. There were so many road deaths, around a thousand every year, that Miller said it was 'as though we are operating under some immutable law of nature. We make funny noises, but none of us really understands what's happening. The USA has its gun culture, we have our car culture.'

Mad Max upholds this view of technological carnage as natural law. After Max's wife and son are slaughtered on the open road by a biker gang, he seeks revenge. He steals the police force's fastest car, a Ford V8 Interceptor, and brutally kills the bikers one by one, running them off the road or chaining them to homemade bombs. Max has been stripped of his humanity, savaged by the ongoing car wars and hopelessly addicted to speed and violence (he's like a kid in a candy store when he first sees the Interceptor). He has become as psychotic as the gang he hunts, and when he walks into police headquarters to retrieve his secret weapon, a clever screen wipe shows the Interceptor instantly driving back out, replacing the broken man from a moment before—as if Max has become the machine. To Melburnians, *Mad Max* is not fiction but a documentary.

As I waited within the confines of my car for the end to arrive, I replayed that screen wipe in my mind.

Melbourne's killing fields... an immutable law... We make apoca-lyptic noises but we'll never understand.

I imagined myself propelled to my death by forces I could not fathom, just like the victim in *Crash* who smashes into the narrator's car and is hurled through the windscreen, striking the bonnet. In that frozen moment, as 'Ballard' watches the man die, a pattern forms on the victim's hand, puffed up 'into a huge blood-blister—the triton signature of my radiator emblem'. This stark incident underscores a key insight of the narrator's acid trip: when incomplete bodies, fractured by the demands of capi-talism, are rebuilt, they're bound together by the signs and sym-bols of banal technology.

And as my disordered mind aligned this with the ciphers of Melbourne's auto-death, I received a personal epiphany. Mill-er's immutable natural law was inextricably linked with my own pathetic death-drive, with the reason I'd been prescribed the accursed pills in the first place. Even before reading *Crash*, I'd been fully primed by *Mad Max* and those nasty road safety ads, so that when Ballard's novel finally revealed its secrets to me, I experienced a mighty temporal shift, the outline of my physical body syncing out of phase with my soul, ontological layers rub-bing together and moving apart again like tectonic plates.

I placed my hands under the dull luminescent glow of the car's dashboard display. They took on a purplish hue, as if I'd photosynthesised the electric light through the skin. I sat there for hours, minutes or seconds, basking in the purple light un-til the car battery had drained and the dashboard glow was no more.

Until my skin was full, head to toe, and I could no longer recognise myself.

8

UNFAMILIAR PLANET

Something snapped inside me that night. I'd glimpsed the operating system that propped up reality. *Crash* exposed shape-shifting narratives in media, advertising and politics, where every version of reality has a negative image, a shadow reality, all part of a synchronous system that keeps us endlessly consuming new promises, new lifestyles, new identities, new tomorrows. Endlessly consuming ourselves. What could be more normalised than the metal skin donned every time we enter a car? What could be more pathetic than a roadrager indulging in reckless pursuit of another vehicle after being held up for a few seconds on the public tarmac? Within inconsequence lurks death, as the philosopher Paul Virilio admits: 'When you invent the ship, you also invent the shipwreck; when you invent the plane you also invent the plane crash; and when you invent electricity, you invent electrocution. Every technology carries its own negativity, which is invented at the same time as technical progress.'

Crash is concerned with the logic of the accident, deploying the mechanism of ambivalence to record a vision of humanity simultaneously enthralled and destroyed by its technological environment. It was an equation that Jean Baudrillard, Virilio's fellow prophet of the apocalypse, understood all too well.

'Is it good or bad?' Baudrillard asks of *Crash*. 'We cannot say. It is simply fascinating, without this fascination implying any kind of value judgment whatsoever. And this is the miracle of *Crash*.'

Naturally I subscribed to the 'miracle' and announced my conversion by quitting my deadbeat job. I also kicked the pills, wanting to meet my demons head on, with the aid of *Crash*, of course, my self-help manual for the post-cyber age.

Driven by a fanaticism I'd never known, I enrolled as a mature-age humanities student at Hartwell University, among Melbourne's less prestigious institutes of higher education but the only one that would have me given my poor marks in school. As my undergraduate years unfurled, besides Ballard, I read little beyond Baudrillard and Virilio, hoping their insights would allow me to make sense of Ballard's ostensible subject matter: the interlocking grid of capitalism, consumerism and social control. At least, that's what I told my tutors. In reality I wanted my philosopher-gurus to jailbreak me into the Ballardian mirror-world.

As it happened, I received high distinctions for most subjects and in due course I was offered a scholarship to commence a PhD. This was thrilling news, affording me the chance to focus completely on an earth-shattering phenomenon: the prescience of Ballardian insight.

Soon after accepting the offer, I witnessed the culmination of a disturbing trend: the gutting of cyberpunk. The process had been initiated by Billy Idol's album *Cyberpunk*, a bland, bleeping electro catastrophe punctuated by cock-rock guitar solos and lyrics awash with appalling cliches (such as a jilted cyborg imploring the object of his desire to 'suck on my love meat'). On the cover, Idol, warped by pixelated green-and-purple washes, looked like a badly rendered character in a low-rent video game, an appropriate metaphor for cyberpunk's fate.

The virus was accelerated by the film *Johnny Mnemonic*, scripted by William Gibson, the most iconic cyberpunk writer. I was eager to see *Mnemonic*, since it featured a version of Information Fatigue Syndrome, the phenomenon I'd hijacked to excuse my earlier malaise. In the film, half the world's population suffers from the Black Shakes, a debilitating condition that attacks the central nervous system, induced by overexposure to information and technology. Equating the concept with my own experience, I felt connected to Big Ideas, cementing the (hardly original) view I'd begun to form: that science fiction was the only accurate representation of the era.

Alas, *Mnemonic* was a cinematic turkey, a lazy hack job. The script was not the problem. Rather, the production gorged on tacky cyber special effects, resulting in a messy, overdriven and incoherent narrative, a fast-paced, explosion-riddled ride through Silicon Valley that killed any point Gibson tried to make. Rubbing salt into the wound, it starred histrionic rappers and overacting rock stars. The sum total was nothing more than a big, dumb video clip, ripe for instantly forgettable consumption by its MTV-primed target audience. Cyberpunk had been killed off at last, no longer the preserve of underground adepts but a margarine substitute available to even the most clueless of popcult magpies.

In contrast to this rapid obsolescence, I valorised Ballard's work as a surpassing of science fiction, a mutated form able to avoid absorption by the media landscape because it actively satirises generic baggage. *Crash* forensically examines our fascination with sexualised violence as entertainment, using the wrap-around ubiquity of car culture as an extreme metaphor. Its aim, said Ballard, was 'to rub the human face in its own vomit, then force it to look in the mirror'. Science fiction is that mirror, but *Crash* is not a science fiction novel.

It is not *Crash* that is science fiction, but the world.

9

QUEENS OF THE CYBER AGE

After a year of heavy immersion in postgraduate research, I flew to Madrid to attend a conference on cyberculture. I then travelled to Liverpool, where I presented on Ballard at a conference on contemporary science fiction. The Madrid event promised an advance screening of *Crash*, David Cronenberg's adaptation of the novel, undeniably thrilling news, although the keynote papers were less enticing, covering hackneyed cyberutopian topics such as 'immersive virtual bodies' and 'the new capabilities of techno-humans'. Thankfully, a shadowy group of hacktivists anchored the proceedings in a mood of heavy realism.

Ten in number, they never revealed their names, a thuggish charisma enhanced by their head-to-toe black paramilitary outfits. I was struck by their compelling presence. They were necessary dirt in the bloodstream, distributing photocopies of their incendiary anti-net manifesto to the bemused crowd and holding impromptu talks outside the lecture halls, corralling anyone who would listen before engaging in stylised fights with the security guards that tried to move them on.

I caught one of their guerrilla lectures. A crippling ennui had stained the new cyber dawn, they announced, and the promised dream of universal access to the net had failed to materialise, replaced by stifling commercialism and a divide between the cyber elite (those with access to the net and the power to control it) and the cyber drones (those lacking the cultural capital to break down the virtual walls). Earlier that year, a prominent cyberprophet had gained ascendancy with a declaration that called for the net to become self-governing in a bid to evade corporate assimilation, but his hippy utopianism disgusted the Balaclava People. They saw his declaration as wholly maladapted to the currents of discontent and dysfunction fraying the edges of cyberculture, because for them the net had already gone bad and its final collapse had to be accelerated from within so that something new could emerge from the debris. The Balaclava People championed an emergent net activism that was multifarious, perpetually in conflict and therefore resistant to all sides of the political equation, and I was attracted to their worldview for much the same reason I was attracted to Ballard: they shone a light on an overlooked fold in the overdetermined map of an overly documented world.

After the first day of the conference, I managed to sneak into the launch party, a hedonistic rave in an abandoned warehouse on Madrid's exurban rim. I could never have gained legitimate entry, since I was not friends with the right theorists, who stalked the space like Kings and Queens of the Cyberverse, acolytes hanging from their coat tails to feed them drugs and sex at regular intervals. The rave boasted sadomasochism as routine entertainment. A back room hosted mass whippings of willing initiates, while in the middle of the dance floor a naked woman reclined on a hospital bed as a stream of revellers danced around her. Her expression was one of perpetual boredom, unchanging even as two shirtless muscle men began to pierce her labia, one gently holding back the folds of skin, the other tenderly pushing a large stainless steel needle through her puckered flesh.

Fermented within that turbocharged sexual atmosphere, polymorphous perversity swept through the crowd like a Mexican wave. Seduced by the pulsating animal heat released by hundreds of thrillseekers, I ended up in a plush hotel bed back in the centre of Madrid with two other party people—a New Zealand woman, Dana, and an Australian man, Brett.

For a few hours the three of us formed a secret society. We were strangers in a strange land, swapping down-under slang and the post-ironic attitude that comes from being shunted away in the former colonies, condemned to watch Asia, Europe and America compete for global cultural dominion. We ended up together because I was attracted to Dana, Brett was attracted to me and Dana was attracted by the idea. But I found the three-in-a-bed scenario too artificial, too clinical, too *expected*. After some perfunctory groping, I bid them farewell and walked back to my *pension*.

The next day, I bumped into Dana as I lined up to enter the conference auditorium.

'We made love,' she said. 'It was Brett's first time with a woman.'

Ahead, a rake-thin man raised his head to the sky and barked loudly for no apparent reason. He sported long dreadlocks and wore a PVC corset under his pinstripe suit jacket. Dana said he was one of the keynote speakers, but I didn't stick around to find out. I didn't even stay to see *Crash*. As I watched the Barking Man, I knew I had to leave. I no longer had the stomach for this serried mass of true believers, all of them harbingers of a chromium-plated Valhalla, all oblivious to the dispiriting libertarianism leaking from cyberculture's rotting hull. Although the Balaclava People had distributed their manifesto to the delegates and continued to rudely crash the presentations, their *ratissages* had little effect. Everything was tainted by the most absurd type of cyber cool, and if you didn't know the codes for entry to that world you were erased from existence, ignored and made to feel like trash.

'Goodbye Dana. I'm sure you and Brett will be very happy together.'

I left the auditorium and gave my conference pass to an indigent man. Expecting money, he scrunched it up and threw it at me in disgust. I was convulsed by a sharp current of anger, furious at his insolence, and curled my hand into a fist, only to let it hang impotently by my side. Madrid was hot and dusty and the sun was blood-red, sieved through a shroud of polluted smog. It put me in mind of *The Texas Chainsaw Massacre* and the film's suggestion that monstrous solar flares were somehow the cause of the revolting human behaviour about to unfold.

I stared at the evil sun, receiving its disturbing signal, waiting to be told what to do next.

THE WAR INSIDE ME

I travelled around Europe for a while, eventually washing up in Amsterdam, where I finally saw *Crash*. It was a confusing experience. Although I deeply admired Cronenberg, the film's soft-porn sheen failed to deliver the metaphysical jolt the novel had given me, and its identification with body modification and the sexual possibilities of the practice left me cold after Madrid.

The camera lingers on every fibre, Cronenberg's hypergrotesque style fetishising bodies modified by the car crash. Scars are heightened and bulbous, like extra limbs. Tattoos are inscribed with ritual significance, markers of a secret society. Vaughan's face and torso form a map of scar tissue, sweat irrigating his physical form like rivers and valleys. In heightening the connection between technology and body modification, Cronenberg paid tribute to *Crash* as cyberculture's foundation stone, yet I felt cheated by what cyberculture had become, by its crass appropriation of that relationship. Where was the resistance, the desire to interrogate the world? All that remained was solipsistic narcissism.

Suitably dejected, I checked into a huge, four-storey hostel, nothing but a holding pen for degenerates. One night in the hostel's cavernous bar, I found myself talking to an American. He was short and stocky, with wiry hair and a permanent five o'clock shadow, and he rubbed me raw with an abrasive arrogance.

'I'm gonna make wads,' he said, spit flying. 'I want dudes to come up to me in the street and ask me questions about life and basketball. I'm gonna change cultures like Plato, like Aristotle, like Kareem Abdul Jabbar, like Woody fucking Allen, philosophical slam dunks coated in a candy shell palatable to the masses.'

'What are you? An actor?'

'*Actor?* I'm a comedian, dropping truth bombs like Newton dropped the apple. So remember the name: *Hollywood Dave.*'

I turned away for respite. The bar was a Hieronymus Bosch hellscape, filled with depraved creatures enslaved to the basest of urges. In every nook and cranny of the barn-like space, packed with two hundred people, revellers were engaged in various stages of fornication, vomiting, fighting, crying, screaming.

I winked at Dave.

'Why don't you do a gig here? I mean, if you really want to start at the bottom.'

The girl across the table giggled and Dave scowled, annoyed to be the butt of the joke. Miraculously, for the first time in ages he fell silent. The girl introduced herself. Her name was Alenka. She was Slovenian. I told her I'd recently visited the Slovenian capital, Ljubljana, becoming lost when I tried to take a bus back to the hostel from the city. The bus driver didn't speak English and I couldn't read the signs. When the bus came to the end of the line, I realised we were in the countryside. It was midnight. I was distressed but the driver pointed to the door, his face blank. He would not speak to me, would not answer my questions, and I could not read what was behind his eyes. I disembarked and headed down the nearest road, not knowing in which direction the city lay. There was no footpath so I had to walk on the edge of the road as a stream of cars filled with sadistic youths sped past, hurling bottles and abuse, making me their target. Somehow, I found my way back after a nerve-shredding two-hour journey.

'Yes, that's us,' Alenka said. 'We don't give a fuck.'

'So, what's your story?'

'Me? I'm an angel. My hair fell out, all of it, when I was five, and all my fingernails. Before, my hair was blonde and straight, but when it grew back—curly and black. The doctors don't know

28

what happened, but I know. I'm an angel. That's the only explanation. My purpose is to help people. That's why I was put here. I'm a guide, but I fell down. It was something I did and they took my power away from me. Made me mortal. Something I did. I was only young. Maybe they know in advance.'

She sounded rueful and vulnerable, although she was probably just drunk, and Hollywood Dave leaned in to kiss her, entranced, I suppose, by her magic and loss, powerful exotica that salved his own pain at being a failed comedian. To my great surprise she reciprocated, leaving me to sit there in silence, watching the cut-price bacchanal unspool in that vast pit of spilled beer and pustulent dreams.

The spark between Alenka and Dave soon turned hot and heavy, so I decamped and tried to sleep in a room filled with four bunk beds, all containing loudly fornicating couples. I was sick of Europe, sick of its dayglo colours, fluro orange and lime green, the height of fashion that season. Amsterdam was filled with beautiful people and it depressed me. I was sick with a serious stomach problem, an old health worry that had resurfaced, distending my belly and crippling me with intense abdominal cramps. I felt like a freak. Sex was now the last thing on my mind but it was everywhere in every combination, mirroring *Crash*, where men fuck men, women fuck men, women fuck women and everyone fucks machines.

In the early days, when I'd first read Ballard's novel, I might have acquiesced. By this time, all I wanted to do was shed my skin, release my diseased and spasming internal organs, and swan-dive into the void.

WEIRD DREAM

The remaining days passed slowly, like swimming in molasses, until I caught the ferry to London, where I attended two Ballard events. At a bookshop in Charing Cross, I watched the man himself read excerpts from *Cocaine Nights*, his just-released novel about a typically Ballardian sub-cult: a hermetic group of pleasure seekers in the Spanish coastal resort of Estrella de Mar. Conversing in his cultured tones, he was a theatrical presence, sipping wine throughout, his shoulder-length silver hair swept from his face, his large frame filling out a blue shirt, red tie and check sports jacket.

During the Q&A afterwards, he held court on a range of provocative topics. He spoke with ironic affection about the 'loveable psychopaths' that populate his work and the role they play in exposing the sordid underside of mediatised dreams. He discussed gated communities and the attendant phenomena of 'total security' and private militias, suggesting that suburbia was becoming a low-level warzone. He analysed the banning in London of Cronenberg's *Crash* (one critic called it 'beyond the bounds of depravity'), concluding that 'we're policing ourselves and that's the ultimate police state, where people are terrified of challenge'. Afterwards, he signed my copies of his books and posed for a photo, although I was so nervous I took it in a hurry before he had time to compose himself. That is why my one and only photo of J.G. Ballard features his face half obscured by his hand reaching up to fix his hair. No matter what I did, I could never get a clear bead on him.

The following week, he appeared on stage at the British Film Institute to talk about Cronenberg. During question time, I raised my hand and was selected. In the novel, the narrator's wife Catherine thinks Vaughan is just a pervert, although she is corrected by 'Ballard', who argues that Vaughan is more interested in technology than sex. In the film the reverse is true: it's not technology that Cronenberg is interested in but sex. The proof is in the film's hyperreal fixation on body modification and the sexual possibilities of the practice.

I wanted to ask Ballard what he thought about that reversal of focus, but my heart was in my mouth from nerves and all that came out was incoherent verbiage, the breathless tonal spew of an imbecile. I could not get to the point and droned on and on, stumbling over my words. I grew mortified when the audience began to laugh, although Ballard, ever the gentleman, pretended that he hadn't heard the question before moving onto the next person.

For an anguished moment, I felt as though I was in an anxiety dream, the kind that generates panicky scenarios where no matter how many times you call a phone number it fails to connect, or you just miss a bus, or you can't make it to an exam on time.

Ballard was always just out of reach, the connection fading at the last frustrating instant.

12

SPATIAL DYSLEXIA

Depressed by my failure to connect with the man who was effectively my spiritual advisor, I immersed myself in London's night life. At a jungle club in Brixton, I purchased two ecstasy pills from a weasel-faced dealer who wore a Burberry cap. I thought he said they were called 'doves' and I felt my body shudder as I recalled my former medication with its crude avian engraving. But although the pills were mauve, a dislocating detail, their surfaces were smooth and blank.

I swallowed them and fell into a mental black hole. The walls of the club receded and the music echoed distantly. I couldn't feel my body, exactly what I wanted because I loathed it and its useless failings, and at that point I was closer to the body-as-meat-and-mind-over-all cybercultists than I'd dared imagine. I hated dancing at the best of times, but given my spatial disarray there was no chance of that happening. I slumped into a corner and watched the people around me.

The club was a shrine to jungle, the new and thrilling dance music that was unlike anything anyone had ever known. The five-level building was a rabbit warren of different dance floors. Each floor contained different beats per minute. Different dancers. Different pills. Different ideals for living. Yet all were linked in a cornucopia of psychic energy, a multiverse of mind-bending complexity. The DJs were incredibly exciting, their hyperfast hands wired to the decks. The music was phenomenal. Clattering metallic percussion that injured the brain. Skittering, liquid-synthetic bass lines that ruptured the bowels. Helter-skelter rhythms pierced with dialogue samples from *Blade Runner*, *Predator*, *Robocop* and *The Terminator*. It was a sci-fi dystopian soundscape, an alien planet brought to life by artificial mind-states and synthetic beats.

As I sat there, catatonic but incredibly present, plugged into the pulsating grid that enveloped me, I realised I'd forgotten my humiliation at the feet of Ballard. In fact I was greatly looking forward to giving my paper in Liverpool, if only to prove to myself a point about my argument—that science fiction was dead in any kind of prophetic sense. The club was proof. Science fiction had become the air we breathed and Ballard had predicted it.

An attractive girl sat by my side. She wore full clubbing regalia, complete with purple wig, and I was startled to realise it was Alenka, although when I spoke her name she corrected me.

'Hush now, love. Everyone calls me *Lamb*.'

'But how did you get here? You're in Amsterdam.'

She didn't answer. She just kept staring at me and stroking my hand. The ecstasy was so overwhelming, I panicked about how disembodied I felt. I was about to tell her that I couldn't feel my body, that I wanted to go downstairs, leave the club and return to the hotel, but how could I when I had no legs?

She spoke first, but not in the broken English I was used to hearing from her in Amsterdam. In Brixton, she was word perfect.

'I know, my love. You can't feel your body. You want to go downstairs, leave the club and return to the hotel, but how can you when you have no legs?'

I must have looked like I was about to pass out because she whispered in my ear.

'*Come back to the music. Everything's alright. Resurface. Tune into the signal.*'

A vicious breakbeat ruptured the sound system.

'You might recognise that,' she said.

I began to babble.

'You're an angel... my guide... your hair fell out, all of it, when you were five... what's under the wig... curly and black... let me see your fingernails.'

I noticed a badge pinned to the breast of her blue vinyl jacket. In a black font on a cream-and-blue background, beneath a mysterious coat of arms, it read: NSK. LONDON VELEPOSLANIŠTVO.

'The badge. What does it mean?'

No answer.

I closed my eyes and leaned in to kiss her, desperate to experience the sublime pleasure Hollywood Dave must've felt when he'd entered her heavenly inner sanctum. I opened my eyes but Lamb had disappeared. The music de-escalated, and as it slowed to a treacle pace so did my heart, until it seemed like there were ten seconds between each beat and I thought I would die on the spot.

Then the music sped up, along with my entire mechanism. My body was electrified, coursing with adrenalin.

I'd been cured, it seemed.

Just like that.

13

THIS ALIEN EARTH

The Liverpool conference was supposed to stimulate debate about the value of science fiction in the contemporary world, but I knew it would attract a battery of academics forming a palisade of tedious theory that would repel any investigations of my own. To my disgust, a phalanx of hardcore science fiction fanboys also turned up, armed with an embarrassing devotion to space opera and little green men from Mars. The academics had political boundaries to patrol and ideological agendas to serve. Fine, they were a known quantity. But the fanboys were devoutly uninterested in science fiction's radical function and treated the conference as if it were a role-playing convention, arriving in *Star Trek* and *Star Wars* outfits, in stark contrast to the art-terrorist chic of the Balaclava People, which I'd suddenly become nostalgic for. The odds were stacked against me. All I had was Ballard, the cult author, and a series of trite observations about his prescience that barely did him justice.

My presentation was a disaster. I thought I'd be able to effortlessly produce a startling hybrid of theory-fiction, like Baudrillard and Virilio, but I simply wasn't talented enough in either theory or fiction. All that emerged was tortuous, meaningless phraseology crudely shoehorned into an incoherent framework. At the expense of deploying rigorous academic analysis, I screened advertisements and other popcult artefacts, intending to highlight Ballard's contention that true science fiction is the language of the everyday, secure in the belief that I was charismatic and talented enough to hold it all together. Swaddled within this slow dive, this epic descent into obscurity, lost among its spiralling, messy intricacies, I became black-dogged by the most pathetic of psychological untruths: the addled delusion of creative genius. Yet I was powerless to apply the brakes.

'Science fiction is dead,' I announced to the audience, 'stripped of its capacity to predict the future.'

How did I know? Because I'd seen it on TV. To prove the point, I screened an advertisement made by Telstra, the Australian telecommunications conglomerate. A man is led into a room containing banks of TVs, watching in amazement as the wonders of advanced telecommunications are demonstrated on the monitors: fibre-optic cables, satellite communications, modems. Awestruck, he exclaims: 'This was all science fiction not so long ago.'

I regaled the audience with the benefit of my insight.

'Since science fiction is now a report from the coalface of the media landscape, the air we reflexively breathe, we need new tools to combat the colonisation of our psyches. What better weapon than *Crash*? To record the uncanny present, the novel appropriates science fiction's base tropes: estrangement, cognitive dissonance, inversion of reality. For example, when the narrator's wife Catherine has sex with Vaughan in his vehicle as it enters a car wash, refracted light from the soapy windows covers their bodies with luminescent hues, "like two semi-metallic human beings of the distant future making love in a chromium bower".

'Yet *Crash* defies categorisation. As far as Ballard was concerned, he'd abandoned science fiction in the late 60s when his experimental novel *The Atrocity Exhibition* was published, but he didn't "have any substitute terminology to offer for what I actually write". All he could suggest was that "for some years I have been trying to show the present from an unusual angle". As a result, Baudrillardian simulacra become ripe for inscription with brand-new auratic powers. In *Crash*, science-fictional tropes transform the narrative into a subversive agenda, the negative value seeping in and invading the commercialised, conventionalised shell.'

Auratic powers. Negative value. Conventionalised shell.

What did any of it mean? The audience didn't know. I didn't know. It was simply words smashed together, an artless stab at significance. I pushed on regardless, trying to sound mysterious, as if I were a techno-shaman able to hotwire the zeitgeist with a sagacity unavailable to mere mortals.

'Today,' I droned on, oblivious to my impending doom, 'global events are couched in the logic of dreams, mediated by cinematic, visual language. Angles and fields of vision are alternated, transmitted via textual pans and zooms, a multi-televisual universe.'

In the audience, a woman (Princess Leia) winced. Behind her, Captain Kirk snored. Under blinding stage lights, my arguments evaporated into vaporous tentacles of nothing. I withdrew into a deep inner space and blanked out the external world.

Time passed.

I don't know how long.

Eventually, my voice took shape around me.

'Recently, I watched a concert by the Rolling Stones live on TV. They were playing in some huge, impersonal stadium when suddenly Mick Jagger caught a glimpse of himself on the Sony Jumbotron high above the stage. For the first time he could see what the audience saw when they watched him: a hyperactive stick-figure engaging in the most ludicrous pratfalls. For an instant his craggy face rippled and stained with confusion, like a twig dropped in cement, as if the image of himself was not what he'd imagined he was projecting to the world, but like a true

36

professional he recovered swiftly, the cement-face reforming as if nothing had happened. He pranced off to the other side of the stage and never went near the Jumbotron again.

'I changed channels. On *The Oprah Winfrey Show*, Oprah was contemplating her existence, debating the true nature of her mediated reality. She looked lost, in a daze, talking to herself and ignoring the audience. In a strangely uncomfortable moment, she discussed her life as a mega-celebrity and how it had warped her sense of self. She referred to her televisual persona as the "Oprah-Oprah Thing" and marked it as distinct from her real self, asking the audience: "Why would you confuse *it* with *me?*" No one answered. Her acolytes were as stunned as she was.

'After an extended period of silence, she changed the subject, dissecting some mindless piece of celebrity gossip that had recently made the news, desperate to remove herself as quickly as possible from whatever satanic psychological force she'd just uncovered, nuking it with trivialities. I was struck by these megastars and their confrontations with their virtual doppelgangers. They treated their media clones with extreme suspicion, as if the doubles could somehow trick them and their audiences, as if the clones *could take their place* and no one, not even themselves, would know.'

I watched a group of people fleeing the auditorium. Among them was a well-known scholar, a superstar in the small academic cult that had begun to form around Ballard. He looked over his shoulder at me with disgust and I was overcome by a razor-sharp anxiety attack, his pure disdain for my work exposing my ego like nerves at the root of a diseased tooth.

Wait... don't leave... there's more...

But he was gone.

I considered making an exit stage left, to stalk him, to plead with him to stay, but I decided to tough it out for reasons I didn't fully understand.

'Ballard foresaw the metaphysical affliction that blighted the working lives of Jagger and Winfrey. In 1962, operating as a radical science fiction writer, he announced: "The only truly alien planet is Earth." In the brave new dawn of mass advertising and mass communications that had detonated in the 60s, Ballard claimed the psychological subconscious, or "inner space", was becoming a more compelling subject for science fiction than the genre's traditional arena of outer space.

'Turbocharged by this insight, he joined forces with Michael Moorcock to lead the British New Wave of Science Fiction. As the movement's figurehead, Ballard composed a series of experimental, non-linear and highly interiorised short stories that addressed the schismatic psychosocial effects of mass media. Collected as *The Atrocity Exhibition*, these established his reputation as a dark magus, a writer able to face the most extreme aspects of our culture and divine a hidden logic within the chaos. With their film-script layout, absence of linking narration and collaged formal quality, the *Atrocity* stories were an imaginative response to the alien terms and conditions imposed by the media landscape.

'The central character is a psychiatrist suffering a nervous breakdown. He's referred to by different names, all beginning with "T"—Travis, Traven, Talbot, Trabert. This shifting identity reflects his fractured personality, an affliction generated from exposure to pop culture and mass media, and each chapter functions as a retelling of that breakdown, filtered through different angles and perspectives, sieved through his multiple identities until there is no solid grounding anywhere for "reality" to find purchase.'

I barrelled on, lost within the sonic vortex of my voice, as if I were listening to someone else, someone without fear, my thoughts welling up from somewhere nameless, disconnected from my terrified brain.

'Throughout the 60s, politicians like Ronald Reagan became expert in the use of advertising tactics to sell their dubious messages, while TV screens were saturated with coverage of John F. Kennedy's assassination, the Vietnam War and Marilyn Monroe's death. All were shrouded in conspiracy and multiple retellings. One shooter or two? Legal war or illegal bloodbath? Overdose or suicide? Blanket coverage of these events, in between mind-numbing commercials and vacuous sitcoms, blunted the effect. Horror and empathy were replaced by spectacle and ambivalence, heralding what Ballard calls the "most terrifying casualty of the century: the death of affect"—the loss of feeling and emotion in the face of tragic events. For the first time, the world was enveloped within a schizophrenic buzz of media fictions that touched, reordered and reshaped even the most intimate details of everyday life. *Atrocity* revealed the fragmentation of consciousness and the overlay of numerous realities and identities that ordinary people experienced from that first toxic blast, irradiated from ground-zero exposure to what we now understand as mass media.

'*Atrocity* examines the ceaseless flow of media imagery and asks what happens on the subconscious level when we watch disparate TV images in rapid succession: actors making love in a soap opera, followed by documentary footage of a child dying of disease, followed by a mindless ad for car insurance, followed by the beheading of a hostage in some guerrilla war, followed by an ad for luxury apartments, followed by a news report of a tsunami sweeping away an entire town. Ballard compares the process to the act of dreaming. Just as the sleeping brain weaves together fantastical narratives from the memories of random events, so too the waking mind must knit together narratives from the new overlay of media fictions it encounters.

'If configured correctly, Ballard argues, the new narrative becomes a type of survival tactic. "The most prudent and effective method of dealing with the world around us," he says, "is to assume that it is a complete fiction—conversely, the one small node of reality left to us is inside our own heads." If misconfigured, of course, psychosis ensues, a precipice that Winfrey and Jagger almost stumbled over when they stopped just short of allowing media simulations to replace reality—indeed, to replace *themselves*.'

I paused. Given the temper of the crowd, what I was about to say next might start a riot.

'In the face of this cultural tidal wave, what is science fiction? Does it matter anymore? Does the genre *matter?* What possible purpose could be served by marking its boundaries if the only alien planet is Earth? Forget outer space. It doesn't exist. Inner space is a vast new cosmos about which we know little, if anything. Reality has haemorrhaged uncontrollably, rendering genre policing a pointless pursuit, the preserve of those unwilling or unable to confront the fluidity of a phenomenon that threatens to erase us at the same time as it promises to liberate. By contrast, *Crash* and *The Atrocity Exhibition* confirm that we *all* speak science fiction and that questions regarding the health of the genre are best left to fanboy networks and the precepts found in *Star Wars* and the like.'

A volley of catcalls erupted from the audience, drowning me out. A shrill voice cut through, loudest of all.

'WANKER!'

What did these people expect to hear? If only I'd presented on the iconography of Mr Spock's ears. Morons. I remembered an old Ballard interview. Typical science fiction fans, he said, are 'a collection of very unintelligent people, almost illiterate', with 'no interest whatever in the serious and interesting possibilities of science fiction'. Locked into an ultra-conservative view of the genre, especially the juvenile fixation on outer space, they would always hobble its potential to shine a light on the present.

I was bolstered by the master's command.

To hell with it. I won't let these nerds get the better of me.

I filled my lungs with air and yelled back.

'For the rest of us, there is WORK TO DO!'

14

PARALIPSIS

After the conference, I was an empty shell. Despite the revolutionary zeal with which I'd approached *Crash*, despite how it had transformed my thinking, I knew my thesis could not progress. Yes, there was work to do, as I'd promised the audience, but deep down I knew I was not the man to undertake it. The glorious high from my rebellious confrontation with the Liverpool crowd had dissipated into abject self-loathing and a deep internal wound had begun to fester. Rocked back on my heels by this intellectual crash, I became lost trying to plot my route back to the hotel and found myself in a side street near Liverpool Cathedral. It was dark and I couldn't see much. I heard a swift 'whoosh'—how I imagined a samurai sword would sound when sliced through the air. Behind me, a young man was swinging a long bike chain above his head. He possessed an abnormal dress sense, sort of a mashup between Dickensian street urchin and modern youth. He wore a hoodie *and* a top hat, dayglo trainers *and* baggy plus-fours, and his weapon glinted menacingly under the street lights.

'Hear that sound?' he hissed, whipping the chain through the air, centimetres from my skull. 'That's the sound of you: *dead.*'

I hurried ahead and stumbled into a busy main street, losing him in the crowd. I remembered a strange theory I'd read online about a Liverpool street, one of the super-virulent urban legends that the internet had allowed to proliferate. Apparently, the street was a portal to an alternate reality, a present-day version of Liverpool yet different in vital details. On a paranormal web forum, a variety of witnesses had testified that they'd seen this portal manifest before their very eyes. Even upstanding citizens such as pilots, doctors and police officers had come forward. A fuzzy discharge would ripple the air, they said, dissipating to reveal people going about their everyday business. Yet these people were dressed in anachronistic clothing, entering shops that no longer existed or that had never existed. After a few minutes, so it went, the scene would fade and normality would return, occluding the alternate reality like an overlay of mist.

Although I couldn't recall the name of the street, I wondered whether I'd stumbled onto it. Was the chain-wielding thug part of the same phenomenon? Obviously, the witnesses had taken leave of their senses. I suppose even pilots, cops and doctors can lose their grip on reality from time to time. Whatever the case, the implications were grim. Say for argument's sake there was an actual portal to a parallel dimension. Everyone that saw it spoke only of the materialisation of a peaceful street scene. Not me. I was almost beheaded. Say the theory was nonsense. In that case, I'd been in Liverpool just over a day and already I was attracting steampunk street toughs. The message was crystal clear.

I didn't belong there, not in *either* reality.

It was that obvious, that simple.

15

MOB RULE

I escaped Liverpool, resuming my death march around Europe's hedonistic backpacker circuit, but the effort drained me completely as I trudged from hostel to hostel, bar to bar, hookup to hook-up. In a halfhearted attempt to reset my mind and follow some vague mental compass, I unmoored myself from the party scene and caught the ferry from southern Spain to Tangier, hot on the trail of 'Interzone', the setting for William S. Burroughs' novel *Naked Lunch*. Interzone is a dark realm of the imagination, a drug-induced parallel universe where the novel's 'William Lee' hides after shooting his wife. Somewhat reminiscent of Ballardian inner space, Interzone is suspended between dreams and reality, a surreal environment awash with interspecies sex (between aliens and humans, no less), bizarre terrorist groups and rogue doctors trafficking in human flesh and black-market narcotics.

Interzone was based on Tangier during the period when it was partitioned between France, Spain and Britain from 1923 to 1956. Declared an 'international zone', Tangier was a hybrid city beyond laws and regulations, notorious for unrestricted trade in drugs, smuggling, sex and espionage. It wasn't the promise of vice that attracted me but the very idea of the place, its reason for being. Interzone, this nebulous state, was immensely attractive to the sort of blurred, in-between man I had become, a dilettante scholar neither here nor there.

However, my enquiries annoyed the locals. Near the train station I was stalked by a gang of moody, malnourished youths who did not appreciate my enquiries as to the whereabouts of Dr Benway, *Naked Lunch*'s sadistic antagonist. When I dived into a taxi to escape, they ran to their car and followed. As we drove deeper into the labyrinthine casbah, I realised I would be lost if I didn't make a move, since the taxi driver showed no sign of stopping or slowing, even after we'd escaped the angry mob. I had no idea what his intentions were—he would not speak to me or answer my questions. I repeated the name of my hostel but we drove further away in silence as the meter ticked over. Desperate, like a cornered animal, I took a deep breath, opened the door and jumped from the moving vehicle. I landed on a grass verge, but the only injury I sustained was a bruised elbow. The taxi sped away without stopping, as if I'd never been inside it.

Somehow I found my way back to the hostel, but I was too wired to sleep. I sat on the bed in the dark, listening to the sounds of the street, syncing my thoughts to the rhythmic hum emanating from the high-voltage distribution box grafted to the powerlines outside the window.

16

SEE YOURSELF GOING BY

The next day I wandered the streets before settling at a cafe atop a high cliff overlooking the Atlantic Ocean. The vast expanse of water, dotted with sluggish cargo ships, generated an immensely peaceful scene and I sat there drinking glass after glass of mint tea, apparently the only customer around. After two hours, I felt pangs of hunger and consumed a garden salad. Only later did I learn that it was unwise to eat food washed under Moroccan tap water, given the parlous state of the country's sewage system. An hour after the meal, I became violently ill with unbelievable stomach cramps. I managed to return to the hostel, crawling the last few metres, and collapsed onto the bed. I was delirious and hyperventilating, dripping with sweat, and suffered a severe disorder of perception in which I appeared to take leave of my own body.

First, the bed began to shake. Then, the clothes I'd discarded at the foot of the bed began to whirl around in the air, as if caught in a mini-tornado. Finally, I began to fly around the room (although my actual body remained inert down below). I crashed into the wardrobe, then bounced upwards, becoming wedged in the angle between two walls. Disengaged from my physical self, observing my diseased mortal shell from above,

I could see that the cracks were showing, that my PhD was nothing more than a set of rusted and broken callipers for a crippled mind. My mode of enquiry was scattershot, attempting to weave too many popcult reference points into an inexpert attempt to pitch Ballard as a hero for the times. Why couldn't I write about him with clarity? Why was it all so messy and diffuse?

The madness was unrelenting. It was the sickest I have ever felt, and by the time the illusion had evaporated and I'd returned to Earth I was a wasted and defeated creature, albeit gifted with true insight. Although I was intellectually out of my depth, I knew in the cleansing torture of my food poisoning that if I could only reveal the mechanism by which *The Atrocity Exhibition* worked then I would solve the puzzle, since it had become quite apparent that, even supplanting *Crash*, *Atrocity* was the urtext, a volume that worked in truly mysterious ways.

In *Atrocity*, fragments of stories contain the informational density and complexity of much longer pieces and can even subvert and rewrite themselves. One chapter, 'The Death Module', comprises a disjunctive series of impressions rather than the standard chain of linked paragraphs. It is a bricolage of snapshots from the media landscape, giving the impression of a viewer changing TV channels every few seconds. Texturally, the sections are very brief, yet culturally they represent a super-dense compaction of meaning. Ballard dubbed such paragraphs 'condensed novels', borrowing the term from Borges, and in that form they appear throughout *Atrocity*, retrofitting nominal literary devices to become portals to past and future works, even to parallel worlds that explode the main narrative.

In the critical chapter 'Why I Want to Fuck Ronald Reagan', Ballard analyses the media image of Reagan, the Governor of California at the time and a former actor who sold personal style over political action. Reagan's homely, TV-salesman body language and voice masked his reactionary politics, an elemental deceit that Ballard reflects across the chapter. Seven 'condensed novels' are preceded by seven apparently unrelated subheadings, yet if the reader stitches these subheadings together a full sentence is revealed, a substratum that cuts against the grain of Reagan's public image in the dominant narrative, calling out the disturbing undercurrents that powered his political career.

'The motion picture studies of Reagan,' the excavated sentence reveals, 'created a unique ontology of violence and disaster.'

As this black magic preyed on my diseased mind, I imagined a matrix of overlapping time tracks, a hypertext of such complexity that it seemed to hold the key to Ballard's entire output. Not only were the paragraphs themselves dense with meaning, they also supported the weight of Ballard's entire oeuvre, including novels and stories he'd already written and those that were yet to come. For example, the subheading that introduced one condensed novel, 'The Concentration City', was also the title of a short story published thirteen years *before*. The subheading that presided over another, 'The 60-Minute Zoom', would become the title of a story published seven years *later*.

How many portals were available?

How many parallel universes?

Zones within zones?

Where did the Ballardian multiverse begin and end?

In trying to parse this cosmic mechanism, it was as if I were the hapless man in M.C. Escher's famous lithograph, *Belvedere*. Escher renders the eponymous building as a three-storey architecture of uncanny dimensions, its interior folding into its exterior at regular intervals. Sitting on a bench outside, the man stares thoughtfully at a cube built to the same specifications as the structure. At his feet lies a diagram from which the cube seems to have been built, or perhaps both diagram and cube have been constructed to explain the impossible building, which has always existed. Next to the man, an anguished prisoner pokes his head through the bars of a dungeon at the base of the belvedere. Perhaps he'd tried to decode the mystery and was driven mad by the task, locked away for his own safety. Perhaps the man in the dungeon was me.

Although I had seen the past, present and future of the Ballardian universe, this was useless knowledge, for what could I do with it? Analysing *Atrocity* was like dissecting a hologram. When a hologram is cut in half, the cross section reveals the same information as the hologram in its entirety, as in genetic sequencing where the divided cell contains the entire code that allows a clone to be made. Holographic information can be dissected this way infinitely—just keep cutting the cross section.

In *Atrocity*, information encoded in one part contains information that explains the whole. Yet the more I attempted to track and contain these connections, the more his entire body of work dispersed until in the end I had nothing.

There was nothing.

I was nothing.

17

DISMAL JARGON

I recovered from the illness and flew home, but there would be no respite. I walked straight into a burst of friendly fire delivered by my PhD supervisor, Anthony, who gave me a copy of the journal *Science-Fiction Studies* in which Ballard had been interviewed. I read it eagerly, only to discover a broadside aimed squarely at the dominant theoretical fad of the 90s: postmodernism, an intellectual fraud, according to Ballard, 'elaborated by people with not an idea in their bones'.

As the standard bearers for my critical review of his work, I'd championed Baudrillard and Virilio. In Liverpool I'd even tried to emulate their opaque, futuristic style, yet Ballard spared no bile for the sort of pseudointellectual I aspired to become, launching a blistering attack on the lumpen mass of cybertheorists that were using him, and other science fiction writers, to make sense of the postmodern condition. Ballard excluded Baudrillard from the carnage, it must be noted, stating that he admired his writing greatly, reserving his ire for those who tried to be Ba(udri)llardian. Instead, he denounced postmodernism as a sad, desperate and directionless trifle promulgated by 'an over-professionalised academia with nowhere to take its girlfriend for a bottle of wine and a dance'. He ended his rude missive with a desperate plea: 'You are killing us! Stay your hand! Leave us be! But I fear you are trapped inside your dismal jargon.'

Like a model paranoiac, I believed Ballard's global 'you' to be directed squarely at me as I recalled the 'dismal jargon' that had emanated from my lips in Liverpool.

Auratic power.

Negative value.

Conventionalised shell.

I entered a deep depression, mortified that my chosen analytical model was the subject of so much derision—not only from fanboys but from Ballard himself.

This uncomfortable truth pierced my brain like a prison shiv, wreaking maximum damage in the crudest possible fashion.

18

THRESHOLD MOMENT

That night, I drove to the summit of Arthur's Seat, a hill on the Mornington Peninsula overlooking Port Philip Bay. I was accompanied by Alyssa, an on-again-off-again girlfriend. I had no real purpose in mind other than to go for a drive, to clear my mind, to try to work out how to get my life back on track. At the top of Arthur's Seat, we parked in the lookout area, taking in the magnificent view across the bay towards the You Yangs mountain range.

After half an hour, my forehead began to throb softly. The sensation was odd yet pleasurable, like a rubber band stretching beneath the skin. I was filled with a micro-dose of excitement, as if I was about to greet a loved one for the first time in years, and became fixated on the horizon at a point just beyond the You Yangs. I heard a neutral voice inside my mind, weirdly genderless, echoing distantly.

Something will happen over there.

Instantly, four bright orange orbs appeared in the sky over the mountains, arranged in a quarter circle. After a few minutes they reformed into a cross, then a square, then a triangle trailing a single orb. Periodically, they would 'switch off' and reappear in another part of the horizon, many kilometres away, zigzagging across the sky at impossible speeds. A group of strangers were at the lookout. They all saw the display. One woman dissolved into tears, repeating the same question over and over.

'What is it? What is it?'

We shared an electric feeling, beyond the limits of understanding. It was a threshold moment. I surveilled the orbs through the pay telescope. Up close, they looked like fireballs, all swirling, angry energy, each with a ring of red around the middle. It wasn't a natural phenomenon. The orbs were intelligent, their formations saturated with purpose. Then without warning, they switched off, vanishing forever. We were tired and wanted to go home, and as we drove away we watched the group of strangers. They were rooted to the spot like waxwork dummies, mouths agape, still transfixed by the experience.

The wind was incredible, and coming down off Arthur's Seat our car was buffeted. As we turned into the Nepean Highway, we entered a dense patch of fog. The fog was unnaturally still, despite the wind, and as we drove through it my throat and chest became constricted. I felt cold and clammy, and caught my face in the rear-view mirror. In the reflection, I suffered a dislocating visual hallucination. I thought I could see a doctor's surgery behind my face, not the car's familiar interior. A white-clad nurse was visible for a micro-instant, before disappearing to the side. I could see my eyes: they were wide and startled, inflected with animal fear, and I had difficulty breathing. I was on the verge of telling Alyssa about it when she spoke first.

'I know, love. You want to breathe but how can you when your throat is so tight and your chest is killing you?'

I stared at her.

'What did you say?'

'I said, *I can't breathe*. My chest is killing me and my throat is really tight.'

'Same here,' I replied, but I was beginning to doubt everything around me. I returned to the mirror. The car's interior had been reinstated. Now, it was clear. I was at fault, not Alyssa. My brain was broken.

We arrived at her house. The drive had taken longer than expected, so in the morning we retraced the route at the same speed. It took 15 minutes. We'd lost half an hour that night, victims of missing time.

A few days later, we were in bed. Alyssa looked troubled. She said there were three scars at the base of my spine, like incision marks, arranged in a triangle. She said she'd never noticed them before and I was positive I'd never had an operation there, but I checked with my parents.

'An accident from when I was little?'

'No. What scars?'

I'd read plenty of books about UFOs and was more than a little paranoid about the combination of scars and missing time, although the thought of alien abduction was too ridiculous to entertain. I was interested in the subject of UFOlogy not solely because of the obvious science fictional connections but also because it was such a compelling psychological phenomenon. Regardless of arguments about the provenance of anomalous sky objects, why were so many people reporting sightings worldwide? The 90s was a hotbed for UFO activity. Was it a mass psychosis? Was it the decade when popular culture had reached such saturation that mediated dreams were bleeding out into the skies? Nonetheless, to satisfy my deep curiosity about the incident, I searched the phone book and found the number for the local UFO hotline. I rang and explained the sighting and its aftermath. The operator, as calmly as if he were a plumber describing a malfunctioning toilet, said it wasn't extraterrestrials that had scarred me but 'psychic witches'—evil cultists who enslaved their victims with mind control.

He told me about his 'holographic' theory of the universe, returning me to Tangier and my sickness-inflected *Atrocity* theory. Reality is a hologram, he said, and every now and then certain parts become broken and need repairing. He said the orange orbs were 'bleeding through' into reality, courtesy of a kink in the holographic system that mind-control cultists could somehow exploit. I was livid with rage and couldn't believe he was fuelling my fear. Why couldn't he tell me the orbs were a weather formation or hot-air balloons? He continued to question me, asking whether I'd associated with any unsavoury types at university who might have had cause to mess with my head, but I couldn't understand his nonsense and became most concerned when I realised how much it was costing me to listen to it. The hotline charged three dollars per minute and I'd been on the phone for 40 minutes. I hung up and tried to forget everything that had happened, but the effort was wasted.

In the following weeks, my research was entirely derailed into musings on the UFO phenomenon, and in due course Alyssa stopped seeing me altogether. We were never a serious item, but she distanced herself completely, refusing to answer my calls. She'd accepted a version of the reality we'd experienced, believing the orbs were nothing more than Chinese lanterns released into the sky by pranksters and the scars relics of a long-forgotten childhood surgery, but she couldn't handle how it had affected me. I'd allowed my research to crumble, and with my scholarship almost exhausted I was nowhere near completing my PhD.

With crushing inevitability, I withdrew my candidacy and Alyssa withdrew from me, for I was dead inside.

No thought, no feeling, no life.

And now completely delusional.

19

SUB-BALLARDIAN

Throughout my postgraduate years, I'd eked out a meagre living as a sessional tutor in the Centre for Comparative Cultural Studies at Hartwell University, but after quitting my PhD there was no more work. I signed on for unemployment benefits and wasted my days drinking, clubbing and writing sub-Ballardian fiction, since I was still in thrall to Ballard's benign influence yet no longer had recourse to an academic structure that could exorcise it. Let me be clear. These fictionalised excretions could hardly be called 'stories', more exactly stream-of-consciousness drivel that poached superficially Ballardian elements and molested them like a teenager bursting blackheads.

At the core of these efforts was a narrator who engaged in bestiality on freeway median strips, watched by bored passengers in onrushing motor vehicles while UFOs patrolled the skies. Indeed, my sighting was becoming a real problem, an obsession that would not abate. I seized any available chance to tell friends, even strangers, about the orange orbs. I would draw them on napkins, drink mats, tissues, scratching out the formation over and over. That insidious quarter circle was significant somehow, the shape of it, and I could not drive it from my mind, like the man in the film *Close Encounters of the Third Kind,* who cannot explain why he is obsessed with the shape of the Devil's Tower in Wyoming where an alien starship eventually lands.

Anthony thought I was deranged. Instead of giving papers on Ballard at important cultural studies conferences around the world, I'd chosen to read my demented fictional leavings at minor spoken-word events in Melbourne where they were met with embarrassed silence every single time. On and on it went, as if I was possessed, unable to stop despite the crushing uselessness of my efforts. Taking leave of the academy was just the beginning. Abandoning my senses was the logical extent.

The millennium came and went, and in the wilderness years that followed, as I decompressed from academia and attempted to regroup, I found myself inexplicably returning to the cyber elements of sadomasochism. For some reason, it had entered my head that I desperately needed to publish an anthology of science fiction stories about alternate sexualities.

I suppose it was a combination of factors that drove me to that point, namely my delusions of grandeur, my UFO obsession and my still-smouldering desire to defeat the worst excesses of cyberculture, since I was convinced I could colonise the future-human terrain that *Crash* inhabits.

What a feeble plan. What an embarrassment to Ballard.

Yet the impulse remained.

20

KILL THE HEAD

Seeking seed money for the anthology, I found myself in the front room of a fetish brothel along with my co-publisher, a poetaster named Davis. We were waiting for a decrepit madame to emerge from the back room. We could hear her torturing someone, a high-flying businessman we later learned, for we saw him as he skulked out of the building and subsequently identified him from a newspaper story that featured his corporate mugshot. We sat on Madame's black-vinyl couch like two turnips fallen from the truck, hoping we could persuade her to funnel some of her sordid profits into the production of our anthology. The subject matter, we were certain, would delight her.

A seven-foot-tall butler-gimp served us tea and biscuits. He walked on his hands and knees, the tray resting on his back in a delicate balancing act as his huge pot belly touched the ground like an overfed Labrador retriever. Sporting a shaven head, he must have been in his 60s and was clad only in PVC underpants and a spiked dog collar. Stopping at our knees, he remained silent as we gingerly lifted our cups from this human Lazy Susan.

Eventually, Madame completed her duties and joined us in the parlour. She wore a blood-red corset and pink garters. Although she was quite elderly, I was surprised to discover she was very beautiful. She took one look at us, squares in sneakers, jeans and band T-shirts, and shook her head.

'No. I am afraid I cannot help you.'

She clapped her wizened hands with surprising force for her bird-like frame, causing us to flinch in our seats.

'Boris! See these gentlemen to the door.'

The giant, fat human retriever sprang from his resting position by our feet, the tray on his back clattering to the ground as he uncoiled to a standing position. He pointed soundlessly at the front door. Once again, I had misread the codes for entry into this shadowy underworld.

'It's okay,' I whispered to Davis as we beat an ignominious retreat. 'My mother has some money.'

To my eternal shame, I persuaded my poor mother to fund the anthology, although I was careful to conceal the exact details. She thought it was a PhD project and didn't even know I'd left university, unaware she was bankrolling a volume of such depravity that the printer removed the company name from the inside cover at the eleventh hour, mortified at the content and unwilling to be associated with it in any way, since the book detailed every perversion, and then some, in lurid fantastical prose written by contributors responding to the call for submissions we had placed in underground zines. I myself was later to disown it, losing my nerve and burning what I thought were all remaining copies to spare my family embarrassment, although a few escaped onto eBay, released by some mysterious person, where they sat as unloved, unnoticed and unsold as they had been at the time of publication (the book was far from a success, with sales so disappointing it was as if it had been boycotted).

Although cyberculture had dissipated, sadomasochism remained the popcult flavour of the times, used as window dressing in films, TV and advertising, and it fuelled a delirium from which I never emerged. These were my people, or so I thought. In graphic detail, in words and artwork, the anthology featured stories about sex with aliens, alienating sex, sex with clones, sex with artificial humans, confused sex, violent sex, sex with inanimate objects, sex with hallucinations, images, colours. As editor, I composed the introduction as if it were a manifesto for living, promising the book would reveal a secret society of gender-bending, alt.sex cyber-warriors, a brave new world of sexually recombinant adepts telepathically communicating with high-tech aliens on a hyperstimulated orgasmic plane of existence. If anything, I had only succeeded in herding an enervated crew of misfit writers united solely by their failure in the real world to connect emotionally, spiritually or sexually with any other human being.

I contributed yet another sub-Ballardian blackhead to the anthology, since I was still so delusional as to believe the stream of rejections I had received from real publishers was due to their failure to recognise my talent (after leaving university, I'd been consistently knocked back for philosophy essays, film and book reviews, fiction, poetry—the lot). Naturally, self-publishing would exact sweet revenge, but this time, instead of aping Ballard, I turned his methods against him, channelling my frustration with the repetitiveness of his later novels, especially *Cocaine Nights*, which seemed to repeat themes and motifs from his previous work at the expense of new ideas.

I massaged that stupid rage and idiot energy into the story like a two-bit parlour whore, producing a cheap cut-and-paste job smuggled inside a straight medical documentary. Online, I'd found a doctor's report about a patient undergoing voluntary penile enhancement. I simply reproduced the text wholesale, substituting the patient's name with 'Ballard'. This type of surgery, I reasoned, was an appropriate metaphor for Ballard's supposedly waning narrative powers and his (in my mind) desperate attempts to rejuvenate them.

I'd copied the idea from his own 'surgical fiction' series, which included the stories 'Mae West's Reduction Mammoplasty', 'Princess Margaret's Facelift', 'Queen Elizabeth's Rhinoplasty' and 'Jane Fonda's Augmentation Mammoplasty'. Ballard lifts whole passages from medical textbooks, changing nothing but the patients' names, which he replaces with those of the respective celebrity figure, the ultra-realism of this method forcing a confrontation between the reader and the forensic detail of hyper-celebrity bodies immensely familiar from the media landscape.

For Ballard, a celebrity's face, mediated via the close-up lens of a TV or movie camera, is as intimate as a map of our immediate urban neighbourhood. It becomes a virtual 'landscape' that we can remake and remodel with the power of the imagination, enabled by the metaphor of plastic surgery and emboldened by a new 'stick-to-the-skin' relationship to images forced upon us by mass media's wraparound ubiquity.

But despite the brilliance of Ballard's technique, I was unable to acknowledge it and could only steal, misappropriate and parody it. In the postscript to the story, I even had the temerity to suggest that I and my depraved literary cohorts could pick up the baton he had so 'evidently' dropped, since I believed that by turning his own method onto him I was free to destroy his relevance and thus his importance to my thinking. But what is parody in its purest form if not an obsessive-compulsive desire to render inert an aspect of a person that has caused annoyance or has sparked a painful moment of self-revelation in the mind of the 'accuser'? Why not simply ignore that aspect, turn the other cheek? The parodic tormenter cannot, and the obsession smoulders until the object of derision is tamed, imprisoned and ultimately inhabited.

I was disgusted to realise that my attempts to 'kill my father' in this useless experiment bore the stench of the horrific film *Silence of the Lambs*, which incarnates the extremities of such compulsion in the serial killer Buffalo Bill, who mocks his female victims in a subterranean prison before slaughtering them, flaying them and wearing their skins as the ultimate prize. Yet while the killer wears the skin, the victim's soul remains forever elusive, something Bill realises as it dawns upon him that he will never, no matter how many women he slays, become a woman himself—a transformation that remains his secret desire. The film's extreme psychological force painfully underscored my disastrous attempts to divine the essence of Ballard's work through academic assessment, then fictive imitation, then inarticulate rage.

With sick force, I was reminded that each phase of this escape plan had failed spectacularly, miring me deeper in the thick mud of depression.

21

PATHOGEN

My anthology of alien sex failed to find an audience but succeeded in destroying my friendship with Davis. To drum up sales, we took the show on the road, coaxing a few of the more outré contributors to give spoken-word renditions of their stories. As master of ceremonies, Davis inhabited a series of characters marked by outlandish costumery, spurred on by my demands for more controversy, more extreme states of being. His personas included an insane astronaut wearing a nappy, and a deviant monk sporting a robe studded with bloodied baby dolls and brown-stained dildos.

One night, at an after-party, Davis snapped when I criticised him for not pushing his performance far enough. I wanted him to provoke the crowd, to start a fight, but he was growing tired of all that. He saw himself as a poet, a pure artist who had no need for crass circus tricks. Bolstered by his own self-importance and his repulsion at my unsound methods, he punched me in the face before drunkenly stumbling out onto the street, still wearing his astro-nappy. I never saw him again.

Someone I did see a lot more of was Catherine, a friend of a friend. I'd met her a few times before but we'd only exchanged brief pleasantries. Nonetheless, I was having vivid dreams about her. In fact, I'd dreamed the same dream three nights in a row. I would be standing outside a building at night, part of a large crowd milling about. Catherine would appear from nowhere.

'Hello,' she would say. 'Remember me?'

Then we would start talking, but I could never remember the details. Then the dream would end. Three nights in a row. Always the same.

The after-party was held in a bar in a large warehouse. The fire alarm went off and the manager hustled us outside. I stood among a large group of people. A woman emerged from the crowd. It was Catherine.

'Hello. Remember me?'

I froze, stunned by the dreamworld bleeding into reality, embarrassed by my nocturnal attraction to her.

She stared at me.

'What is it? Your face is pale.'

'It's nothing. Good to see you, Catherine.'

I watched the crowd return to the bar.

'False alarm. Let's go inside. I need a drink.'

Catherine was striking, with shoulder-length brown hair and high cheekbones. She was interested in critical theory and philosophy, and we shared an appreciation for Baudrillard and Virilio. She had never read Ballard, although I managed to stimulate her interest in his work (I was careful to emphasise the Baudrillardian and Virilian correspondences).

We started seeing each other, but six months in, after the initial sexual and intellectual spark had died, she began to keep me at arm's length. She was emerging from the ashes of a long-term relationship and her heart, I knew, still lay with the other man. I suspected she was seeing him on the side, which caused me to want her even more.

Previously, I'd had semi-serious relationships with women

but they were never intense. This was different. I'm not sure how it happened, but I became utterly consumed by her, for Catherine entering my life was nothing less than an invasion, a viral takeover. Or rather, Catherine entering my body was a pathogen that consumed me from within, a flesh-eating disease that, once given licence to feed, could never be quelled.

PART II
ZONES

22

DEEP ASSIGNMENTS

J.G. Ballard's best-known novel is the semi-autobiographical *Empire of the Sun*. It tracks the adventures of an English boy, Jim Graham, who lives in Shanghai with his expatriate parents and survives the Japanese occupation of the city during the Second World War. *Empire* is drawn from Ballard's own life. Born in Shanghai, he lived in the International Settlement there, a zone within a zone. Shanghai, lawless and decadent, wasn't like the rest of China, and the International Settlement, full of sheltered expats erecting a simulacrum of England in the colonies, was nothing like Shanghai. Then the war came, Japan invaded Shanghai and the Ballards were interned in Lunghua, a civilian camp. Lunghua was another Interzone, another nested reality—a zone within a zone within a zone. During the occupation, Ballard witnessed horrors that would never fade. Public stranglings in the city square. Chinese soldiers beheaded in the street. Coolies beaten to death. Bodies floating in canals. He roamed abandoned houses and derelict streets, and the apocalyptic scent of death would later warp his fiction, forming a lightbox of imagery cloned in story after story.

The ripples from that autobiographical shockwave refused to dissipate. In 1987, when Steven Spielberg turned *Empire* into a big-budget motion picture, he shot it partly in the studios at Shepperton, the Surrey town where Ballard lived. When the film was released, Ballard speculated about his subconscious motives for moving there thirty years previously. Had he done so knowing that one day he would write a novel about his Shanghai childhood and watch it come to life in these studios?

'Deep assignments run through all our lives,' he concluded. 'There are no coincidences.'

Deep assignments.

Soon, I would understand the devastating implications of that occult phrase. I would learn how everything is deeply connected in ways the conscious mind cannot possibly fathom.

23

BENDING TIME

Despite the uneasy, compromised nature of our union, within a year Catherine and I found ourselves living together in Japan. She had landed a job teaching English in Osaka and I had followed to eke out a living as her assistant. I performed menial chores such as typing up tests and researching classroom topics in return for a modest stipend from the school. Outside of work, I tried to make sense of my environment. I embarked on long, aimless walks around Osaka, allowing myself to feel as displaced as possible. Knowing little of the Japanese language, I survived on instinct, drifting from moment to moment like a speck of dirt buffeted by the churning bubbles in a glass of Alka Seltzer.

I was fascinated by micro detail, such as the way Osakans stand to the right on escalators while Tokyoites stand to the left. I asked our Japanese friends about this but there was no definitive answer. Some said it was a hangover from the feudal era. Tokyo was dominated by samurai, who preferred to draw their swords to the left, while Osaka was home to merchants, who opened their money bags to the right. I spent hours people-watching, trying to solve such elemental mysteries, and at night I experimented with long camera exposures, trying to catch every fibre in the visual overload that was neon-lit Osaka, bending light through the aperture to bathe Osakans and their city in alien hues.

I hoped that eventually I would bend time as easily as I did streaks of light. But that superpower was beyond me.

I remained depressingly mortal.

24

TOHOKU RISING

One evening, we were watching TV in our small apartment when the living room began to violently shake. I was holding a red soft drink, which jumped from the glass as if it were trying to escape. Trapped in that micro-moment of panic and confusion, the airborne liquid reminded me of the sentient alien blood in the film *The Thing*, which leaps into the air when touched with a red-hot wire. Under stress, I always immediately reached for parallels with film, especially science fiction film, a habit that drove Catherine mad (she regarded it as a total abandonment of reality).

'Earthquake!' she yelled, diving under the kitchen table. I scampered after her as plates and glasses flew from the shelves. Breathless, on all fours, we stared at each other like wild animals. The quake shook the apartment with violent force. My vision was blurred and the floor felt like rubber. Then it was over. We switched on the TV. The news anchor said the quake's epicentre was in the ocean. Catherine translated the report.

'Osaka: all clear. Tokyo: all clear. Tohoku: multiple tidal waves and tsunami alert.'

That night, I couldn't sleep for thinking about my life. The quake was the perfect metaphor for all the draining emotional turmoil passing between myself and Catherine. We knew we were finished. Aside from Catherine's ongoing issues with her previous partner, she'd grown tired of my negativity and chronic self-doubt, of my permanent regret at leaving my thesis unfinished, of the way I could only view life through the lens of science fiction films. Lying immobile beside her in the dark, knowing we would never be intimate again, I resolved to travel to Tohoku. I wanted nothing more than to enter the eye of the storm, to test myself, to travel in an environment where I wasn't relying on the support of a dominant partner who felt utter contempt for me.

I was fascinated by Tohoku, this agricultural region in northern Honshu, and its status as a backwater feared by outsiders. Travel books painted a picture of an insular, depressing place blighted by drab industrial towns and hostile, superstitious locals living resolutely in the past. Occult myths saturate the fabric of the place. According to local legend, chameleon foxes live in the mountains, as big as ponies when seen from the front and as small as a human baby when viewed from behind. These creatures exist side by side with *kappa*, violent water spirits of low intelligence who can be easily tricked, and fertility goddesses with a penchant for marrying horses.

In a way, Tohoku was like Tasmania, the Australian island state. In the 70s, Tasmania was unloved, forgotten and ignored, the butt of jokes about inbreeding and general redneck behaviour. Like Tohoku, it was a 'backwater' where occult tales were common. The hunt for the extinct Tasmanian tiger caused fanatics to lose their minds in order to prove the animal had not vanished, with reports emerging of unnatural creatures hiding in the hills. Tasmania was also Australia's busiest UFO hotspot, with sightings all over the state, and for decades ships and aircraft vanished off the coast with alarming regularity.

One of the most famous disappearances occurred in 1978, when the young pilot Frederick Valentich flew his Cessna from Moorabbin Airport in Melbourne on a routine flight over Bass Strait, the channel separating Tasmania from the mainland. His destination was King Island, a tiny outpost just off Tasmania's northwestern tip, and his last radio transmission was terrifying. With his voice cracked and trembling, he told the control tower that he was being stalked by an enormous UFO. The object, he relayed, was a 'long shape', flying 'at such speed', but then it began to hover right on top of him. An abrasive noise was heard—metal on metal—and the radio went dead. No trace was ever found of Valentich or his plane.

As a boy, I lived near Moorabbin Airport and the story haunted everyone who lived in the area, cementing the perception of Tasmania as a zone of high strangeness surrounded by a cut-price Bermuda triangle. Tasmania's remoteness was romantic to someone as withdrawn as I was then, just as Tohoku appeared to the awkward, directionless adult I'd become. No one rated untouristed Tohoku, but for me, now that it was quake ridden, it seemed deliriously exciting. There was nothing like the possibility inherent in a disaster zone, with its promise of rebooting society from the ruins, for luring someone as disconnected from reality as myself.

The next morning, I quit my dispiriting job as Catherine's research slave. She wasn't happy.

'If you go to Tohoku,' she warned, 'don't bother coming back to me.'

She fell silent, biting her lip in contemplation.

'Actually, we're through,' she said. 'Good luck with your life. You'll need it. All I did was try to help you but you're incapable of receiving love. You're a blank clock, a dead fish. I've never seen anything like it.'

It was the last straw for her. My urge to travel spontaneously to a dangerous place was the final vindication of her suspicions as to my emotional immaturity. Feeling the life-force drain from me, I gathered my few possessions and trudged off to the internet cafe, where I used my dwindling savings to book the bullet train to Aizu-Wakamatsu, a small town in Fukushima prefecture and the gateway to Tohoku.

I slept the night in a capsule hotel and stared at the room, amazed at how the boundaries of my world had suddenly shrunk to minuscule dimensions: two metres long, one metre wide, one metre high. I passed out and when I awoke, hours or minutes later, the power had gone off. I opened my eyes to pitch-black confinement. Groggy from half-sleep, I was convinced the capsule was my coffin.

Trapped within that delusion, as I waited patiently for my air to run out in the final seconds of forever, I tried, unsuccessfully, to make peace with myself for all the mistakes I'd made in my life.

25

DISASTER ZONE

In the morning, I boarded the bullet train. When I arrived at Aizu-Wakamatsu, it was midnight and I became confused about the directions to the hostel. I thought the streets were empty and was astonished when a mob of rake-thin youths emerged from the shadows thrown by the train station. Ten in number, they were dressed head to toe in skintight black outfits, each with long black hair spiked to the heavens like deep-space antennae.

'*Sumimasen*,' I said to their leader. 'Youth hostel?'

He bared his teeth. They'd been sharpened to fangs and I had a foreboding that he was about to lunge forward and bite me. As I stepped back in fright, he snapped his fingers and the gang reached en masse for their hoodies, pulling them over their faces. Walking backwards towards the station, they disappeared into the shadows, merging with the night. As I stumbled away, I had a nasty flashback to the steampunk street thug in Liverpool, to the Tangier youths. Why did I always attract such *weird* violence? The menace was never straightforward, always bizarre and tinged with a palpable sense of unreality.

I was still trying to process the phenomenon when I bumped into an elderly fishmonger returning to his van. He wore white rubber boots, a white smock and white cap, and in the darkness his uniform shone with a heavenly glow, in contrast to the void-black of the gang's outfits. The effect was enhanced when he passed under some street lights and his clothes shone like ice. I was as stunned by this apparition as I had been by the gang.

He pointed to his van.

'Youth hostel?'

'*Hai*. Youth hostel. *Arigato.*'

We drove off. He was quiet the entire time, in contrast to the synthetic voice of the GPS, which guided him all the way.

After ten minutes, we arrived at the hostel. Aizu-Wakamatsu was desolate and bleak. I disembarked and was greeted by the hostel manager, who was full of conversation, but I was tired and made my excuses, collapsing into bed fully clothed. The wind that night was savage, battering the structure of the hostel with a horrendous banshee wail. The next morning I was a wreck.

'Bad night. The wind. No sleep.'

The manager laughed.

'Don't cry. Thirty-four people dead on coast overnight during treacherous typhoon. Tohoku hit by ten typhoons this year. This only your first!'

I panicked at the thought of what I was getting myself into, but I knew I had to push on. My destination was unknown. I wanted to keep moving until I couldn't take it anymore.

26

THE MAN FROM MORIOKA

I left Aizu and kicked around the northern towns for a few days. In Morioka, I visited an *izakaya* and met a local man. He wore an anonymous denim shirt and a ridiculous blow-waved hairstyle, yet somehow radiated a powerful charisma. He told me I looked out of place.

'What do you mean? Because I'm Australian?'

I'd barely seen any other Westerners in Tohoku.

'No, because you are lost.'

He meant spiritually lost. And by spiritually, he wasn't referring to God.

'You have lost your bearings in time and space. You will be dead by age forty, if not careful. Heart attack or something else.'

I asked him how he knew this and he said that he was telepathic, that he came over to talk to me because 'in my mind' I'd asked him to.

'I don't understand.'

'It's okay. You have interest in magic, in alien life. I know this. You have told me, in your mind. Well, let me help you realise potential. I can call UFOs at will. Let me show you.'

For five minutes, he sat stock still, his face a stone mask.

'Look outside.'

I did so. High in the sky, three white blobs appeared from nowhere, not much bigger than stars yet intensely bright. They zigzagged around the atmosphere as if an impossibly powerful laser pointer had been aimed at the heavens.

'Any one of us can use telepathy. Any one of us can call into being UFO with telepathy. This seems madness to Westerners but not to Japanese. In Japan psyche, there is principle of non-verbal communication. Deeply found in every social interaction.

Deeply embedded in language. For example, Japanese word *ishin-den-shin* means "communicating with unspoken meaning, with no voice".'

I looked again. The sky lights had vanished.

'Try to relax,' he said. 'You make too much of everything. Preserve your life. Stop drinking. There is much more to come. Human understanding begins with acceptance. UFOs answer my call and appear when I please. But anyone can do same. I am not unique person. Not many people watch the skies day and night, every day. I am just ordinary man who never gives up. When it happens, I receive soft vibration on my forehead. Throbbing yet pleasurable. Like rubber band. It is very exciting and makes me grateful. It is like lover you have not seen for some time. After it happens, I am filled with knowledge. I can understand concepts I never knew before. UFOs I think are trying to open our minds to something hidden, yet essential to our future.'

I tried to rationalise what I had just seen, even though the light display confirmed what I'd always known to be true.

'I don't know,' I spluttered, 'The idea of telepathy, let alone UFOs—it seems ridiculous.'

For some reason, I thought of Ballard. Despite everything, he refused to leave me and on this occasion even appeared to issue a warning. In his story 'A Question of Re-Entry', a man disappears into the Amazon jungle, where he is worshipped as a god because of his ability to commune with sky spirits. In reality, the man has duped the indigenous people by consulting a logbook of transit times for an orbiting satellite. Just before the satellite passes across the night sky, he gathers the tribe and pretends to summon the spirits. When the satellite flashes overhead, right on cue, his legend is assured.

Had the Man from Morioka pulled the same trick? Were the zigzagging lights simply manmade objects that he knew were due to appear? In the interim period since my own sighting, I'd become a full-blown sceptic and had accepted Alyssa's viewpoint. The formation of orange orbs was just a prank played by kids. Nothing to it. This must be a con, then. It was too similar to the Ballard story. Had I been conned by a fellow Ballardian? That would be the ultimate indignity.

But how could he know I'm a Ballardian? Because he's telepathic.

Such were the mental contortions I put myself through to make sense of my life. I thought of the UFO hotline operator and his insistence that I'd opened my mind to malevolent forces. No doubt, I was a very gullible man. It was a longstanding failing that made me susceptible to even the slightest hint of paranormal activity. My academic training, my supposed ability to think critically and analytically, was of no use and only exacerbated the problem. It convinced me that paranormality could be rigorously catalogued rather than debunked, and I had to fight such temptations, otherwise I was a dead man walking. So what exactly was happening here? If it was a trick with scheduled satellites, or maybe drones under his control, what was the point of it all? Would I be scammed, robbed, hoodwinked into revealing personal details that could be used against me? Brainwashed? Enslaved? What did this person want from me?

'I want nothing from you,' he said, 'except for you to understand that telepathy is not voice in my head. I feel it, it vibrates deep inside my mind, and it is my job to translate it into words, but it is not relying on any type of language.'

I rose from my seat.

'I have to go.'

My head was swimming. I had no desire to enter this hell-world again.

'Please,' said the man. 'When it happens, try to relax. Tune into signal. Understand, it is not language.'

He tapped his temple.

'Remember: I can hear you. Nothing escapes.'
This time, his mouth did not move: *Deep inside your mind*.

27

BESET BY DEMONS OF THE WEST

I caught the night bus back to Tokyo. Tohoku had defeated me. I hadn't even found the ruins I so desperately craved, the devastation and destruction that, perversely, I believed could reanimate my diseased soul. It was as if the tsunami had never arrived. Yet on the TV inside the bus, a news reporter told a different story, portraying a reality that somehow had completely eluded me—or so I thought. She was explaining how small towns in Tohoku had been submerged by tidal waves. Trucks, cars and houses had been overturned by the quake and many lives had been lost in the chaos. But it would be her next observation that dealt the killer blow.

'In the aftermath of the disaster, the Ghosts of Tohoku have been sighted. Reports are streaming in of apparitions wandering the neighbourhoods of small towns. They knock on the doors of random houses, waiting to be invited in for dinner, their skin bloated and green from drowning in the tsunami, their clothes soaking wet. Then, without warning, the dead turn on their heel and walk away, melting into the night, depositing puddles of water on the doorstep. Taxi drivers have been flagged by spectral passengers whose heads have been ripped apart by flying debris from the quake. When the drivers hurry the victims to the hospital for treatment, upon arrival they discover that the victims have vanished at some point on the journey, leaving behind only specks of blood on the upholstery.'

Was the Man from Morioka another Ghost of Tohoku? Although he bore no obvious marks of trauma, our entire conversation had been shrouded in a powerful sense of unreality, a sort of lucid dreaming, as if I was awake but deep within the dreamworld.

When the bus reached Tokyo at 6.30am, I still had no definitive answer and felt tired and confused. I had no place to go and no one to see. Desperately needing to rest, I remembered how Japanese kids often sleep in internet cafes after a big night out. As long as you can pay, you'll be left alone in your tiny cubicle.

Two girls walked past the bus stop, dressed identically in the weirdest get-up I'd ever seen. Of course, outlandish costumes are the norm for a certain strata of Tokyo youth and no one, not even the most decrepit senior citizen, bats an eyelid. Even so, I was amazed. They wore shiny skintight bondage outfits, one red, one black, with what looked like frosting on the shoulders. They sported bizarre masks complete with beaks—one black metal, the other red metal. Completing the look, huge razor-sharp claws were attached to their hands in their respective liveries. They looked like Edward Scissorhands emerging from a meat locker.

I caught their attention.

'*Sumimasen. Internetto?*'

My little weirdos pointed their claws in the direction of the internet cafe. I thanked them and took off. Once there, I paid and slumped into a comfortable leather seat. I looked around the room. On the far side was a cubicle in which someone had been living for some time. There was a suit jacket on a coat hanger over one partition and a pair of shoes by the chair. Two dirty towels were slung over the opposite partition and a tarpaulin had been placed over the top of the cubicle, pinned to the flimsy walls and obscuring the sleeping occupant. Japan has no welfare system for people who lose their jobs and homes, and 'cardboard cities' for the homeless can be found outside many of the major train stations (in Japan, homeless people use large cardboard boxes to sleep in, although I'd never heard of it happening in net cafes).

I drifted off until a loud American voice jerked me awake.

'Buddy. Hey, buddy!'

The voice belonged to a porky man in a cheap suit. He leaned over from the adjacent cubicle, sporting a bowl haircut that in its perfect, shiny roundness was utterly ludicrous, even in this land of shadow gangs, telepathic UFO hunters and scissor girls.

'Where've you been, man?'

'Tohoku.'

'Tohoku! Say, what's that island up there? Fire Island?'

'Never heard of it.'

The American was fit to burst, jumping up and down in his seat.

'Say, they're breeding cyborg dogs up there! Some kind of whacked-out research facility.'

I waited for him to continue but he fell silent, as if he'd drained his brainpower too quickly.

'What are you doing here?' I asked.

'Me? I work in Guam. Own a hotel there. Lotsa Japs in Guam, man. It's like a second home for 'em. I come to Tokyo for business, to drum up trade, promote the hotel. I'm telling ya, if you can tap into the Jap tourist market, you've got it made. Filthy rich in no time.'

When he said 'Guam', I felt a shiver of recognition. Years ago, while researching my thesis, I had come across a reference to this North Pacific island in a passage from *The Atrocity Exhibition*. When T-, at the height of his madness, crawls into a derelict hut in a portside industrial area, there is an extended description of the urban wasteland with its old tyres, beer bottles and burst cement bags. Inexplicably, the passage is interrupted by the intertitle 'Guam in 1947', which I assumed was a signifier of T-'s troubled relationship with the war (he is a former air force pilot), as if the trauma of violent conflict was a permanent sub-stratum of time that could be revealed by rubbing away the top layers of reality.

In 1898, after the Treaty of Paris, Spain ceded Guam to the US, which held it until the Second World War, when the Japanese invaded. Japan occupied Guam for thirty-one months, renaming it Omiyajima ('Great Shrine Island') and forcing the indigenous Chamorro population to submit to Japanese culture. In 1944, the Americans returned with 55,000 troops and retook the island, a conflict that claimed 17,000 Japanese and 5,000 American lives. However, in the postwar era, as my American friend gleefully highlighted, Guam had morphed into a haven for Japanese tourists attracted by this tropical island in their backyard. I asked him how the locals felt about the Japanese today, given that brutal history.

'Yeah, war's pretty fucked up, but it's all about the moolah now. When you're talking millions of dollars pumped into the economy year on year, what's a little genocide between friends?'

He stared at the ceiling.

'Hey, you know Tohoku's fulla ghosts, right?'

'Yes, I know.'

'You like samurai castles?'

'Sure, I guess. I visited the replica castle in Aizu, but it looked like what it was: prefab and fake.'

He gave me a distant look.

'I saw a ghost in a Jap castle once. Little midget ninja dude.'

He held his downturned palms four feet from the ground.

'He was only this big. Jesus! He ran straight at me, waving this huge freaking sword at my knees, but I managed to hurdle him, and he just disappeared. Vanished.'

Silence.

'So, you like Tohoku?'

'I suppose, but I feel a little unusual right now. I've had no sleep, I've been on too many trains and buses, and I just saw two girls dressed like sexy nightmares.'

'Hey, don't sweat it. You don't need trains to travel around Tohoku. You just need *this*.'

The American tapped his temple, like the Man from Morioka had done but on the opposite side. He grabbed my shoulders and fixed me with a level stare. His lips moved but I could no longer hear what he was saying. His voice sounded like he was underwater.

I passed out from fatigue in my little cubicle, and when I awoke the American was gone. Despite his overbearing manner, he'd said something that stayed with me.

You don't need trains to travel around Tohoku.

He'd tapped his head. I'd assumed he was talking about the mind, the imagination. This Ballardian trope, the examination of inner space, placed the Man from Morioka's monologue in deeper perspective. It was as if the two of them were in league. How does the mind negotiate time and space, they seemed to ask. Telepathy on the one side, or imagination on the other? However, I would not allow myself to follow that train of thought and instead wallowed in useless nostalgia for Catherine and my former life.

Thus infected, I visited the discussion forum for the English school that had once employed me. Someone had posted an ad for Rough Planet, the world's largest travel publisher, calling for writing samples from aspiring travel writers. With the memory fresh in my mind of everything I'd seen and experienced in Japan, I wrote up my misadventures and sent them on, accompanied by a timid query: 'Is this the sort of writing you're looking for?'

I'd pitched my essay as an outsider's view of Japan, a cliched angle to be sure and one that did not fill me with hope that it would be accepted, since no matter how I tried to articulate my adventures they sounded like ludicrous pulp fiction. Unable to escape that defeatist mindset, I flew home to Australia; further pursuit of Catherine was futile. A week later, I checked my emails. A Rough Planet editor had answered my call.

'Yes. This is the sort of writing we're looking for.'

I was back in the game.

28

DREAMS OF THE WEAK AND PUNY

My initiation was quick and painless. On the strength of my Tohoku sample, I was contracted by Rough Planet as a freelance guidebook author, working mainly on country-specific publications. It was not that I wanted to be a travel writer as such, but I was addicted to writing and after my ejection from academia I had to find an outlet for it. The impulse was like gas in a bloated stomach that had to be expelled before severe cramp set in. On another level, I suppose I wanted to distance myself as completely as possible from my inglorious failure by selecting a writing career with no connection to the objective truth and machine-tooled language that academic discourse strives for. Yet far from providing an escape from my former life, my travel-writing adventures would be underwritten and stitched together by my Ballardian awareness, allowing me to travel instantaneously through wormholes to any point in inner space.

For my first job, I was dispatched to the Netherlands to cover the main cities: Amsterdam, Utrecht, Den Haag, Rotterdam, Maastricht. I didn't know much about the Dutch, except for a few standard reference points: film and football. I worshipped the science fiction movies Dutch director Paul Verhoeven had made after moving to Hollywood—*Robocop*, *Total Recall* and

Starship Troopers, an unholy triptych that became a touchstone in my undergraduate essays, underpinning my laboured points about resisting the Americanisation of popular culture. I deeply admired how Verhoeven destabilised standard action-film tropes to create a pure, unflinching critique of American values using the tools of Hollywood itself, like the square-jawed jocks in *Starship Troopers*—introduced as all-American heroes by dint of their privileged upbringing and wholesome good looks, in the end they are nothing more than cannon fodder, massacred wholesale by their fearsome alien enemy.

I associated Verhoeven's iconoclasm with the qualities of his homeland, an indomitable national psyche that values freedom of expression above all else. That vital spirit was reflected in the great Dutch football teams of the 70s. These wizards of the pitch deployed a system known as 'Total Football', in which players performed in any position, switching from attack to defence and back again with ease, their mercurial skills making them impossible to mark, counteract or categorise, much like Verhoeven waging his one-man war on Hollywood.

Dutch footballers carved up the opposition with unexpected and beautifully executed moves, expanding the pitch into a fourth dimension, an ability the writer David Winner traces back to the nation's longstanding efforts to rescue and protect its land from the sea. The Netherlands is an artificial world, reclaimed from water over hundreds of years. Surrounded by 2,400 kilometres of dykes, dunes and a complex infrastructure of locks, surge barriers, canals and pumping stations, the nation has performed a topographical sleight of hand, creating a habitable landscape where previously there was only water. In confounding the opposition by playing out of position, in conjuring up space on the pitch where previously there was nothing at all, Total Football expresses the historical propensity of the Dutch to make the most of a restricted topography.

It wasn't long before I ditched the cliched sights I was con-tracted to cover, such as Amsterdam's canals, coffee shops and mindnumbing tulip fields. I'd had my fill of them all those years ago when I was wasting my days with Alenka and Hollywood Dave, and I could easily write about them by drawing upon their ubiquity in popular culture. Instead, I focused my energies on the hidden banks of water beyond the artificial boundaries that perpetually threaten to overwhelm the nation.

Ballard pushed to the surface again, although I hadn't read anything by him in years. After my academic disaster, I could barely stand to see his name in print, let alone read an entire Ballard novel. His work reminded me of everything I was not. It was a painful memory of a future that had never materialised, of a time when I'd fantasised about spearheading a movement that positioned him as the Patron Saint of the Cyber Age, so convinced was I of my ability to interpret his unparalleled ge-nius in a way others could not. What a puny dream. What an embarrassing memory. What an insult to Ballard. Yet I saw the world through his imagination, whether I liked it or not.

I remembered an interview he gave long ago, when he re-vealed the genesis of *The Drowned World*, his novel about a future London submerged in swamps and lagoons after solar radiation melts the polar ice caps and raises the planet's temperature. In the 60s, after arriving in Shepperton, he had been struck by how the town was effectively a marine landscape hidden from view. Shepperton is beneath the flight path to London. From the air, if you look towards the town, a watery landscape is revealed, domi-nated by the Queen Mary reservoir—the centrepiece of a network of smaller reservoirs, canals and settling beds. According to Bal-lard, Shepperton's streets are 'causeways' between the reservoirs, but the vast expanses of water are not discernible at street level, since they're concealed by high dunes and fencing.

'One is aware of a sort of invisible marine world,' he explains, 'of living below the water line. It works on you imaginatively after a while.'

When it worked on him, *The Drowned World* was born, a strange and beautiful novel in which Shepperton's 'submerged' landscape becomes a potent metaphor for a world that has lost its bearings in time and space. Triggered by the inundation of London and the attendant threat to civilisation, the main character, Kerans, becomes obsessed by dreams of the sun and the obliteration of all life within its intense corona. Rather than retreat to the cooler northern hemisphere like everyone else on this climate-changed planet, he follows his solar dreams and heads for the hellish inferno in the south, where it has become too hot for life to survive but where he believes the last vestiges of the old world will be shed forever. Is his quest merely a futile, mythic drive towards death, or does it signify the evolution of a new mode of being? Whatever the case, for Kerans the blasted landscape functions as a 'zone of transit', harbinger of 'a radically new environment, with its own internal landscape and logic, where old categories of thought would merely be an encumbrance'.

Critics often perpetuate the myth that Ballard writes in the classical dystopian mode, mining pessimism, repression and the negativity of a post-industrial age, but such an assertion is a category error. His characters prefer to remain within their 'dystopia' rather than react against it, and if such a union isn't mischaracterised as dystopian it is invariably dismissed as nihilism, a fatal acceptance of the brutality the world has fallen into. But they are not disengaged from the world. They want desperately to change it for the better, even if that means accessing the rate of change via extreme imaginative ends, embracing disaster for the chance it affords to strip away old modes of being and begin again.

Kerans hurtles single-mindedly towards a seam of transcendence that radiates out from Ballard's intense documentation of decay, entropy and ruins, and, in its own way, my impulse to travel to tsunami-wrecked Tohoku was underwritten by his personal odyssey, a fact that I was not fully aware of at the time, given that I was operating as a sheer reflex mechanism, a human insect incapable of rational thought or deed. It was only later, with the full benefit of hindsight, that I could understand exactly what it was that I had been seeking after I'd traded the cyber conference for the Madrid sun. I was dimly reiterating Kerans' solar dreams, subconsciously preparing myself for the day when finally I would be able to face oblivion and begin again. In that sense, Ballard's fictions anticipated everything I felt, everything I did.

They anticipated me.

29

HYPER-CONVENIENCE

Distracted by my remembrance of the future past, I detached from the cities to travel throughout the provinces. In Zeeland, I explored the Delta Project, a vast storm-surge network designed to avoid a repeat of the 1953 North Sea Flood that overwhelmed Zeeland's estuaries, submerging most of the land and killing 2,551 people. The psychological impact of the Netherlands' reclamation from the sea, of living below the water line, recalled Shepperton's sub-aquatic ambience. Walking the N57 motorway perimeter between Noord-Beveland and Schouwen-Duiveland, I photographed this 'invisible marine world', a landscape peppered by surge barriers, artificial islands, moveable inlets and long, thin causeways. The subliminal fear of the embankments breaking again colours every aspect of Dutch life, and in its desire to avert future inundation the Netherlands has become a nation defined by infrastructure, yet an infrastructure so vital, so present, it has become a form of architecture in itself—an overt display of miraculous fortitude.

After wandering Zeeland's motorways, storm networks and wind farms for a week, I reluctantly returned to my Rough Planet schedule, boarding the train to Den Haag, where I stayed at the Hotel Imperial near the Holland Spoors train station, a shabby part of town frequented by men with shifty eyes. The area was in stark contrast to the centre, which radiated a stately air befitting Den Haag's old-world status in art and society (I didn't know much about this quiet city except that it was once home to Vermeer and is the Dutch seat of government). The Imperial was a classically compact, brown-brick Dutch building, barely a few metres wide and sandwiched between two taller buildings. The proprietor handed me the key and gave me instructions in bad English, an unusual detail, since everyone I'd encountered in this country spoke better English than I did. Upon departure, I was to drop the key into a secure container in the hallway. I never saw the proprietor again.

My top-floor room was tiny and musty. The one window overlooked the main street, which was filled with clattering noise at all hours, although mysteriously there didn't seem to be many people about at any particular time. That room struck me as a place where a person utterly defeated by life would go to die. No wonder I'd ended up there.

Deep assignments.

Through the window, I saw a 7-Eleven across the way and wondered whether it sold razor blades. Unlikely. One would need to be more creative in order to liquidate the self in the age of hyper-convenience.

One day, I promised myself, I'd put more effort into finding a solution.

30

SYNC ERROR

The following morning, I ticked off the major sights. The small Mauritshuis museum was a highlight, I suppose, with its collection of Dutch and Flemish art, including Vermeer's *Girl with a Pearl Earring* and Rembrandt's *The Anatomy Lesson of Dr Nicolaes Tulp*. All I really knew about the latter was that it had induced such rapture in the narrator of W.G. Sebald's novel *The Rings of Saturn*, who, standing before it, entered a kind of fugue state as a result of his deep contemplation of the work and imagined the wartime horrors of the past rising to the surface of the immediate present. As I tried to absorb meaning from the painting, I felt less affinity with Sebald's avatar and rather more with Scarlett Johansson's character in the film *Lost in Translation*, when she visits an ancient Japanese temple.

'Am I shallow?' she asks her husband, assessing her ambivalent reaction to the temple. 'I didn't feel anything.'

Similarly, I was not versed in the lore of Rembrandt's work and the context in which it was created, and the feeling of time-travel gifted to Sebald's narrator would not come.

I found the Mondrian and De Stijl collection in the Gemeentemuseum a good deal more stimulating, as I did the collection of works by M.C. Escher housed in the Escher in Het Paleis Museum. However, upon sighting the original print of *Belvedere*, I received a sudden hit of my food-poisoned incomprehension at the mysteries of *The Atrocity Exhibition*. My body recoiled at the memory. I knew that my failure to sync with Rembrandt had marked me for what I was: a popcult idiot savant paddling in the shallows, far distant from the likes of Sebald, not well-read enough to be an intellectual, too disconnected from reality to be a cultural commentator, too absorbed in the familiar to be a philosopher.

A travel writer was just about my level, corroborating my decision to leave Ballard and academia far behind. Yet I could never be content, for something deep and unnameable continued to corrode me from inside.

31

BUNKER LOGIC

Bored and restless after a morning of museums, I caught the quaint tram to Scheveningen, a northern district of Den Haag. Although this seaside strip attracts ten million visitors a year, the weather was inclement that day and there were just a few souls wandering up and down the elongated beach. I walked to the end of the once-famous pleasure pier. It was deserted. Pleasure piers, such as the iconic structure in Brighton, England, have always instilled a deep melancholy in me. Their decrepit state in the modern era stands in sharp contrast to their lost function as repositories of amusement and fun-filled dreams, and their sad projection into the sea is a baleful invitation to immersion in an unknown dimension of time. The Scheveningen pier was especially forlorn, its old, rotting rafters and beams providing a dank frame for unused vending machines and crumbling posters promoting Hollywood blockbusters to an audience of ghosts. Repulsed by the miserable spirit that infested the pier, I returned to the beach and walked east.

Eventually, I passed a WWII bunker half hidden by dunes. It was part of the Atlantic Wall defence system built by the Nazis from 1942 to 1944 to repel an Allied landing, a chain of 1500 bunkers lining coastal Europe from southern France to northern Scandinavia. I nearly missed it, since it was hidden behind long grass. However, unlike *The Anatomy Lesson of Dr Nicolaes*

Tulp, once sighted it captured my attention in an instant and I scrambled over the high dunes to gain a closer view. The squat, ominous structure was green from weather and decay. In the mid-section, concentric semi-circles were stacked on top of one another. At the bottom was the gun encasement. A rusting gun turret was visible through a wide, thin slit. On either side of the semi-circles were two enormous bulkheads pressed up tight, as if the squat bunker were a concrete creature fighting the crushing gravity of an alien planet in a futile bid to avoid implosion. For once the inevitable science fiction metaphor was apt—the bunker's compact, spherical shape was oddly reminiscent of the killer robot ED 209 in Verhoeven's *Robocop*.

Perhaps this was no coincidence. Verhoeven was born in Amsterdam but moved with his family to Den Haag in 1943, when construction of the Atlantic Wall was in full swing and the Netherlands was occupied by Germany. In Den Haag, the Verhoevens lived near a strategic Nazi military base under continual attack from the Allies. Like Ballard in Shanghai, the young Verhoeven witnessed gruesome scenes of violence and destruction. He remembers war as an action-packed adventure that tested his mettle and developed his apocalyptic mindset, fuelling the vision behind his brutal science fiction blockbusters.

'I was a small boy during the war,' he said, 'but the mind takes these images like a sponge at that age, and the images were so extreme: bombs exploding, buildings collapsing, the whole sky turning red because the city was on fire.'

Amid that devastation, it is not hard to imagine the young Verhoeven sneaking off to Scheveningen beach, echoing Jim in *Empire*, who, in Lunghua, makes sport of his ability to give adults the slip. Perhaps Verhoeven had even encountered the same bunker I had, his memory of the concrete sentinel flowing into the future design of ED 209. This possible connection transfixed me and I tried to make sense of it, but I lacked the brainpower to do so in any meaningful way.

My quest was especially futile, since the Atlantic Wall continues to beguile men and women much smarter than myself, including Virilio, the greatest theorist of war ruins. In *Bunker Archaeology*, his book-length photo essay on the development of military technology, Virilio records his walks among the remains of the French portion of the wall. On his first encounter with a wartime bunker, he immediately became overwhelmed by 'a feeling, internal and external, of being immediately crushed' by the structure's relationship to time and space. The bunker featured an imposing base set deep into the earth, but its interior had been colonised by sand from the encroaching dunes, creating a claustrophobic narrowness amplified by half-buried, abandoned objects such as rusted bicycles and ragged clothing. It was as if he'd stumbled onto a subterranean civilisation, the bunker's impervious modernity offset by its abandoned state, rendering what was once contemporary, the architecture's brutal lines, thoroughly ordinary and forgotten, 'a collage of two dissimilar realities'.

Like Ballard and Verhoeven, Virilio was a war child. He lived through the blitzkrieg of French cities, the supreme unleashing of technology's potential: total destruction.

'For a kid,' he recalled, 'a city is like the Alps, it's eternal, like the mountains.'

But the war changed all that.

'One single bombardment and all is razed. These are the traumatising events which shaped my thinking. War was my university.'

Likewise, the annihilation of war had impressed upon Ballard 'the sense that reality itself was a stage set that could be dismantled at any moment, and that no matter how magnificent anything appeared, it could be swept aside into the debris of the past'. As did Virilio, and, one suspects, Verhoeven, Ballard channelled his bunker obsession into his work. Clearly, the refusal of these structures to disappear appealed to these men who'd each felt reality disintegrating before their very eyes.

From time to time, Ballard took his holidays in France. One day, walking along Utah Beach in Normandy, scene of the Allied landing on D-Day, he noticed an edifice in the near distance, partially obscured by mist. It was a bunker, part of the Atlantic Wall, and his immediate thought was that it was like the pyramids, that is, eternal, a structure completely outside of time. The bunker's decrepitude pitched it beyond history. Its modernist form had been corroded by urine, ossified faeces and the campfire remains left by decades of tramps. But within that form, or rather within its decay, Ballard had glimpsed an echo of contemporary England, since the bunker recalled the crumbling high-rise blocks and motorway overpasses back home, designed by bored planners indifferent to the long-term demands of a socially inclusive, robust urban form.

Architectural materiality and cultural atemporality are the abiding themes in the bunker meditations of Virilio and Ballard: the collapse of the past into a dystopian future as seen from the present—the contemplation of ruins. That super-dense black hole would also define my experience of the Netherlands, and very soon after encountering the bunker I was struck down by a cruel and unusual disease: time sickness.

32

THE VIRILIAN GAZE

I retreated to Den Haag and walked to Madurodam, one of the many boring tourist attractions I had to endure in order to complete the assignment that was my ostensible reason for being. Madurodam is a theme park that is essentially a 1:25

scale model of the Dutch landscape, with heavy emphasis on the attractions that in their life-size incarnations inspired such yawning indifference in me: canals, windmills, tulip fields, all the rest. Yet, bracing myself for a tacky experience, I came away deeply shocked. Gazing at Madurodam's Dutch landscape in miniature, I felt as though I'd *again* taken leave of my body. The memory of my Tangier ordeal flooded back and once more I imagined myself floating above my physical self, adrift in inner space, looking down upon the entirety of the Netherlands, able to see it all in microscopic detail, as if nothing could escape my gaze. Struck by a feeling of desperate unease, I removed myself from the theme park, the experience of Madurodam coming on like a torture knot cutting off the circulation to a limb the more I struggled to free myself.

I stalked the streets until I found my next port of call, the Panorama Mesdag, a 360-degree painting of Scheveningen beach completed by Hendrik Willem Mesdag in 1881. I entered the building in which it was housed, but the artwork only intensified my fevered state. From within a cylindrical, sand-covered room, the painting is viewed from wooden bleachers atop an artificial dune in the middle of the space. The dune is surrounded by period-replica beach chairs, with birdsong and the sound of crashing waves emerging from the sound system. As I took in the panorama, a simulacrum of the beach I'd just visited, I could not shake the sense that I was watching myself traversing that lonely strip, out of my mind with grief and self-doubt, battered by the ghosts of my past failures. At the same time I (the man on the beach) could quite clearly see my desperate and lonely future, which I was enacting in the present—marooned on an absurd fake dune. Just as Mesdag's simulation superimposed a crude double onto the real beach, I laboured under two out-of-phase bodily outlines, for I was so removed from the world I could no longer locate my true self.

33

MAGGOT BRAIN

Exhausted from trying to parse my confused inner state, I returned to the Imperial, where I caught an early episode of the reality TV program *Big Brother*, which asks strangers to live together for weeks on end in a microsocial war of attrition until only one is left, their every move filmed and broadcast to the world. I was stunned by what I'd found. The episode was shot in the Netherlands, although that fact was not remarkable in itself as the show's wild popularity has delivered the franchise worldwide. No, it was the fact that, judging by the clothes and set design, it was clearly filmed in the late 90s, a time well before the format had become famous.

I was so puzzled by this that I braved the bleak night-time streets, locating the nearest net cafe in order to research the origins of *Big Brother*. To my amazement, I discovered it was in fact a Dutch invention, developed in 1999. I thought it had originated in the US and far more recently, given its all-American premise of surveillance as entertainment. The original Dutch season even had a survivalist feel, featuring a sparse house devoid of the creature comforts that characterised later series. Unsurprisingly, this distorted domesticity triggered a deep psychosis, a quintessentially Ballardian notion, with contestants reportedly suffering post-traumatic stress disorder upon leaving the house.

The discovery turned my world upside down. Admittedly, in those days it did not take much to plunge me into a deadly tailspin. However, when I quelled my mind enough to think straight, I realised that the concept of watching other people's lives is endemic to the Netherlands, Europe's most densely populated country, with seventeen million people jammed into an area of just 41,526 square kilometres. Many Dutch people leave their curtains open day and night for everyone to see their domestic activities. Is this odd national trait an admission that there is nowhere to hide? In that case, *Big Brother* would make total sense to the Dutch, with its promise that everything will be visible.

As I considered these matters, the research on surveillance culture I'd conducted for my thesis returned to me. Ballard had predicted the merger of CCTV and TV entertainment, extrapolating a near future when surveillance would be so integrated into everyday lives that it would be impossible to trust unaided vision. To do so would be resolutely dangerous, even life-threatening, as essayed in his short story 'The Intensive Care Unit', set in a near future where ordinances are in place to prevent people from meeting in person. All communication is conducted via TV monitors, although it is never explained why these restrictions have been imposed. The narrator is a doctor who only ever sees his patients via the screen. When he first 'met' his wife, he had no idea whether 'she was five miles away from me or five hundred'. When he makes love to her, they switch to a private channel, away from the prying lenses of their family, and swap footage of themselves naked. Children are produced via artificial insemination and raised in solitary creches, nourished in their formative years by a diet of cartoons and educational programs rather than hand rearing.

Ballard presents television's inherent functions as surveillance and control, encapsulated in the literal meaning of the story's title: as a descriptor of medical practice. In hospitals, the way an actual intensive care unit protects at the same time as it strips away privacy, invading the body with probes and signals to keep it alive, confirms Ballard's view that we welcome the dissolving of our physical being. In the story, every human action is monitored and recorded, yet the narrator notes the 'admirable conventions' and 'liberating affectlessness' of his world.

91

These qualities afford him a range of benefits, including the chance to 'explore the fullest range of sexual possibility' through clandestine pornographic channels that cater to all tastes. In every way, he feels safe, protected and satisfied, deliriously happy 'within the generous rectangle of the TV screen'.

'The Intensive Care Unit' was published well before CCTV was adopted widely in the UK, yet there seems to be a form of surveillance guiding the story's networked reality, an uncanny sense that, although the characters' televised broadcasts are ostensibly for private and personal use, what they are recording is being transmitted elsewhere, the cameras part of a linked grid. Indeed, the narrator refers to the key events of his life as having occurred under the 'benevolent gaze of the television camera', as if the camera has the power to confer life or withdraw it.

Eventually, the narrator becomes bored and decides to enact the unthinkable: he brings his family together to meet in the flesh. However, they cannot handle the thought of being disconnected from their screens and become profoundly disorientated. Lost between worlds, they experience a kind of reality overload. Overcome with bloodlust at the sight of one another's unmediated selves, they hack each other to pieces using household scissors. Of course, the narrator's video camera records every slash, every cut, as even death, the final release, is performed for the benevolent lens. The narrator wishes to make a 'complete record of this unique event', referring to the controlled slaughter of his family as 'the ultimate home movie', since there is no question of escaping the screen or trying to find a world beyond the gaze. That is undesirable or even impossible, about as improbable as an astronaut leaving the boundaries of the universe to see what is on the other side. Any transcendence through death must still be enacted according to the logic of the electronic gaze.

Today, Ballard's vision is complete. 'The Intensive Care Unit' reads as though it is the transcript of an alt-world *Big Brother*, a more intense and violent variant transmitted from a parallel universe. The invasion of the corporeal self by the image has become so thoroughly integrated into our lives that it is repackaged as entertainment of the most pervasive and personal kind, as Virilio argues in his bleak essay 'The Vision Machine', which suggests that we are suffering a dissolution of the body into the electronic gaze, the result of the exponential sophistication and ubiquity of surveillance technology. That outcome, Virilio explains, is not induced by mere simulation (as when virtual reality substitutes for actual reality, producing two competing realities) but by an invasion of the actual by the virtual—a *replacement* of reality. Such is the collateral damage arising from the 'wide-awake dream of a population of objects all staring at you'.

In this strange new era, a significant proportion of the population exists solely within the gaze, a readymade supply of entertainment for the rest—pathological voyeurs like myself. Indeed, I'd become hopelessly addicted to trawling live CCTV footage online, hunting down real-time feeds from the numerous surveillance camera networks squirrelled away across the web. I did this mainly when I was bored or depressed, when I couldn't help but live in the past and dwell on my failures. I wanted to have dominion over at least a tiny portion of the world. In its pathetic way it was a form of revenge, for I needed to feel omnipotent, to have numerous feeds open at once, to indulge in anything that could impart the illusion of seeing god-like across dimensions, as opposed to hopelessly drifting out of control in a narrowcast world (my default setting). As well, I was a latent sadist, a sick personal trait that surfaced whenever I became disgusted with myself, and it was my desperate hope that one day I'd be privileged to witness spectacular crime spontaneously emerging from the shadows of these secret locations like maggots from rotting meat. Maybe even death.

For Ballard, reality TV is 'absolutely fascinating', especially the subgenre of found-footage surveillance feeds. Most people, he claims, are 'so desperate to find what they believe to be "reality" that they will happily watch programs of CCTV footage filmed in underground car parks, rainy shopping malls and motorway junctions ... the drabber the better'.

In acknowledging the truth of that statement, I was only too willing to recognise within it the sad spectre of my own unhealthy and wicked self, for what I was really searching for on the CCTV trawls was me. A different version of me, in a different universe, a different reality—a *superior* reality. A clone that had surpassed myself in every way. Smarter, sexier, stronger, more masculine, more charming, more confident, less paranoid.

But all that emerged were the maggots.

34

BIOMECHANOID

On my trawls, I'd been guided by an app called Surveillance Stalker that cycled through thousands of internet-enabled CCTV feeds. I installed it on the computer in the net cafe, where the cybersecurity was non-existent, and when it spluttered into life I immediately felt restful and calm, like a strung-out junkie melting into the first hit of the day. Grainy feeds of indeterminate locations spooled into view, far beyond the reach of my unenhanced optic nerve. Business parks at night. City squares cast in gloomy shadow. Empty swimming pools. Hooded hospital entrances. The city-like expanses of airport perimeters. Freeway feeder roads where human interaction had been factored out of the landscape and the only transactions were between speed and machinery. Surveillance Stalker was my privileged window onto Ballardian space.

The app had a chat feature so that anyone logged on to a particular feed could communicate with anyone else watching it, but the conversation always consisted of sky-crushing banalities, for live CCTV feeds attract the lowest class of human being (I include myself in that taxonomy). But I didn't know how to turn the feature off and the constant interruptions polluted the experience. That night in the internet cafe, as the hours wore on, I became absorbed in the app's sparse, jerky action and pixelated frame-by-frame movements. My back became hunched and sore, my body moulded to the chair like a biomechanical creature ripped straight from the demonic tableaux of the artist H.R. Giger.

A frozen scene appeared on the screen: a city square somewhere in Eastern Europe. As a man walked across the 'set', a sodium street light flickered off, the laggy software rendering his movements like a stop-motion creature from a Ray Harryhausen film, trapping his legs in the molasses-like gravity of CCTV time sickness.

The interjections of an entity called 'Breeanna the Beauty' invaded the screen.

> *There's sumthin in the back of the square!!! It's shakin its head!!! Check it out!!!*

But there was nothing and no one.

I clicked on another feed: a grey and forbidding overpass.

'NoFace666' was with me, like the uncoordinated id of my digital psyche.

> *Were creeping on people. Hahaha now ever time I look at traffic cam or etc I'm goin to wonder if some one is watching lol.*

I winced at this creature's hideous 'lolspeak', yet I knew exactly what it meant. Throughout the night, I had been alert for the offices, university computer labs and library reading rooms that cycled across the screen, lusting for the uncanny shock of catching someone I knew watching their computer. Would they be using Surveillance Stalker? Would they be watching for me?

Perhaps I would even see myself on their monitor as I sat there in that squalid net cafe, a desire for self-recognition that was nothing more than a forlorn digital dream. Hunting for my ghostly double was like trying to find a pixel in a CGI haystack, yet I became immersed in the idea and could not let it go. I was sick, obsessed with doppelgangers, trapped under the passive gaze of the CCTV cameras in the internet cafe (above my head, behind me, to the right), helpless to prevent my image leaking out to some unknown, unpatrolled quadrant of inner space.

As I watched the feed, a scene from *Crash* came to mind, in which Vaughan receives a blow job from a prostitute in the back seat of his car, which is driven by 'Ballard'. As they traverse an airport overpass, 'Ballard' passively watches the sex act in the rear-view mirror—but there was nothing of the sort here. The overpass was as dead as my soul.

As I scrolled through the menu to a construction site on the far edge of some remote American town, a new entity, 'Stump-jumper', piped up.

> *Where are the girls?*

The feed switched to an unoccupied apartment block on the construction site, recalling a scene from *Cocaine Nights* in which a porno film is shot in an apartment amid the ever-present 'defensive nervous system of security alarms and surveillance cameras'. Relentlessly seeking any deviation from the norm, I examined every inch of the feed, its colours leached almost to monochrome by the overworked software.

Again, nothing.

When a video store replaced the construction site, I hoped for a casually dressed urban professional to scope the aisles, a mysterious brown package under his arm, picking his moment to bomb into oblivion the suburban ennui of the franchise as the anti-consumerist revolutionaries do in *Millennium People*, Ballard's satirical novel of middle-class revolt. But the scene was devoid of action, underscored by the crass ejaculation of a new playmate, 'Pounder'.

> *Fuuuuuuuuck. Boring.*

Then came an office building in the dead of night and signs of life at last. A woman at her computer, dressed in a power suit, slumped backwards in her chair. Perhaps she'd inject herself with painkillers, unable to bear the thought of returning home to whatever it was that awaited her there, echoing the habits of the enervated corporate class in *Super-Cannes*, Ballard's novel about a new breed of cyborg—the modern-day office worker.

Not according to 'Dirty Millsy'.

> *Are we supposed to just sit here watching? What if she got murdered?!*

But Millsy was weak. That was precisely why we were there.

I grew agitated at the lack of action and stabbed at the keyboard, advancing the menu until I came across a posse of mannequins in a store window. I recalled the Kraftwerk song, 'Showroom Dummies': mannequins come to life, break the window of the store that imprisons them, find a club and start to dance.

'Shazza69', bored and sarcastic, was less inspired.

> *Wow. A shop window. Haven't seen that before.*

Then tundra, somewhere in Siberia. Naturally, my attention turned to UFOlogy. In Tunguska in 1908, an unidentified flying object detonated in the low atmosphere, flattening two thousand square kilometres of Siberian forest. Channelling the Man from Morioka, I willed a similar object to appear and explode, only to encounter the usual dead sky, the same dead time. Then came a pig in a pen on a remote farm, the animal's fleshy snout filling the screen, followed by a dolphin swimming in a zoo, followed by the underside of an obese woman's body as she struggled with laps in a pool.

I needed a break from the suffocating nothingness and surfed the web, alighting on a story about a man in New York who was stuck inside an elevator for forty-one hours. Thrillingly for a creature of my proclivities, his every tortured movement had been recorded on CCTV and the time-lapsed footage had been uploaded to YouTube, overlaid with melancholy piano music. Inset into the main screen were three supporting scenes: transmissions from cameras in the building's other elevators. Apparently, the security guards had failed to observe that the elevator had stalled or to notice the trapped man losing his mind on the monitor before them. They'd locked the building and gone home for the weekend, trapping him in his tiny cell.

Calmly, he laid down on the elevator floor, expecting someone to find him soon, but as time wore on he began to unravel. He smoked cigarettes, banged on the door, pulled his hair, slapped his face. Cleaners went about their business in the other lifts, visible on the split screens, unaware he was there, their workaday tasks contrasting sharply with the escalating panic in the adjoining lift. The sad tinkling of the piano soundtrack and the slapstick sped-up footage ironically distanced the viewer from the man's true torment as he nervously paced the elevator car. He forced open the doors only to find a brick wall (the car had stopped between floors). He sat down, slept for a while, then woke up, panicking and screaming soundlessly, since there is no soundtrack to CCTV and in inner space no one can hear you scream.

I wondered how I'd react if I encountered his torment in real time. It would be sweet relief after enduring umpteen feeds of farm animals, dank underpasses and spotty students watching porn on university computers. Probably, I'd applaud and cheer as if it were panopticon performance art. After all, I was so desperate for reality, as Ballard had foreseen, that I'd happily watch a man disintegrate for entertainment.

I could picture the scene: I'd turn in for the night and log on in the morning to find out how he was doing, to see whether he'd expired overnight. The thought made me so giddy with excitement, I even fantasised the premise for a new reality TV show. Trap unwitting citizens in urban environments: elevators, office toilets, car washes, factories, high-rise garbage enclosures, concrete islands. Leave them there for the weekend. Beam the CCTV feed to the world. Guess their fate, their actions, their next move. Do they die? Play with themselves? Talk to God or to the camera? Record their emotional response, their physical torment. Rate it and vote on it.

The end.

Years ago, the SETI project, which searches the galaxy for extraterrestrial life, released a program that allowed home computers to crunch and analyse a tiny amount of the data gathered from outer space by SETI's high-powered radio-telescope array. The program then sent the results back to headquarters. The software could be downloaded and installed by anyone and became massively popular for a while, everyone mucking in to do their bit for the ET cause. As I amused myself with the prospect of my reality show, I realised that instead of installing SETI we should all be downloading Surveillance Stalker instead. It seemed a far more important tool in the advancement of human knowledge, able to scan the fathomless expanse of inner space where intelligent life is even more elusive than in the outer reaches of the cosmos.

But my insight did not last and was replaced by a crushing hopelessness. I remembered an interview with Virilio, in which he relates the plot of a science-fiction story: artificial snow is seeded with tiny cameras and released by planes, and 'when the snow falls, there are eyes everywhere. There is no blind spot left.'

But what, he is asked, will we dream of when we can see everything?

'We'll dream of being blind.'

That was *my* dream, for I had become burdened by the

thought that I could see everything at once, that CCTV had allowed me to see under, over, inside and out.

Until there is no blind spot left.

As I admitted my situation, the lights in the internet cafe went out. From the shadows, the man behind the counter made a throat-slitting gesture: *Closed.*

He booted me out, forcing me back to the Imperial, and as I traversed the bleak streets Virilio's prediction of our future wide-eyed dreamstate refused to leave my mind, rendering even the pus-yellow glow seeping from the street lights as controlling alien entities, assaulting my retina with a terrifying intensity.

35

REPETITION

I arrived at the hotel. It was 3am. I laid down on the bed. The lights were off but the fluorescent glare from the convenience store seeped into the room. I was beginning to connect the dots between the mirror worlds, the UFOs and the time fugues, and as I did so the feeling of leaving my body returned, the sensation that had afflicted me at Madurodam and the Panorama Mesdag, underpinned by the memory of the full-on body horror in Tangier and the thudding dislocation of my latest CCTV trawl.

The trawls always left me languishing in a state of profound unreality, as if everything around me were a projection, an illusion—even my own body. This time the sensation was exacerbated by the store light, which beckoned me into the beyond. I imagined my body wasting away to nothing until I was just a matrix of brain waves under the control of someone else. Scared witless, I dug my nails deep into the palms of my hands, puncturing the skin. The light grew wider and brighter until it engulfed the room completely so that even in the dark I could see.

We will dream of being blind.

Something was forcing itself upon me, paralysing me with fear. Unable to move a muscle, I remembered the real-life horror stories of those poor souls under general anaesthetic who wake up during surgery but are unable to let the surgeon know and therefore feel every excruciating cut of the scalpel in real time. A surge of the purest terror spread from the base of my spine to my neck, rising and rippling across my back like Jacob's ladder transforming the heated, ionised air above a malfunctioning power station. I could sense a presence in the room, another intelligence, and although I could not move my neck, I could see my hand from the corner of my eye. Astonishingly, every bone and vein was visible in a reverse image, as if I'd passed it under an X-ray. I knew then that not only had I lost control of my body, I'd finally lost my mind, and I prayed for the end to be swift and soon.

But there would be no end.

36

REPLICATION

Suddenly morning was revealed to me, a wave of light flooding the room from a bright and sunny day. I had not stirred from the bed and was still in my street clothes. I tested my fingers. To my utter relief, I could move them, although the palms of my hands were cut deep from my serrated nails. I checked the time: 6am. Somehow, daylight had forced its way into my world, as if the black of night had been bypassed, rolled back in time. What was this? A vicious epilepsy? A type of waking madness? A soft veil of confusion swaddled my mind, a sense of missing time, for I could not recall having gone to sleep. I'd closed my eyes the moment the store light seeped into the room and when I'd opened them I was four hours into the future, staring at the sun. It was as if a button in some distant control centre had been pressed, turning night into day. What did this hotel episode represent? Another sighting (another 'abduction')? Another psychotic episode? Another day pass from reality? Or were such connections meaningless? I hadn't thought about the orange sky orbs for years until the Man from Morioka had triggered an apparently related telepathic phenomenon, and even then I'd put the incident down to mind games played by a disarming huckster.

I blinked, trying to resolve my vision. The room shimmered with a sickly purple phosphorescence, bathing the outline of the hotel furniture in a queasy glow. I watched the mystifying haze fade as the sunlight seeped in. The utter strangeness of the kaleidoscopic dimension before me was fascinating but also confronting in its similarity to a disturbing accident that had befallen me as a child, an event that somehow I'd long forgotten, despite its obvious relation to everything that had happened to me, and which was only now being excavated after years of desuetude.

I could picture the skies that day. It was just before sunset and the clouds were streaked with every colour. I was ten years old, riding my bicycle down the steep hill that formed our street in the sterile suburb at the foot of the Dandenong Ranges. My eye was drawn to a cigar-shaped white mass, flecked with grey, almost camouflaged among the billowing cloud configurations. The mass remained stock still in the middle of a bank of fast-moving clouds, and as I turned my gaze to it I saw that its appearance was actually metallic. It moved as if responding to my attention, inching slowly sideways at first, before performing an impossible perpendicular manoeuvre at blazing speed. It took on the colour of burning steel, as if it had been dipped into a furnace, and as it drew further away it glowed a bright red, ascending to become a dot in the sky until it was gone.

I was so absorbed in its morphing qualities that I careened into the back of a parked car. I was travelling downhill at a rapid clip and performed a half-somersault, bouncing off the vehicle's rear and smashing my head on the tarmac. At the moment of impact, a blinding flash of purple light engulfed my field of vision, followed by an intense white sheet of strobing light that caused the blood vessels in my eyes to flare up like miniature, iridescent worms. The neurological fireworks lasted for minutes and induced a headache of such magnitude that I was doubled up in the foetal position. When my mother ran from our house in distress, all I could see was the outline of her body picked out in the same flaring purple glow I would encounter many years later in that grotty Den Haag hotel. I stared hard at the maternal apparition until the outline slowly resolved and my mother's familiar shape resolidified, and for a few hours afterwards I suffered crippling headaches and bouts of vomiting that sapped my will to live.

I knew I'd been concussed when I crashed the bike, making the clarity of my recall even more perplexing. Usually, the immediate lead up to severe concussion is erased from memory, but even without the occluding effects of a blow to the head to reckon with, the mechanics of memory retrieval made it highly likely I had invented some if not all of the striking details. Often, people confidently declare they can remember the weather conditions when a significant childhood incident occurred, even the precise hour and date of the event, yet with the passage of time this type of minute detail is the most difficult to recall without external validation. In actuality, the brain invents bridging memories to fill in the gaps with false details. Every time we remember something, we overlay new information onto the memory. Traces of the original are available, but they become increasingly fainter the more we dredge up the memory and overwrite it.

Moreover, the confirmation bias that exists in every person's individual belief system warps childhood memories. Our recall of events is shaped by the way our older selves wish it could have been resolved, and as we age that wish fulfilment hardens into an inflexible version of reality. The aura from treasured personal artefacts further falsifies the recollection. Photographs taken around the same time colonise and replace the memory, since a photo is more immediate and permanently fixed in time and space.

My memory of the skyborne anomaly was sharp and clear and involved the weather in great detail, sure signs of false memory retrieval. As for the controlling influence of neurologically hardwired belief systems, no doubt my former hardcore interest in UFOs and the occult influenced the way I'd remembered the 'sighting'—and the cloud (for that is almost certainly what it was). But despite everything, the scars on my spine remained. Their existence could not be denied even if their origin would not yet be revealed to me. Not for the first time, my mind turned to *La Jetée*, Chris Marker's legendary film about the recall and overwriting of disturbing childhood memories (*La Jetée* is effectively a transmission from God, since nothing can touch it for the truth it reveals about the nature of existence).

A line from the film spoke to my experience.

'Nothing sorts memories from ordinary moments. They only claim remembrance when they show their scars.'

Had I believed in the UFO reality of my memories so much it had physically manifested in the form of a trio of scars—popcult stigmata?

I stared at the Imperial's shit-brown wallpaper, encrusted with a bloody constellation of squashed flies orbiting a large grease spot, like a map of the solar system designed by the village idiot from found materials.

The answer evaded me. Who was I trying to fool? I *never* had any answers—for anything.

I was just an empty vessel.

Rubbish in, rubbish out.

37

STAR CULT

As a child I was painfully shy, profoundly afraid of the outside world. It was this feeling, I'm sure, that began to foment my future interest in the paranormal and my fascination with the possibility of alien life, an impulse I now recognise as a lust for transcendence, for some guiding principle to deliver me from confusion and uncertainty. Perhaps the transcendental manifestation of the cloud I saw was simply a variant of Jung's 'Christ Principle'—just the same old religious template of yearning for salvation from above to transform the mundane terror of the everyday, but transplanted into a modern, technological context. Instead of the Star of Bethlehem, a fast-moving UFO. In another life I might have joined a radical church, a star cult. In this one, I attempted a PhD.

Perhaps this was no accident. In *The Atrocity Exhibition*, a minor character, a lecturer, tells his students that 'cosmic space vehicles may have been seen approaching the Earth two thousand years earlier'. He asks: 'Are they Jung's symbols of redemption, ciphers in some futuristic myth?' Like so much in this strange book, the passage is left unexplained and its themes are never returned to, just one of many apparently disjointed paragraphs in a seemingly randomly plotted work. Yet *Atrocity* works a strange kind of magic. Skimming its pages, suddenly these drifting passages seem to connect to a wider narrative, as the reader fills in the gaps according to personal experience. Indeed, it hypnotised me in precisely that fashion, as if, through the act of reading it and joining the dots according to my own internal logic, Ballard was writing the story of my life. But if that was the case, the narrative had reached a critical juncture and plot holes had to be filled before the shocking denouement could be reached, and in order to do that I needed to retreat to my past—and to my obsession with stargazing.

When I was young, my parents would take me to the Melbourne Observatory near the Botanical Gardens. I remember reading a plaque there. It announced that the observatory was open to the public for viewings of the night sky through its large telescope. I was too young to attend a viewing so I made a promise that when I was older I would book myself in. As the years flowed by, I forgot about that promise although my passion for the heavens endured, albeit diverted into the cultish pursuits that so consumed my mind. As an adult, I lived near the Botanical Gardens but had forgotten about the observatory. One day, I went jogging around the gardens and happened upon the observatory tucked away to the side. As I passed through the gates, everything came flooding back, vivid in every detail.

I remembered the exact wording of the plaque: OPEN TO THE PUBLIC. BOOK NOW FOR NIGHT-TIME VIEWINGS. I remembered the weather and season: fine and sunny with blooming flowers. The clothes my parents wore: shapeless suburban uniforms of beige slacks and cable-knit jumpers in brown and yellow. But as I approached the main building, a sign told a different story: CLOSED TO THE PUBLIC SINCE 1945.

I reread the sign many times, expecting the words to reorder themselves into the message I'd seen as a child. I couldn't believe what I was reading and felt supremely cheated. More than that, I felt outside of time, as if the parameters of reality had shifted when I wasn't looking, a more intense and dislocating version of the feeling that enveloped me when I discovered *Big Brother* was Dutch and not American. I was overcome by the strangest sensation, as if I was in a foreign land, lost and alone, unable to speak the language. I scoured the observatory grounds for clues to the mystery, exploring every corner, every blade of grass, every angle of every wall, but came up short.

It was only when I returned home and googled the Observatory that I was able to reconcile the hole in space-time that the grounds had generated. I found a newspaper report from the mid-1800s, which confirmed that time in Melbourne had indeed gone haywire.

'Never was a city so doomed to having great varieties of or variations in time as Melbourne', the report said. 'There is no true or recognised, or proper standard of time in the place. The Post Office Clock, which should be, par excellence, the best and always right, is barely right, except twice in the twenty-four hours by accident. Ten minutes slow one day, and the same number fast the next, is perfectly common ... the writer once having seen the hands moved on fifteen minutes at one stretch.'

In 1863, the Observatory was established to keep order in that temporally lawless place, and its weapon was standardised time. The Observatory deployed a transit telescope linked to a master clock, which observed the movement of 'clock stars', celestial bodies whose positions had been recorded accurately. With this system, the Observatory controlled clock time throughout the state of Victoria by means of telegraph signals and then radio technology, although political factions ensured the allocation of time would be sabotaged. Some towns set clocks to local solar time in defiance of the central authority and found themselves marooned in the past compared to Melbourne, which had been propelled ten minutes into the future. Because of that, Melbourne grew stronger—culturally, politically and temporally. Despite closing down long ago, perhaps the Observatory still controlled chronological reality, in particular *my* reality. Control time and you control the world.

The feeling that swaddled me, time out of joint, intensified when I discovered a website devoted to something called 'The Mandela Effect': the phenomenon of shared false memories. The effect is named after the belief many people hold about the circumstances of Nelson Mandela's death: that he died while imprisoned in the 80s. Of course, not only did he survive long after that, he was released from prison and became President of South Africa. Other shared false memories reported to the website include geographical locations that have supposedly changed. For example, people had testified that New Zealand was north of Australia on maps they'd seen as kids, an amazing detail to Australians like me who knew otherwise. Celebrity deaths were later discovered to have never happened. Movies and books were found to have had plot details altered when rewatched or reread.

'The Mandela Effect' was first studied by the paranormal investigator Fiona Broome, who concluded that when large numbers of people have a shared collective memory that differs from the majority view, the divergence can be regarded as evidence of an alternate universe. But most testifiers were American. Surely many of these reports could be attributed to the culturally insular nature of mainstream American life. Despite my scepticism, I couldn't dismiss the theory completely after my observatory and *Big Brother* experiences, even if these, technically, were not manifestations of the Mandela Effect, which must comprise a *shared* false memory to qualify.

Aside from Mandela, the most enduring example of the effect is the title of the popular American children's book series, *The Berenstain Bears*. On Broome's site, a parade of people had sworn that when they were growing up the correct spelling was *Berenstein*. Some claimed that they had the books to prove it but that when they went to the attic to retrieve their treasured volumes they were devastated to have found them 'altered' with the suffix *-stain*. These lost souls felt as cheated as I did at the gates of the Observatory. After all, nothing is as emotionally devastating as a childhood memory that proves to be false, for so much is invested in our formative years be they good or bad.

Although the bears were hardly a phenomenon in Australia, I had heard of them as a child and was in no doubt as an adult that the correct spelling was 'Berenstein', a remarkably vivid recall for a cultural artefact barely seen on our shores. I was therefore amazed to discover that official histories have it as 'Berenstain' (even typing that induces a shudder) and that it has always been that way. Some say the collective imagination defaulted to 'Berenstein' because '-stein' is much more common in American surnames, but why would that be so memorable for me, an Australian?

Since so many people have this false memory, the Berenstein cultists insist, they must be sharing a parallel reality. So the story goes, at some point someone must have time-travelled to the past and for some inscrutable reason altered the name of the bears, sending a slight but detectable ripple through space-time to the present day and retroactively rewriting a tiny slice of history. But there was a glitch in the process and the transition to the new reality was bumpy so that many retain a memory of *-stein* while others only remember the 'new' spelling. There are as many deniers as believers in this fight. For the former, it has always been 'Berenstain' and there is simply no argument, no conspiracy.

One might attribute this divide to human nature. Our memories are unshakeable in their foundations. They define the way we perceive reality. When those foundations are blown away, when a memory is proved to be incorrect, the natural instinct is to dig deep into an unfalsifiable theory (such as being born into a parallel universe) in order to explain the divergence between perception and reality, since the shock of having one's memories of the past proven wrong is simply too great to bear when they have been carried as unassailable truths for so long. But although I could follow this line of reasoning, my default position would always be conspiratorial, for I had never quite shaken the fear of the outside world that had defined my childhood, the fear that reality was a rug that could be pulled out from under me at any moment, plunging me to my doom.

I spent days and nights wandering the observatory grounds, trying to detect any shred of evidence for the way my mind had remembered the sign, but there was nothing. I wondered how many more childhood memories would prove to be false if examined closely enough. Perhaps they all were. There was no easy way to independently verify them, for my father had since died and my mother had succumbed to advanced dementia, her state a source of great distress to me as I tried to negotiate the strange twists and turns in her circular, self-erasing language and logic, her nonchalant, clinical disengagement from time and space.

As I laid on the filthy hotel bed, I allowed my paranoia to claim me, a savage claustrophobia that trapped me as surely as a luckless miner in a collapsed coal mine. Despite my suspicions as to his motives, it was exactly as the Man from Morioka had said. Following the example of my poor, doomed mother, I had lost my spatial and chronological bearings and was drifting aimlessly in inner space, like an astronaut on a spacewalk cut adrift from the Mothership, receding further and further away from the diminishing pinprick of light that was the distant sun of my imaginative solar system.

38

SCAR TISSUE

I searched for my scars. The trio of indentations, their familiar shape, calmed me and the outline of the room began to settle. The sickly purple haze dissipated and a noxious odour filled the air. It was sulphurous, somewhat like rotting eggs, but mixed with an unexpected scent. What was it? Burning electrical circuits? With immense effort I raised my head from the bed and looked outside to try to determine its origin but the street was quiet. No people, no traffic. I slowly gathered my senses, packed my bags and walked downstairs. The proprietor, as usual, was nowhere to be seen, nor were any other guests. In fact, apart from meeting him on arrival, I'd not seen another living soul in the place.

Except for myself.

I remembered the great filmmaker Andrei Tarkovsky, who in his diary had transcribed an observation from the Renaissance philosopher Montaigne.

'We do not move in one direction,' said Montaigne, 'rather do we wander back and forth, turning now this way and now that. We go back on our own tracks.'

Montaigne lent support to a theory Tarkovsky had been nursing about UFOs: that instead of pointing towards extraterrestrial life, the phenomenon reveals a crisis of the self.

'That thought of Montaigne's', he explained, 'reminds me about something I thought of in connection with flying saucers, humanoids and the remains of unbelievably advanced technology found in some ancient ruins. They write about aliens, but I think that in these phenomena we are in fact confronting ourselves; that is our future, our descendants who are actually travelling in time.'

Tarkovsky had been considering such matters since 1975, when his wife and son saw a UFO outside their home. An odd mushroom-shaped light appeared in the sky. It seemed to head straight towards the Tarkovskys, growing larger, bathing everything in its glow before dissipating. Tarkovsky thought that it might have been a nuclear blast, maybe some kind of weapons test, but the mystery was never solved. Whatever the case, the family sighting confirmed what he had always known to be true: that when we look towards UFOs, we are looking deep within ourselves.

Three years before the sighting, Tarkovsky's film *Solaris* featured phantasms of the past that are plucked by an alien entity from human memories and made flesh. The characters stare down their psyches with horrendous results, confronted by dead lovers reborn over and over or the unkillable fetish objects from their depraved subconscious minds. In *Stalker*, the film he made four years after the sighting, a ragtag group of strangers becomes lost inside 'the Zone', an ambiguous landscape filled with ruins, abandoned buildings and rusted machinery. In the Zone, we're told that the laws of human engagement cease to apply. Gravity can be bent and levitation can occur, and for much of the film it is implied that this is because the uncanny landscape has been irradiated after an alien landing. Eventually, the viewer begins to suspect that the Zone is actually a projection of the damaged psyches of the people wandering among it, again forcing them into a confrontation with their own worst impulses—what was initially thought to be an alien intelligence originates instead from within the dark depths of the human psyche. As I worked my way through these connections, I knew that Tarkovsky's hunch was correct. Obsessed by anomalies in the sky and ruins on the ground, whenever I looked skywards or stalked the urban landscape, what I was searching for were reflections of myself.

I dropped the key in the slot and walked to the train station, weaving past stray dogs, split rubbish bags and a small posse of drunks. Rotterdam was next on my itinerary, and as I boarded the train at Holland Spoors I caught the reflection of my face in the carriage window. It resembled a waxwork dummy melting in the heat, an effect induced by the oily window glass and summer glare. As I stared at my ghostworld doppelganger, I had the sudden impulse to zigzag my head up and down and from side to side, like an electrocuted bird, trying to trick my reflection, as if I might trigger the time lag that occurs when you watch yourself on a buggy webcam and your representation moves a split second after you do. But it was no use. I was welded to the exact rhythm of the molten horrorshow before me.

At the precise moment that I completed this experiment, I had the strangest sense of remembrance, but not of anything that could place my immediate thoughts in context. Ever since I was young, I have had a recall in dreams of previous events, but these are not events that have taken place in the waking world. In the dream, I might enact something or say something with an immediate awareness that I am following on, either in words or actions, from something that has happened or that I have thought previously—*but within the dream world*. The continuous, causal sequence of events, including the memory, is entirely contained within the dream, as if I have been living a parallel life, enacting an alternate chain of events to waking reality. Occasionally, such 'memories' seep into the waking world and whenever that happens I am stopped in my tracks, stunned by the contradiction of remembering something which I have no recall of previously enacting in any kind of conscious reality.

The webcam connection was like that. The action, and even the location that hosted the action—aboard a train—seemed all too familiar, as if it had arisen from a previous thought, from a prior impulse, but not one that I'd formed in my waking life. As that realisation swept over me, the dislocation I encountered was so intense that I clasped my head as if suffering migraine, prompting an old woman to offer me a handful of pills. I stared at them for some time, transfixed by their corroded edges, which seemed like the terrain of distant moons.

'Where did you get those?' I shouted, causing her to flinch.

She stuffed them back into her bag and left the carriage, just another bystander repelled by my shambolic condition.

One of the pills had fallen to the floor.

I picked it up, noting the dove engraved on its surface, and swallowed it, waiting to be shunted into the next phase of existence.

39

CARTOGRAPHIES OF THE INFINITE

The train arrived at Rotterdam. I disembarked and was struck immediately by the large office building a few metres away. Its mirrored facade seemed to fold the structure back into the sky and clouds, and as I stood before it I again caught a distorted reflection of my face enveloped in the yellow glare of the overhead sun. The bright white light that had engulfed me in Den Haag seemed connected to the Neverland of mirrors before me, and in a moment of madness I imagined I had travelled to Rotterdam on a beam of light, emerging through the building's reflective skin to become lost within an internal maze of infinite dimensions.

I deposited my bags at the hotel and made my way to the downstairs bar. It was full of merry people talking loudly, and as I ordered a drink I resolved to finish the novel I'd started a few weeks before, *Requiem for a Dream*, Hubert Selby Jr's horrific tale of drug abuse, tortured dreams and broken humanity. It had been impossible to read anything at all lately. I couldn't focus, couldn't concentrate, my attention span wandering from the page so frequently I felt illiterate. I needed to try again, if only for my self-esteem. After all, I was a former scholar of literature, and even though I hadn't graduated I intended to use that training like a suit of armour to distinguish me from the plebs.

Suddenly everyone in the bar fell still and silent, but I continued to turn the pages of my book, confused by the abrupt soundlessness. I was the only one in the place not frozen to the spot and felt as dispossessed as a leper who'd entered a beauty clinic by mistake, my scholarly pretensions now an embarrassing mark of shame. After a brief interval, everyone resumed their carousing as if 'switched' back on. It was unnerving, even after the barman explained that they'd paused for a national minute of remembrance to honour dead war heroes.

The experience chilled me to the bone and forced me onto the street. Was this the way it was to be—everyday interactions becoming more and more difficult to negotiate? Something had happened to me in Den Haag, but what? A major malfunction of some kind. A flipped switch. A broken circuit. Hunger pains. Lack of sleep. Overwork. Who knew?

Block it out. Show no fear. Be a real man. Forge ahead.

On autopilot, I wandered around the harbour before washing up at the Overblaak development, a strange architectural outcrop near Blaak metro station, designed by Piet Blom in 1984 and comprising three discrete, theatrical sectors. Blaaktoren (Black Tower) is a thirteen-story hexagonal apartment block shaped like a pencil. Spaansekade (Spanish Quay) is a complex of buildings surrounding an inner courtyard. And the Kubuswoninge (Cube Houses) are a series of interlocking apartments. The Overblaak's unique design upholds the future-forward vibe Rotterdam has projected since the war, when it was bombed flat by the Nazis and rebuilt from the ground up. For postwar architects, the destruction was a green light. With nothing left of the old world, anything went in the built environment.

I thought of the locals who had lived through the war. What was their experience of the transformed city? As urban space changes our memories change with it, and I have always been compelled by the disruption to one's treasured grip on reality that occurs when visiting a particular part of a city for the first time in a number of years, only to find it changed completely. A row of shops might have been demolished or rebuilt, a building knocked down and never replaced, an alleyway walled off and hidden from view. When the association is strong (perhaps the alleyway was home to a favourite bar, where many good times were had), it can feel as though you have lost your mind, as if the memory was implanted, as if the bar never existed and you were never inside it. The impact is fierce and abrupt, as if a chunk of your temporal lobe has been sliced away in real time.

I had submitted to one such experience in Melbourne, just before leaving for the Netherlands. Visiting the docklands, in the shadows of a toxic twilight, I watched an interlaced grid of illuminated yellow piping crawl across a corporate building, some kind of kinetic design feature. The building had replaced a patch of open space that I fondly recalled, which once provided a beautiful harbour view, and with a jolt I realised my memories of the space had been replaced with someone else's.

The destruction of Rotterdam must have made many war survivors into amnesiacs, no longer able to recall how the city used to be, so confronting was the damage. Yet undoubtedly there were many others who didn't have amnesia but the opposite. Perhaps they recalled the city all too well, but the problem was that their memories had to be superimposed onto the scorched landscape. How could the rebuilt city ever live up to these overlapping layers of expectation? Could future cities be 'tuned' to produce a kind of stereoscopic urbanism? Could they combine the overlay of mental associations from a particular space or building to form a three-dimensional reality part constructed (in the architecture) and part imagined (inspired in the mind by the architecture)?

The Cube Houses seem like the first real flowering of Future Rotterdam, the stirrings of a new sensibility that solved the dilemma of the past by setting it free. The project, borne of a startling theatrical sensibility and unencumbered by history, is a pure representation of Blom's personal philosophy: to rethink housing by infusing it with mythological significance in a world that no longer knows how to dream.

In the 70s, a prototype of the Cube Houses had been realised in Helmond, a small city in the southern Netherlands. There, Blom dubbed the first floor 'the street house', the second 'the heaven house' and the third 'the tabernacle'.

'For each moment of the day and every state of mind,' he expounded, 'there is a different floor to ease one's mind.'

Presumably, for there to be a heaven and tabernacle there must also be an opposite dimension—perhaps the street as the depths of hell. What better environment to test that theory than the urban grit of Rotterdam?

The Cube Houses are a sequence of apartments tilted on an angle of forty-five degrees, anchored to hexagonal poles and attached to one other in modular units. End to end, set against the skyline and viewed from above, each cube perched atop its pole is supposed to symbolise a tree, while the jagged tops of the houses, locked together, evoke the ceiling of a forest. The interconnected apartment roofs are arranged around a publicly accessible courtyard, and the apartments attract so many 'architecture tourists' that one has been converted into a 'show cube' open to the public. Inside the show cube, one can see Blom's standard three-level fit-out, with the topmost level (the 'tabernacle') forming an ideal observation deck for spying on the courtyard rubberneckers below (the devils in the depths). Standing in the centre of the courtyard, looking upwards, one can see a star-shaped patch of sky formed by the central convergence of roofing. The upper levels of the cubes surround the star shape, from where it seems certain the occupants are watching you. The exteriors of the cubes are anthropomorphised by two porthole windows in the middle, one at the top and one at the bottom, forming the rough outline of a human body.

Immediately upon sighting the apartments, I wrote in my notebook that they 'seem wrenched straight from the novels of J.G. Ballard'. Why did I think of them as Ballardian? After all, there are no cube-shaped flats in his stories with colour schemes straight out of Mondrian. Yet I intuited that the complex was designed to affect the behaviour of its inhabitants in some unsounded way, like the building in *High-Rise*, Ballard's vicious novel of urban decay, which describes the breakdown of social values in a London apartment block and the subsequent full-scale descent into tribal warfare. In *High-Rise*, there is the sense that the architecture itself possesses the residents with a caged, animal urgency and a ruthless territoriality, but I had to work hard to make any kind of connection with the Cube Houses. I had not read a Ballard novel for so long and I was rusty and out of practice, although my backbrain Ballardian awareness eventually kicked in, as if I were a shamanistic caveman dredging up ancient ancestral memories of life as a lizard in the primordial swamp.

Think.

It was something to do with *Super-Cannes*, with the setting, Eden-Olympia, a high-tech business park near Cannes. Eden-Olympia is nominally a gated community but effectively a micronation. It is occupied by rich businesspeople who live in luxury homes, where they enjoy a private medical system and private security force.

Think it through.

Eden-Olympia is an exercise in social engineering where the architecture controls how the inhabitants think and behave.

'The moral order,' Ballard writes, 'is engineered into their lives along with the speed limits and the security systems.'

There is no separation between private and public space. The business park's new breed of corporate workers use their onsite homes merely to 'refuel', as if their homes were filling stations for automated bodies, with comfort and leisure of secondary concern.

Make the connection.

Eden-Olympia's modular buildings and modular people fulfil machinic functions that serve a higher purpose. The business park exists both within and outside of Cannes, fully integrated yet wholly apart due to its socio-spatial logic. On one level, the architecture forces the residents into a unified, sterile conformity. The business park is a metaphor for end-state consumerism, when every urge, every desire, has been mapped and commodified and the only way out, the only way to feel alive, is through metered doses of violence. Consumerism, the novel warns, must tap into extreme states of psychopathology so that it can continue to flourish. Accordingly, Eden-Olympia's stressed-out executives take pleasure trips to the edge of town to beat up immigrants living in makeshift camps.

Tune into the signal.

Eden-Olympia is self-regulating. It polices itself. There is no law enforcement, no religion. Its systemic efficiency means that any violation of that system is immediately apparent, standing out like tracer bullets in the night sky. The architecture in *Super-Cannes* is a cyborg interface between body and technology, and behind the pale walls of the office buildings lies a disturbing psychopathology that seems enhanced by the sterile environment, as if the endless white facades are magnifying glasses that channel a demonic sun into a vaporising heat, forcing the residents into a volatile, intense and fatally inward state.

Resurface.

The well-ordered strangeness of the Cube House complex seemed designed to repel the outside world even as its unique outline marked it as a local icon. In the courtyard, as I looked up through the star-shaped porthole to the sky, I imagined with a jolt that once again I could see myself down below, that I was in the Show Cube watching my tired and hunched frame trudging through the courtyard, for I had not quite divested myself of the nagging and profoundly disorientating out-of-body sensation that a few hours earlier had been all-encompassing. Like Jagger and Winfrey perched atop their respective stages— febrile celebrities confronted by their ghastly, ghostly selves—I could see that while I was on the inside of the complex, I was also the outsider failing to conform, watched by faceless people behind those sinister slanting facades.

Suddenly my attraction to Escher over Rembrandt, and to Ballard over everything else, made total sense, and I took these architectural observations as an affirmation that the way I had chosen to make a living was pre-ordained. The travel writer and the architect are quintessential Ballardian professions. Architects stalk the pages of many Ballard stories, using the city as a petri dish to mutate the psychology and physiology of its inhabitants, and while the job description 'travel writer' makes just one appearance (in *Cocaine Nights*, in the form of the character Prentice), almost all of Ballard's anti-heroes are travellers of some description, whether through inner space or the external world. And there I was, the dilettante wanderer, with a foot in both camps.

I could see a rootless life unspooling ahead of me as I wandered the globe on assignment after assignment, studiously avoiding relationships and commitment, writing about architecture and infrastructure while under cover as a travel writer, shunning human contact and preferring the ambience of buildings and freeways, doggedly determined to bury the pain and confusion I carried about the loss of both my academic career and the woman I loved.

Pathetic self-indulgence, it seemed, had become my life's work. And I was brilliant at it.

40

CUBIST DREAM

In the late afternoon, I rented a bicycle from a gruff man with a yellow beard in a small kiosk at the train station and rode to the Museum Boijmans Van Beuningen. After three days, the sights and sounds of Rotterdam were in my pores, and my ears rang with the ceaseless clatter of bicycles toppling over, a frequent occurrence, so tightly packed were they at every available parking point in the city. Outside the museum, I attempted to lock my bike but bumped the one next to me, starting a chain reaction as ten more fell over. A man was parking his Vespa. He flashed me a toothy grin.

'Relax,' he said. 'It's Holland. We're made of bikes.'

A mob of kids ran by, tipping over every bicycle they found.

'See? If not you, then someone else.'

I entered the museum. The fun sport enjoyed by the kids was echoed by two installations. One, a bicycle compacted into a cube. The other, a bike folded into a quarter of its size. Dutch spatial logic was again on show—how much could be done with so little and with such common items? I explored the surrealist wing, which collected works, ephemera and artefacts from Dali, Duchamp, Breton, de Chirico and Kandinsky. The surrealists were a touchstone for Ballard and he valorised their art for its conflation of the inner world of the mind with the outer world of reality. Dali's influence on *The Atrocity Exhibition* is palpable. Ballard and Dali share an interest in the rejuvenating essence of the paranoid mind to interpret reality in a more meaningful way and in the ghostly doubles that stalk the mental alleyways of modern life. *Atrocity* even includes a sequence in which T- imagines himself lost inside the actual landscape of one of Dali's most famous paintings, *The Persistence of Memory*, with its bizarre imagery of melted clocks set against a bleak desert back-drop. If Dali had remade the external landscape in the image of the mind, then Ballard had returned Dali's mindscape to the quotidian map of reality.

After two hours in the surrealist wing, I was spent. I went outside, laid down on the lawn and returned to *Requiem for a Dream*. I had almost finished it, and as I stared at the cover, re-minding myself of the juncture I was at in the story, I recalled its inexorable rush over the last few pages into unimaginable private hells for each main character. I put the book down and closed my eyes. A feeling of falling, of descent, struck me, and in this half-life I remembered I was from Australia and that Aus-tralia is on the bottom of the Earth and that I was currently on top of the Earth or somewhere near it. I was due to fly home in a week, and as the time drew near I felt myself falling back down under.

I became tired and giddy. The heat was intense and I was dehydrated from the two glasses of wine I had consumed at lunch. The alcohol, combined with the afterburn from Selby's horrific book and the psychic jolt from the surrealists, cast me adrift in a potent stew of nightmare imagery. I thought of novels of madness forged in European summers, such as Camus' *The Stranger*, a tale of sunblind murder and universal indifference, and Mann's *Death in Venice*, about the pathetic writer Aschen-bach, who sits on a sweltering Venetian beach and wilts from his fruitless lust for young male beauty.

The Dutch sun beat an oppressive tattoo on my eyelids, and as I passed away into the world of sleep I was deposited on the rooftop of the Osaka apartment I once shared with Cathe-rine. This did not seem strange, even though I understood that I was in Rotterdam. It was like the scene in *Solaris* where a char-acter drives an autonomous car from a house in Russia to the freeways of Tokyo, a geospatial disjunct that is never explained, never explicitly referred to, but simply *is*.

Catherine was inside somewhere. Even after all this time I still desired her, although I did not have the courage to act honestly and rectify the flaws in my character that had driven her from me. I was drunk as usual, swigging from a *sake* bottle as I leaned over the guttering. Peering through the window, I saw her in her dressing gown, eating breakfast at the wooden table in the kitchen. I called to her. She looked up.

'Oh. It's you. Yes, what is it?'

I drew breath, composing myself. For some reason (it was the first thought that came to mind), I asked her to imagine she was an astronaut living on the first space station in deep space, in the proximity of the Hubble telescope.

'Catherine, you are on a ten-year tour of duty. You are homesick and you can see the Earth from time to time through a super-telescope. The Earth looks very small but blue and green and recognisably home. You yearn for it, for your lover waiting for you back there, for your friends and family, but you have to finish your ten years in deep space. Finally, the time comes. At last, you are free to go home.'

I waved the *sake* bottle, gesticulating dramatically at the early morning sky. Catherine regarded me with barely concealed distaste.

'You undergo an exit medical and the result hits you like a shot through the heart. Owing to the ten years you've spent in artificial gravity, your limbs and musculature have altered irrevocably. One step under Earth's heavy gravity and your bones would snap like twigs. You would be a quivering jelly. With no skeleton to speak of, you would collapse inwards. Your internal organs would implode. You would drown in your own juices.

'Now, you are condemned to spend the rest of your life in the space station with the other unfortunates who came with you. You were the first crew. No one knew the effects because humans had never ventured that far into space before and for that long, and you will likely be the last, unless technology can assist our passage in the future. How would it feel, Catherine? How would it feel to gaze upon that blue-and-green orb, knowing that it is your home but that you can never return to it?'

She remained silent throughout that part of the proposition.

'Catherine, what would be your final act? Would you stay on the station, aimless, rootless and disconnected? Would you put your eyes out, unable to bear the sight of Earth and the lover that awaits you there, who you will never see again, and so serve out the rest of your days blind and insane? Or would you knuckle down and decide to make a good fist of it, perhaps intermarrying with a colleague from your damnable crew, while living forevermore with the heaviness in your heart of your true loved one, who you would never see again? Perhaps you'd commit suicide, hoping to meet your lover in the afterworld, where time has no purchase, is as meaningless as an apple in a wheelchair, as insignificant as a sewing machine making love to an umbrella on a hospital operating table.'

Finally she spoke, for the first time since I had called to her. Her pretty, round face poked through the window frame and looked up at me as I flailed theatrically on the rooftop. She crooked her finger, beckoning for me to follow.

'Come inside,' she said, so softly that I strained to hear.

I climbed down from the roof and scrambled through the window, still swigging from the bottle. I was drunk and shaky on my legs. She grabbed me to steady my descent, her hands around my waist until my feet struck the floor. My heart skipped a beat at the pressure of her long fingers on my hips. I felt a deep, sharp stab of nostalgia, a remembrance of loss that destroyed my composure, exacerbated by the sight of the painfully familiar kitchen. I stared at the table under which we'd crouched during the quake. On the bench, I saw the cup I'd been sipping from just before the tremors began—the vessel from which the 'alien blood' had sprung—imprinted with faded Japanese characters that said 'hello goodbye'. On the fridge door, I saw a photo of Catherine and her former lover. My image was nowhere to be found.

Despite those psychic wounds, I still loved her. I always would. I desired her madly but the manner of her embrace was that of an annoyed mother tending a wayward child and it doused my fire. She grasped my shoulders firmly and looked me directly in the eye. Neither her grip nor gaze were sexual or loving, rather they were matter of fact, tasks to be completed.

'I can't give you much time,' she said. 'You demand too much already and I have things to do this morning. But I will answer your question because I have suffered to sit through your proposition until the sheer weight of exposure to your drunken rambling forced a state of interest upon me, purely to find out the point of it all. In the end, it's a mildly interesting equation and I'll do well to answer it, if only for my own mental wellbeing, for I do not often like to think that *you*, of all people, could put such a conundrum to me to which I could not answer.'

She breathed in, exhaled.

'Yes, I would end it all. But I would do it my way. Not with pills or gun. No. I would go for one last spacewalk.'

I watched her speak, watched her full lips forming the words as I basked in the glow of her radiant inner light.

'I'd float for a while around the space station, taking one last look at my home for these last ten years.'

I drank more *sake*, intrigued. As she spoke, her round face was wide and expansive with wonder and I imagined the Earth's circumference superimposed over it, a graphic match in the mind: Catherine/Mother Earth.

'And then I'd push off the station in the direction of Earth and let the rope loose. Perpetual motion, Einstein's law—the vacuum of space would propel me home.'

I took her hands from my shoulders and clasped them in mine.

'But,' I spluttered, incredulous, 'your air supply would not last a day—two at best! It would take you weeks, months to return!'

'Yes,' she said, and a radiant energy sprang forth from deep inside her, an unquenchable spirit in the face of empirical reality and scientific rationalism. The glow on her face, the wattage from her smile, was as brilliant as the sun, and just as I had imagined the Earth superimposed over her face, I imagined that heavenly solar body performing the same function: Catherine/Goddess of Heat, Harbinger of Light.

'Yes, that is true. What you say is indeed the truth. But it would not matter if I died since the vacuum of space would preserve my body. It would reach the Earth in perfect condition, and as I died with the last of my air disappearing, I would strain to do so with grace, with a smile worn upon my face, despite the spasms of a failing, defeated vessel of flesh. And that, my body at rest, my face smiling—*that* would be my last gift to my loved one.'

'Oh, Catherine.'

I shook my head softly, immensely grateful to have the upper hand.

'Dear Catherine, your body would burn up on re-entering the Earth's atmosphere. There would be nothing left for your loved one to receive. You would be crisp and cinder.'

And then the light died. The wattage ebbed and her smile was gone. There was no more power to be drained. She pushed free of me, and as she did so I recognised this as the most terrifying moment of my life. She continued to push away and upwards, her hands spreading outwards from the force of her rage like the wings of a great bird shot through with the bullets of vicious hunters taking aim from below. And she cried. She gave birth to great heaving sobs instead of to the baby I desperately hoped I'd have with her one day. I had never seen her cry like that before. She was stricken, consumed with primal grief.

'Get out! I never want to see you again!'

She turned her back to me, her face hidden, that face which I'd derived so much satisfaction from watching, with its map of wonder and innocence drawn in her cartography of blood, nerves and facial tics. With her face turned away, like the dark side of the moon, unavailable to me with my limited means, I was like primitive man, a stumbling, blind, plague-ridden peasant man, and I hadn't yet invented the telescope that could see across to the far side of the moon.

With waning force, she turned around and repeated her command.

'Just leave. *Please*. You must leave. It's too late.'

It was dusk. A security guard prodded my shoulder.

'Sir, please, you have to go now. The grounds have closed. The museum is closed. You must leave. It's late.'

I rose and walked to my bicycle, which again had been knocked to the ground. I picked it up, rode to an internet cafe and typed up the dream in one go.

Then I emailed it to my friends back home with the subject line: 'Cubist Dream'.

41

URBAN SPLINTERS

Somehow, despite not following the brief, despite my interior thoughts overwhelming reality, I managed to deliver a manuscript that was acceptable to my editors. They even retained my obscure architectural references to Ballard, and when the Netherlands guidebook was published I marvelled at how I'd managed to build a new career from the ashes of my former life. More assignments followed, including a return to Japan, where I covered the sights of Tokyo, and a traversal of Australia's east coast, where shopkeepers and hotel managers were so eager to be reviewed by my prestigious employer that they stopped just short of offering me their daughters in return.

But after that first flush of success, I became thoroughly disillusioned with travel writing. The profession was nothing more than a confidence trick in which reviewer and proprietor colluded. Oh, I was content enough to describe the landscape, the sights, the architecture, but when it came to assessing the service in hotels and restaurants I didn't have the stomach for waxing lyrical or playing the game. If a small-town hotel manager offered me free accommodation, I felt intense pressure to deliver a favourable review. If I refused the offer, I felt the eyes of the locals upon me, burning with suspicion that a bad review was imminent. In any case, travel writers are redundant, for these days anyone can book a trip on the web and research anything they want to know about their destination. Mass travel has shrunk the world and dirt-cheap air fares have wrapped the planet in a tentacled grid of route maps, itineraries and carbon trails. The romantic notion of 'untouched areas' has become extinct, with package tourists following guidebook trails mapped out in advance.

In Ballard's novel *Millennium People*, a movement of deracinated middle-class urban professionals operates out of a central London gated community. They campaign against the mind-numbing effects of consumer society, bombing travel agencies in protest against mass tourism, which they deride as 'the great soporific'. The tourism industry is a con, they claim, deluding jaded suburbanites into thinking that by going somewhere, anywhere, they'll be able to hotwire their lives with mainline excitement, whereas in reality 'all the upgrades in existence lead to the same airports and resort hotels. There's nowhere to go. The planet is full.'

Ballard once said, 'no travel writer I have known has ever written about the importance of parking'. Was this a call for the profession to uncover new experiences in the barren age of mass tourism? If so, it was a challenge I wanted to pursue, given my fervent desire to reinvent my new career, little realising I was sliding back into the old one. In between assignments, I returned to the Ballard novels gathering dust in boxes under my bed. I scoured them for clues, cataloguing and cross-referencing countless passages featuring car parks. This urban typology was almost an unhealthy obsession for him, as he acknowledges in *Super-Cannes* when Sinclair, the narrator and Ballard avatar, is told that he 'needs a lobotomy' because he's 'obsessed by car parks.'

In *Atrocity*, there are numerous references to car parks. Their slanted form mirrors T-'s stylised movements through the media landscape and their 'inclined floors' function as a model of his 'oblique personality, forever meeting the events of time and space at an invisible angle'. Car parks are cornerstones of Ballard's post-industrial exotica, a type of homogeneous urban space that engenders fleeting moments and temporary states of being.

The anthropologist Marc Augé coined the term 'non-place' to describe such spaces, particularly transit zones that lie on the edge of awareness as we pass through them—car parks but also airport terminals, hospital waiting rooms, hotel lobbies, freeway underpasses. For Augé, the late twentieth century is characterised by 'supermodernity'—that is, the 'obverse of postmodernity'. Whereas the theoretical construct of postmodernity describes a loss of meaning, narrative and identity (subsumed within an endless play of images), supermodernity describes the superabundance of narratives and identities, and a *deluge* of meaning—a fundamental warping of our perception of time by the supersaturation of events bleeding out from media, TV and advertising. The architectural effects of non-place are merely by-products, an invasion of the material realm by a malignant infospace.

Non-place is fractured, incoherent, on the edge of perception. It is beyond history, beyond time, beyond identity. Non-place projects the illusion of connectivity but in reality forces us into a confrontation with ourselves, since the connectivity it offers is mechanical and uniform, like the disquieting similarities between major airports when, travelling from one to the other, it is as if one has not travelled at all. Non-place spreads like a disease because every non-place is a step on the way to somewhere else, part of the same synchronous system that *Crash* identifies, the tightly sutured matrix of consumerism and social control that keeps us perpetually hungry for new identities, new products, new promises, new lifestyles, new versions of ourselves.

And yet it is utterly seductive. In *Cocaine Nights*, whenever the travel writer, Prentice, crosses national borders, he is drawn to the 'no-man's land between the checkpoints, zones of promise, rich with the possibilities of new lives, new scents and affections'. I too was deeply attracted to such zones and never felt more alive than when I found myself in non-place, whether the duty-free zones of international airports (hazy, indeterminate yet strictly causal by-products of late capitalism) or capitalism's leavings, such as the industrial edgelands that ring major cities with their mutant amalgam of nature, ruins and functional architecture. The titular Stalker, Tarkovsky's guide to the Zone, also feels it and is unable to resist the powerful seductions of that ruined landscape, and through that analogous attraction I have come to understand how my own life has been defined by undecidability and my subconscious efforts to resist categorisation.

I've changed professions so many times that I never know what to say when people ask what I do for a living, sabotaging any chance at career progression, and when I find physical manifestations of that condition in the urban landscape—that sensation of being between, of existing in null space—I feel untouchable, charged with cosmic energy.

That attraction connects me to a wider, deeper dream. In the age of hypersurveillance, where privacy is non-existent and there is no point on the map that has not been surveyed, colonised or invaded, the dream of finding hidden folds in the cartographical matrix is immensely powerful, an impulse that helps to explain the phenomenon of micronations, so-called 'model nations' that claim dominion over forgotten corners of the map. Mostly, micronations are hobbyist exercises, although some have serious political intent, and almost all mimic the structure of independent nations and states. The most famous micronations are Sealand, which claims an abandoned WWII gun platform in the North Sea, and the Principality of Hutt River, located on a secessionist wheat farm in Western Australia. Perhaps, then, the most radical strategy of all would not be one of 'becoming known', as the wide-awake visibility of social media would have us believe, but of refusal and withdrawal: embracing obscurity and banality by inhabiting the greyed-out, blurred zones of hypercapitalism.

The point would not be to disengage completely (and risk entering a suicidal inwardness, as Ballard repeatedly warns) but knowing when to stop and when to withdraw. When to resist classification and when to exercise choice. When to re-form and when to re-emerge.

42

UNTOURISM

The more I thought about my swelling dissatisfaction with travel writing, the more I realised how much I'd been primed by Ballard, and with this realisation I felt my priorities begin to shift. For the first time in living memory, I experienced a kind of liberation, an unexpected feeling that accompanied me on my next assignment to Auckland. One evening, as I was walking across the public pier that bisects Viaduct Harbour, the footbridge rose to let a massive yacht through. Passers-by stopped in their tracks, strangers struck up conversations and children squealed in delight at the multi-sensory spectacle of the rising structure. The footbridge's tolling alarm bells and flashing hazard lights formed a vivid backdrop for the movement of the super yacht, creating a motion sculpture of languid beauty. Here was a spontaneous happening that engaged the people in random play, a readymade antidote to the tedious, top-down tendency in urban design to plan for every single human interaction.

Naturally, there was a Ballardian charge. In Ballard's work the amorphousness of the urban environment inevitably rises up to defeat the architect who dares impose his desires from on high. The emergent, the chaotic, the random always wins. However, on the subsequent assignment, to Barcelona, I found chaos and more. In Barcelona I found the spark that lit the fire that almost killed me.

Originally, I was enamoured with the place, especially the rhythm of its roads, completely different to that of Melbourne's, a measure I obtained via traffic flow, the true index of civility. In Barcelona, I observed how cyclists were treated with equal rights on the tarmac, as opposed to Melbourne roads, where cyclists are considered vermin and the only law is eat or be eaten.

In the brief moments when there were no cars, pedestrians crossed against the lights and the reverse was true for vehicles, although the congestion would invariably ramp up within seconds. The police didn't appear to mind. It was organised chaos (the traffic flow was dense and perpetual, balanced on a knife's edge) but as a social contract it worked. Barcelona was an organism that knew when to breathe in and when to breathe out, regulating its system for a stress-free life. Melbourne was a heart-attack victim with fatty arteries and severely constricted airways.

Barcelona was convivial, a city made for wandering, for inspiring reflection and thought. I walked many kilometres each day, directionless but always finding something to inspire in the alleyways and back streets, such as stencils of Kafka and graffiti that quoted Brecht. During one such foray, an elderly lady appeared. She saw me taking photos of buildings and stopped right in front of me, smiling radiantly but remaining silent the whole time. She was dressed impeccably, wearing a red beret, shiny red shoes and a beautifully tailored pink jacket and skirt.

Her face was obscured by the glare from the sun and I suffered the stark delusion that she was my mother. They were around the same age, of similar build and fashion sensibility. But the sun disappeared behind clouds, the old lady's face was revealed and I saw that she was not who I believed her to be. I took a step backwards, confused by my mistake, enduring a painful reversal of the process by which my mother had appeared to me during my childhood bike accident. The old lady jammed her cane into the ground and extended her arm outwards as if to say: *Hey! What about me? I'm the finest architecture here.* I took her photo, and as soon as the shutter clicked she turned on her heel and walked briskly away.

In the evening, I visited a few bars before returning to the hotel. Three girls approached me. They began to pat my chest and arms, stroking my hair and whispering in my ear. I was flattered. I wasn't thinking. I was drunk. I was stimulated. I hadn't been touched by a woman for a long time. Suddenly the girls broke away and turned a corner at lightning speed, and I knew my wallet had gone with them. I chased them down a side street. A short, stocky man stepped from the shadows, smashing a beer bottle into my face. I fell backwards, cracking the back of my head on the ground, shards of glass showering my body. I put my hand to my face, blood streaming through my fingers. My attacker stood over me. Although my eyes were filled with blood, I could just make out his features. His face was black with stubble and his hair was wiry. He was a dead ringer for Hollywood Dave.

I managed to speak, although the effort was difficult through cracked teeth and wads of blood and saliva.

'Dave...'

He spat in my face.

'Remember the name,' he said, before scurrying away to join the girls in the shadows beyond.

I addressed the empty street.

'Help. Help me, please. I'm in trouble.'

But there would be no help.

It was a long walk back to the hotel. I was angry and in extreme pain, semi-concussed and bitter to the core. No one assisted me or took the slightest bit of notice, despite my nasty head wound. I was made to feel invisible, shunned—a pariah. On that death march, as I re-entered the populated zone, I noticed for the first time how many young Barcelona men were on crutches. I realised I'd been seeing them everywhere, even at that time of night. No one was helping them, either. Perhaps they'd been run over where they stood, victims of the lax traffic laws. Perhaps the harmonious traffic flow I'd observed earlier was just a projection, nothing more than wishful thinking, the utopian distortion of a stupid outsider with his head in the clouds, blind to what was really going on. Perhaps the city had turned against these young men. Certainly, it had turned against me and that was a lesson I resolved never to forget: how quickly white can become black. Instead of admitting me as an equal partner, the streets had devoured me. Never again would I become so complacent, so disgustingly happy.

What was there to smile about?

Fuck all, I reminded myself. *And don't you forget it.*

I thought of Viaduct Harbour. Perhaps at that moment a fresh group of people had been stopped by the rising footbridge. Perhaps, drunk and belligerent, annoyed at being held up for a few minutes on a pub crawl or some other idiotic pursuit, they'd picked on a mild-mannered family man out for an evening stroll with his brood. Perhaps the family man had been pushed into the icy waters below. Perhaps he'd struck first, ripping one of the miniature fibreglass public-art cows from the ground, using it to smash his tormentor's face to a pulp.

Back in Melbourne, two weeks later, I downloaded my photos and discovered that following the assault they were all of roads, buildings, car parks—hundreds of photos with not a single person or 'normal' tourist landmark in any of them. That violent night in Barcelona had shifted my perception entirely. From the moment I'd picked my teeth up from the ground, it was as if I was the last man on Earth, documenting my surroundings, leaving photographic traces of my existence for discovery one day by a future race with more reason to live than me.

Utopia had been defeated. White had become black. Utopia was dead.

Long live dystopia.

PART III
MIRRORS

43

FROZEN TIME

Ballard said that he had a 'divided mind'. The Ballards had em-
igrated to England when he was young, but he was not English.
Shanghai was too vivid. The war was too real, too dirty, too insane. He could never go back (the past was 'another country',
he said), but Shanghai would always be with him. He would
rework the ruins of Shanghai into a private mythology, a rep-
ertoire of symbols coalescing into motifs repeated throughout
his stories, instantly familiar to any Ballardian worth their salt.
Drained swimming pools. Derelict runways. Deserted buildings.
Symbols imbued with a powerful ambiguity, radiating the mys-
tique of an abandoned humanity and the psychological reduction induced by apocalyptic events.

When *Empire of the Sun* was published, the critics rejoiced.
At last, Ballard's autobiography! *Empire* was believed to be a
high-resolution scan of his life but it was nothing of the sort. It
was a Xeroxed version, a degraded, tenth-generation copy, no
more blessed with ultimate biographical truth than the rest of
his stories. When he came to write about Shanghai, the symbols
stood in for the reality, since they had come to replace reality.
Empire, he said, was a reflection of 'the life reconstituted from
the fictional footprints that I left behind me'.

Lunghua was central to the mythology. It was the wellspring.
The camp was utterly removed from the world. Psychologically,
it was divorced from the conflict once Japan stopped maintain-
ing it in the face of crushing defeat. Spatially, it was isolated by
surrounding acres of paddy fields, deserted villages and barbed
wire. As Ballard recounts in his 'official' autobiography, *Miracles
of Life*, one morning, towards the end of the war, the internees
woke to find that all the guards had disappeared and that the

skies were empty of fighter planes. Most chose to stay within Lunghua, despite the freedom to leave (the camp had come to be all they knew, defining the boundaries of their world), and young Ballard did the same, although occasionally he travelled to and from Shanghai before returning to the camp (walking, hitchhiking, riding army trucks).

Viewed from certain angles, much of his fiction can be seen as a reworking of that biographical detail—the insular conditions of Lunghua and the strange behaviour it engendered. Pick a story, any story. In *Crash*, London's enclosed motorway system seals Vaughan's cult from the outside world after they imagine themselves merging with the road network's physical coordinates. In 'Thirteen to Centaurus', a group of people believe they are in a spaceship to Mars when in reality they are part of a controlled experiment inside a warehouse on Earth. Only one 'astronaut' has discovered the truth, a teenager, Abel, who leaves and enters the capsule as he pleases, although he keeps this knowledge to himself and chooses to remain with his people, preferring the illusion to whatever the outside world has in store. In *Concrete Island*, an architect, Maitland, crashes his car on a motorway and drives off an embankment, landing in a patch of wasteland beneath a spaghetti junction. Injured and unable to leave, he is effectively marooned, cut off from the view of the passing motorists above. Although he eventually heals, even then he remains, choosing to embrace the new sense of psychological freedom that envelops him the more he is distanced from his enervating job and loveless marriage.

In 'The Day of Forever', the Earth has stopped rotating, causing time to stand still. A young man, Halliday, haunts the abandoned hotels of an African town, scavenging for food and hoping he will once again be able to dream, an ability he inexplicably lost when time stopped. Before he washed up in Africa, Halliday lived in 'the international settlement at Trondheim in Norway', an obvious reference to Ballard's childhood. In *Empire*, the circle is complete. The childhood events that inspired his writing are returned to his biography as if they are elements of Ballardian fiction. *Empire* was published seventeen years after 'The Day of Forever' yet depicts a time decades in the past. Like *Atrocity*'s bewitched chapter titles, it obliterates the past and future.

In *Empire*, young Jim internalises the earlier story's fictionalised sense of frozen time, regarding his existence within the International Settlement as life lived 'wholly within an intense present'—as if time had indeed stopped. The fictional device in 'The Day of Forever', encasing Ballard's real-life Shanghai within a science-fictional metaphor, becomes a poignant comment on the unreality of the expatriate experience when transplanted to the Shanghai novel, where class and privilege shelter Jim and his family from the past (Shanghai's relationship to its Chinese history) and the future (the spectre of impending war).

Empire describes the abandoned, drained swimming pools of Shanghai's elite as if they were the mise-en-scene of a post-apocalyptic world. The cruelty of the Japanese guards is recorded with the same ambivalence as the willed violence in *Crash*, and Jim's exploration of ruins is guided by the same detached viewpoint adopted by Abel in his fake space station. *Empire* is not the story of Ballard's life but the story of his life viewed through his fiction. Fiction shapes reality. Shanghai came first, followed by the fiction that reworked those turbulent years, then the 'semi-autobiographical novel' about Shanghai that could not help but be shaped by the fiction originally trading off that life.

Empire plays fast and loose with the facts of his biography, generating a type of psychological realism—a mirror of the soul. As the Japanese war effort implodes, supplies are cut off and scores of internees starve to death, yet Jim does not fear war but rather embraces it for the evolutionary tests it brings. He's resourceful, forming a black-market trading network with the

American servicemen in the camp. He's idealistic, admiring the singleminded bravery of the Japanese soldiers. He's a dreamer, deeply possessed by the machinic beauty of the American and Japanese fighter planes that infest the skies.

Above all, he's a survivor. When he is separated from his parents, he is forced to live on his wits as he negotiates Shanghai's blasted landscape. In reality, Ballard's parents did not go missing in the war (nor was he an only child), although he said they were 'missing' from him in an emotional and empathetic sense. As a teenager, he simply felt he was coping with the war more effectively than they were, hence their removal in the novel and the amplification of Jim's personal qualities. The original life, the real Ballard's life, could never be accessed again. The life lived first, before any semblance of a writing career, remained a zone within a zone, a world within a world. *Empire* is a third-order simulacrum, a copy without an original that erases reality and replaces it with itself. Ballard could never go back. How could he when he was lost in the future?

In *The Kindness of Women*, the sequel to *Empire*, Jim emigrates to England. Ballard's real-life acid trip (the inspiration for his novel *The Crystal World*) and the car accident he endured after writing *Crash* take place within the fictionalised narrative of *Kindness*, so that the semi-autobiographical man inhabits two lives at once.

The novel is obsessed with the symbolism of mirrors, and Jim repeatedly frames his own actions and those of the people around him within their reflective gaze. A friend watches him through a mirror, 'as if the reversed image might give a clue to my sinistral dreams'. When he makes love to his girlfriend, 'with every glance in the mirror a small part of us died'. When his novel about his childhood in Shanghai is turned into a movie, he is filmed in conversation for 'a documentary about the production, a film within a film that took its place in the corridor of mirrors'.

He even speculates that one day he may write a sequel about his life in England, this imagined work triggering an infinite recursion effect when evoked within the reflective pages of Ballard's fictionalised sequel about his actual English life.

Even *Miracles of Life* is contaminated with the writer's imagination. The sudden death of his wife Mary from pneumonia takes up barely a page, but his dream of her returning to him to say goodbye takes up considerably more, as does a discussion of *The Atrocity Exhibition*, the writing of which was partly his attempt to sublimate the hurt and anger he felt at losing her so unexpectedly. Motifs from his fiction bleed into the autobiographical frame. When he describes how he was originally drawn to science fiction because it examined the trend towards 'politics conducted as a branch of advertising', we recognise echoes from *Crash* where the phrase was first used in the introduction. How is this 'autobiography' more truthful than *Empire*?

Ballard was a time traveller, revisiting his Lunghua memories in numerous stories, blurring the edges in each incarnation, incrementally shifting the background scenery, erasing forever the demarcation between fiction and reality. When Spielberg filmed *Empire*, these fictional footprints reconstituted themselves like a tulpa shaped from the imaginative clay of the mind's eye. Spectral afterimages leaked from the Shepperton studios as the ectoplasm of memory engulfed the immediate area like tar. Spielberg used the streets around Ballard's house to recreate the Shanghai neighbourhood where the Ballard family lived. Ballard's Shepperton neighbours were recruited to play his fellow Lunghua inmates.

On set one day, Christian Bale, cast in the role of Jim, approached him.

'Hello, Mr Ballard,' he said. 'I'm you.'

A divided mind. A copy without an original. Shanghai overlaid onto Shepperton. Ballard vs Ballard. None of this was by chance. On the contrary, it was quite deliberate. Ballard dreamed this future into being. He created the conditions for his own replacement. He knew he was expendable and that this was an inconsequential detail.

Nothing was more important than the story, the words on the page.

44

NEW VICTIMS

Baudrillard said that the desire to be a clone is the ultimate fantasy expression of the society of simulation, that is, 'the fantasy of being able to circle around one's self' by way of advanced technology. Virtual reality, social media, augmented reality—all allow us to project perfect images of ourselves to the world. What is left but sexless reproduction?

'No more mother, no more father', writes Baudrillard, but 'a matrix, that of the genetic code. The subject is also gone, since identical duplication puts an end to division.'

Ballard knew this. He practised it. He was the alchemist. In *Empire*, Jim, finally rid of his parents ('no more mother, no more father'), bests all the adults and exposes their petty games, flowering into a psychological being fully formed and primed for adult life. The fantasy of the clone in this context is not simply about a perfect reproduction but a reproduction that is perfect, more so—a surpassing of the self.

But if *Empire* is Ballard's anti-autobiography and his most famous novel, then *Crash*, his most infamous work, is the anti-*Empire*—his anti-anti-autobiography. A narrator called 'James Ballard' in a novel about psychopathic sex addicts? What the devil is he playing at? It's a joke, it must be. Jim in *Empire* is the real Ballard.

So they say.

Think.

When Mary died, Ballard was stalked by the black dog. Outraged at the indifferent universe that had taken her from him, for the next ten years he channelled his grief and anger into an extraordinary body of work. Across that dark decade, he produced the dislocating cut-up chapters that comprised *Atrocity*. He designed a series of 'advertisers' announcements' and even bought advertising space in magazines to place the ads and 'sell' his morbid obsessions (one featured a bondage photo of a bound and ball-gagged woman alongside inscrutable text: 'In her face the diagram of bones forms a geometry of murder.').

He conceived a play about the psychosocial significance of the car crash. He devised a gallery exhibition of crashed cars, hosted by a stripper, that culminated in the drunken destruction of the exhibits by an audience enraged at the casual violence underpinning his art. He starred in a short film called *Crash!*, playing another version of himself. Half fiction, half documentary, the film is a waking dream. The Ballard avatar—a sort of clone—stalks a spectral woman across the motorways, overpasses and car parks of suburban Watford, and as she fades in and out of his mind's eye he imagines her fetishised body broken and brutalised in a parade of car-crash scenarios.

All told, it was a disturbing body of work but even so it was merely a prelude to the ultimate statement: *Crash*. The novel.

'Do not publish.'

Crash's narrator is called 'James Ballard', not because Ballard himself had a history of crashing cars for sexual kicks but because he considered the controversial subject matter to be the final exorcism of his pain after losing Mary. *Crash*'s extreme material, he said, was a valid index of his inner life and emotional turmoil. It was his true autobiography, he added, not *Empire*, mocking those who took his Shanghai novel to be the

Real McCoy, and in interviews he embraced *Crash*'s authorial confusion.

'*Crash* is my psychopathology,' he once said. 'The book is a psychopathological hymn and I'm singing it. Attaching my name to the protagonist reminds the reader where these ideas are coming from: a real human being, a "real" reality.'

Lost in the mantra of stylised violence, Ballard hypnotised himself, exorcising his grief with the ritual repetition of automobile trauma, exploring it from every conceivable angle across every artistic discipline available to him. But isn't it the case that artists dabbling in the black arts, mediators between worlds, tend to lose themselves in the glare after flying too close to the sun? For incantations of this kind, repeated often enough, can bring something back with them when the voyager, the cosmonaut of inner space, re-enters our world. There are ruptures in space-time. Matter collides and there is fallout, like a Sumerian demon woken from the dead and hungry for souls.

After considering the uncanny similarities between the dark desires of *Crash* and the death of Princess Di, the writer Iain Sinclair asked of Ballard: 'Had he activated a demonic psychopathology that could only be appeased by regular sacrifices?' As everyone knows, the Princess died in a high-speed collision pursued by a blood-frenzied media scrum, but it was as if Vaughan himself had planned it. After all, in *Crash* he is obsessed with filming the death of a Hollywood 'princess', Elizabeth Taylor, in a staged car crash.

But if Ballard had activated a demonic dimension, then with crushing inevitability it tried to claim him too, once the clone had set the parameters for his demise. In the short film *Crash!*, the clone warns that the car crash is the most significant event that will happen to most people, aside from death. Is it completely meaningless, the clone asks, a random act of violence, 'or does it in fact take place with our unconscious, and even conscious, connivance?' For the clone, car crashes are 'arranged deaths' brought on by a collision between 'the technological landscape' and our 'unconscious fantasies about power and aggression', and the crash itself is the logical by-product of consumerism and the immersive fictions it generates—of our willingness to become subsumed by them.

And so it happened that, shortly after delivering the manuscript of *Crash* to his publisher, James Graham Ballard rolled his Ford Zephyr on a divided motorway. A blowout forced the vehicle into oncoming traffic and it landed upside down. Petrol was leaking everywhere and Ballard was trapped—the roof had jammed down and the doors would not budge. With desperate shouts from onlookers of 'Petrol! Petrol!' filling his ears and the realisation the car could explode at any second swamping his mind, he managed to reach deep within himself, somehow pulling body and soul together to force a window down and escape before he was engulfed in the flames of full-tilt autogeddon.

Having lived with the concept of *Crash* for so long, did Ballard, like the narrator of his novel, experience cathartic relief after finding himself at last in an actual accident?

That was not the end of it. Once invoked, the demon could never be put back in the bottle. Ballard's accident would be immortalised in another version, enacted by another clone, shot in the uncanny valley of location filming. When Cronenberg made *Crash*, he dug deep into Ballard's real-life mythology, fashioning a scene in which the film's 'Ballard' (a clone of a clone, the novel's narrator transmuted into celluloid—the real Ballard twice removed) crashes his car on a divided motorway and swerves into oncoming traffic. Ballard had told the story of his personal crash to several interviewers and the film event plays like that recollection rather than the equivalent scene in the novel, further blurring the boundaries between his life and the unquenchable artistic monster he'd unleashed. For his sins we were given a new crash (a new *Crash*), a new clone (a new 'Ballard') and a new director (Spiel/Cronen/berg), as Ballard and his ghastly obsession were killed off and reborn in the inferno of repetition.

As Sinclair observes: 'The same crashes happen over and over as new victims are initiated into the vision.'

New victims—including myself.

45

FUGUE STATE

People would often gush with envy when I told them what I did for a living. Travel writing must be the best job in the world, they'd invariably say, but one of the biggest misconceptions about the profession is that guidebook authors swan around on holiday and then do a bit of writing as an afterthought. In reality, much of the job involves gathering facts and figures and updating perishable information, such as currency rates or the phone numbers of tourist offices. There is little time for sightseeing as you're always battling the quick and savage clock, on your feet for twelve hours a day during torrential rain, baking heat or whatever testing local conditions you're parachuted into. I was paid a lump sum for each job and all expenses were taken from that. The amount of money I'd make for a particular assignment was determined by how long I spent in each location. If I missed a bus or train or spent too long in the pub, I might have twenty hotels to review the next day instead of ten. But whatever I did, there would always be another brochure to collect or another hotel toilet to inspect.

I took the frankly absurd out-of-body experiences as proof I was working too hard and becoming unhinged. I needed to slow down, stop travelling, find a partner, settle down and get a desk job, anything to anchor me in the real world. I was ready to throw it all away when the company made me an offer too good to refuse: they invited me to become their North Pacific correspondent.

When they sent me the offer, they also sent me a map of the North Pacific. I scanned it. Most of the islands were specks in the ocean separated by vast distances. I thought of the isolated pub that existed in the apex of the two major freeways back in the bleak tarmac desert of my childhood suburb. The pub had always reminded me of a remote Pacific island, an association driven by its location. You couldn't walk up to it, since there were no footpaths. The only way to reach it was by car. It seemed a location of impossible appeal amid the chaos, noise and speed of the freeways, an association that deepened the first time I read *Concrete Island*, where, in the introduction, Ballard considers the common fantasy of being marooned on a desert island. Why does it carry such appeal?

On one level, it affords the chance to return to our primitive being, to test ourselves and survive on nothing but our animal cunning. Mostly it will remain just a fantasy, and yet, he claims, while 'the Pacific atoll may not be available ... there are other islands far nearer to home ... surrounded, not by sea, but by concrete, ringed by chain-mail fences and walled off by bomb-proof glass'.

Subways isolated by power failures; elevators trapped in office buildings. Could such situations be engineered?

'Marooned in an office block or on a traffic island,' Ballard theorises, 'we can tyrannise ourselves, test our strengths and weaknesses, perhaps come to terms with aspects of our characters to which we have always closed our eyes.'

I suppose I had always viewed the remote pub in that way, even as a child—even before I'd become a Ballardian. Judging by the impossibly angry men that went in and out of it, and the seething rage they unleashed on the world once they'd become intoxicated, the pub was a lawless interzone, an effect intensified by its location, which seemed to transform completely the damaged souls that passed through it.

My assignment offered a rare opportunity. In *Concrete Island*, Ballard compares Maitland's patch of wasteland to a Pacific atoll. Eleven years earlier, in 'The Terminal Beach', he'd described an actual Pacific atoll, Enewetak, as 'synthetic, a man-made artefact with all the associations of a vast system of derelict concrete motorways'. (Enewetak had been used for nuclear testing by the Americans during the 40s and 50s, irradiated by nuclear slagheaps and pockmarked with concrete testing bunkers.) The urban wasteland and the Pacific atoll are inversions, forming in their totality an ambivalent state where conflicting ideas are held simultaneously—where black becomes white. The remote pub, as it existed in my memory, its Pacific metaphor intact, was but one side of the reflection and therefore only half the story. By actually travelling to the Pacific, perhaps I would be able to finally enter the mirror-world that I had long sought.

I itemised the islands that Rough Planet wanted me to visit. Palau. Yap. Chuuk. Pohnpei. Kosrae. Saipan. Rota. Tinian. And Guam.

Guam.

Yes, I knew about Guam.

I remembered the American in Tokyo and the picture he'd painted of Guam as a tropical theme park for Japanese tourists. Because of his stench, the idea of the place was less than appealing, yet overlaid with the Ballardian matrix an overwhelming aura radiated from the cartographical grid. Ever since the Netherlands, Ballard was back on the menu, no doubt about it, but in a different form. Gone was the fanboy hagiographer who had first attempted that ridiculous thesis. In his place was a man possessed by the spirit of Ballard, animated by the Ballardian.

Invested with this new power, I made an inventory of all the Ballard stories set in the Pacific, a subset that included the novels *Empire of the Sun* and *Rushing to Paradise*, the short stories 'My Dream of Flying to Wake Island' and 'The Terminal Beach', and parts of *Atrocity*. I found them fascinating, since the characters experience fugue states that correspond with the extraordinary slipstream the Pacific itself inhabits, caught between a tribal past and a forestalled nuclear future.

Pacific islands have always suffered from unstable identities and volatile nationalism, from perpetually coup-ridden Fiji in the South Seas to the permanently colonised islands north of the equator. Palau is frequently cited as an archetypal tropical utopia but it also embodies the root definition of 'utopia'—*no place*. It has been a pawn in the hands of colonial powers continuously since the late seventeenth century, diluting its traditional culture and replacing it with a melange of other cultures. Spain enforced Christianity on the Palauan people. Germany commanded them to work as plantation slaves. Japan forced Palauans to speak a subservient form of Japanese and turned the main island into a heavily fortified military base. The US bombed Palau in a series of bloody battles with Japan before claiming it as American territory until 1994.

For Ballard, the Pacific is compelling. The terrain around Lunghua, he explained, had been bombed by US planes based in Guam, an act that birthed the Ballardian multiverse—the blasted conditions of Lunghua were the seeds from which the psychopathology of his characters grew. Because of this link, he said, the abandoned wartime runways of Pacific islands retained 'a potent magic', filled with 'extreme states of nostalgia and possibility, doorways into another continuum'.

'My Dream of Flying to Wake Island' captures that mystical feeling. A concrete story arc never coalesces, rendering the narrative in perpetual fugue, much like the Pacific itself, and a constant yearning envelops the central character Melville, a former astronaut who flew a solitary mission in space during which he suffered a mental breakdown broadcast live to millions of viewers on Earth.

I detected a parallel between his public humiliation and my still-raw dismissal by Catherine. If Melville had imploded in space then I had crash-landed in inner space, an illogical, childish metaphor that summed up the scale of my delusion. Humiliated and wanting to remove himself from the world, Melville resolves to fly to remote Wake Island in the North Pacific, possessed by the island's geographical isolation and 'psychological reduction', the latter a product of its role as a WWII military base and the fact that it has never had a permanent indigenous population. Like Melville, Wake Island was lost between worlds.

Melville prepares for his journey by collecting photos of the war ruins that festoon Wake Island and I did the same, copying the behaviour of this damaged astronaut in preparation for my own trip. I was drawn to one particular series taken by a US military officer stationed on Tinian. He'd developed the photos during the war in a clandestine photo lab on the island, dramatically capturing apocalyptic flashpoints. Pockmarked runways. Plane and tank wrecks half concealed by jungle. Mass military graveyards. Bombers submerged in sand. Damaged bunkers and air force shacks.

In the end, I accepted Rough Planet's offer. After all, the trip offered the chance to drop completely off the grid, which was fortuitous given that erasing myself from public view was my secret desire, while comfy domesticity would be just another sop to the ghost of Catherine. Like Melville, I knew the Pacific held the key that would unlock my final escape into a different dimension.

46

STRESS TEST

On 16 July 1945, the first atomic bomb was detonated in New Mexico on the Alamogordo Test Range. For an emergent breed of scientists, this event signalled a new epoch, which they dubbed the 'Anthropocene', marking the moment when humans began to make an irreversible impression on the entire planet and its resources. The dawn of the nuclear age was chosen as the historical start point for the Anthropocene because of the devastating impact radioactive isotopes have had on the environment, coinciding with massive population spikes and the development of destructive global technologies that have contributed to irreversible climate change.

Ballard developed the notion of an historical nuclear hinge-point in both *Crash* and *Empire of the Sun*, well before the term 'Anthropocene' was coined, although his focus was on metaphysical rather than physical effects. In *Empire*, as Japan's war effort crumbles, Lunghua is evacuated and the internees are led on a death march to Nantao Stadium, supposedly to find rations but secretly to be executed. After near-fatal run-ins with roving bands of American scavengers, Jim ends up in the destroyed stadium, now filled with prisoners of war, and watches as the horizon is illuminated by the unearthly light from the atom bomb over Nagasaki. Jim understands that he is on the cusp of a world-rending event, an unprecedented historical divide: 'He had seen the start of World War III, and realised that it was taking place around him.'

What then is the real 'empire of the sun'? Not the rising sun of Japanese nationalism but the nuclear sun and the birth of the postwar era. In effect, Jim has witnessed the Big Bang: the birth of the Ballardian universe.

In the introduction to *Crash*, Ballard spells out his proto-Anthropocenic thesis, asserting that the post-war world is indeterminate precisely because there is no precedent for the nuclear age in the safe nostalgia of the past. The future, he declares, has become 'a casualty of Hiroshima ... devoured by the all-voracious present'. Today we are in thrall to a disorientating atemporality that renders history nonfunctional, seeping down from the planetary scale of climate change into the minutiae of our everyday lives. Who listens to a single album anymore? We listen to every album from across a musician's multi-decade career—the soundtrack of the Anthropocene is an eternity of songs blancmanged in shuffle mode on our devices.

In 'The Terminal Beach', Ballard predicted the fusion of all cultural inputs into one homogeneous mass. The story marks the first appearance of T-, the troubled psychiatrist who would later stalk the pages of *The Atrocity Exhibition*. Here, he's known as 'Traven', a radiation-sick air force pilot wandering the ruined bunkers of Enewetak after it had been blasted by American nuclear testing. Crazed and hallucinating, Traven detaches himself from reality and imagines himself communing with dead bodies as his psychology and physiology mutates among the irradiated bunkers, a transformation framed as an explicitly post-war condition, induced by thermonuclear weapons, that results in 'the total fusion and non-differentiation of all matter'.

The Pacific has been warped by nuclear testing. French Polynesia was used as a testing site for almost ten years, so saturated with nuclear fission that high radiation levels were detected 4,500 kilometres away in Fiji. Bikini Atoll was rendered uninhabitable by American nuclear tests, its inhabitants forcibly relocated, never to return, and the same fate befell Enewetak, although its people, relocated in 1948, were allowed to return in the 80s after the US government caved under global pressure and cleared the main island of active waste. Stripped of the past by the American war machine, these islands were turned into fortresses from which the twenty-first century was born and then left in an elastic time-space continuum once the war had ended.

On Runit Island, part of Enewetak Atoll, there is an enormous 46cm-thick concrete dome, known to locals as 'the Tomb'. The dome covers the nine-metre-deep crater formed by the 1958 Cactus nuclear test, containing tonnes of plutonium waste with a half-life of 24,000 years. There are photos online that show children playing on top of the dome, indifferent to its deadly contents. When the human race disappears and Runit is uninhabited, the debris will remain. The dome has begun to crack and scientists fear it is only a matter of time before a major typhoon damages it further, causing its lethal contents to spill into the ocean. In any case, climate change and rising seas will ensure that Pacific islands like Runit will be underwater before too long. The plutonium waste will be submerged. Water pressure will stress-test the cracked concrete, and when it fails and the waste cascades into the ocean, the planet will be the tomb.

Runit's concrete dome, overlaid with Ballardian significance, became an extreme metaphor for my trip, its dark toxicity contained by layers of burial, nuclear waste corkscrewing down into the collective cultural subconscious, out of sight but always threatening to ooze out insidiously.

47

BLACK HOLE

Guam was the hub for my Pacific mission, this US territory with its northern half dominated by the imposing Andersen Air Force Base. During the war, Guam was a sleepy backwater. Today it is part mini-Florida, part WWII theme park and part American suburb, riven with temporal displacement. There are US flags and fast-food restaurants everywhere, the locals have American accents and consider themselves American, and the indigenous Chamorro culture has been almost subsumed (today, only a quarter of the population speaks the language).

The drive through the southern region is beautiful, winding through jungle-fringed hills and coastlines, and there are atmospheric old villages steeped in the architecture of another invading power: the Spanish from the time of Magellan. Near the southern beaches, fifteen metres under water, lie the wrecks of Japanese Zero fighter planes. I swam out to one of the wrecks, and as I stared at its morphing outline beneath the deep blue, rippling water, I found it difficult to reconcile Guam's violent history of invasion with what I knew of Japan and its people, which, judging from my Tohoku misadventures, seemed more slapstick than belligerent.

When I drove to the War in the Pacific memorial park at Asan Beach, I was educated in what the Japanese had done. On the radio, a man from Yap, among the North Pacific's most traditional islands, was describing the concept of *rai*—stone money. *Rai* are highly symbolic 'coins', four metres in diameter, that were carved centuries ago in Palauan quarries five hundred kilometres away and brought to Yap by outrigger canoe.

The man detoured into a history lesson.

'When the Japanese occupied Yap during the war,' he said, 'they smashed *rai* as punishment if we didn't cooperate, then used the broken pieces to pave their roads. If that didn't work, they just murdered us and dumped our bodies outside the villages. By the end of the war, our population was down to 2,000, although today it's 11,000. Still not that much but better than total extermination.'

He delivered this information without rancour but rather in a detached fashion, relaying historical fact. It reminded me of Ballard's descriptions of the Japanese in occupied Shanghai, a topic he frequently turned to in interviews. With similar detachment, he would tell the story of how he'd witnessed Japanese officers in the street slowly strangling Chinese prisoners to death with telephone wire, or how he'd watched Japanese soldiers ride in a coolie's rickshaw before refusing to pay, taking it in turns to smash the rickshaw to bits before kicking the coolie to death. When asked how such brutality had influenced his fiction, Ballard pulled no punches.

'Violence is seductive in that it has a logic of its own; one almost misses it when it's gone ... One tries to recreate episodes of violence because they do tell a kind of truth—a final truth—about human beings and what we are.'

The host of the radio program, fired up by the Yapese man, began to admonish Guamanian and American politicians for holding out on reparations for Guam's war victims, a raw reminder of how the Chamorro people had themselves suffered, first as victims of the Japanese, then as US 'citizens' drafted into the gory theatre of war. When the Americans retook Guam from Japan in 1941, Asan Beach was one of the flashpoints of that bloody battle. Today, it is a peaceful stretch of deep-blue water with rocky sands fringed by swaying palm trees, although the various monuments scattered around the War in the Pacific Park leave no doubt as to what had happened.

War ruins festoon the North Pacific, symbolising how the memory of the conflict is kept alive at the deepest structural level so that the region can never find peace. The ruins are black holes that absorb all the light, sun and sand from their surroundings, and the islands are double agents weighed down by an impossible trauma that can only be glimpsed at the edge of perception. Most of the islands I visited on that trip were idyllic, yet their tropical surface was flimsy, a veil that could be torched at any moment.

As I explored the War in the Pacific Park, I considered the

casual way everyone on Guam leaves rubbish lying around, locals and tourists alike, adding another layer of undecidability to the island's cultural strata. Empty cans of Asahi, the famous Japanese beer, were discarded on the ground next to cans of Budweiser, America's 'King of Beers'. I watched Guamanian kids drinking Budweiser in the remains of a Japanese WWII bunker as the flags of Guam, the US and Japan flew in the background. Like its Scheveningen counterpart, the bunker was compelling, its great bulk staring down time and space, and the simple actions of those kids and the cultural flashpoints they represented embodied the essential mystery of both the bunker and the Pacific.

No place.

48

METANOIA

As the evening approached, I drove to Tumon Bay, which once boasted a thriving beach-bar scene consisting of numerous huts on the sand that sold triple-strength island cocktails. The huts were no more, although some hotels maintained beachside bars in an attempt to recreate that heady atmosphere. There was one genuine holdout, 'Jimmy Dee's', founded by Guamanian singer and island legend Jimmy Dee. I made my way there, sat down at the bar and heard laughing from the other side. It sounded familiar and I peered around the palm trees in the middle to see who was there. It was none other than the American from Tokyo, the one with the bad haircut, his arm draped around a female companion. When he saw me, his face lit up and I braced myself for the verbal diarrhoea that would surely follow.

'Buddy!' he spluttered. 'Ha, it's *you!* What the hell? How are ya, man? I knew you'd turn up here one day. Get over here. Pull up a seat.'

I sat next to them. He jerked his thumb at the woman, a rude gesture I thought.

'Hey, this is Connie.'

Connie was very drunk. She was sipping a large cocktail topped with a miniature paper umbrella and seemed much older than him.

'About time we all got acquainted, right Connie?'

'Sure thing, Rob.'

So that was his name.

During our entire Tokyo encounter, 'Rob' had never told me his name or given me a business card—unusual behaviour for such an egotistical bigshot. He tried to make conversation.

'So, my Aussie mate—ever been to Tasmania?'

There was something indecent about him and I wanted to stop his inane patter dead in its tracks. I started rambling, spouting anything to shut him up.

'Yeah, I have. I was there last month, in fact. In Hobart, on assignment. Well, I say "assignment" but really I was just looking for disaster porn.'

Rob stared at me like I was something he'd dug out from his ear, while Connie seemed turned on at the mere mention of 'porn', her cheeks flushed with red.

'See, Tassie has always interested me. I like how it's so isolated from mainland Australia. Like Tohoku. You remember Tohoku, don't you, Rob?'

This time, it was my turn: I jabbed a thumb in his direction and turned to Connie.

'We met in an internet cafe in Tokyo. I'd just come back from Tohoku. I think Rob was looking at porn. Not disaster porn— the real stuff. Anyway, he tried to freak me out with insane stories about midget ninja ghosts and cyborg dogs.'

Connie glared at him and Rob fixed me with a dead expression, waiting impatiently for his turn to speak, but I stymied him by refusing to pause and extend a gap in the conversation that he could exploit.

'For as long as I can remember, I've been morbidly fascinated by collapsing bridges. I was a toddler when the Westgate Bridge in Melbourne collapsed during construction in 1970, killing 35 workers, and although I was too young to really remember it, I knew how the city was affected afterwards. Bridges are powerful when they fail, signifying a deep psychological rupture in the social contract, a sense of disbelief that the systems that hold us in place can be so easily breached.'

Rob shifted uneasily and Connie scratched her nose.

'Five years later, the midsection of Hobart's Tasman Bridge collapsed when it was hit by an iron ore tanker. I can vividly recall photos of the ruined bridge in the newspapers. One photo showed two cars hanging over the edge of the huge gap where the middle of the bridge used to be. Four cars had already gone over, killing seven people. When I went to Hobart recently, I wanted to bathe in that feeling of disaster, to imagine what it would be like to witness a bridge fall down right in front of me, to watch the world split apart.'

'Uh, okay,' Rob said, forcing his way into the conversation. I knew I'd weirded him out and felt a momentary sense of triumph.

'So, anyway,' he prattled on, 'Australia's best death metal scene is in Hobart. Not many people know that.'

I couldn't stand him, so I refocused on Connie.

'How long have you been here?'

'Seven years and it's driving me nuts. There are *no* men on Guam.'

Now it was her turn to jerk a thumb at Rob—he was the type of insect you just wanted to squash under your finger.

'Except for *this* guy. Well, there are but they're all married with kids by the age of fifteen.'

'So what do you two do for kicks, besides hang out at Jimmy Dee's? I'm writing about Guam and looking for inside info.'

Rob scoffed.

'You won't find any culture here, my friend. There's not even a film industry! Well, there was one big blockbuster filmed here, but then it got canned and no one ever saw it. It was funded with dirty money or something like that. They couldn't even get that right.'

Connie leaned in, a conspiratorial air about her.

'There's this red-light joint around the corner we always go to when things get dull. Courtney Love used to strip there. It was the only way she could make money when she was trying to be an actor.'

'Why Guam?'

'Don't know. It was after she auditioned for the part of Nancy in *Sid and Nancy* and didn't get it. Maybe someone on the production told her to do it. You know how sleazy these film types are.'

She looked at her watch and the movement parted the lip of her handbag, which was dangling from her arm. Inside the bag I saw makeup and a purse, as well as syringes and a big box of doves.

'Where did you get those?' I said, pointing to the pills.

She snapped the bag shut.

'None of your business. Rob!'

Rob came over and grabbed my arm. His grip was surprisingly strong. He whispered in my ear.

'*Hey buddy, what's with all the questions? Can't you see the lady's trying to show you a good time?*'

As I backed away, Connie's demeanour softened.

'I'm just going home to powder my nose,' she cooed. 'Join us there in fifteen minutes? You'll like this place, I promise. Courtney's knickers are framed on the wall.'

'We love us a bit of Love!' Rob bellowed.

Without waiting to hear my answer, Connie departed and I took the opportunity to make my excuses and leave. Assuming I was reading the vibes right, the thought of a threesome with these people was nauseating.

As I left, Rob yelled at me.

'Hey buddy! You've changed since Tokyo! What's wrong with you? Antisocial little prick!'

But I've always been antisocial, you idiot. You were just too self-absorbed to notice.

I stepped outside. Connie had driven away. A trail of doves was laid out on the ground, snaking from the entrance to the spot where her car had been parked. It was absurd. Was there a hole in her bag? The pills reflected the moonlight, tiny pinpricks illuminating a cartography of pain, and for once I resisted the urge to ingest them, instead crushing them under my feet, one by one. I caught Rob watching from the doorway. He was talking on his phone. When he saw that I'd noticed him, he scurried inside.

I made it back to the hotel. The coffee shop opposite was filled with light and activity. This was unusual, since it was typically a dank place and never seemed to be open or to have any life about it whatsoever. I went inside to see what was going on and found men and women in suits and formal dresses moving in and out between the back room and the front. They were arranging tables and carrying plates of food. I was greeted by a woman with a German accent.

'Hello there. You look tired.'

'I am.'

'We're not really open tonight—we're hosting the local church group. But you're staying across the way, aren't you? I've seen you come and go. Why don't you join us? Meet some new friends?'

A church group was an unsurprising development, given that Guam is staunchly Catholic and the signs of faith are everywhere.

Crucifixes. Statues of the Pope. Roadside Baby Jesus dioramas illuminated three months ahead of Christmas. Before I could say I wasn't interested, a public-service announcement came on the radio. I turned to listen, recognising it instantly as I'd been hearing it all over Guam. It featured Robin Zander and Rick Nielsen from the band Cheap Trick, their glory days far behind. As the opening power chords kicked in, I turned to the woman.

'Can you believe it? This is what it has come to for these guys. They used to be actual *rock stars*. OK, wait for it...'

She smiled indulgently. As the music died down, Robin spoke.

'Hi, this is Robin from Cheap Trick. Don't drink and drive. You *know* it's dumb.'

Then Rick piped up.

'Hi, I'm Rick from Cheap Trick. Yeah, don't drink and drive. It really is dumb. Remember, music lives and so should you.'

Music lives.

In the dull, blunt setting of that clandestine church group meeting, the radio announcement brought the enigma that is Guam into sharp focus. Now I understood the island's real function. Guam was purgatory, a place where everyone goes to find redemption for their sins. War ghosts, Japanese tourists, faded rock stars, exiled Americans like Rob, failed academics like me. With that realisation, I told the German lady I would be happy to stay.

'Excellent,' she said, pouring me a glass of premium apple juice. 'Now the real fun can begin.'

49

LOST IN SAIPAN

Despite the German lady's kind offer of plentiful juice and prayer, I had failed to achieve spiritual nirvana. After interrogating me at length, she had decided I was too removed from the world to be properly saved. She advised me to go nowhere near Saipan, the next stop on my itinerary, claiming it was a den of iniquity and the cesspit of the Pacific, with its notorious strip clubs. She believed I would be highly susceptible to becoming a victim of violence there, but Guam had its share of vice, too, as my encounter with Rob and Connie had hinted.

I ignored her and flew to Saipan. I checked into a cheap hotel in downtown Garapan, unwittingly ensconcing myself in the red-light district. The woman was correct. I could not do anything without being wrapped in the tentacles of degradation. My room was cramped and airless. It was one of the hottest nights of the year, and with no air conditioning and only a tiny window, I opened the door to let the air in. Across the way, I saw a gaggle of hookers, barely wearing anything, sitting on their balconies in the building opposite. They laughed and waved, asking if I needed a massage. I shut the door and tried to sleep, but the rooms had been subdivided and the walls were paper thin. A couple on one side was having extremely loud sex and someone on the other side was watching very loud television. There was an acrid stench of mould from the walls and the toilet would not flush. I was in red-lit hell.

Sleep was impossible, so I read up on Saipan's history. During WWII, the occupying Japanese forces wiped out whole villages and most of the Chamorro culture, replacing them with facsimile Japanese towns, bars and restaurants. From what I'd seen of Garapan, I wondered if they'd ever been kicked out. Japanese restaurants and sushi houses were everywhere, the signage was in Japanese and many of the locals spoke at least a smattering of the language.

According to the guidebook, the north was Saipan's most beautiful region, filled with rolling hills and lush beaches. The next day I drove there to see it for myself. In the mid-morning, I

164

arrived at Banzai Cliff, Saipan's northernmost point, where I not only found natural beauty, as promised, but also discovered the full extent of the psychic scars from the Japanese occupation—a map of pain surveyed from numerous monuments, statues and homages to the war-dead. Oddly, there was a happy-go-lucky atmosphere at these monuments. I noticed the same busloads of Japanese tourists making the circuit from cannon to cliff, from early morning to late afternoon, laughing and joking, taking photos and eating snacks. During the war, hundreds of Japanese families committed mass suicide at Banzai Cliff rather than surrender to the Americans. The youngest child was the first to go, pushed over the edge by the next youngest, and so on, until the mother pushed the last child over. Finally, the father pushed the mother over before leaping to his death. This pathetic, pointless sequence sums up the futility of Japan's war effort, especially considering the return of the Japanese today in greater numbers and as valued customers.

Looking over the cliff, I was compelled by the sight of the raging water swirling below. I tried to imagine how those damned fathers might've felt, staring at the sea, absorbing the horror of the intimate murder they'd just committed, preparing for their own miserable end. But I was so stained by my obsessions that all I could think of was Ballard's 'Intensive Care Unit' and its final scene, when the father leads his family to their self-imposed arena of domestic carnage and their horrific slaughter by household scissors. He looks on approvingly as his wife and children are hacked to pieces, allowing the logic of the world in which they live to decide their fate, a far cry from the desperate suicides of the trapped and hapless Japanese. What an absurdity. Even sombre moments of reflection had to be viewed through the Ballardian lens, but still I couldn't draw any meaning from the connection. It just resurfaced, hanging in the air like a noxious gas. In hindsight, it was the onset of a kind of psychosis.

I heard giggling and turned around to see a young Japanese girl dressed in fashionable camouflage pants and cap. She was posing by one of the monuments. An older Japanese man in his late thirties was taking her photograph. He wore baggy pants, a leather jacket, feather-cut hair with bleached blonde tips, John Lennon sunglasses and a red baseball cap. She pouted sexily, twirling her hair seductively and tilting her head at a come-hither angle, before revealing her nipple to the camera. She mounted an old WWII Japanese cannon and pretended to lick the barrel, totally unselfconscious as she looked me directly in the eye with a dazzling smile. I began to understand where these pictures might end up, perhaps at the end of a Google image search in a few months' time: 'saipan banzai nipple gun barrel'.

Retreating from Banzai Cliff, I drove past the Hotel Nikko Saipan, an abandoned building notable for its futuristic design. The hotel seemed modelled on the domed city from the 70s science-fiction film *Logan's Run*, and clearly, by dint of that design, it was meant to usher in a tourist-driven wonderland that would transform Saipan and embrace the future. There it was, in the jungle, by the beach, rising in the twilight like the remains of a wartorn city. The well-appointed chapel to the rear was still in use as far as I could tell, apparently by wedding parties. As I took photos, a young Japanese couple emerged from the foliage, he in tuxedo, she in gleaming white dress. They were oblivious to my presence, skipping barefoot across the beach before melting into the ever-widening shadows, disappearing so rapidly I began to doubt they'd ever existed.

When the Hotel Nikko Saipan opened in 1988, the island was at the height of its popularity with Japanese tourists. The Chamorro had traded in their cultural heritage for a stake in this utopia, only for the gamble to backfire when the bottom fell out of the Asian tourist economy a few years later (although Guam, owing to its proximity to Asia, retained the trade). Saipan's devolved Chamorro culture had been replaced by the rusted hulks of abandoned consumerist monuments.

Across the road, the La Fiesta shopping centre was sure to follow. In the guidebook, La Fiesta was touted as a major community hub, but things had obviously changed in the five years since that had been published. The centre was like derelict San Francisco at the start of another apocalyptic film, *The Omega Man*: I could see cars and other signs of civilisation but no indication whatsoever of human life. Inside, I discovered abandoned Japanese restaurants and computer-less internet cafes filled with wires and cables, recalling a passage from *Cocaine Nights* in which Prentice, passing through a mall, walks past 'an untenanted retail unit, a concrete vault like an abandoned segment of space-time'. At La Fiesta, space-time had not been abandoned so much as recalled, a faulty and defective product.

A Japanese man stepped from the shadows. Well-dressed and genial, he was the first human I'd seen in the complex for half an hour. He smiled and winked at me, then disappeared into an office. For one hot second, I thought he was an apparition, like the tenebrous married couple skipping across the beach, but then I saw his colleagues inside, busily typing away at their desks. The scene was infused with a leaden melancholy, as if these office workers, like the last survivors of a nuclear war, had holed up underground and were trying to restart civilisation on a scorched Earth, clinging to Saipan's dreams of a tourist utopia and desperately trying to kick-start the economy all by themselves.

In Ballard's final novel *Kingdom Come*, a shopping centre is overrun by consumers, sealed off by an ad-hoc guerrilla force and declared a 'micro-republic'. I wished I had access to Surveillance Stalker so I could track the movements of the lonely La Fiesta workers at night. Perhaps in time they too would secede from the outside world, scavenging the remains of the old order, forever ready for the empty horizon where they would be free to test and refine the limits of their humanity.

50

TIME WARS

After a few days I flew to Rota, a small island with a population of 3,000, where the main attraction is diving. At a cafe, I met two Americans, Hank and Chuck. They'd been on the island for decades, seduced by the charms of a place where nothing changes from day to day. Hank said he could feel time slowing to a complete halt, as if he'd been commanded to wake up and repeat the same tasks and activities for eternity. In his case, it was diving and spear fishing, jobs so rewarding he was grateful to be caught in a rip in the time-space continuum if it meant pursuing his passion forever. Chuck said he'd learned many skills to survive. A carpenter by trade, once everything on the island had been repaired he installed cable television for the locals. When the last super-typhoon tore down all the cables on all the houses, he became a dive guide. When the economy went stale and dive tourism dried up, he became a fisherman. In a bar, I met a Rota-born man who also followed this pattern. He had owned the local store, then he had been a farmer, then he had managed a tour company and so on.

I stayed at the Reef Palace Hotel in Songsong village, where my room was appended to a commanding balcony view of the Philippine Sea. I awoke at 7am each morning, looked towards the sea, filled my lungs with air and sat down to write. With each new dawn, I felt myself slipping into the Micronesian Time Slip that held Hank and Chuck in thrall. In the evenings, I sampled Songsong's surprisingly numerous restaurants and bars, where, almost without fail, I would be the only customer.

Rota was beautiful, friendly, relaxed, archaic. There was nothing to do but drive around the hills and mountains looking for the ruins of Japanese cannon and historic *latte* stones, or explore the ancient underground grottoes, including Tonga Cave on the northeastern outskirts, a massive cavern criss-crossed with stalactites, stalagmites and tunnels snaking into the endless darkness (the cave served as a Japanese military hospital during the war, then a typhoon shelter). In the evenings, I swam along the thin, elegant beaches on the island's eastern side.

One day, I sat on the beach reading *The Pacific*, Simon Winchester's exhaustive history of postwar social, cultural and political changes in the region. Winchester describes his visit to the Pacific island of Tonga and the view he'd enjoyed of Mount Silisili in Samoa just across the water. Because of the International Dateline, clock time was exactly the same on both islands yet Mount Silisili was a day behind. With a start, Winchester realised he was staring into the past. Analogously, in Ballard's Pacific fictions, a state of atemporality is overlaid upon the post-war world. In the author's note that precedes *Empire of the Sun*, he explains that although the Japanese bombing of Pearl Harbour occurred on the morning of 7 December 1941, in Shanghai it was morning on the following day. There is no further extrapolation of this paradox, although the meaning seems clear. In the Pacific, time is haywire, a temporal Bermuda Triangle, a black hole of time.

Today, the Winchester Paradox no longer exists. Time is as malleable as clay. After Winchester's book was published, Samoa changed timezones, jumping forwards (westwards) in time. This was intended to improve the island's local trading prospects, as it would be aligned with Asian rather than American time. When the change happened, the island's population of 200,000 went to sleep on Thursday and woke up on Saturday. What happened to Friday, that extra day? Where did it go?

When traders send digital signals across the world, they use fibre-optic cables, which transmit data at ninety per cent the speed of light. This is called 'high-frequency trading' and the common unit of time is a millionth of a second, since traders deal in microseconds to gain any advantage over rivals. It has been discovered that light-speed 'latencies', the delay a signal takes to reach one global financial centre from another, can be reduced even further by originating financial transactions midway between two major financial hubs. This maximises the capability to buy low in one centre and sell high in another. Remote places—at high latitudes, or island chains in the middle of the ocean, like the North Pacific—could become major financial centres due to light-speed latencies. Time and the ability to cheat it could become the Pacific's most valuable natural resource. Will America want Samoa back in its timezone one day? Future wars may not be fought over oil or water, but time.

Control time and you control the world.

I remembered the Melbourne Observatory and what it had done to my sense of time. Back then, I was so delusional that I imagined I'd been born into a parallel universe. Now, all of those moments of madness were returned to me via Winchester's book and I began to withdraw. On my last night in Rota, Hank invited me to a barbecue at his place in the hills. I said I would drive there in an hour but I never left the hotel, for I was afraid I would never be able to leave the island if I did. That night, I listened to my phone ring five times as Hank tried to contact me. I never answered.

My flight to Guam was the next day.

I woke and caught it without saying another word to those people.

51

MALIGN POTENTIAL

The North Pacific is the origin of Ballard's atemporal end-states, and I was determined to stand at the locus: the bomb pits on Tinian, where the Little Boy and Fat Man A-bombs were loaded onto B29 superfortresses to destroy Hiroshima and Nagasaki, creating the crack in the sky that had so transfixed Jim. I travelled to Tinian from Saipan aboard a derelict, single-engine five-passenger plane. We were buffeted all the way by heavy winds, the plane dipping and swaying like a rollercoaster, and the knuckles of the frightened man next to me were almost translucent as he gripped his briefcase. As a card-carrying claustrophobe, I wanted to jump, half believing anything would be preferable to the slow, suffocating fear of the cramped and crowded cabin, but then Tinian came into view and the panic subsided, sliding back down my throat to dissipate into the corpus.

As the plane slowed to land, I glimpsed the tiny, peaceful island rushing up to meet us. The tropical image made it hard to come to terms with Tinian's violent past, which will always haunt it, pulsing through the palm trees and sand dunes like a repressed phantasm. Tinian is the smallest of the three main islands in the Northern Mariana chain, yet during the war it was the world's busiest military base—the springboard for the most significant flashpoint in Western history. As we descended through wispy sheets of cloud, I felt as though we were passing through chronological layers in Google Street View, as though I could peel back layers of time and peer into the past. This one-village island, just a dot in the Pacific Ocean, was once steward of the most destructive force the world has ever seen, an impossible concept undermining the very fabric of reality.

Touchdown.

As we disembarked, the frightened passenger vomited and I had to sit down to catch my breath. Once I'd composed myself, I hired a car at the airport (barely a shack in the sand) and headed towards the abandoned North Field, the former US air base. I drove down Broadway, a two-lane road on the island's east side. When Tinian was captured by the US in 1944, the Americans were struck by its shape, similar to Manhattan Island, and named the roads after New York streets: 8th Avenue, 86th Street, Broadway. The Ballardian resonances were inescapable. In *Empire*, a simulacrum of London is erected in Lunghua, complete with signs (including 'Regent Street') that demarcate the paths between huts as the British inmates attempt to block out the war. Tinian's 'Manhattan' shared that impulse, although today it is a palimpsest that demonstrates how the island is unable to escape its history, for there is a cancer stirring beneath the surface, mostly dormant yet infused with malign potential. 'Broadway' is no longer just a quaint nod to the past. It is a primordial swamp from which we have emerged, a sea of time threatening to drag us back into its maw, so thick and strong is its pull.

I arrived at North Field, hot and sweaty from the humidity. There was no life, save for the monitor lizards flitting between the cracks in the abandoned runways. In fact, I hadn't spotted a single soul since leaving the airport. I went for a swim at Chulu Beach (naked, because I had no swim gear), which I misread on the map as 'Cthulhu Beach', a mistake that would assume dark significance as my journey unfolded. In horror writer H.P. Lovecraft's story 'The Call of Cthulhu', the submerged alien city of R'lyeh is home to Cthulhu, an alien god, and R'lyeh's design was inspired by Nan Madol, the ruined, half-sunken city on Pohnpei, the island I would soon be visiting.

After my swim, I drove to the atomic bomb pits. Today, the empty concrete pits are covered with plexiglass to deter souvenir hunters from breaking them up and absconding with the pieces, yet they retain an iconic power, for it was from these holes in the ground that my formative nightmares stemmed. I was a teenager in the early 80s when post-nuclear holocaust dramas were common, including *The Day After*, *Testament*, *The War Game* and, most frightening of all, *Threads*, with its ultra-realistic scenes of global nuclear devastation leading to the absolute end of human civilisation. These terrifying visions plunged ordinary suburban environments into chaos and destruction, and Tinian was the springboard for them all, with the fear of the bomb spreading via Hiroshima and Nagasaki to feed the nuclear psychosis of audiences worldwide. I stood before the bomb pits in frightened awe, remembering the stunning conclusion to *Threads*: the birth of the last baby on Earth, a horribly disfigured mutant.

Driving back to the airport, I glimpsed a ruined WWII aircraft half-hidden in the jungle. I stopped the car but I couldn't make out the plane's country of origin. The wreck evoked ghosts of war, of materialism, of nationalism. How many ghosts pass through one's own body at any one time? How many wi-fi signals? How many time travellers? One can never know. Across the North Pacific, ghost stories are abundant. I heard many tales of Pacific colonisers establishing themselves in fortified micronational bases like kings, only to die of disease, invasion or mutiny. These people were said to haunt the islands, alongside water monsters and ancient alien races like those dreamed up by Lovecraft.

Surveying the wrecked plane, I thought about the presence of ruins in Ballard's work. In wartime Shanghai, the Japanese subdivided the city so that inhabitants could only be in certain zones at certain times. In the borderzones, Ballard encountered whole buildings abandoned, even whole districts. At a ruined casino, he and his friends marvelled at the huge roulette tables that had been tipped over, necklaced by overturned game chips in a bizarre tableau, everything junked in a stylised fashion as if advertising the absolute end of human activity. This fascination with decay is woven throughout his writing, materialising in the submerged London cityscapes of *The Drowned World*, the crumbling concrete jungle of *High-Rise* and the lifeless New York of his novella 'The Ultimate City'.

In the novella, the city is in ruins from massive pollution and industrial waste, abandoned in favour of the bland idealism of Garden City across the harbour, a sterile, rural ecotopia that disavows technology but breeds a robotic conformity in the populace through total fidelity to green ideals. A young boy, rejecting the values of Garden City, flies his glider to New York and attempts to restart the city singlehandedly, revelling in the ruins and destruction, thriving on the latent power and implicit grit of urban life. Once, an interviewer asked if 'The Ultimate City' signalled a certain relish for decay, but Ballard denied the charge, suggesting that instead it signifies *potential*. The boy, he explains, is 'trying to recapture something of the dynamism, aggression and freedom for the imagination to soar that was so lacking in the small rural town where he was brought up ... The city is abandoned, and with it, suspended in time, is a whole set of formulae for expressing human energy, imagination, ambition. The clock has stopped, but it will be possible for the boy to start it up again.'

Ballard's obsession presages Western society's compulsion towards 'ruins lust', the fetishisation of destroyed, once-grand symbols of permanence. Ruins lust is intrinsic to the popular pastime of 'dark tourism': voluntarily visiting ruined and abandoned places inscribed with trauma, such as Chernobyl and Auschwitz. In any dissection of urban devastation, whether natural or manmade, we must admit its appeal, for ruins lust highlights our deep desire to stare into the sublime, to swim both within and against the chaos at the heart of the post-traumatic city.

But as I reminded myself, I had no swim gear to hand. As always, I was woefully unprepared.

52

AIRLESS AND CASINO BLACK

I drove from the bomb pits to the village of San Jose, passing a crumbling tower, all that remained of the old church. Outside the tower, two stone tablets were etched with the Ten Commandments. At the end of the road, the Tinian Dynasty Hotel and Casino loomed large, a garish neon-lit temple. Outside the casino a sign was imprinted with a single commandment: NO THONGS OR SINGLETS. The casino and hotel complex was a strange vision, a monument to excess amid a languid tropical setting: this remote island with its sparse population, a place untouched by tourism save for the 'dark' variety—atomic rubberneckers like myself.

The largest market for North Pacific tourism is Asia, but there are no direct flights to Tinian from any Asian country. Why was the casino built here and not on Guam, or even Saipan, where the money and tourists are? I sat on the steps to the casino's entrance, pondering this elemental mystery, beneath the shade thrown by a pair of big pink dice atop a gold-inlaid marble tower. I could see inside to the lobby. There were no punters, only downtrodden staff wearing miserable expressions (I later heard that many had not been paid for months as the casino was in severe financial difficulty). I walked across the driveway to the grass verge and laid down. The sun was high in the sky, returning me to Rotterdam, Camus and Mann, and when I closed my eyes I could see the red blood vessels in my eyelids, brightly lit like tracer bullets in a war-torn sky.

Casinos, these airless worlds, fascinated me. Melbourne's

own Crown Casino was a lightning rod for all kinds of high weirdness if you knew where to look. In fact, a few weeks before flying to the Pacific, I had designed an experiment in which I tried to unlock that code. I wanted to function as a cosmonaut of inner space within the Crown complex, a massive rabbit warren filled with hotels and restaurants and as many stories as there are gangsters on the premises. The parameters of the experiment required me to remain within the complex for twenty-four hours, eating only from the food court. How much money would I spend? Could I resist gambling? Could I snatch a few minutes' sleep here and there without attracting attention in a space designed to negate sleep? Would my senses become totally warped?

I saw Crown as the ultimate acceleration of capitalism, the ideal to which all Western cities would aspire if only they could. Think of the public benches designed so that homeless people cannot sleep on them and the almost total domination of public acoustic space by noise pollution. What is the end game? The instilling and maintenance of hypersensation and hypertension so that the body is always awake with no time for rest, with no time for leisure activity except to spend money as quickly as it is earned. Of course, if you have no money or are unwilling to spend it, then a phalanx of security mobsters will terminate your tenure in the promised land with extreme prejudice. That is how the casino functions and that is how hypercapitalism operates in principle. Hypercapitalism scorches everything that passes by, just as Crown did on its grand opening night. When the huge gas jets outside the entrance were turned on for the first time to impress the crowd, a flock of pigeons flew straight into the billowing flames, the roasted birds dropping dead from the sky to pelt the thronging masses below.

As the psychiatrist Maxted declares in *Kingdom Come*, hypercapitalism, or more exactly consumer culture, is like a 'soft police state'. Those who fail to buy more bear the mark of failed citizens.

'If anything,' Maxted says, 'fascism is the form that consumerism takes when it opts for elective madness.'

To prove the point, I was prepared to risk precisely that brand of insanity.

The experiment began at noon, and it was my intention to call on various acquaintances to accompany me over the next twenty-four hours, sort of like control subjects, anchoring me in some kind of external reality so that I did not go entirely mad. The first friend, Sam, arrived at 4pm. She was a sound artist, interested in the acoustic dystopia that casinos generate. She brought a high-definition directional microphone and sophisticated portable recording gear. Sam and I walked up and down the casino in ritual contemplation, our heads bowed, trying not to let the visual overload jam our reception of the acoustic environment. Everywhere inside the casino, carefully sculpted soundscapes increased the perception that anyone could win, from constant announcements of massive jackpots to be won, to recorded, looped and amplified sounds of coins crashing down poker machine chutes. After an hour and a half, Sam declared her interest over and left. I think she was overwhelmed by it all but I couldn't worry about her for long. I sat down, trying not to look suspicious.

A second friend, Daniel, arrived at 8pm. By then I was suffering from extreme boredom onset with mild delirium. I hadn't eaten for five hours as I was intent on conserving money, although the only ways to counter boredom and hunger in a casino are to spend more, to gamble more. I'd met Daniel on the internet through an excellent blog he maintained about Melbourne's new breed of city-like shopping malls and the animated state of suspension they engender in the people passing through them. He was a very interesting person, young and well read, with a sardonic sense of humour that highlighted the essential absurdity of consumer society, which we were both repelled and fascinated by. He brought with him a ground plan of the casino. Mindful of Ballard's warning about consumerism's 'soft police state', we sat down at the Sports Bar and inscribed a swastika over the ground plan. We decided we would walk the swastika's arms, no matter where they led us, hoping to unravel the subliminal fascism powering this virtual city state.

I remembered seeing Ballard in that London bookshop back in the 90s. He'd spoken of the advanced leisure resort in *Cocaine Nights* and how it functions to atrophy the senses and strip the body of agency.

'It's a unique phenomenon,' he'd told the crowd. 'A metropolis utterly devoted to leisure, something close to suspended animation. And it's very inviting. But people lying on their backs are very vulnerable to predators.'

That *frisson* of vulnerable fear was precisely what enveloped Daniel and I as we became absorbed in the casino's otherworld. The effect was total. There were no clocks anywhere, creating a timeless zone in which the breakdown of the biological cycle was the only indication of chronometry. We were in the Zone, where the casino's audiospatial chaos generated a deadly illusion of lazy disconnection, and the only remaining link to consensual temporality was the schedule of the televised horse racing on the massive floor-to-wall TV screens that spanned several levels above our heads (horses and horse racing haunted the interior, the casino as shrine to this towering pillar of the gambling industry).

There was no natural light of any kind, no windows. Mirrors took up entire walls, distending the innards into infinity. The long walk across the mid-section of poker machines and blackjack tables seemed endless. Hovering alien ectoplasm, the sickly UV of Giger-style nightmares, fell into view. Magic mushrooms hung from the ceiling, glowing lysergically—someone's idea of contemporary light fittings. We were in a bunker far below the Earth's surface, or so it seemed, drinking, gambling and watching spooling televised sports. My palms began to itch maddeningly but I ignored the sensation, distracted by many other things, for it seemed we could not turn a corner without some kind of Ballardian connection springing forth, so potent was his foresight.

In *Kingdom Come*, when the shopping centre has seceded, the dissidents construct altars for directionless shoppers out of abandoned consumer items like white goods and kitchen utensils. Sure enough, we discovered a full-scale Harley Davidson replica motorcycle hanging from the ceiling. Below it was a large sign bearing the legend: DISPLAY VEHICLE ONLY.

'What have we here?' Daniel intoned, in the mock-theatrical voice he'd adopted upon arrival, which he thought appropriate to the atmosphere of unreality in the place.

'A shrine to technological carnage. The sign warns the initiates, lest they confuse the fake with reality.'

Trinkets were piled up on the carpet around the altar, burnt offerings of cigarette butts, condoms, coins, keys. Passing cleaners made no effort to remove the detritus, which was arranged in a perfect concentric ring. Coin idolatry was everywhere, even woven into the fabric of the carpet, which bore in its design endless swirling motifs depicting coins of all denominations. The motif was interwoven so tightly that if you were to drop an actual coin onto the carpet you would have trouble locating it, so absorbed into the illusion would it become, like everything else in this blighted place.

Daniel and I had been in the casino together for two hours, ten in total for me. I was beginning to feel decidedly unusual, and in this state I imagined the resilient, supernatural carpet was custom designed to soak up blood, vomit and semen without leaving any visible trace. As I explained this 'theory' to Daniel, a man loitered nearby, listening in. Eventually, he approached us. Once closer, he told us that he knew the man who'd made the carpet and that he had made a fortune from this and other sales. He said the man also designed body bags for porn queens addicted to cocaine and ultraviolent bondage.

'Did you know there are sliding compartments in the toilet cubicles that can quickly open to dispose of suicidal high-rollers who have lost the lot? This is so they don't have to bring the corpse back through the main arena, where it would spook the punters.'

'But how many people kill themselves on the can?' I said. 'Aside from Elvis.'

He tapped the side of his nose.

'You'd be surprised. Common enough for it to be worked into the design. And Elvis didn't kill himself. His great heart simply gave way.'

'That's an opinion, I suppose.'

Suddenly he became distracted by what appeared to be, judging from his uncoordinated actions, an insect buzzing around his ear. He batted at it repeatedly but there was nothing of the sort. He scurried away without another word, swatting invisible bugs from his ears.

Moving further down the swastika's central arm, we paused before a display in a glass case: an expensive handbag draped in gold chains (bizarre 'art' was everywhere in the casino, always cash- or horse-themed). Riffing off the scene, Daniel boomed at passers-by, like some kind of blood-and-thunder prophet.

'Listen up! The masses think they are free but they are forever enslaved. Chains no longer shackle their bodies but decorate their pathetic consumer goods instead!'

I pulled him aside and told him to shut up in case the security guards came. If that happened, it was game over. We would be ejected from the casino zone and my experiment would have failed, while everything around us would reform and continue on as if we had never existed, all that groundwork evaporating into nothing. I hustled him away from the crowd that had formed around us. We slipped through a passageway to another dimension—a room where a cabaret act was in progress. The stage and the vivid red curtains surrounding it were so removed from the gambling noise that it seemed not of this earth, like a purgatorial side room in a David Lynch film into which the anti-hero stumbles by accident.

We sat down at a table and ordered drinks. On the wall next to us, a large poster advertised the food court. It featured a man performing an exaggerated running-forward-on-the-spot dance, the type beloved of vaudevillian performers. He wore a yellow suit, dark-green waistcoat and purple bowler hat. His clothes were festooned with sparkly sequins. Strangely, his skin had a purplish hue. That was bad enough, but when I clocked the poster's hideous Comic Sans font I felt like sicking up my drink. I thought of Ballard's fantasy novel *Hello America*, set in a post-apocalyptic, overgrown Vegas where casinos are maintained as elaborate displays—a 'lake of neon signs' lit up in garish hues by the few surviving inhabitants. Magically, the purple-skinned hep cat came to life, as if emerging from my Ballardian fever-dream.

'Come with me to the Food Court', he moaned in my ear. 'I know a mystical place, a snack bar, where they spike the slushies with alcohol and Viagra, where cyborg men with vat-grown muscle can inflate their pecs with a bicycle pump to 150 psi. It's called Food and Booze Express City and it's open 24/7, natch, because you know it, don't you man, that Dreamland never sleeps. Oh, and dig: the women are *unfuckingbelievable!*'

I could feel my eyes popping right out of my skull and leapt from the chair, trying to tear the poster from the wall, only for

Daniel to hustle me away from the crowds. He shoved me down the hall and slapped my face.

'What the hell? Yelling at people is one thing but tearing down the walls? You almost got us arrested! You haven't eaten for hours. Let's get some food.'

'No, no. I'm okay. No food...'

We were in a dark alcove. There was no one else around. I leaned on his shoulder, out of breath.

'Let's keep going.'

'Are you sure?'

'Yes. Believe me, I have no choice.'

53

BROADCAST SIGNAL INTRUSION

At the end of the hallway, we reorientated ourselves by the lower left arm of the swastika. We decided that once we reached the end of it, we would turn around, walk back up and trace the opposite arm. As we waited for a noisy bucks' party to disperse, we brushed up against another manifestation of the equine spirit that haunted the casino: a brass horse's head mounted on a marble plinth. An old lady was staring at the head. Daniel adopted the parodic pose of a stereotypical art critic, chin in one hand, elbow resting in the other.

'Here, it is no longer enough to elevate the horse, to allow it to destroy a man's livelihood through the dark art of gambling. No, the situation is beyond that. Instead, the Crown Prince has decapitated the horse and mounted its head as a warning to the devotees: *Spend and spend again. Spend until your life expires or we will expire your life for you.*'

The old lady regarded him with distaste, beating a hasty retreat. We resumed our drift until we reached the swastika's centre and then began to travel down the lower right arm. Soon after realigning ourselves with these new coordinates, we encountered a glowing tube that stretched from floor to ceiling. It was filled with thousands of illuminated coins, another kind of artwork, we guessed, another ridiculous display in an environment full of them, for the 'art' in Crown was as surreal as anything Dali could have dreamed up.

In my parlous state, I imagined the glowing tube was a mega-computer, an artificial intelligence that ran on pure cash, and that pulsing throughout that pile of super-compacted currency was a liquid charged with megawatts of electricity and data, a new technology of viscous fibre optics drawing upon the inordinate strength of abstract social wealth to create simulated neurological pathways with highly complex processing power greater than military mainframes.

I turned to my friend.

'You know what this is, don't you? A computer that runs the whole operation here at Crown.'

There was disjointed music on the sound system. I couldn't hear it properly and the snatches that pulsed through the ambient noise of the poker machines sounded for all the world like 'Venus in Furs', the Velvet Underground song about sadomasochism, with its insidious refrain 'Severin, Severin', a reference to the central character in Leopold von Sacher-Masoch's novel *Venus in Furs*. Severin is obsessed with a woman called Wanda and desires nothing more than to be her slave, no matter how debased the act. I thought of Catherine and tears ran down my face.

I will always be your slave. Always.

The likelihood of the song being 'Venus in Furs' was millions to one in that land of Top 40 tunes, muzak and yacht rock, but although I'd clearly misheard, inspiration struck and adrenalin buried my sadness.

'The supercomputer here is called Mr Severin! Mr Severin's word is law and *he will not tolerate any deviance from that law at any time!*'

Daniel nodded, warily. During our time together in the Casino, we'd quickly learned not to question anything the other said, no matter how absurd the utterance, for who was to say what was real and what was not in a place where illusion was everything? Thinking about the neon unreality of the abandoned casinos in *Hello America*, I became touched by a presence that was almost indescribable, an alien intelligence reaching deep into my soul to finger my pathetic humanity with a cold machinic rationalism.

A mystical vision appeared. A monolithic slab slowly descending from the ceiling. White light growing and growing. In the Zone.

'What... what is that?'

I pointed to the monolith, which was enveloped by a corona of neon light.

'What?' Daniel said. 'It's lights. Just a light fitting. A *tacky* light fitting.'

'No, no, you damn fool! It's covering everything! Where is it coming from?'

The light was so bright I could not see the wires holding the fitting in place from the ceiling. It hung inside a wide glass dome of super-reflective intensity, giving it the illusion of suspension in mid-air. I had no idea of its purpose. It was metallic and inscribed with glyphs that matched no known language. It was a true mystery and I needed to move away from it, for I had the fear, riven deep in my bones, that I was in the presence of the supernatural.

Daniel was yet to read *Kingdom Come*, so to distract myself I explained the plot as we hurried away. I told him that it concerned a brand of consumerism that promoted catharsis through violence, an uprising that begins at the local mall and is fuelled by hunger for violent, nationalistic sport. As Daniel absorbed the details, he waved his hand airily at some burly manual labourers who were drinking beer and watching the massive sports screens.

'Look at them: gathered in a dungeon to celebrate the waste of their lives. A dungeon in which to drink, lose more cash and relieve the pain of being alive. Their women are probably at a poker table somewhere, siphoning the kids' inheritance on bad odds.'

A gloom permeated the air. Condensation seemed to drip from the walls, thick like blood. One sensed brutal violence might break out at any moment, especially as Daniel's theatrical provocations were, as usual, attracting the wrong kind of attention. On the sports screens, some rugby players were celebrating a victory. They tore off their shirts and punched each other on their bare, muscled arms as if comparing biceps, and for one hot moment it seemed like the whole casino crowd might follow suit, so worked up and restless were they, jostling each other and spilling their drinks. Only one measure could quell this mood—a variety show.

'*Mr Severin,*' I whispered. '*Call on Elvis.*'

We had seen a poster advertising an Elvis floor show and remained in a state of high anticipation for the moment when the great *men* would appear, for the poster promised not one Elvis but many Elvises, from every phase of his career. Young Elvis. Matinee Idol Elvis. Fat Elvis. Maybe even Dead Elvis. As I had commanded, the Elvises took to the stage in front of the sports screens. We were immediately transfixed by the besequinned, dolled-up women in the chorus line that followed, who had massive variegated feathers attached to their bottoms and their heads, vixens conga-lining to within an inch of the menfolk's lives.

'Completely Elvis!' the MC moaned. 'Yeeeeeeeesssssss! The Elvises are in the building! With their authentic performance, you'll really believe the King is singing just for you. So why not give it up for Elvis? And Elvis? And of course, ELVIIIIISSSSSS!'

The combination of the plural 'their' to denote a singular entity, 'the King', added to the air of unreality, as if the King was composed of multiple, competing personalities. I thought of the man possessed by invisible bugs.

If only he was here to see this.

Daniel pointed at Fat Elvis.

'Look at this man, this pneumatic freak. He is not copying Elvis but a mirage.'

For a moment, as the amazing spectacle unfolded, I thought I could see my beer boiling in the glass. Then suddenly the Elvises and their women were gone, and in their place was an incredible sight projected high above on the biggest sports screen. As the reporter covering the horse racing read the results, the digital feed stuttered and shuddered in vertical hold, flickering madly before splitting him straight down the middle, as if his true appearance was being revealed beneath a suit of human skin.

'Amazing,' Daniel said. 'A veritable twenty-first century schizoid man.'

The reporter kept talking as if nothing had happened while his image became a snarling, digitised mutilation. One side of his body was normal, the other raging and spasming. Half his face was blackened, depthless and devoid of all features. Half his shirt was a lurid purple instead of the regular green.

'Mr Severin has had a breakdown!' I yelled. 'Someone in here has won far too much cash. The system can't cope! It's stuck in an infinity loop, cracking and breaking!'

The noise of clinking coin and tolling fruit-machine bells reached unbearable levels, for we had pierced the veil and seen beyond, out into the Racecourse of the Real. Yet there were no gears and pulleys behind the mask, no puppet master pulling the strings or pushing the levers that made the android race-horse reporter work—just a roiling black void of utter nothingness. This horrible mutation, this glitch in the TV signal, had ripped apart before our eyes to reveal a monstrous face beneath, like the ghouls in *They Live*. Perhaps, as in that film, someone had jammed the masking signal, forcing us all to see the aliens clearly.

As they really were.

For the very first time.

I turned to Daniel, desperate to know his thoughts, but he was nowhere to be found. I panicked and raced to the toilets to hide in a cubicle. I sat on the toilet with the door locked, wide eyed, panting, my shirt soaked through with sweat. I thought of the secret doors. If I died in there, I would be ejected and no one would ever know. I wouldn't even be granted the theatre of a dramatic exit.

Daniel texted me.

'Sorry. Headache and bowel movement. Emergency retreat. Good luck for rest of voyage. Remember the pigeons.'

It had been four hours since he'd entered my world. I'd been in that hellhole twelve hours in total. Twelve more to go.

I put the phone away, recovered my composure and left the toilet, walking the swastika in reverse.

54

TRIPWIRES

The next stop was Koror, capital of Palau. I stepped off the plane into an apocalyptic climate zone. I went to bed and was woken at 2am by sheet lightning and eardrum-shattering thunder. In my sleep-addled state, I thought that Palau had been re-captured, that the thunder's metallic percussion was the sound of bombs. I wandered the hallway, trying to reset my mind, and bumped into the concierge.

'This weather,' he muttered. 'Most unusual for Palau.'

He made an ominous statement about global warming destroying his island, hinting that an even darker force was starting to manifest, a malevolence seeping out through an enraged supernature. Although his face gave nothing away and his eyes could not be read, it was all in the tone of his voice, which betrayed a kind of resigned fear. He slithered away into the darkness at the end of the passageway and I returned to bed. Sleep claimed me at last, and I wandered into an extremely nasty dream.

I was on an interminable search-and-destroy mission in an unknown jungle, fighting in a war I'd long forgotten the name of. The mission was critically important, that much I knew, the stakes as high as could be.

I remembered the commander's warning: 'The terrain is a minefield. Watch your step.'

But I was too tired to search for tripwires, having been on guard in a foxhole for three days and two nights, staying awake (shielding my mind from the horror) on a suicidal cocktail of amphetamines and LSD.

I took a step forward and heard a deafening blast. I was thrown onto my back, my ears ringing. I could smell blood, cooked meat and mud, a disgusting medley of odours that forced me to retch. When I'd finished, everything was deadly still and strangely quiet. I couldn't hear a single sound except for the beating of my heart. I saw a nearby flower. It was intensely beautiful, its colours too vivid to be real, its beauty intensified by a necklace of sharpened metal filaments on the ground surrounding it, glinting in the bright sun. Just beyond the flower, I saw a bloody human foot.

The enemy must have caught one.

I was overcome by an overwhelming desire to run back to our camp and to safety. I stood up and fell onto my stomach.

Something's wrong.

Then I understood.

That's my foot.

Still there was no pain.

I picked it up. Rolling over onto my back, I tried to re-attach it to my ankle but it kept falling off. I could see my other foot. Most of it was gone and the bones that formed the one remaining toe were visible. I giggled at the sight of it and the stump began to glow and throb. It was a warm feeling, fuzzy around the edges. As I sat there, I returned my gaze to the flower. It was so pretty, with an enormous variety of colour and mottled leaves of infinite complexity.

I don't know how long I stared at the flower.

The stasis was broken when a fellow freedom-fighter found me. She looked me up and down, her face contorted with distress. I wondered what the problem was, and then I understood.

I have no feet.

The pain, hitherto unimaginable, broke its shackles at last.

I regained consciousness in the hotel bed, screaming in terror. My sheets were spattered with blood from where I'd been clawing at my ankles, trying to reattach my phantom feet. It was a hideous dream, one of the worst I'd ever suffered, and it soured my time in Palau, for I knew I'd succumbed to a baleful energy that swamped me with absolute self-loathing.

For as long as I remained in the Pacific, the fear it induced never left me.

55

SYNTHETIC VIOLENCE

I departed from Koror, taking the state boat a few kilometres south to the tiny island of Peleliu. In 1944, Peleliu was torn apart by one of WWII's bloodiest battles. Fifteen thousand people were killed in two months and the forests and jungle were destroyed. Today, the greenery has returned. Exploring the jungle, I found rusted pillboxes and burnt-out tanks, an eerie sensation when combined with the whistle and song of the tropical birds that lived in the regenerated vines and foliage. The lush cornucopia had largely healed the devastating battle scars of old, yet the uncanny combination of beautiful nature and the psychic overlay of carnage exhumed my nightmare. After encountering the shell of a wartime Japanese army hospital, I was convinced I saw a man run through the undergrowth towards me, but the outline of his body was blotted out by the sun flaring through the vines and the apparition was no more. I sat down on the stairs of the former hospital, which led to an upper floor that no longer existed. I felt exhausted, highly strung and emotional, and my body became racked by great, heaving sobs.

I tried to analyse the dream, always arriving at the same conclusion: I didn't have the right stuff. When faced with real hardship, I would crumple and fold. I thought of Ballard, Verhoeven and Virilio, graduates from the University of War who'd emerged from conflict as stronger people. They spoke of the senses stripped back, of fighting to survive, of having nothing when you once had something, of the trauma of war and destruction shaping their personalities and testing their inner strength.

I'd had it far too easy in life and yearned for similar encounters. Like a soft, flabby middle-class type in a Ballard novel, I longed to strip everything away and start anew. But where could

I find a disaster zone back home in my safe suburban world? I would have to manufacture one in order to survive, a dark thought I managed to suppress until a year later, when I found myself in the grip of synthetic violence of my own design. But in Peleliu that seed was yet to germinate. Instead, the stark realisation regarding my crippling inadequacies threatened to destroy me. Yet I could be persistent and resourceful, up to a point. It was the only thing that kept me going. For example, needing to defecate, I opened Rough Planet's Pacific guidebook, ripped out a few pages and used them as toilet paper.

As I squatted amid the ruins of Japan's wartime occupation, wiping myself with a map of the Pacific Ocean, I wondered which phantasms would stalk me next.

56

SECRET AFFINITIES

A few days later, I returned to Koror and drove to the village of Ngermid. The jungle near Ngermid contained the abandoned Hotel Nikko Palau, which had closed down after guests reported seeing in the rooms the ghosts of Japanese soldiers killed in the war. Yet, like the Hotel Nikko Saipan, perhaps it had closed simply because the bottom had fallen out of the economy and a hotel in the jungle was no longer sustainable. The shells of these discarded Japanese hotels were as significant as war ruins. They too spoke of a former hostile occupation—the ghosts of consumerism they evoked were every bit as significant as their wartime counterparts.

The Hotel Nikko Palau was foreboding. It was older and more traditional than the Nikko Saipan, and for once I was reluctant to explore, for the Palau dream was still vivid in my mind and the jungle surrounding the hotel was the jungle of that nightmare. It featured an identical canopy of trees fanned out in a U-shape, the same dappled sunlight filtered through the leaves, the same marshy undergrowth, the same green vibrancy.

The jungle was a green hell, a verdant inferno.

Stay away.

I had to keep moving, had to retreat from whatever it was that was trying to devour me, so I returned to town, hired a 4WD and drove to the island of Babeldaob. Joined to Koror by bridge, Babeldaob is three-quarters the size of Guam, imposing and impenetrable. It dominates the map of Palau, a striking, massive blob to the north of the main island cluster, although it is sparsely populated as most young people move to Koror for work. Ancient stone footpaths connect the villages and most roads are dirt. The Koror resorts might as well be a galaxy away.

I drove to Ngarchelong in the north, where enigmatic, four-foot high basalt monoliths sit in an open field. I sat among the monoliths, known to the locals as *badrulchau*. Unlike Yap's stone money, there is no origin story. No one knows how the *badrulchau* were constructed or what they signify. The guidebook fell from my bag, opening at the map of Pohnpei. Luckily, it had not been disfigured during my emergency ablution in the Peleliu jungle. I spotted Nan Madol on the map. It connected Cthulhu and Lovecraft. And Ballard? Maybe. Once, an interviewer asked him if his work bore 'secret affinities' to that of Lovecraft, specifically an 'emphasis on alien geometries, the outsider and landscapes as symbols of mental states'.

'I've never read him,' Ballard stonewalled, 'but there may well be correspondences.'

Although he'd given nothing away, I couldn't let it go. Even this straightforward assignment to a beautiful island paradise would be burdened with my Ballardian awareness, for I knew that Ballard was the decoder ring that could unlock the central mystery of existence, opening the door to an interzone, a non-place, where everything was interconnected.

It was the only faith I had left.

57

BALLARDCRAFT

Ballard's stories teem with apparitions. In 'One Afternoon at Utah Beach', 'My Dream of Flying to Wake Island' and *Atrocity*, pilots inhabit a purgatory between life and death. The ghosts of dead astronauts, a metaphor for the collapse of the Space Age, haunt 'News from the Sun', 'Memories of the Space Age' and 'Myths of the Near Future'. In 'The Terminal Beach' and 'The Dead Time', characters commune with the dead and even receive advice from them. In *The Unlimited Dream Company*, a pilot crashlands in Shepperton. When he regains consciousness, somehow he has developed supernatural powers. Is the entire narrative a fantasy generated by his dying brain, or his spiritual rebirth? One might ask the same of Maitland in *Concrete Island*.

Despite this overwhelming body of evidence, Ballard said that, rather than paranormality, the dislocated realities endured by his characters were merely the result of dissociative fugue states. Ever since I'd returned to his work, I had been considering this conundrum, weaving it into a more complete picture of his war years. Perhaps the apparitions were manifestations of Ballard's own post-traumatic stress disorder, a psychic overlay generated by Lunghua's devastating memory-seed.

On another level, I suppose I was trying to bury the embarrassment of my previous interest in the paranormal by channelling that interest into something more 'worthy'. Believe me, when you tell people you've seen a UFO, you renounce all credibility in any intellectual endeavour you might subsequently attempt. Alas, I didn't have it in me to ground my research in facts and instead lapsed into fatal habits.

My research took me to a blog named *English Heretic*, maintained by the shadowy 'Doctor Champagne'. One post detailed his discovery of an 'Aviation Ghosts & Mysteries' database on a paranormal website. The database lists hundreds of hauntings and UFO sightings at English airfields, a 'rather Ballardian catalogue of dead airmen', according to the Doctor. In one incident, the ghost of a headless American pilot spooked the roads around Hadstock, trying to hitch rides into town. In Felixstowe, the spectre of a WWII pilot appeared daily in the back seat of a man's car, but only when the man took a certain turn in his journey from his house to his office. When he changed route, the apparition disappeared.

Doctor Champagne compared the Felixstowe haunting with a passage from *Atrocity*, which describes the sudden appearance of an extra pilot, 'Lieutenant 70', on board a bomber that landed at the military air base at Ohama Beach, Normandy, on 'December 25, 197-'. The pilot carried no identification and had no recall of how he came to be there. When he was taken in for X-rays at the base hospital, he suddenly disappeared and the plates he left behind were of a human foetus that had been X-rayed thirty years before. Doctor Champagne drew parallels with an unsolved incident that occurred on 25 December 1980, when air force troops at the Bentwater RAF base near Rendlesham Forest, on England's Suffolk coast, saw a glowing red UFO on the ground.

For the Doctor, the mystery of Lieutenant 70 is a prime example of Ballard's precognitive ability. *Atrocity* was published eleven years before the Rendlesham incident but the two events share the same date, and the entity captured on the X-ray plates presages the experiences of modern-day UFO abductees, who frequently describe their capture by 'grey' aliens that are foetal in appearance. Doctor Champagne also compared Lieutenant 70 with the figure of LAM, the godlike entity seen in transcendental visions by the infamous black magician Aleister Crowley, and many conspiracists have drawn connections between LAM's physicality and that of 'greys'.

According to the occultist Kenneth Grant, Lovecraft was also in contact with other dimensions. Whereas Crowley had unlocked the dark realm via black magic, Grant said that Lovecraft's portal was revealed within the fever dreams he'd endured throughout his adult life—the same nocturnal visions that had inspired his uncanny tales of cosmic horror. Had Ballard stumbled onto the same portal? What if he too was not consciously aware of the process? What if he was a 'conduit', unwittingly transmitting messages from other dimensions that manifested in the parade of ghosts haunting the margins of his work?

At the time, I knew little about Lovecraft, having long ago dismissed his writing as adolescent fantasy, and it was only on the plane from Koror to Pohnpei that I read 'The Call of Cthulhu' for the first time in preparation for Nan Madol. I found it deeply unsettling, with its depiction of the alien geometries in the sunken city of R'lyeh, which cause such terror in the humans that discover them, driving them to madness as a result of their utter inability to reconcile the architecture's impossible angles.

I tried to follow the line from UFOlogy to Crowley to Lovecraft to Ballard. Lovecraft and Ballard speak to different audiences—or do they? In fact, there is a slight critical tradition equating them. In 1959, when Ballard's story 'The Waiting Grounds' was published in *New Worlds* magazine, editor Ted Carnell wrote that 'Ballard has a touch of that same genius which eventually made Lovecraft great' (the story is about mysterious space visitors leaving cryptic messages for baffled humans, imparting a cosmic incomprehensibility similar to that of Lovecraft's confounding aliens). Much later, Ballard's 'Prisoner of the Coral Deep' appeared in an anthology, *The Starry Wisdom: A Tribute to H.P. Lovecraft*, although the story itself was not conceived by Ballard as a 'tribute' to the horror writer but chosen by the anthology's editor, D.M. Mitchell, because it shares Lovecraft's sense of the universe as an eternal and alienating force.

The twinned entity had gained critical traction since then. Academics had begun to present papers on the synergies between Ballard and Lovecraft, and critical-theory blogs were riffing breathlessly on the relationship as if they were analysing Lennon and McCartney. Even I, with my limited intellectual means, could sense some similarities. Both writers generate highly memorable inner worlds, where the fevered imaginations of the central characters absorb and reinterpret reality. These inner landscapes are rendered so vividly that each author has birthed a neologism, 'Ballardian' and 'Lovecraftian', instantly descriptive to those in the know. Also, both writers outlived the genres that originally defined them, although they moved in opposite directions, Ballard renouncing the science fiction label as his career wore on, Lovecraft embracing science fiction in his later years.

I remembered Ballard's denial of these 'secret affinities'. He may not have cared for the association but I did, and I was prepared to risk everything to excavate the truth.

58

CONNECTED TO MACHINERY

From 1100 to 1628, Nan Madol was the capital of the Saudeleur Dynasty, a permanent home to royalty, political figures and priests. The ancient city, spanning a hundred artificial islets, was a complete world, a labyrinthine micronation divided into residential, food, construction and mortuary sectors. The latter, a 'corpse city' within the complex, covers fifty-eight islets, over half of Nan Madol's territory. It is an area of occult resonance filled with burial tombs, including one that supposedly caused the death of a German governor in 1907 after he excavated its remains and fell foul of an ancient curse. The malodorous, sub-aquatic presence of this ancient charnel house bewitched Lovecraft, the mortuary's powerful superreality informing R'lyeh's baleful coordinates in time and space: 'The nightmare corpse-city was built in measureless eons behind history by the vast, loathsome shapes that seeped down from the dark stars. There lay great Cthulhu and his hordes, hidden in green slimy vaults.'

'Nan Madol' means 'the spaces between', referring to the canals that link the islets, and the translation signalled to me like a beacon, given that ever since my Ballardian reawakening in the Netherlands I had desired nothing more than to disappear into liminal space. When I arrived in Kolonia, the Pohnpeian capital, I hired a guide to take me to Nan Madol. His name was Arthur. He was gruff, bearded and wore filthy blue overalls, an expatriate Australian of all nationalities, originally from the outback town of Broome, and as we clambered aboard his boat he related a local legend: Nan Madol is the inverted mirror image of a long-submerged sister city, itself part of the lost continent of Lemuria.

'Nan Madol is filled with secrets,' he said.

A pause.

'You're Australian.'

'Yes. From Melbourne.'

He glanced at my open bag. The Lovecraft anthology was visible.

'Lovecraft is connected to Melbourne.'

'How?'

'In 1910, Harry Houdini flew the first powered flight in Australia. At Diggers Rest.'

'Yes, I know. Just outside Melbourne.'

He stared at me, a nasty glint in his eyes, like a prison guard annoyed at an inmate speaking out of turn and plotting the appropriate punishment.

'Fourteen years later, Lovecraft ghostwrites a story for Houdini called "Imprisoned with the Pharaohs". You know it?'

'No.'

'Houdini's the main character. He's on holiday in Cairo, but he gets kidnapped and thrown into a huge pit.'

'By who?'

'Don't know. Doesn't matter. Look, don't interrupt me again, you got that?'

I studied his face, trying to ascertain whether he was serious, but he stared me down, his features impenetrable.

'Down below, in the pit, he gets lost in a maze of tunnels, which turn out to be under the Sphinx. He stumbles around the maze, falls into a ceremonial chamber, and in the chamber he sees a pack of freaky creatures—half-man, half-beast. The freaks are worshipping some kind of monster with hundreds of tentacles, and they're being told what to do by two pharaohs. They're in a trance so they don't notice Houdini, but he's not about to hang around and be invited in for tea, right? So Houdini does what Houdini does best: he escapes.

'When he's a bit further away, he looks around and realises that this thing with the tentacles is actually the paw of an even larger beast, and this beast looks exactly like the Sphinx. When he gets outside, he thinks maybe he's hallucinated the entire thing. Maybe he got smacked on the head when he was kidnapped and it made him dizzy, but whatever, something's bugging him all the same. His guide, the guy who brought him to Cairo, looks exactly like one of the Big Chief Pharaohs back in the pit.'

'Nice twist. But what's the link with Melbourne?'

'The story is set in 1910, right? The year of the first powered flight in Australia. Houdini's flight. In Melbourne.'

I had no idea what he was driving at.

He sighed.

'The story is about demons hiding in plain sight. And these half-animal freaks, they're like zombies—under the influence of someone else. Drones. Remote control. You get me? Alright, look, the story is about Houdini's flight. Lovecraft wrote it in code. In the story, Houdini is actually travelling to Australia. Cairo is just a stop on the way. And I'll tell you something else: Houdini's flight wasn't the first in Australia. No. The year before, in the Dandenong Ranges, a priest saw two bright rotating lights zigzagging across the sky. He said there were five other lights behind the two main ones, just hovering. This went on for three hours and he said the lights looked like they were "connected to machinery". But what does that mean? "Connected to machinery" suggests a "powered flight", right? But don't the history books say Houdini's mission was the first powered flight? So, what were those lights?'

My blood froze and I was cast back to the day when I'd smashed my bike and my head, cold-cocking my brain into a different plane of existence.

I lived near the Dandenong Ranges.

'That's absurd. Are you suggesting Lovecraft knew what the priest had seen and had encoded that into a story about the Sphinx?'

'Lovecraft knew many things.'

'Look, I haven't read it, but still I don't think so.'

Arthur became tense and was about to retort when, suddenly, Nan Madol, decaying and half-ruined, loomed ahead of the boat, requiring him to focus his energies on negotiating the narrow canal leading to the entrance. The complex is constructed from criss-crossed basalt pillars, which locals believe were summoned by black magic, and as I observed its deep, etched exterior, scarred from centuries of weathering, black-green and slimy from the waves—Lovecraft's description of R'lyeh incarnate—I couldn't shake the sense that, yes, it was hewn from a material originating far beyond the earthly plane.

We reached the banks and disembarked, and as we walked around the complex I kept slipping in the marshy ground, my feet disappearing in moss and mud, my anchoring on the terrain as tenuous and treacherous as the grip on reality I was trying to maintain. I knew I was cursed. I had thought my internal dislocation had long passed, ever since my UFO obsession had faded, but it seemed my return to the occult had activated it again.

I felt ill and asked to be taken back to Kolonia. We left Nan Madol. Arthur was silent all the way, and when I tried to engage him in conversation, to find out more about Lovecraft and Melbourne, he just grunted. At Kolonia, he shoved me off the boat, and I tumbled face first onto the beach. I felt my essence dimming, like car headlights slowly running down. It was night and I was alone. I was sick of my own company, sick of thinking about Ballard and Lovecraft, and spooked by my encounter with Nan Madol and the thug-guide. I hadn't even seen much of the complex. I'd felt repelled by it somehow, unable to participate in the usual disengaged tourism my profession demanded. There was something on the edge of perception holding me back, and everything Arthur had told me exacerbated the sensation. It was maddening. I just wanted to live a regular life, to be domestic, to have a wife and kids one day, to be interested in sport and read the papers over breakfast, to have normal hobbies like interior decorating and gardening.

Anything but this, dragging me under the surface again and again.

59

BLACK SHADOW

In order to relax, I visited the Jungle Bar, a mellow, open-air establishment that served *sakau*, a narcotic drink made from the roots of pepper shrubs, which are strained through hibiscus bark, giving the end product a gritty, muddy consistency. *Sakau* is like *kava* from Fiji or Vanuatu but with a greater kick. In the old days, it was of great religious importance and could only be drunk in the presence of the high chief. Today, its consumption is egalitarian. I sat down and ordered a cup. A group of men were watching a pool game, and at regular intervals a younger man would offer the *sakau* bowl to each spectator. No one spoke and the atmosphere was completely still. For *sakau* drinkers, loud noises or bright lights are intolerable. That is why everyone consumes mostly in silence, in dark spaces.

After a time, the waitress came to my table.

'You know how to drink *sakau*? There's nothing to it. All you need to do is this.'

She closed her eyes.

'You mean close my eyes?'

'Yes. That's it. That's all you need to do.'

The *sakau* was so clammy I nearly vomited, but I pushed through, drinking some more until the narcotic effect kicked in and I could no longer feel my tongue and lips. Time appeared to stretch, and I knew that even the smallest actions, like scratching my nose, would take forever, so I didn't bother moving a muscle to do anything at all.

There was music on the sound system. No drums. Treacle-slow bass runs. Fuzz guitar. A high-voiced man wailing over the top. The waitress said the band was Black Shadow from Chuuk, an island with a fearsome reputation for drunken, random violence. The music featured a strange type of rhythm, clearly designed to be heard while on *sakau*, perhaps as an antidote to the Chuukese stereotype. Later, when I returned to Australia, I searched for 'Black Shadow Chuuk' on YouTube and found a number of songs by the band. These, I was shocked to discover, were uniformly upbeat, positive and fast-paced, underpinned by a cheesy cod-reggae rhythm. That was the only style they were known for, according to the YouTube comments, and they never deviated from it: upbeat rockin' vibes. What I heard in the Jungle Bar had no correspondence whatsoever with that particular reality.

On the third cup, I fell silent, like the men around the pool table. Further conversation was unnecessary since I knew, at long last, that I could read minds. The waitress nodded approvingly, her mission complete, and I thought of the Man from Morioka. Was he out of range or could he 'hear' me? I took his advice and tried to summon UFOs with the power of my mind. For ten minutes, I concentrated on the night sky visible through the thatched roof but nothing materialised.

I left the bar. There was something I needed to uncover, something on the edge of reality. Nan Madol had prised open a neural pathway and I needed to return to the hotel, to get online and conduct more research, but I became lost trying to find my way back. Following what was supposed to be a simple twenty-minute route, it took me an hour to return to my lodgings. This time, I knew I wasn't the victim of missing time (or maybe I was—perhaps the phenomena were related). *Sakau* had simply fried the most basic neurological functions.

I ended up in Porakiet Village at 1am. Puzzled locals wondered why I was out so late. I couldn't explain and didn't ask for directions, since I had a powerful determination to find my way home, to try and solve the enigma of why I was lost. That single-minded focus was engendered by the *sakau* but so was the fuzzy logic. As I left Porakiet, a pack of wild dogs chased me, then an intense flash storm flattened me to the ground. I gave up and asked a lady sitting on her porch the way home. Once back at the hotel, I consulted a map and saw that I'd walked past the turnoff at least four times. I had been going round and round in circles.

Annoyingly, the lights in my hotel room were playing up, adding to my unease. Wet and bedraggled, I sat in the lounge area in a confused state, trying to work off the *sakau* effect. There was a mirror on the wall in front of me, which I could not stop staring into, thinking about the legend of Nan Madol's sunken mirror-city. I placed my chair in front of the reflection, the lamp behind me. The room lights had blown and the lamp was the only light source but it barely illuminated the space, bathing everything in a queasy yellow glow. The lamp was hidden by my back from the mirror, a placement that wreathed the room in strange shadows, yet I could not rouse myself from the chair to reposition it.

As I stared at the mirror and the flickering shadows that stained my face, my features became gradually deformed. The shadows morphed my face into my father's, specifically the uncanny visage he wore in the coffin at his funeral, after his jaw, wide open at the time of death, had been deliberately broken by the undertaker and stitched back together to form a 'natural' expression (of course it was nothing of the sort, resembling the countenance of a waxwork dummy with human skin stretched across it). His face became my own, which then transformed into the face of a stuck, dying pig. Then it became me again but this time a younger version—a gormless teenager.

Each face returned my stare with an expression that was enigmatic and startling. Each face, no matter how familiar, was impossible to decode, as if imbued with the cold malevolence of an alien god. Nan Madol may have opened a neural pathway, but perhaps it had also let something in. I tried to avoid forming the word 'possession' in my mind, for the implications were too horrifying, and I felt that even by naming the threat I was submitting to it.

I tried to halt the process, tried to self-exorcise by forcing my features to follow my own design, attempting to will into place the facial structure of some kind of masculine ideal, such as the image of the perfect male found in mens' magazines. But as I concentrated on the mirror, something even more shocking was revealed. In the reflection behind my heathen death mask, I could see the wall of the lounge room in my apartment back home.

I moved closer to the mirror, closer to the reflection. My face dissolved, but the apartment wall remained.

PART IV
IMPLANTS

60

REVERSE ANGLE

I stared at the reflection again to be sure. Yes, there was no doubt about it: the wall behind me belonged to the Kolonia hotel room I'd occupied a year ago. I smashed the mirror on the floor, fearful of the hallucination, unnerved by the sensation of looking *backwards in time*. 'Damn you,' I muttered, an oath directed at my friend Charles, who'd been over with a supply of virulent hash, which, to my great regret, I had avidly consumed. I loathed dope for the absolute state of paranoia it instilled in me, but even so I'd acquiesced, since oblivion was much on my mind. Charles said the hash had been 'dusted', laced with some synthetic drug. I didn't bother to ask for the details, didn't care. But after an hour he'd departed, bored with my catatonia and refusal to leave the mirror. The man who was supposedly my closest friend had left me to fight that wave of existential terror alone, marooned in my stinking apartment.

I was living in East Melbourne, a patch of inner-city suburbia divorced from the world. Nothing changed in East Melbourne. It was wedged decades in the past. The suburb was mostly occupied by rich doctors, retired actors and their manservants. Even the ectoplasm was posh—local mansions were said to be haunted by spectres in top hats and tails. I rented a crumbling art deco apartment in one of the last remaining residential pockets that could be inhabited cheaply. Slumming it among old-money merchants and trustafarians amplified my sense of isolation, since I'd chosen to live in a place where I felt ostracised so that I could destroy my mind in a slow, controlled experiment.

The hash high eventually dissipated and I was startled by the ringing of my phone. It was mutual acquaintance of Catherine's.

'Just to let you know: she's back in Melbourne for a family visit.

Don't do anything stupid.'

I hadn't seen Catherine for three years, and I knew I would expire at the thought of being in the same city as her. As long as she was overseas the breakup was barely manageable. Disregarding my friend's advice, I persuaded Catherine to meet me for a drink, clearly against her better instincts because she took a long time to agree. It didn't go well. I was out of my mind on a deadly mix of Jagermeister, Red Bull and vodka, a Molotov cocktail I'd become partial to consuming in enormous quantities. The memory of her had given me licence to go crazy on a brew of such severity that I was surprised to have found myself alive at the end of those terrible binges. I can only attribute that good fortune to the strong heart that runs in my family, since everything else was conspiring to push me into the grave as I stalked the streets at night, blind drunk on my nasty brew, hulking in the shadows, always searching from the corner of my eye for something to give flesh to the ghosts of my life.

We met at a bar, and after a few drinks I asked her to spend the night at my apartment. She refused. We had a blazing argument and I remember nothing after that. My rocket-fuel binges would often see me lose hours, sometimes days at a time. As a prelude to these periods of missing time, I would experience again the blinding headaches and light flashes that had afflicted me in Den Haag, flaring and overwhelming my vision so that I could see nothing else. These would be my last memory until I woke up wherever I found myself. In a park. On the pavement. In someone's front yard.

That night, I witnessed purple-and-white flashes crawling across Catherine's physical outline, like the last remnants of an electrical discharge. They formed the same phosphorescent halo that had grafted onto my mother when she'd appeared after my childhood bike accident, but Catherine didn't resolve into fleshly permanence. Her outline simply winked out, disappearing into the void of my drunken haze. I remember nothing else of that night, and afterwards she wouldn't return my calls or answer my emails.

Stricken with grief and desperate to dull the pain, I called the doctor who'd treated me for depression over ten years ago, conveniently forgetting my earlier misadventures with prescribed medication. Rather than the receptionist, the doctor himself answered, as if he'd been expecting my call.

'It's you.'

I spoke an incantation.

'Doves.'

He summoned me to the clinic, and when I arrived he gave me a lecture about how I should never have left his program of psychoactive therapy. I emerged from the clinic twenty minutes later, remembering little else of his diatribe but clutching an unmarked box of doves.

That night I ingested a couple and the familiar hallucinations returned, manipulating me like a psychotic lover. The walls crumbled. The floor disappeared. The usual high jinks. It vaguely occurred to me that I should tell the doctor about the severity of the side effects, but in the end I refrained. I *wanted* reality to crumble.

It was what I'd been lusting for all my life.

61

INSIDE THE SKULL

One day, groggy after being smacked around by the pills, I dozed off on the bed. When I awoke I found myself trying to smash through the window with my fists to escape the collapsing floor. I wrapped a grotty bandage around my gashed hand and went for a walk to try and work off the effects. I was still in my dressing gown, a filthy madman adrift in a suburban wasteland. I passed a travel agency, one of the few still operating in the area, since most had been digitally disrupted by online bookings. This bricks-and-mortar outlier was as archaic as a fax machine, as superseded as a VCR, something the proprietors must have realised given the poster they'd placed in the window, which carried a perplexing tagline: I WAS ROBBED IN MEXICO. BRING BACK THE STORIES NOT THE BILL. BOOK YOUR HOLIDAY WITH US TODAY.

I stood before the poster for some minutes, my senses battered by the crude signal. The message seemed a last-ditch bid for relevance. The travel agency, a national chain, had built its reputation by targeting young backpackers with party-hearty advertising, all cornball humour and sexual innuendo. But in that new, brutal and unforgiving era, promoting Mexico with the usual cliches like tacos, tequila and sombreros was doomed to failure. If they'd continued down that path, they'd surely attract the type of bomb-happy anti-tourism revolutionaries found in *Millennium People*, with their mission to erase 'the great soporific': mass tourism.

The demographic was beyond street smart. They'd seen and heard it all before. The logical next step was to market their nightmares, and the only place left to visit when the world had been stripmined of experience, when every angle had been exhausted, was the inside of their skulls and their deepest fears. In that sense, the travel agency was simply following the logic of hypercapitalism. As Ballard once said: 'To keep us happy and spending more as consumers, capitalism is going to have to tap rather more darker strains in our characters ... look at the way in which the more violent contact sports are marketed ... and of course the most violent entertainment culture of all, the Hollywood film.'

I studied the poster. What would be next in the series?

Perhaps a local variant: I WAS LEFT FOR DEAD IN MELBOURNE BY FERAL ALPHA MALES HIGH ON CRYSTAL METH. BRING BACK THE HOSPITAL BILL—AND THE STORIES. BOOK YOUR TRIP TO HELL WITH US TODAY.

For a demographic brought up on Eli Roth films, that would trump the taco-and-tequila-style cliches of 'Melbourne: World's Most Liveable City', a slogan used so often by the tourist board it had been drained of all meaning.

That year I lived in perpetual fear, divining signs everywhere of an imminent suburban apocalypse. The poster was but one example of the monstrous sigils all over the city summoning the blood-hungry masses to war. Another was a billboard that advertised Hummer vehicles, the suburban armoured war machine popular with plastic rappers, low-class politicians and trashy wedding parties. The Hummer was a chaos agent. Every time I passed the billboard I was palsied with fear. The angle of the photo emphasised the vehicle's bulbous grille, reflective body and fat tyres, evoking the gaping maw of some killer robot poised to strike. The windscreen was obscured and all traces of human occupancy were erased. It was all about the gleaming machine, a nasty package capped with an aggressive slogan: NOW GET LOST.

What was the billboard really saying?

Admire me, love my vehicle, and then get out of my sight, otherwise I will destroy you.

I texted a photo of the billboard to my friend Mike, who was researching neo-fascist imagery in *Kingdom Come*. He divined its meaning straight away. The billboard, he said, was a direct copy of a Mercedes Benz ad from 1943, right down to the raised nose, invisible windscreen, monstrous tyres and reflective surface. The ad had been published during the war in the Nazi propaganda magazine *Signal*, and Mike reckoned the Hummer version continued the lineage by following a Ballardian trajectory.

After all, as I'd learned in Crown Casino, *Kingdom Come* carries a prescient warning: 'fascism is the form that consumerism takes when it opts for elective madness'. But how to enlist the people? Ballard knew: encourage them to take part in mass rituals, like shopping.

'It's a way of voting not at the ballet box,' he reckons, 'but at the cash counter. The one civic activity we take part in is shopping, particularly in big malls. These are ceremonies of mass affirmation.'

At heart, consumerism feeds on a state of boredom. That's why such ceremonies are important, although in themselves they are never enough.

'What people are looking for is their own psychopathology,' Ballard concludes. 'They're bored, and they want to start breaking the furniture.'

All it takes is a dominant personality, an alpha force, to harness the energy whipped up by consumerism. It need not be a leader, though, as in classical dictatorships—it could be a *brand*. Enter Hummer, the vehicular equivalent of a political strongman.

Soon after the billboard appeared, the papers reported the story of a man who was admiring a Hummer in Melbourne's central business district. When he said to the driver 'I love your car', six people emerged from the rear of the vehicle to beat him senseless with an iron bar. Their motive was not recorded, although one wonders whether they emitted the war cry 'Now get lost' as they brought the iron bar down upon his head. Even the cops were in on the act. Not long after the beating, they took possession of a custom Hummer pursuit vehicle bequeathed to them by the company as a 'promotional tool'. Would they too follow the logic of the billboard, of corporate Nazi propaganda? A police state sponsored by Hummer—it could only happen here on Earth, the one true alien planet.

Was my apocalyptic mindset a reflection of the volume of violent events or of the fact that 24/7 rolling news coverage made violent incidents more visible? Inner-city Melbourne seemed increasingly lawless. Each day brought more reports of roving gangs attacking passengers on trams, of refugees bashed senseless in the street, of drunken nightclub patrons targeted for severe, sometimes deadly muggings. However, despite my righteous anger at the unwashed masses and the carnage they'd unleashed, a difficult truth began to emerge. After enough exposure to media-driven violent events, I was starting to get off on the spectacle, lapping it up as if I was playing an immersive video game that shielded me completely from affect. I wanted nothing more than to watch the world collapse as I sat on the porch in my filthy dressing gown, dosed up on hyperextended depression pills, washing them down with dirty-bomb cocktails.

However, after a time, I grew bored with passivity and began to purge myself of it. Bit by bit, I found myself initiating the program of synthetic violence that had first called to me back in the Pacific jungle.

Nearly there.

62

SICK MUSIC

In the rare gaps when my mind wasn't sedated and I could think clearly, I rationalised the ominous strains in my personality as a by-product of Australia's ruling John Howard government. I'd convinced myself that what I was experiencing was an allergic reaction to Prime Minister Howard's hardline, divide-and-conquer style. In the eyes of Howard, you were either for his right-wing party and everything it stood for, or you were 'un-Australian', a peculiar insult popular with Australian politicians since

1925, when the reigning prime minister, Stanley Bruce, used it to demonise striking sailors. But Howard took it to the next level, wielding the phrase like a weapon, scything down the messy intricacies of contemporary life that threatened like noxious weeds to overwhelm the black-and-white dualities he had so skilfully erected to keep chaos at bay.

Towards the end of Howard's reign, it was reported that of all mentions of the phrase 'un-Australian' in the nation's newspapers, 28.2 per cent were attributable to him alone. Striking dock workers were 'un-Australian' in his eyes, as were anti-globalisation movements, anti-Iraq-war protestors and 'hoons' (an Australian slang term for anti-social youths in cars, the object of an ongoing moral panic concerning drag racing in suburban streets). Staring down the barrel of the latest opinion polls, which showed waning support for his government, Howard seemed to pray for another enemy to stoke the fires of indignation that had kept him in office for the past decade. I was far from being a Howard supporter and if the Prime Minister wanted to brand people like me as 'un-Australian' then I supposed I'd better live up to it.

However, I became hopelessly trapped in a demonic feedback loop. On the one hand, I could see through the media beat-up surrounding hoons on the roads and violent young men on the streets, and I was appalled by the dishonesty and lying complicity of journalists in feeding and exaggerating the *Clockwork Orange*-style mass panic. Yet increasingly I found myself under attack whenever I left home, forcing me to side with anti-hoon sentiment. I was an obsessive cyclist, and at the height of my mania I rode 250km every week. This prolonged exposure to the road brought me into contact with the worst excesses of Melbourne motorists, who revealed a latent psychopathy at the mere sight of a cyclist.

I'd seen it all. I'd been knocked off the bike and into onrushing traffic by car doors deliberately opened in front of me. I'd had bottles aimed at my head from fast-moving cars. I'd been pelted with eggs that impacted with the force of rocks, intentionally squeezed out of bike lanes by countless vehicles and verbally abused by any number of drivers.

I talked myself into believing that death was near and became militant about cyclists' rights. I was dirt in the machine, an antibody racing through the urban bloodstream, squeezing between the cracks in peak-hour traffic lanes, negotiating the Melbourne sprawl with its endless freeways and dual carriageways. Melbourne suburbs are built on the rubble of autogeddon and cyclists flirt daily with death in that system, a vulnerable lower class dehumanised in the media as 'rats' with no place on the roads, victimised for the crime of holding up a car for a few seconds when ill-conceived and inadequate bike lanes vanish suddenly at intersections.

In the papers, shock-jock columnists bellowed that cyclists had no place on the roads because they didn't pay road taxes, even though in reality income tax pays for the roads, not vehicular tax. But such subtleties were lost when the scent of blood was in the nostrils, and B-grade celebrities, terrified by their waning popularity and willing to do anything to bolster it, had joined the war, issuing faux death warrants against riders, using their popular platforms (social media, radio, newspaper columns) to whip their followers into a frenzy—insane behaviour described approvingly by one tabloid columnist as a 'jihad against cyclists ... the emerging civil war on our roads'.

The columnist had plenty of company. On national TV, a famous comedian urged her audience to deliberately open car doors onto cyclists, to 'just take them out'. A leading Melbourne football commentator cut off a cyclist on the road with his car before leaping from the vehicle, grabbing the cyclist in a bear hug and breaking the rider's finger. In his high-profile newspaper column, a prominent Australian novelist fantasised about installing weapons on his car to deal with cyclists who annoyed him on the road, before publishing a post-apocalyptic novel in which the punishment for riding a bike was amputation. Another well-known columnist pontificated that motorists were not culpable if cyclists were killed or maimed on the road. In fact, he seemed to say, it was a motorist's *right* to act in this fashion, underscored when he sent a tweet to a professional racing cyclist that simply said: 'Beep, beep. THUMP.' Yet another 'journalist' with a large readership wrote of how cyclists bring upon her the overwhelming urge 'to swerve towards'.

On and on it went, a catalogue of high lunacy capped when a celebrity ex-cricketer tweeted a story about a cyclist aggressively hogging the road in front of his car. When the cyclist threatened to sue, claiming the celebrity was covering up his own aggression towards him, the ex-cricketer's Twitter army of two million followers did the rest, flooding the cyclist's account with insults and threats.

Faced with that tidal wave of hate, I recoiled in horror, yet I continued to march headlong towards it, for here was the chance to capture another image of myself, if only from an oblique angle.

What sort of psychosis would emerge when my back was up against the wall? Total capitulation or mindless, unfounded aggression?

Either way, I was utterly doomed, defeated by my own worst impulses.

63

STRANGER DANGER

One night Charles and I were walking home from the pub. I was drunk and ranting at my poor friend.

'Australia is the Wild West writ large upon the global stage, a country unformed like a foetus, built on a tradition of bloodshed forged at the birth of the nation, a psychic schism festering like an open sore.'

I was referring to the genocide of Indigenous Australians from the start of white settlement and the societal conditions that continued to place the remaining indigenous population at an enormous disadvantage. This original sin, I tried to tell him, which had never been resolved, was why violence was still so entrenched in the day-to-day fabric of Australian life. I was so immersed in this tirade that I failed to look ahead of me, bumping into a passing stranger.

'Watch it, dickhead,' I said.

The stranger stopped.

'What?'

'You heard me. Moron.'

He crash-tackled me, knocking me flat on my back. I was winded, fighting for breath, the situation worsened by his hands tightly wrapped around my throat as he did his level best to strangle the life from me.

'Why did you say that?' he screamed. 'I've done nothing to you!'

For some reason, I was not scared and instead laughed in his face, or at least issued an approximation of a laugh, given I could scarcely breathe.

'Back off!' Charles yelled, reaching for his phone. 'I'm calling the cops!'

The stranger went into shock, perhaps realising how far he was prepared to go, and released his grip. He spat in my face and disappeared into the shadows. Charles helped me to my feet, but I was weak from pain and the task proved difficult. We sat on the kerb, his arm around my shoulders to stop me slumping to the ground.

Charles was shaken.

'Jesus. Your face went purple. I thought he was going to kill you but you just laughed at him. What the hell is wrong with you?'

I managed to regain the power of speech, although the pain in my throat was excruciating.

'So what?' I rasped, my voice a death rattle. 'I'm right, you know I am. Australia's real national anthem is not "Advance Australia Fair" but the sick music of skulls cracking on pavements. How many times have you read in the paper about fights at pubs and people punched to the ground, their heads caved in on the sidewalk, haemorrhaging to death, blood mingling with rivers of beer and vomit?'

Charles was deeply unimpressed.

'That's just blood sport, common as muck. I thought you were better than that but now I see you for who you are. You're just another thug with a fragile ego, just another hooligan filled with self-loathing, rattling your cage to make a big noise and prove you're still alive when really you're dead inside.'

He was right, he always was, but I didn't want to listen. All I could see around me was a mirror-world reflection of Brooklands, the fictional London satellite suburb in *Kingdom Come*. I identified with the narrator, Pearson, a former adman who had become bored with his job and lusted after a dose of insanity to make him feel alive again. Pearson travels to Brooklands to investigate the death of his father, shot in the Metro-Centre shopping complex by a gunman who opened fire on the lunchtime crowds, but he quickly becomes embroiled in the dark undercurrents of Brooklands' social strata, where everyone is obsessed with football and shopping and every resident seems to be a rabid nationalist.

The plot was eerily reminiscent of the beach riots in Cronulla, a Sydney suburb, which had erupted on Australia Day the year before. White racist surf gangs, waving Australian flags, attempted to defend 'their' beach against immigrant Lebanese 'intruders'. Of course, they were blind to the insuperable irony of defending white turf on Australia Day, known as 'Invasion Day' to many Indigenous Australians in painful recognition of the fact that white people violently took land from black people under the pretence of settling the nation. *Kingdom Come*'s clockwork mobs mirrored the behaviour of these beach defenders, except that with a typical Aussie touch the Cronulla violence was organised around surfing not football.

Around that time, a documentary had been released about an infamous Sydney-based surfer gang, narrated by a well-known Australian actor. We see the gang's home videos. In one, they beat up other surfers for daring to drop in on 'their' patch of ocean. In another, they swarm all over a bus in peak-hour traffic, refusing to let the bus move and harassing the driver, who can only stare at the camera in a helpless mix of terror and resignation, trapped and abused for the crime of going about his job. Yet the actor wanted to make a feature film about the gang, these genuine Aussie heroes.

The image of a mob of roaming thugs, egged on by a celebrity ringleader, is mirrored in *Kingdom Come* in the form of David Cruise, a forgotten actor who becomes the popular host of the Metro-Centre's cable TV channel. Cruise commands newfound fame and extreme loyalty among the mob, and when Pearson ingratiates himself into Brooklands' social scene, he 'rebrands' Cruise to sell the Metro-Centre, casting him as a tortured, nihilistic anti-hero in a series of billboard campaigns and TV spots.

The campaign becomes so popular that it leads to the secession of the Metro-Centre from Brooklands, a radical movement that begins when Cruise's followers use the act of shopping to instil political control. They understand that in this new metropolis shopping has so invaded the urban that it fulfils all civic and social functions, allowing the Metro-Centre to become a virtual city-state even more influential than standard institutions.

But the secession of the centre is more than mere fantasy. It is rooted in the way contemporary shopping centres operate. The Metro-Centre's real-world equivalent, the Bluewater complex, sits on the outskirts of London, a monstrous shrine to consumerism, enormous in scale. When it opened, the developer, Eric Kuhne, tried to justify it by saying that he never saw it as sounding the death knell for old-style regional communities but as a first step in creating a new kind of city, one that would provide a 'luscious experience' for those who submit to it.

When Ballard is interviewed in Iain Sinclair and Chris Petit's film *London Orbital*, he recognises the enormous implications of this social experiment.

'Iain,' he commands. 'I want you to blow up Bluewater.'

Finally, we rose to our feet. I tried explaining all of this to Charles.

'Blowing up Bluewater may have been dark sarcasm on Ballard's part, but I need to take him at face value. I need to do what Pearson did: to harness the shape of rage, to light a fuse under the vectors of violence and form a counter-movement from the debris.'

To kick the dog.

Charles was still disgusted with me for dragging him into that nasty bout of street theatre, and his compassion for my injured state had completely evaporated.

'Oh yeah? Well, harness *this!*'

As his fist smashed into my face, I saw stars and went down

for the count, and just before I did, I remember thinking: *Finally, someone has slowed me down.*

64

DANGEROUS BENDS

Sport and violence are galvanising forces in *Kingdom Come*, where support for a football team becomes endorsement of a bland mono-culture. In Melbourne, the idea of sports fans supporting consumerism over and above any notion of 'team' or 'community' is institutionalised. The big football teams play out of the same few grounds. There is no suburban specificity in Australian football anymore, no unique signifiers, just a differentiation predicated on sponsor logos. East Melbourne was in the eye of the storm and I could not avoid the repercussions of sport, of this monotheistic cult of blind worship. My apartment was near the city's sporting precinct, which included the Melbourne Cricket Ground, the hallowed turf of Australian sport, and the newer, city-like tennis and rugby stadia. Whenever a big game was on it became prudent to avoid the seething sports zone, since I never knew what kind of juiced-up knucklehead I might encounter in the small hours.

One night, I could hear a crowd of rugby supporters streaming down the street on their way to Olympic Stadium. They were overturning rubbish bins, ripping mirrors from cars, urinating in gardens—a suburban zombie army of the damned. I was used to such disturbances and thought nothing more of it until a couple of hours later, when I turned on the television and caught the tail end of the news. As the station wrapped up the big game, an incident occurred that was shattering in its implications. It was as if war had been declared but no one had noticed because we were all too glazed over and self-absorbed to care.

As the news anchor cut to Olympic Stadium, I watched the remains of the match-day crowd melt into the night. A sports reporter faced the camera, itemising the game's key moments, while a group of young men loitered behind him in the large shadows cast by the arena. Over the ambience of the gang's mocking laughter, which rose steadily in volume, the reporter dribbled out cliches, secure behind his armour of trusted TV-speak.

'For the Rockhampton Rodents, this game was like climbing a tall mountain. They were trapped in a snowstorm, unprepared for the avalanche that flattened them.'

I can recall every detail of what happened next as if I'd watched it in excruciating slow motion. A young man emerged from the shadows where the mocking gang lurked. He was short in stature, with a thick neck, heavy, overhanging forehead and caterpillar eyebrows. He wore a Rodents jersey and his beefy face was accentuated by a rough-hewn page-boy haircut. Extending his arms, he lunged nearer until he was centimetres away from the reporter. Then he pretended to lick the man's ear. I was fascinated by this strange, confused ritual playing out on live television. It was narcissistic and aggressive, signalled by the peacock dance of outstretched arms and puffed-up chest and the self-loathing eroticism of the proffered tongue.

As the reporter felt the man's hot, drunken breath on his vulnerable neck, he looked around, but his tormentor had lurched back into the shadows, laughing uproariously with his friends. Visibly unnerved, the reporter paused, waiting for the studio anchor's cue to come in over his earpiece as a volley of hooting and whistling erupted from the darkness. At length, he resumed.

'Rockhampton shouldn't have been in the finals. They were missing most of their forward line and the madness only got worse when the game started.'

Brow Man returned, assuming his position behind the reporter. He wore a mock-thoughtful expression, his head nodding exaggeratedly in sarcastic agreement with the hapless victim. Another man joined him. Both made offensive gestures behind the reporter's head before disappearing, while the man at the centre of it all shifted uneasily, a good-natured smile on his face. He seemed determined to ride it out, occupying himself by talking up next week's games, although he could sense that explosive violence was in the air.

We all could.

Once in an interview, Ballard revealed the role of his fiction: 'I'm trying to say: "Dangerous bends ahead. *Slow down.*"'

Later he revised the statement.

'But of course, there's a small part of me which has always said: "Dangerous bends ahead. *Speed up.*" Because I'm curious to know.'

There, in one fell swoop, he'd forged a disturbing footnote to his work, a terrible hyperlink that, once followed, undermined his main thesis, sealing off forever the manhole by which we'd entered his strange new realities. Now we were expected to *enjoy* his perversions. Taking the advice to heart, I willed these young idiots to ride the savage beast that had possessed them all the way to the end.

Speed up!

'Well, now,' the reporter continued, 'attention shifts to the Broome Bandicoots, who last night made it to the semi-final.'

Brow Man sprinted back into the frame, jumping on the reporter and wrapping his stocky arms around his neck. He nearly dragged him to the ground, but the reporter recovered and shrugged him off. He attempted to joke about it but lost composure. Staring at the ground, he swore under his breath, resigned to the helpless inevitability of what was to come.

Right on cue, he disappeared like a puppet jerked on a string, punched to the ground by the entire gang. Animalistic whoops and hollers filled the air as the cameraman stepped away, although he managed to record the assault, refocusing the lens as he stumbled backwards. A tall man with a shaved head and wide shoulders moved around the scrum at a hyper-rapid clip, unusually quick for a man of his stature. He pushed away anyone who tried to come to the reporter's aid, hopping up and down like a possessed jackhammer, his glassy bug eyes and sweaty, gleaming head caught squarely on film. The reporter was somewhere amid the whirling mob, lost under a welter of flailing arms and legs, and then the cameraman was attacked too, falling to the ground and dropping his equipment, although the camera continued to record as it pointed upwards, capturing a dead night sky punctuated by echoing voices and the sound of clashing bodies. Mercifully, the feed was cut as the station returned to the studio, where the shocked anchor attempted to regroup.

The sequence of events lasted just under two minutes yet contained an entire universe, and my guilty exhilaration at the violent spectacle dissolved into abject panic. I felt trapped as surely as the reporter, for this is what it had come to: spontaneous bashings in full view of the media glare, a performance for the cameras, random acts of senseless violence repackaged as the ultimate thrill. These men had not even bothered to hide their faces from the camera during the whole time it had beamed the incident to a nationwide audience, and that fact fascinated me as much as the attack repelled me.

I thought of Virilio, who once proposed to build a 'museum of accidents' but then decided that the museum already exists—it is television. We have not, he claims, adjusted to the saturation of images in our society. Instead, we are 'forgetting our body. We are losing it. This is an accident of the body, a de-corporation. The body is torn and disintegrated.'

I refused to see the attack on the reporter as a simple case of drug-fuelled idiocy. On the contrary, we, all of us, including Brow Man and his moronic gang, were becoming lost in Virilian virtual space, allowing our bodies to waste away under the sleepless gaze of televised surveillance.

65

PSYCHODRAMA

My apartment had become stifling and I needed air. I decided to risk a late-night run to the supermarket for provisions, anything to remove myself from the coordinates of the TV eye. At the store, as I negotiated the checkout lane, I found myself in front of an inebriated man who was swaying all over. He was unable to hold his balance, and I could feel his hot breath on the back of my neck, so close it was as if he wanted to bite me on the jugular. It reminded me of Brow Man's fat tongue slithering out of his mouth, on the verge of licking the reporter's neck, and I experienced a strange, electric sense of dislocation, as if I'd swapped bodies with the reporter and had been sucked into the digital signal, my flesh compressed and floating away into the aether.

The invasion of personal space repulsed me more than the secondhand stench of stale alcohol and body odour assaulting my nostrils, and as I tried to move away the man pushed his fist roughly into the small of my back, delivering a punch of such intensity I staggered a few steps forward.

'What're you up to, mate?' he slurred.

I turned around, stung not so much by the punch as the attempt to rope me into fake pleasantries.

'I'm not your mate and I'm not doing anything. Piss off.'

'You're clearly doing something, cunt.'

'Okay, yeah, you're right. I'm doing something. *Now* can you piss off?'

He laughed.

'Alright, tough guy. What's so bad in your life that you're acting like a miserable bastard?'

'My dad's got terminal cancer. Glad you asked?'

It was a lie (my Dad was already dead) and he knew it. My heart was in my throat, for I was no fighter, which he could also sense.

'Bullshit!' he screamed, spit flying through the air. 'I'll smack your fucking head in, then you'll have something to whine about.'

The terrified checkout attendant left to alert security and I left without my goods. The meathead's friends were outside, drinking bourbon. He was held up by the security guard and signalled for them to follow, but I was extremely fit from cycling and they couldn't catch me. As I ran into the cold night air, watching my breath expelled in pale clouds ahead of me, I knew that something of extraordinary significance was also in the air. I was convinced of it. The attack on the reporter seemed to have intensified this feeling, to have signalled it like a flare. Personal space could be invaded at any time, the threat of surveillance no deterrent to Brow Man or to the idiot in the supermarket but rather an *encouragement*, a lusty come-on, the chance for them to star in their own psychodramas.

Once I'd lost my pursuers, I stopped to catch my breath, staring at the night sky. There was no activity. No planes, no birds. The sky was dead. I thought of my former UFO obsession and laughed at how distracted and disconnected it used to make me feel. Down here was the real struggle, right here on Earth.

Time to light a fire.

66

MELBOREA MORONICA

When I arrived home, I booted up the computer and tried to capture my thoughts. Ever since my return from the Pacific, I'd been writing obsessively on Ballard, more so than when I was studying, trying to make sense of the world. I often wrote on autopilot, well into the night, barely aware of the process. The next day I'd be surprised to discover three thousand words on the screen. After a few months I had a total of 60,000 words and realised I'd been rewriting my long-abandoned thesis, updating it for a new age of personalised surveillance and street-level terror. The positive message of affirmative dystopias that once possessed me had taken a darker turn. Ballard's characters, I realised, sought out extreme situations, even stoked them, so that something new could emerge from the chaos. It wasn't a question of merging with dystopia, as I'd once thought, but of accelerating it, of pouring petrol onto the fire. In principle, that's what the rugby thugs had achieved, although I doubted they had a program of social change in mind. Instead, they'd succumbed to fatal inversion, allowing the logic of the image to dictate to them, as if they had forgotten that their actions in the virtual world could have corresponding effects in the actual space of lived experience.

I attacked the keyboard, a torrent of thoughts rushing to cohere, refocusing my mind as I tried to contextualise in Ballardian terms the events of that strange evening. When Brow Man and his gang went on the attack, there was a forgetting of the body that absolved them of all responsibility, a subliminal belief that if the cameras are rolling then anything and anyone is fair game, that it is all staged, a performance. These boneheads would probably be arrested the next day, since they hadn't bothered to hide their faces from the camera the entire time. In fact, they'd stared it down, proud of who they were. Absorbing the heightened tenor of surveillance, they'd allowed television to serve up the means of their control as the ultimate form of entertainment.

The circumstances that gave rise to their rampage were presaged in *High-Rise*, in which a man named Wilder attempts to record the building's descent into anarchy with his all-seeing 'cine-camera'. Proud of his working-class roots, he dreams of making a documentary of the social workings of the high-rise, but as violence takes hold and tribal warfare pits floor against floor, the camera is broken in a skirmish without having record-ed a frame. Yet he continues to carry it with him, gripping it like a weapon. Wilder is obsessed with the idea that everything must be recorded in visual terms, even if the actual act of re-cording is a mere illusion invested in a broken-down piece of equipment. Violently catalysing the savage events, Wilder delib-erately drowns a resident's dog, triggering the chaos to come. As the building succumbs to total savagery and people are brutally killed all around him (sometimes by his own hand), his only thought is to capture the madness on film, ostensibly as part of a documentary he's making on the building, although his real motivation is the deep-seated need to fulfil his own 'personal bi-ography'. He wants to capture a record of his ascent through the high-rise from the lower floors where he lives to the architect's opulent penthouse, shaming those he feels inferior to along the way: his neighbours, members of the hated middle class.

Ballard describes Wilder as having 'rugby scrum man-ners', and in my newly possessed state, in which anything and everything could be perceived as Ballardian, that descriptor was like a ley line connecting the past (when the novel was pub-lished) with the present (32 years into the future) and the attack by *rugby* fans on the television reporter. The connection was ten-uous, ridiculous, but I could not let it go. I became so delud-ed I imagined I could see ley lines everywhere. These mystical alignments, points on a mental map with no defined boundaries, joined anything and everything with my Ballardian awareness, linking any coordinate with any other.

Watching the attack on the reporter, I had become aware of an extreme 'Wilderian' life force oozing from the television, a callous, brutal and selfish masculinity that had mutated to destroy those it was subjugated to. Brow Man and his gang were descendants of Wilder, a vicious thug who had bloomed under what Ballard describes as the 'true light' of the high-rise: the 'metallic flash' of cameras that record the violence the residents crave, storing it for fetishistic viewing later on.

'What depraved species of electric flora,' he writes, 'would spring to life from the garbage-strewn carpets of the corridors in response to this new source of light?'

In fact, that 'depraved species' was growing wild in the cracks between the concrete and tarmac in Melbourne. Brow Man and his antics had cemented this certainty in my mind, because I'd been exposed to 'this new source of light' myself, way back when I'd photosynthesised the purple glow from the car dashboard into my skin.

I'd even given this mutant species, my people, a biological classification.

Melborea Moronica.

67

SUICIDE BY THUG

Charles lived in a bedsit in Preston, in a liminal zone wedged between the trendy main streets. The bedsit was in a block populated by perverts and drunks, plonked in the middle of the zone like the desert monolith in *2001: A Space Odyssey*. It was the only residential building around, an object of alien wonder viewed with amazement by the beggars, junkies and homeless people inhabiting the cracks in urban space. The zone was perpetually under construction in its bid to be gentrified under the great hipster experiment engulfing inner-city Melbourne, although that scenario had its upside. The bedsits did not have en suites, just a shared toilet block for the entire building, so disgusting and rundown as to be unusable, yet most residents were able to find relief in the Portaloos of the nearby construction sites.

The night after Brow Man went on the rampage, I visited Charles. We had made up after our spat, and I wanted to discuss the Ballardian ideas that had fermented in my mind since I'd been attacked on the street. As I climbed the steps to the building's second floor, I gagged at the smell of methylated spirits and vomit permeating the fabric of the place. I waded through the rubbish and faeces in the hall leading to Charles's bedsit, tripping over the legs of a topless man supine on the floor. His torso was filthy, as if he'd been rolling in shit, and he was wanking in semi-darkness, his piston-pumping hand rendered in yellow horror-film hues by the hallway's flickering lights. Backing away from this revolting apparition, I knocked on Charles' door. He opened it, and in the sliver of light emanating from the crack in the door I saw a cockroach scurrying over the onanist's foot.

I hustled inside, squeezing past the unplumbed bathtub that took up most of Charles's single-room quarters. His small bed was tucked away to one side. Charles was a handsome man, in his early thirties. He had longish brown hair, a largish nose and a quizzical expression, features that resembled the French actor Jean-Pierre Léaud. He even dressed like Léaud. Like a uniform, he always wore a grey overcoat and a shabby yet well-tailored blue suit.

'Nice jacket,' he said as I entered. It was identical to his. Indeed, I was beginning to dress like him, for I not only admired his style but deeply appreciated how he was as alienated as me.

Charles was an intensely nervous man. Once, I saw him walking towards me on the street. He saw me too but hadn't realised I'd spotted him first. Thinking he had gone undetected, he ducked into a nearby alley to avoid conversation—and I was his closest friend. Somehow our relationship endured, although I had to go to great lengths to see him, since he never returned my calls.

Charles was studying towards his PhD at Hartwell, which concerned the use of dystopian motifs in the work of the French novelist Michel Houellebecq. He was as obsessed with Houellebecq as I was with Ballard, and in his wallet he carried a photo of his idol smoking a cigarette butt and carrying a plastic shopping bag—Gallic homeless chic. The previous week, at a lunchtime presentation, he had given a paper on the iconography of that photo. I was in the audience when, halfway through his talk, he excused himself to go to the toilet, an unusual move in itself, but then he never returned. All that was left was that mad image of Houellebecq blown up on the lecture screen. As the minutes wore on, the audience became dumbfounded and I was stricken with embarrassment for him. My visit to his apartment was the first time I'd seen him since that fateful day.

I sat down on his dirty, unmade bed.

'What happened?'

'Nerves. Those lights shining in my face, all those ignorant people. How could I justify Houellebecq to them? They'd only go back to reading *The Da Vinci Code* tomorrow.'

I let his rant die down and didn't mention the incident again. I knew it was futile to ask him to explain his erratic behaviour. For Charles, it was up to others to decipher the mystery of his existence. We were both poor and would bring food whenever we visited each other, supplies we invariably stole. I had pinched some bread rolls and wine from the local deli, which I laid out on his tiny, cracked table.

'Charles, I'm bored with travel writing, ashamed at what I've become. The company has ruined me, with its editorial imperative to write with "colour and flair". It's meaningless. Every travel writer makes the same dumb jokes and we all sound like brain-dead hipsters. They never give you enough time to review everything. It's a slog and I'm bored with writing about endless chain hotels, sick of trying to find new ways to describe "spectacular" sunsets, ashamed of glossing over the existential horror of identikit pink-and-blue floral bedspreads. The entrance to hell is wreathed with floral bedspreads!'

Charles reached over to his bookshelf and fished out the Japan guidebook I'd contributed to. He found the chapter on Tohoku I'd written and read aloud.

'Morioka makes a good base camp.'

My words.

'You haven't read *Platform*, have you?'

'Houellebecq? No, only *Atomised*.'

'Well, *Platform* is Houellebecq's attack on the tourism industry, on guidebooks like *this*.'

He twisted the knife, waving the Japan guide in my face.

'Including their elitist view of which destinations are worthy, the sheer banality of their descriptive writing.'

He retrieved *Platform* from the shelf and read from it.

'The first stop was Kanchanaburi, which all the guide books agree is a lively, animated city; the *Guide du Routard* considers it a good base camp.'

I was filled with self-loathing but Charles refused to back down.

'You've become a walking cliche. I used to admire you because you were so single-minded and refused to sell out. But this, what you do now—it isn't writing.'

'I know.'

'You should finish your PhD. The department has surplus funds and needs to spend them by the end of the year. Don't you regret not finishing?'

'Of course. Ballard won't go away.'

'Yes, you're obsessed and it won't let you go until you finish this thing. You'll never get your life back on track until you write it out of you.'

I sat there, mulling over his 'advice'. It was the blind leading the blind, since Charles couldn't stand before an audience without wetting himself in fear. But I knew he was right. Returning to study offered the chance to absolve myself of all my failures and disappointments, even regarding Catherine. If I could graduate, perhaps I might win her respect. However, I was too enervated to find out whether his claim about department funds was true and I knew I'd do what I always did: let the opportunity slide through inaction until it evaporated. That way I wouldn't run the risk of failure. I finished my wine and left.

In the hallway, the onanist was nowhere to be found. That was a shame. I wanted to kick him full in the face on the way out. I wanted to break his nose, to spread it right across his filthy face. I wanted to know what that felt like. As I stepped into the street, I looked around for someone I could pick a fight with. Anyone would do but preferably someone big and tough, for I desperately needed to fulfil the impulse I'd allowed to surface the night I was strangled half to death. What I wanted was not to prove a point about street violence, as I'd told Charles, but to enact my version of suicide by cop.

Suicide by thug.

The streets were deserted.

Not for the first time, I was left alone with my wretched self-destructive thoughts, too cowardly to act on them myself.

68

HOSTILE TAKEOVER

It had been a year since I'd returned from the Pacific and there were no other assignments on the horizon. I'd lost my appetite for the pitch, for selling myself to disinterested editors. For the freelance writer, that is fatal. Starving and on the breadline,

I finally landed a couple of straightforward, desk-based travel-writing jobs, the first being a contribution to a faux guidebook on micronations.

Micronationalism was an interesting fad and one that, I would learn, had darkly Ballardian overtones. In fact, it would be my future obsession with micronations that would eventually pitch me into a final confrontation with the spectre of Ballard, but for now I could only write about the phenomenon with ironic detachment, mocking the sad nerds all over the globe who'd declared their bedrooms as independent states, studiously ignoring the serious political implications of the movement. To add insult to injury, when the book was published, it received wide exposure and good reviews, and a famous comedy actor even optioned it for a feature film, although myself and my two co-authors, as indentured content monkeys, never saw a cent of this shiny deal. We'd signed away all rights to the publisher in return for a lump sum, leaving me as broke as ever.

The second job was writing about the attractions of northern Japan for a Chinese inflight magazine. In principle it was easy. All I had to do was rehash my Tohoku experience to provide an account of the regional sights, such as the hiking trails and replica samurai castles. Instead, bored with the task, I turned in *fiction*—a short story into which I'd inserted myself, 'the travel writer', as an agent gone rogue on the road, patterned after the anguished assassin Willard in the film *Apocalypse Now*. Like Willard, the narrator was blind drunk in a seedy hotel room, driven mad by the absurd nature of his assignment, droning on and on to himself about how he is unsuited to the work, about how travel writing has made him insane. The attractions were barely mentioned, except in bad verse (the narrator fancied himself as some kind of punk poet), and the story, naturally, was never published.

It was the last travel-writing assignment I was ever offered, and I can scarcely imagine a more pathetic act of psychological self-sabotage, detonating your own career just for the hell of it, since the stakes are so low as to be invisible to anyone but your own miserable self. Everyone else just wants you to do the job you've been paid to do. Here, yet again, was another echo of my original sin: the derailing of academic ambition into trivia, facilitated by the utter impenetrability of Ballardian discourse and my insane obsession with examining every single aspect of my life under that unrelenting microscope.

Although my cards had been well and truly marked as a travel writer, I was still able to sell the occasional non-travel piece in niche markets where my name had not yet been tainted. A month later I had a book review published in a local literary magazine, and when a copy of the magazine was sent to me I was surprised to see Anthony, my former supervisor, listed as a contributor. I emailed him to say hello, casually mentioning Charles' advice.

'Yes,' he replied. 'There is a surplus of departmental money, and yes, it could be used to bring you back to finish your PhD. If that's what you really want.'

It was.

Anthony checked the records. I had eighteen months to finish the thesis before the window closed. Once you quit a PhD, you have ten years to re-enrol and complete it, but beyond that you must reapply and start all over again. I always did things at the last minute, like uploading job applications just before the online system closed, a constant death race with my soul. With little else going on in my life, I accepted.

A few weeks later, I visited the university to enrol, accompanied by Charles. At the library, I located the same hardback first edition of *Crash* I had valorised when contemplating my thesis all those years ago. I opened it at random, expecting to become immersed all over again in the fervour of Ballard's words, only to find immature aphorisms scrawled in pen and linked by arrows to the text:

Ballard DESTROYS →
        ← YES!!! That is the postmodern condition!

As I discovered more of these juvenile ejaculations, I pitied the sad undergraduate who had felt compelled to declare his hand in such a public and embarrassing fashion.

Charles laughed.

'That's your handwriting.'

I recoiled in terror. I hadn't realised, but when I looked closer I had to accept the truth. It *was* my own hand. It *was* me who had defiled the pages of *Crash* all those years ago. I was repelled by this confrontation with my younger self, who seemed to have taken the book as some kind of punk manual for smashing the state. I located *The Atrocity Exhibition* and *High-Rise*, only to encounter more of the same, and my heart almost stopped for I had long ago wiped clean that phase of existence and erected a new person in its place. To be reminded of that skin again, to inhabit that naive persona once more, was an elemental horror.

I am that person, but I am not me.

I remembered the murder scene in the cyberpunk film *Strange Days*. A young woman is hooked up to a virtual reality device that is also linked to her killer, forcing her to experience his sadistic pleasure in torturing her, as if she is inhabiting his body and senses while simultaneously undergoing the most excruciating pain. Thinking about that disturbing scenario, I became intensely sorry for the hapless readers who had borrowed the book after me in that ten-year gap, their experience of Ballard disrupted by the immature mess emanating from my hyperactive pen, yet at the same time I understood that it was I who was the vandal, the tormentor.

At that point, something occurred to me. I turned to Charles, who still wore an insolent smirk.

'Don't laugh. This is precisely the effect of reading Ballard that interests me. People want to own him, to inhabit his writing, to invest it with their own agenda.'

'Why?'

'I don't really know. I think there's something about the writing that causes a kind of fusion with the reader—an invasion by a foreign intelligence.'

But Charles had wandered off to look for Houellebecq first editions, leaving me to my fate: trailing the shadows of men and women infinitely smarter than myself.

69

APPLIED BALLARDIANISM

Upon my return to academia, I'd nursed grand plans of creating a new discipline, 'Applied Ballardianism', that would analyse Ballardian currents in contemporary culture. The twenty-first century had become so 'Ballardian' that the adjective was even defined in the *Collins English Dictionary*: 'resembling or suggestive of the conditions described in Ballard's novels and stories, esp. dystopian modernity, bleak manmade landscapes, and the psychological effects of technological, social or environmental developments'. However, I knew the Ballardian worldview was more than a simple descriptor of cultural norms, more than mere philosophy. It was an ideal for living.

Of course, kickstarting such a movement would not be easy, given that I was trained in the failing discipline of cultural studies, which, a decade before, had peaked in popularity. Bathed in that golden glow, Ballard had become a subject worthy of cultural analysis because his writing—resistant to genre, corrosive of literary norms—had proved such a powerful influence on a battery of artists, musicians, architects, filmmakers and writers. Since then, cultural studies had become a wasteland and Ballard had been absorbed into the mainstream, claimed by newspapers like *The Guardian*, which turned to his work whenever the scent of banal apocalypse was in the air (football hooligans, IKEA riots—the usual suburban dystopia fuelling the latest moral panics).

Cultural studies had peaked and troughed at a rapid pace, devolving into an academic fad tainted by depthless critique and a lack of intellectual rigour, a degraded form bitterly satirised by Don DeLillo in his novel *White Noise*, in which the central character, a cultural studies scholar, founds a department of Hitler Studies in the same building as the Popular Culture department. Cultural studies is so shallow, DeLillo argues, it treats subjects of 'serious' historical worth with the same superficial analysis as pop-cultural artefacts like soap operas and advertising. Worse, the founder of Hitler Studies doesn't speak a word of German, an indictment of cultural studies as utterly divorced from history and context.

That represented one end of the spectrum, fighting off the pungent smell that had attached itself to the discipline and robbed it of its credibility, a stench amplified by the ludicrous popularity of academic volumes that apply classical philosophy to the lyrics of Metallica, Led Zeppelin, Pink Floyd and other stadium-rock acts. At the other end, where serious work was being conducted, lay another battle, a struggle for funding and support, a brutal war that trapped the last few cultural studies academics at Hartwell University in a rearguard action, watching with helpless terror as the field was gradually absorbed by more profitable disciplines. Their futile battle reminded me of the resistance fighters holed up in the abandoned shopping mall in the horror film *Dawn of the Dead*, and their fight to stay alive against hundreds of zombies breaking down the doors in search of fresh brains.

These remaining battle-hardened veterans wanted to make cultural studies relevant again, but instead they were preoccupied with warding off the undead army in an unwinnable war that ground them down and enslaved them to paperwork and administrative tasks to justify their research. They came under intense scrutiny from the powers that be because their research was not directly indexed to pure revenue but to the vagaries of 'cultural capital', forced to justify its existence with ridiculous and obscure metrics, until in the end the paperwork took up more time than the research. Inevitably, the department was broken down and assimilated, reduced to a couple of courses attached (for some inscrutable bureaucratic reason) to a new and more lucrative school, the Centre for Cryogenics, Plastic and Reconstructive Surgery, a department that had absolutely no connection to literature or philosophy. No one beyond the resistance fighters questioned this, however. The Centre's very existence seemed a natural rule of law.

Meanwhile, sessional tutors like myself (the only regular work I could find when I returned full-time to the PhD) were exploited ruthlessly, the carrot of tenure forever out of reach as the pressure increased to teach, study and publish while also trying to obtain a qualification. Aside from that harsh economic reality, there were philosophical questions I had to resolve before I could move forward. Why did I always shove aside the positive implications of Ballard's work, the message of resistance it carried, in favour of the dark desires that had driven his characters to reach that point? I suppose it reflected my own cynical worldview, my own fatal inwardness that ensured I found little joy in anything. The light in Barcelona, for example, had quickly turned dark. Yet wasn't there liberation in the embracing of dystopian states? Is that not a form of resistance? The trick, as

Ballard explained so patiently, lay in knowing when to apply the brakes before self-immolation occurs, to stop just short so that a creative *frisson* could illuminate the shining path.

All fine in theory, but I wasn't even sure I had it in me. Given the choice between brake and accelerator, I knew which impulse would win out every single time.

Like a Melbourne driver ramming into a cyclist, I was powerless to prevent my fate.

70

ROARING MICE

I was three months into my second coming and already deflated anew. What was the point in continuing when I'd been outed as a zombie academic, intellectually undead? The situation was grim but it was Anthony who turned me around, making amends for his inadvertent derailing of my ambition back in the 90s. He told me about an exciting conference on Ballard that was to be held at the University of Ipswich in England, and when I read the call for submissions I was galvanised, convinced I'd finally found solid ground on which to stake my ideas. The organisers had provided stimulating thought starters and possible topics for aspiring presenters to consider, a laundry list of themes found in Ballard's fiction. The psychological power of urban space. Memory and time travel. Utopia and dystopia. Political terrorism and meaningless violence. Surrealism, consumerism and fascism. Pornography and science. As such, the conference represented an opportunity to test my theory of Applied Ballardianism, offering a chance to root it in *reality* and ram a stake into the cynical heart of my shady alterna-self.

I tried to leverage some of the momentum from the micronations book I'd worked on, submitting an abstract on 'Ballard and micronations' to the organisers, since I'd always been interested in the way his writing evokes a vivid spatiality couched in the language of secession. The urge to form micronations, whether as a joke, a political experiment or a religious utopia (all modes have found wide purchase) can in some ways be attributed to globalisation and the failure of political action to ignite the mass imagination, a process that Ballard was fully aware of. In end-stage capitalism, he once said, the 'overriding power of the global economy threatens the autonomy of the nation state, while the ability of politicians to intervene as an equalising force has faded'. Within such a vacuum, micronational enclaves thrive.

In Ballardian terms, there are parallels in the suburban phenomenon of gated communities, sealed-off suburban areas guarded by surveillance technology and private security firms, predicated on the unease that particular social groups feel regarding a certain quality of life and welfare that they believe governments cannot guarantee. It is under such conditions that micronationalism erupts in Ballard's final quartet of novels. Fermented in the self-sufficient resorts and business parks of *Cocaine Nights* and *Super-Cannes*, the phenomenon morphs into full-blown secession in *Millennium People*, with its 'anomalous enclave' of middle-class discontents, and in *Kingdom Come*, with its consumer-driven revolutionaries.

Millennium People charts an uprising in Chelsea Marina, an exclusive gated community in London where middle-class citizens, rejecting their perceived role as the 'new proletariat', revolt against a meaningless society. They turn their community into a miniature war zone but the action is doomed to fail, since the revolutionaries are too indoctrinated by consumerism to consummate their insurrection. They even tidy up once their uprising has been quashed, sweeping away broken glass and pushing destroyed vehicles off the road and into designated parking spaces.

Having made it all too easy for the authorities to move in, martial law is declared and Chelsea Marina becomes 'an anomalous enclave ruled jointly by the police and the local council'. The rebellion that almost causes Chelsea Marina to secede is swiftly reintegrated into the system, an act remembered in the newspapers more for childish, tabloid acts of violence (the novelty of middle-class revolt) than for any sustained program of social change. The transgression of meaningless violence is usurped by the more powerful intervention of state violence, the Simulated State repackaging rebellion to demonstrate the futility of performing actions that can be broken down into news bites, into spectacular entertainment.

So it proved in the real world. In 1967, in one of the more famous examples of a micronation taking on the state, a man named Giorgio Rosa sunk a tower in the Adriatic sea, twelve kilometres off the coast of Rimini. Ringed by a promenade with an area of 120 metres, the tower boasted a post office, bar, restaurant, bank and supermarket. At first, the Italian government ignored the structure, since it was outside established territorial limits. But when Rosa declared the platform an independent republic, the 'Isle of Roses', with Esperanto as its official language, navy frogmen were dispatched to blow it up, the government claiming that not only was the tower a threat to national security but that Rosa was also using it as a tax haven and pornography studio. The only alternative for micronations, then, as the existence of Sealand proves, is to hope for survival as a harmless tourist oddity, tolerated by the surrounding macronations and defanged of oppositional intent.

After the failures of physical micronations, some micronationalists put their faith in Second Life, the virtual reality environment that had maintained a low-level popularity after an initial burst of hype. According to Linden Lab, creators of Second Life, their aim was to develop a cyberpunk-style 'metaverse' where users could interact, build worlds, conduct business, communicate and socialise without the attendant hassles of 'meatspace'. Alas, Second Life fell prey to the same entropic forces that had scuppered numerous micronations, replicating the same political schisms, the same slavery to consumer goods, the same bad blood and intolerance between people who would never see eye to eye. Reports began to emerge of virtual bullying, sexual abuse, paedophilia, neo-Nazi political campaigning—even 'virtual terrorism' directed against Linden Lab.

Despite the danger signs, I became heavily involved with Second Life and the impulse grew to be more than a Ballardian reflex, more than simply research for a thesis.

For in Second Life I lived—and in Second Life I died.

71

ALTER VU

In Second Life, I inhabited a woman's body. I was acting on pure instinct, feeling far more comfortable in this form, re-modelling my avatar's physicality with beehive hair, stacked heels, boob tubes, pneumatic breasts, glittery earrings and huge, silicon-pumped lips. Only in virtuality could I feel more comfortable as a woman than a man, even though the form I assumed was an imperfect pastiche of a woman, as if I was a panicky alien suddenly deposited on Earth and trying desperately to pass itself off as human. I would visit virtual lesbian bondage clubs and score cheap virtual 'sex', wondering if the women I 'made love' to in the pixel S&M dungeons were also men behind their computer screens. There was something inherently Ballardian about the scenario, doubtless part of the appeal for my disordered psyche—the idea of virtual sex, with participants separated by screens, was straight out of 'The

Intensive Care Unit'. But it ran deeper than even that obsession. After all, two men having computer sex behind the shield of opposite genders would be the closest I would ever get to admitting something intrinsic about myself, something that might help me solve the riddle of why I had never been able to form relationships after Catherine had gone. Alas, there was no way of knowing their true identity and so the insight evaporated, leaving me rudderless once more.

One evening, I entered 'Tohoku' into Second Life's search engine. I was still interested in Japan and knew that Second Lifers frequently named parcels of virtual land after their favourite part of the world. Still, I was surprised when an entry for 'Tohoku' appeared, since the place was far from popular. With mounting excitement, I teleported there and found that someone had indeed bought land and named it after the Japanese region. They'd even erected a traditional Japanese temple, which I entered, but with none of the ambivalence that Scarlett Johansson felt in *Lost in Translation* when faced with a real temple, for nothing was as sexy as virtuality. The temple was deserted, so I laid down on an opulent bed and allowed my avatar to idle. Time flowed by. Eventually, a woman and a man materialised before me. They told me their Second Life names: 'Markerian' and 'Kubrickian'. They were the owners of the land, and although they were wary of my intrusion into their space, I managed to befriend them. Over the next month I visited them frequently, careful never to reveal my meatspace name or anything at all to do with my first life.

Markerian offered to be my Second Life guide, and one day we visited an artists' colony founded by people with real-world disabilities. I was moved by the freedom they had found in virtuality and the accounts they related of being able to perform physical feats in Second Life that they would never be able to achieve in reality. It put me in mind of a conference I'd attended long ago, where I'd met a woman confined to a wheelchair.

The woman had told me how *The Atrocity Exhibition* was venerated as a text of spiritual significance by the disabled people in her community. They considered *Atrocity* a forking-branch chronology, a representation of a multiverse in which variations of the same character enact parallel lives, a viewpoint informed by the many-worlds interpretation of quantum physics, which holds that there are infinite variations of our reality existing simultaneously throughout the universe.

In *Atrocity*, T- has a master plan: to stem the avalanche of media fictions invading his mind, such as the official narratives surrounding the assassination of JFK and the suicide of Marilyn Monroe. He restages these celebrity deaths 'in a way that makes sense', reconciling the inconsistencies in the official version with a revised reality that satisfies his conspiratorial, paranoid mind. In these alternate deaths, he casts his girlfriend in a variety of gruesome roles: a dismembered accident victim; a lifeless body at the bottom of a drained swimming pool. Although he kills her in each iteration, she is reborn from chapter to chapter, while T-'s fragmented personality and frequent name changes suggest that he too has been reanimated.

Atrocity had given the woman hope that while her body may have stalled in this reality, there was another she could inhabit in a parallel world where her physicality was quite the opposite. She was determined to find the portal that could lead her there, and I often wondered whether she became part of that virtual community, for her personal philosophy was exactly the same as that of the disabled artists.

It was how they lived their lives.

72

NEW GOLD SUNSET

On another occasion, Markerian escorted me to Ouvroir, Chris Marker's island in Second Life. 'It's my favourite place here,' she said. 'And now you know how I got my name.'

I'd heard Marker had a long-standing involvement with multimedia—he was an early adopter of CD-ROMs—but I had no idea he 'lived' in Second Life. The experience was incredible, as vivid as any real-life event. Given my deep admiration for Marker and his films, I found it overwhelming to step inside a world he had designed. We were deposited on a big mountain made from pictures of Guillaume, Marker's cat and muse (the director was a well-known cat lover). There was no one else about. We followed the signs to a film museum that housed artefacts and ephemera from Marker and other directors including Coppola, Lubitsch and Lang. In the museum, strange creatures wafted through the air, and I rubbed noses with a floating polka-dot shark as atrocity images from wartime newsreels slid beneath my feet, visible through the transparent floor.

Next door was a small, dark cinema devoted to Marker's films. At that moment, it was screening *La Jetée*, a work much admired by Ballard. Shot almost entirely in stills, *La Jetée* tells the story of a prisoner of war in post-apocalyptic Paris, who is selected for a time-travel experiment that returns him to the pre-war era. He is judged to be suitable for the experiment, since he has a particular recollection of the peacetime era that won't leave him—a memory of a woman he'd briefly glimpsed as a boy on the jetty at Orly Airport, her face creased in horror as a man is inexplicably shot and killed before them. Carrying this traumatic memory, his captors reason, will cushion the shock of re-awakening in the past.

When the man is sent back in time, he is consumed anew by his memory of the woman. Somehow he finds and befriends her, although he is never sure whether he is travelling through time, dreaming or reliving his memory of her. He is sent back in short bursts, and on his last foray hurries to where he knows she will be: at the airport jetty. He wants nothing more than to escape with her into the past, never to return to his own time, but standing in the way is one of his captors, who has followed him back. When the captor shoots the man dead, right in front of the woman and a small boy standing beside her, the narration reveals that the boy is the man as a child. The man has entered his own memory and reinhabited it. He has watched himself die.

Once, describing how *Atrocity* works, Ballard reflected on the human process of memory retrieval that gives the book its psychological charge. He coined an evocative term, 'mental Polaroids', to describe our most entrenched memories, such as fond remembrances of family, lovers and friends, even the recall of great pain and suffering. For Ballard, although these mental Polaroids are as moving as family photographs, in the end they are nothing more than 'a ghostly and alternative version of our own past, filled with shadowy figures as formalised as Egyptian tomb-reliefs'.

He may as well have been describing *La Jetée*. Just as the film's protagonist, a war-scarred man interned in a squalid enemy camp, was 'marked by an image from his childhood ... a violent scene, whose meaning he would not grasp until much later', so too was Ballard, who in his writing revisited the morbid stasis of Lunghua over and over, condemning his adult self to eternally re-enact that primal moment of childhood trauma. Like *La Jetée*'s tormented time traveller, perhaps Ballard never really knew if he was dreaming, remembering the past or travelling to the future. In fact, he once claimed that writing was an extension of the dreamworld, firming in my mind the half-baked theory I'd formed in the

Pacific about his Lovecraftian dream portals.

Like Marker, Ballard was obsessed with the question of how to escape or cheat time, a preoccupation rooted in his beginnings as a science fiction writer. In many of his early stories— such as 'Escapement', 'Chronopolis', 'The Voices of Time', 'The Garden of Time', 'Time of Passage' and 'The Day of Forever'— clock time is advanced as an arbitrary, manmade construct that imposes order and control on the liberating chaos of the subconscious. In the 70s, he abandoned this mode of enquiry, preferring to record the urban devastation of *Crash*, *Concrete Island* and *High-Rise*, but then in the 80s he made a surprise return to the battlefields of time, publishing a trilogy of stories about psychologically damaged astronauts: 'News from the Sun', 'Memories of the Space Age' and 'Myths of the Near Future'. In this remarkable series, to inhabit stopped time is to participate in an explicit act of rebellion—it is to refuse the world.

In 'Memories of the Space Age', the populace suffers from a 'space sickness' brought to Earth by returning astronauts. Those afflicted with the sickness perceive time slowing almost to a halt and a few minutes can last a whole day. Every event in the past and future can be accessed in the present, for the passing of events into memories takes place at such a slow rate they accrete into the present and become reinhabited, thus forming a predictive 'memory' of the future: 'The flow of light through the air had begun to slow, layers of time overlaid each other, laminae of past and future fused together. Soon the tide of photons would be still, space and time would set forever.'

These frozen moments provide a chance to escape into immortality 'in a world beyond time', transcending forever the mundane realities of everyday life. Indeed, one character, Hinton, hurls himself to his death from the gantry around an abandoned space shuttle, presumably in an attempt to fly, held aloft in the air by the suspension of time. In 'Myths of the Near

Future', a similar slowing of time causes the body of one man to be 'dressed in a dozen glimmering images of himself, refractions of past and present seen through the prism of time', while his younger and older faces merge in the one visage, forming a 'rendezvous of his past and future selves'.

Yet there is a critical misalignment in the chronesthetic philosophies of Marker and Ballard. In *La Jetée*, at the moment of death, it is clear that the man is liquidated by his pursuer. A weapon is aimed at him and he recoils at the shot. However, when Ballard reviewed the film in the 60s he offered a different interpretation. The man commits suicide, he asserts, and the recoil is the action of him throwing himself from the jetty upon sighting his enemy—much as Hinton does some twenty years later in 'Memories of the Space Age'. But that is a fundamental misreading, since Ballard has invested *La Jetée*'s protagonist with the power to choose his own fate, placing him at odds with Marker's worldview, in which the man is hopelessly trapped within the vagaries of time and memory, haunted by the past and unable to escape it, hunted down and killed because there is nowhere to hide from himself. Had Ballard's deeply held message of resistance so coloured his worldview that it extended to a wilful misreading of the film? Or had he simply misremembered it?

There was no way to be sure, no stable ground from which to judge, a fact that hit me with full force as I watched *La Jetée* in the Ouvroir cinema. I was startled to realise that it was a different cut to the version I knew so well. The opening sequence, in which the man runs across the jetty at Orly Airport, was filmed in *live action* rather than the familiar stills, and the French narration used markedly different intonations (in fact, it was *a different voice*), a disorientating experience that in its totality caused me to doubt my *own* memory of the film. It was a perfect Markerian moment, and I looked for my friend, Markerian, to regale her with that insight but she was nowhere to be found.

La Jetée was referenced all over the island, more so than any other film. Why? In Marker's travelogue *Sans Soleil*, the narrator says: 'Every memory can create its own legend.' Perhaps Ouvroir itself was nothing less than the act of memory, with all its illogic, with all its subjective 'realness', becoming an actual world that engulfs reality, that replaces it by dint of the overwhelming realness of psychosis, a scenario that *La Jetée* and Ballard's work both describe.

I left the cinema and walked to a little bar. On the exterior wall was a series of film posters called *1926: The Great Premakes* that announced impossible productions: '*Rambo Minus One*', 'Wallace Beery in *Breathless*', 'Rudy Vallée sings the popular song "How Green Was My Beret"', '*The Adventures of Rin Tin Tin: It's a Mad Mad Mad Dog*, directed by Oliver Stone Snr'. The bar's interior was also covered in posters—for real films: *The Man Without a Past*, *Breathless*, *Alice in the Cities*, *La Jetée*.

The bar was deserted except for Guillaume, who suddenly appeared beside me, beckoning me to dance. As we completed a tango, I looked out across Chris Marker's ocean. There was a seductive, honey-coloured glow over the horizon. I disengaged from the virtual cat, zooming high into the air in an effort to reach the horizon, but after a few seconds I was denied egress by an invisible barrier, which knocked me to the ground. Marker's world had not been mapped that far, or perhaps it was simply my destiny to be left behind. I returned to the bar. After all, Guillaume was more than enough for me. We danced a little while longer, then I bid the cat farewell.

I looked back over my shoulder and saw Guillaume standing in repose. He wore an infectious smile, his ginger fur bathed in the eternal hues of Marker's perpetual golden sunset, and at that moment my heart was filled with unending love, for I had never seen a more beautiful sight in my entire life.

73

VAT-GROWN

One day, such as 'days' are in Second Life (they can be easily manipulated—a button can turn night into day), I was conversing with Kubrickian. He was pestering me to tell him what I did for a living. Ever cagey about revealing my first-life identity, I attempted evasion, only to be scolded.

'Come on,' he said. 'Tell me your story. I want to know why you quit travel writing. That must be the best job in the world! And Ballard—I *love* Ballard. *Crash* is such a disturbing book.'

Then he spoke my name.

My real name.

And then...

'You're not really a woman, are you? Any more than I am really a man.'

My blood ran cold. How did 'he' know who I was? My former job? My intellectual obsession? My 'true' gender? I thought of the Man from Morioka. Had this virtual Man from Tohoku also read my mind? Calming down, I realised that Kubrickian must have done some digging behind the pixel walls of Second Life, despite my careful attempts to conceal my identity, following the tracks and traces of my online leavings (I maintained a couple of low-key blogs, one on travel writing, another on Ballard, easy to find if you knew where to look). It must have been something I'd said in idle conversation, some detail I'd let slip, but despite rationalising it this way, it struck me that perhaps this was how the real world worked, that there was an operating system propping up reality, some kind of software that could be accessed behind your back.

Had the Man from Morioka also done this, hacked into a metaphysical grid that stored the log-in details for my soul?

Something wasn't right and it wasn't just my fuzzy thinking and intellectual shortcuts or my addiction to cosmic nonsense over critical rigour. This was physical. Nothing virtual about it. I felt clammy all over. Sweating profusely, I logged out from Second Life without saying another word to those people. I never set foot in Tohoku again.

As the Second Life menu faded from view and as the horror of being exposed corroded my senses, I felt as though I was dying, or rather as though a version of me had died, sloughed off like a phantom skin. Language was the murder weapon, Kubrickian's intimate questioning deflating my virtual persona so thoroughly it was as if the life had been sucked from my body, like the male victims in the film *Under the Skin*, reduced to nothing more than limp bags of skin. The Fleetwood Mac song 'Peacekeeper' was playing when I fell back to Earth, and although I hadn't noticed it at all while logged in, at the precise moment of 'death' it became lodged in my brain so that even today I associate the song with the instant when I 'died'—with the point in time when my name was invoked, signalling my imminent demise. Whenever I hear 'Peacekeeper', my blood freezes and I die another death.

I had been in Second Life for four hours straight and felt ill. I fled my apartment, repulsed by what had just occurred, and walked aimlessly around East Melbourne. Near the 7-Eleven, I encountered a gang of muscle men. There were five of them standing there silently, blocking my way and staring right through me with blank, dead eyes. To a man, their physical appearance was uncanny, their biceps impossibly large and bulging under tight shirts. Their identical feather-cut hairstyles were long, glossy and spiky, protruding from their heads like plastic cable ties. Their faces were hollow and sculpted, as if they had undergone reverse implants to sink their cheeks deeper. Their skin was grey, like a mutant tan, and their lips a deep ruby red. I could have sworn they were all wearing lipstick, but looking closer I could not see the boundaries around their mouths where it should have been painted on.

They appeared to be idling, waiting for instructions of some sort. They hadn't noticed me standing on the pavement before them, and I had the strangest feeling I was *still* in Second Life, watching the heroically built gym bunnies that frequent that world. In Second Life it seemed as if every male, once they'd acquired a few 'Linden dollars', had purchased muscle grafts that pumped up their bodies to impossible levels and new skins that glowed a toxic orange. Often, you would catch them inactive, repeating little cycles of behaviour, looped gestures and so forth, the default mode avatars entered while unused and waiting for their meatspace owners to return to the computer to reactivate them. Out there on the pavement, the gang before me seemed to be idling in exactly the same way, as if they were waiting to be reinhabited.

As I tried to move past the group, one of them snapped to attention. He was well over six feet tall and wore an electric-blue shirt, so tight it looked airbrushed onto his torso. He stood in my way, his muscles rippling under his shirt like small creatures trapped under a linoleum floor.

'You miring, brah? You jelly?'

His mates snickered. I had no idea what was being asked of me in this bizarre argot and resigned myself to yet another beating. He handed me a leaflet with a photo of a bodybuilder even more unnatural looking than him, so artificial he seemed made of pixels and wax. His features were sculpted, like those of the men in front of me, who could not have been more than eighteen years old, and the muscle bulging from his body looked like it was grown in a vat. Unpleasantly, I remembered the green-skinned hepcat advertising the food court at Crown Casino and the way he'd come to life in my fever state, telling me improbable tales of Viagra-spiked slushies and men with impossible pecs.

I remembered how I'd been constantly nauseous in the casino and felt a nasty wad of bile rise in my throat.

The man's arms were folded across his massive chest and his bulging veins and disturbing musculature were pumped up and extremely present, like miniature, engorged penises snaking the circumference of his biceps. He wore mirrored sunglasses and an unnerving smile—an undead grimace that split his unnaturally stiff face apart.

The one who'd stepped forward pointed to the photo.

'Brah, this is Bizz. Bizz is the Brother of Hercules, the Son of Zeus. Spread the word. Bizz has left this world but Bizz will return, and then the world will know just how aesthetic the perfect body can be.'

What now? What *was* this? Some weird cult? Promoters for a bizarre new gym? Who *were* these freaks? Finally, I was allowed to pass and I hurried away, although in hindsight it was a relief to have been in the presence of an actual cult (if that's what it was) rather than the ever-present threat of vicious street thugs. After all, I was used to cults. They were self-contained whereas the nature of street violence was random and chaotic, utterly dislocating and devouring, a form of theatre I was highly susceptible to, given my predilection for instant gratification no matter how debilitating.

When I first moved to East Melbourne, I remarked to my new neighbour that the area seemed full of rich old people. That was correct, she said, but these posh degenerates also belonged to a secret swingers' society, similar to the decadent old-money cult in the film *Eyes Wide Shut*. She said you could recognise those 'in the club' by the colour-coded handkerchiefs they all wore, which signalled various perversities, but I never found any trace of this secret society, although I often encountered the damned, ragtag crew that stood outside the abortion clinic on Wellington Parade. They clutched grotesque sandwich boards to which were affixed anatomically correct dolls of pregnant women, cut away in cross section to reveal bloodied, plastic foetuses strangled to death by umbilical cords. Whenever a woman entered the clinic, these demented pro-lifers would incant in unison:

'Prayforherprayforher.'

As distressing as it must have been for the women who had run the gauntlet, at least the pro-lifers had not resorted to violence—yet.

I decided to embark upon a long bike ride. I could always think clearly while riding and I wanted to process the meaning of my encounter with the vat-grown gang. However, after two hours on the road my mind was as blank as ever so I headed back home, mission aborted. As I was travelling fifty kilometres an hour down an incline, a young man (they were always young) jumped out from behind a parked car, deliberately fixing his outstretched fist right in front of my face, while his friend stood to the side laughing uncontrollably. Unable to swerve to the right, where I would be crushed under the wheels of a passing truck, I managed to duck under his arm and avoid disaster.

'Welcome to Melbourne, dickhead,' he said, flipping me the bird as I sped past.

I smiled to myself.

But I never went away.

74

SODIUM ECSTASY

A couple of weeks later, I received an email from the conference organisers. My abstract on Ballard and micronationalism had been accepted, news that pushed me into an exhilarated, panic-stricken state, competing emotions that had always dogged my cracked-mirror intellectual life. Now that the prospect of presenting before an audience for the first time in ten years was all too real, I questioned why I should submit myself to certain humiliation. I wanted to pull the plug, to do a 'Charles' and just disappear. Why put myself through it? When I first attempted my thesis, Ballard had barely penetrated academia. There was little secondary literature on his work, nothing like the torrent of meta-analysis found today. I was helping to blaze a new trail but ten years on everything had changed. The event billed itself as a 'Global Conference on J.G. Ballard', but in the 90s it would have been unthinkable to have staged it with that kind of scope. Back then, his predictions seemed so exotic that studying him one felt part of an exclusive club.

When had things changed? It was hard to say. Probably around the time 'Ballardian' had entered the dictionary to describe a particular societal condition, signifying widespread acceptance of his prophetic powers, although the halo effect from the high-profile Spielberg film adaptation had blazed the trail. Whatever the case, I knew the ground had shifted under my feet. Soon after my return, I attempted a review of the critical literature on his work only to abandon it, so wide-ranging was the discourse. I discovered nine published academic volumes, countless essays, numerous unpublished theses and a welter of blog posts ranging from the adolescent to the insightful. His writing had been used to identify spaces of 'play' in large cities, as a divining rod for tracking changes in post-war London architecture, as an index of the decline of Western civilisation, as a way to 're-articulate the central question of how the law communicates and reproduces itself and the social', as a thesis exploring ethical dilemmas in notions of the self as mediated by technology. *Crash* had been deployed as a tool that forces a 'more productive understanding of psychopathology', while *The Drowned World* was used to compare the efficacy of relief efforts after Hurricane Katrina had submerged New Orleans.

In comparison, my participation loomed as a folly of cosmic proportions. Who was I? Just a minor academic grasping for relevance by attaching an important author's work to some tenuous cultural current. I was a full decade out of the loop. Most presenters would have a battery of critical theory to call upon, a decade of Ballard studies behind them. All I had was trite observations about sports reporters, Second Life and teenagers declaring their bedrooms as independent states.

With two weeks to go, I slipped back into my old habit of stalking the streets late at night in a drunken stupor. It was as if I was trying to renew the violence and chaos that had dogged me earlier in the year, like revisiting an old friend in the face of uncertainty. One night, an unaccountable phenomenon enveloped me, the intensity of which I had not experienced since that extraordinary night in Den Haag years ago. As I neared the completion of my inebriated drift around the suburb, I entered my street. I could see my apartment block in the shadows, faintly illuminated by a row of four sodium street lights. Then as I walked under each street light they extinguished one by one, and the moment I passed they switched back on, one after the other.

It happened again on two further nights and each time, as the sodium lights winked off in sequence, I felt intense pleasure, a sense of achievement that I had the power to trigger this anomaly. However, the elation did not last and was followed swiftly by a crippling pain in the back of my head that rendered sleep impossible. Were the street lights faulty? If so, what were the odds of the fault occurring at the exact moment I walked by—on *three* separate occasions? Analysing the event, I realised that it occurred only when I was thinking about my paper. However, after the third incident, I tried to replicate the behaviour but found that if I *consciously* thought about the paper, with the explicit aim of triggering the episode, it would not work.

I had little recollection of my daily activities across the next few weeks and with two days to go before my flight to England I panicked, believing I had wasted my time with nothing to show for it. But then, combing files for possible material to cobble together, I was astonished to discover the completed paper on my computer. I had no memory of writing it, nor did I have any recollection of arriving at the airport to board my flight to England—that moment also materialised from nowhere, as if I'd coaxed it into being.

Unlike the street light interference, which had proved beyond my conscious control, it seemed that I could, just by thinking about it, beam myself into the future.

75

HANGAR THREE

At the airport, I had time to kill before my flight so I walked to the abandoned Astrojet Centre near the short-term car park. I'd always wanted to break in and explore the place. In the late 60s, the Centre was a museum and exhibition complex devoted to the Space Age and the Golden Age of Flying. In the 70s, it became a popular cinema, where people would catch a film before catching their flight. In the early 80s, its final incarnation, it was a training and convention centre for the now-defunct Ansett Airlines. It had been disused ever since.

I peered through the dusty windows. I could see one of the old theatres, with its rows of cinema seats and medium-sized screen. Ansett had shown instructional pilot films there, and the floors were festooned with ancient paper cups and ring binders from those sessions. The theatre seemed to have been abandoned as is, with all humans suddenly evacuated but signs of their occupancy remaining, and as that thought came to me I received a queer feeling, a tingling that began at the top of my head and crept down my body, spreading across my shoulder blades and spiralling down my spine to the soles of my feet. Although different to the sensation I'd experienced under the street lights, it seemed connected to it, like some kind of sequel. Without understanding why, I felt compelled to focus on one particular part of the sky, beyond the airport's northern perimeter. At the precise moment I adjusted my vision, I felt a long-forgotten sensation: a throbbing in my forehead, a warm current of giddy pleasure.

I heard an interior voice—neutral, genderless.

Something will happen over there.

As the sun was setting, a plume of vapour appeared in the sky and began to spiral downwards. The plume was bathed in a beautiful orange glow, and my first thought was that it was a trail of condensation streaming from the leading edges of a plane about to land, although the plume was a long way from the airport. It was too slow to be a meteor, that much I knew.

The plume began to cleave into two distinct forms. The lower detachment oozed down through the sky—a golden, viscous stream resembling molten lead poured from a crucible. It trailed a circular object that had suddenly revealed itself, studded with four flashing lights arranged around a fifth. The upper form enacted a swift right-angle manoeuvre, travelling upwards until it was abruptly lost from sight, while the circular object, with its molten plume, continued to descend until it faded away to nothing.

I had no idea what I'd just witnessed and was startled when an overweight, middle-aged man materialised next to me. Where had he come from? I'd been alone a second ago.

He wore black-rimmed glasses, a full beard, a green army jacket and a chipper smile.

'That wasn't a plane,' he said.

'No kidding.'

'Strange things happen all the time in the skies above airports but they go unnoticed. People rarely look up. They're too busy trying to get someplace else.'

He said he was at the Astro Centre for a geocaching competition; the cache was somewhere in the grounds of the abandoned complex. He told me all about his hobby, including a recent expedition he'd undertaken to Essendon Airport, once Melbourne's major passenger terminal but now a landing field for mainly light aircraft.

'It was 2am. No one was around. The airport had closed for the night. The cache was supposed to be near Hangar Three so I walked over to the fence. I looked across at the runway, and— I'll never forget this—I saw a dwarf on a pushbike, pedalling like a maniac down the runway. He must have been doing sixty kilometres an hour.'

I remembered Doctor Champagne's occult database. One of the documented apparitions rode a spectral bicycle around an abandoned airfield. I pushed the story out of mind and tried to maintain an armour of cold rationalism.

'But how? Surely it was a motorbike?'

'No, couldn't have been. No sound. Maybe not a bicycle, although it looked like one. It was really fast and totally silent.'

'A pilot, exercising after a long day?'

'I don't think so. He was a *dwarf*, for a start. He'd have to be flying tiny planes. But listen, that's not the weirdest part. When he reached the end of the runway, he lifted the front of the bicycle, like he was doing a wheel stand—actually, like he was about to take off—and just disappeared. Vanished into thin air.'

'Completely?'

'Yes, completely. No trace left. I told a pilot friend about it, and when I mentioned Hangar Three he froze. It's well known among local pilots that Hangar Three is haunted. He'd heard the ghost was a young boy but I saw a man. A dwarf. You know, my age. Maybe a bit older.'

'I don't know what to say.'

I looked at my watch. My plane would be boarding soon. I was about to tell the man I had to leave, but he spoke first.

'I know. Time to leave. Bon voyage, my friend.'

A very loud jet flew over our heads, low to the ground on its landing descent. Its engines emitted an ear-splitting whine and I clasped my hands to my ears.

The man regarded me.

'You might recognise that.'

Due to the noise, I thought I'd misheard.

'What did you say?'

The phrase seemed oddly familiar. Had I dreamed it? I knew I'd heard it someplace else, in some intimate context, but I simply couldn't place it within any known sequence of events in my waking life.

'What?' I repeated. 'Recognise *what?*'

He said something else, which I couldn't hear at all—the jet was directly above us. All I could discern were his lips moving.

He smiled and walked away, merging with the shadows.

Darkness had descended.

As I knew it would.

76

GALACTIC EYES

I sat in the airport bar, thinking about my unnerving encounter with the bearded man. My mind was racing, spewing disjointed thoughts. I resolved to contact airport administration as soon as I could. Surely air traffic control would have seen that strange display? Whatever it was, the sky anomaly seemed a further sign of the apocalyptic event I knew would hit at some point. Struck by the intensity of this conviction, I scrawled an impromptu haiku onto a dirty napkin:

Galactic eyes
Sharper than a poison claw
See into the beyond

Without thinking, I drew four dots next to the haiku. These, I was startled to realise, were arranged in a quarter circle. I hadn't thought about Arthur's Seat in years but now the mysterious formation had forced its way into my world again. What did it mean, this auto-drawing? Was I about to finally fulfil my destiny, as *Crash*'s narrator had done when he found himself in his pre-ordained accident? I was starting to believe that I had been cursed with extrasensory perception. It was the only way I could avoid the alternative conclusion that I was becoming completely insane.

A flat voice announced my flight. I left the haiku under my coffee cup, convinced it would blow the mind of the waitress when she found it. I boarded the plane and took my seat. Ahead, the galley was criss-crossed with light and motion as the cabin crew scuttled back and forth, talking in low code on the intra-plane telephones as they inspected and closed the self-contained food units, which an hour or so earlier had slid along purpose-built rails from the back door to the mid-cabin galley for easy loading. Through the window, I scanned the airport perimeter. It ebbed away in a heat haze yet I knew there was life beyond, an entire world, because my eyes trusted the painted arrows on the airport aprons, which pointed the way towards an interdimensional rendezvous.

I tried to make out the holding points on the main runway where the pilot would stop the plane to await instructions from the control tower: 'all clear' for take-off or 'sit tight' to wait in the queue. I picked out the rubber paint on the porous friction asphalt that marked the holding point at the north end. The paint was non-abrasive, designed to resist perpetual wear and tear from fully laden, 430,000-kilogram 747s. Just beyond were the almost imperceptible surface outlines of precast concrete monoslabs inset into the soil around the holding bays. They were designed to withstand the continuous, enormous blast of hundreds of jet engines per day. Seeded and woven with grass, the surface of the slabs had become one with the landscape, strengthening its capacity to withstand the rigours of non-stop commerce and mass-tourism trails formed by people and machines, so dense and compacted they might yet form collapsing black holes into parallel worlds.

Finally, we were airborne. I booted my laptop to edit my paper. The woman next to me was rocking her little boy to sleep. He was terrified by the turbulence, which shook the plane violently. To distract him, she made conversation. She said they were Melburnians, travelling to see her friend in England who had cancer.

'What are you working on?'

'This? Oh, it's like a literary paper. It's about postmodern fiction, I suppose. It's driving me crazy, trying to reach the point where I'm not ashamed of it.'

I was overcome with emotion, recalling the struggles I'd been through to arrive at that state, but she simply smiled, melting the black ice that occluded my mind.

'Why don't you read it to us?'

'It's not exactly a children's story.'

'That's okay. Maybe you just need to hear it out loud for it to make sense in your mind.'

'No, I couldn't possibly.'

I watched the boy. He was biting his fingers and burrowing into her chest. Although chatty, she was pensive too, probably also scared to fly but holding it together for her son. Droning on about Ballard and micronations might be a welcome distraction for all of us.

'Alright, but stop me if it gets too much.'

'Sure. I'll do that.'

Strangely, I didn't feel embarrassed about the prospect of reading aloud to her. She radiated an intoxicating warmth that made me forget myself.

'Well, here goes: "Zones of Transition: Micronationalism in the Work of J.G. Ballard".'

She chuckled.

'My friend, the one we're going to see, emailed me the other day. She said, "Just once, I'd like to get through the day without something being described as Ballardian." He's in the papers a lot over there.'

'Everyone loves a good neologism: Kafkaesque, Daliesque, Lovecraftian.'

'Orwellian, Kubrickian.'

I stared at her, convulsed by an electric tremor of recognition.

'Yes,' I said. 'Kubrickian.'

I vanquished the reference from my mind, instead returning to the screen and its queasy familiarity.

'Ready?'

She nodded and I drew breath.

'J.G. Ballard grew up in wartime Shanghai, first in the International Settlement and then in a civilian war camp. He described Shanghai's wartime limbo as a "strange interregnum" when "one side in World War II had moved out and the other had yet to move in", an experience that would generate his lifelong fascination with what he called "zones of transition".'

I briefly explained the concept of micronations, trying not to bore her, before connecting Ballard's transitional zones with the phenomenon.

'His novel *Concrete Island* was written at a time when the real-world potential of micronations was being explored.'

She perked up, despite her tiredness.

'Australia has a micronation, right? Even I know that.'

'Yes. The Principality of Hutt River, founded in Western Australia in 1970 by a wheat farmer, Leonard Casley, who was upset about government wheat production quotas. He reckoned they were eating into his profit margin, so he did what any annoyed farmer would do. He bought some royal robes, called himself "Prince Leonard" and declared war on Australia.'

'War? Really?'

'No, not really. Only in his mind, perhaps. It was a non-violent, three-day "conflict" during which he sat around drinking cups of tea while waiting for Australia to strike. Of course, they never did, but he seceded anyway.'

'He turned his farm into a nation?'

'Sort of.'

I began to feel self-conscious. I sounded like a total nerd, like I was describing the history of a particular brand of train set.

'Back to the paper.'

I was embarrassed that I'd let my guard down by displaying my obsessions and longed to retreat to safer ground: impenetrable critical theory, so that I could erect a wall of studied indifference to block out the effect she was beginning to have on me.

'Sure,' she said. 'Hope I didn't break your concentration. Just tune into the signal, but I guess that's easier said than done.'

We've had this conversation before.

'Excuse me. Do I know you?'

She laughed.

'Of course not. We've never met.'

'What did you say just then?'

'Tune into the signal.'

She pointed at the laptop screen.

'Sealand,' she said. 'I've heard of that one, too. Go on, tell me about Sealand.'

I felt ill.

'What's wrong?' she said. 'Your face is pale.'

She took my hand.

'Hey, it's okay. I'm interested. I *want* to hear more.'

She underlined the words on the screen with her finger, reading aloud.

'In the late 60s, the most famous micronation, Sealand, was founded by a pirate-radio DJ, Roy Bates, who claimed an abandoned WWII gun platform in the North Sea and declared it an independent state. In *Concrete Island...*'

I removed her hand from the screen and took over the narration, easing myself back into the world.

'In *Concrete Island*, the architect, Maitland, trapped on a patch of wasteland between a motorway junction, replicates this overt act of reclamation, recovering and recycling lost territory. Like Sealand, the concrete island is a liminal region, an adjunct to civilised society, forgotten and discarded. The island itself comments on the peculiar nature of modern life, where we are required to process a welter of information from an endless number of throughputs so that the recent past, in the words of the anthropologist Marc Augé, "becomes history as soon as it is lived". Appropriately, on the concrete island there are collaged temporalities embedded within the fabric of the place—traces of Edwardian streets alongside the remains of WWII bunkers and the more recent leavings of junked cables, tyres and car parts.

'Today we no longer have time for relationships or meaningful connections before we are required to devour the next moment, the next product, the next lifestyle, the next soundbite, the next belief system. Because we are so consumed by this hunger, we are enslaved to what Augé identifies as "solitary individuality, a communication so peculiar that it often puts the individual in contact only with another image of himself". Again, *Concrete Island* seems to predict this scenario when Maitland announces: "I am the island."'

I looked at the woman and boy. They were asleep; I'd bored them into submission at last. I stared at the curves of her body, thinking about how beautiful she was. Her sheer physical proximity reminded me of the basic human urges I'd suppressed since Catherine had rejected me, and as she slept under the dim cabin light, her shoulder-length brown hair falling over her fine-boned features, I could almost imagine she was...

No.

I buried the thought like radioactive waste under tonnes of concrete, until my mind was once again as barren as the poisoned nuclear surface beneath Runit Dome, thousands of kilometres away across the ocean on Enewetak Atoll.

77

SOLACE IN DYSTOPIA

I fired up the in-flight entertainment system and selected the film *Children of Men*, which I'd never seen. When I came to the sequence in which the forest-dwelling revolutionaries ambush the heroes in their car, I sat back as if punched. The action was vivid, multisensory and all-enveloping, circulating around the moving vehicle in a continuous, 360-degree take filled with chaos and extreme danger, and I kept rewinding that gut-wrenching scene, which heralded a new strain of hypervisceral science-fiction cinema surpassing even Verhoeven.

I dozed off, falling into anarchic dreams. When I awoke on the descent to Heathrow, the woman and boy were still asleep. The weather was cold and grey. I could see urban ruins and billowing smoke in the distance, and as we flew over Shepperton I spotted the massive Queen Mary Reservoir. Ballard's house, I knew, was just a few kilometres east.

He will always be associated with Shepperton, this quiet, nondescript town. In interviews, he playfully ran it down, insisting that he didn't know how he had ended up there, that it was 'the everywhere of suburbia, the paradigm of nowhere'. In fact, he'd moved to Shepperton in 1960 when he was editor of the journal *Chemistry and Industry*. He wanted to become a screenwriter and the chance to live close to the famous Shepperton Film Studios was an opportunity too good to miss, although his only screen credit would be the treatment for the prehistoric potboiler *When Dinosaurs Ruled the Earth*, and even then his name was misspelled as 'J.B. Ballard'.

Shepperton is referenced in many of his stories, but one novel, *The Unlimited Dream Company*, flares more brightly than the rest, so brilliant is its corona. It is a beautiful, lush waking dream wrenched directly from Ballard's cerebral cortex. An airport worker, Blake, seeking to escape his mundane London life, steals a Cessna, only to crash it into the Thames at the bend where the river passes through Shepperton. He is rescued from drowning by a group of locals, and soon after that symbolic rebirth discovers that he is unable to leave the boundaries of the town, as though an invisible force is repelling him.

He develops strange powers. He can fly unaided and can conjure menageries of birds and packs of wild animals from thin air, even pluck them from his orifices. He can morph his body to become that of a bird, a whale, a deer. His sexual appetite becomes all-consuming and he mounts anyone and anything. Galvanised by his raw libido, the people of Shepperton forget about their London office jobs and safe suburban lives, forming a cult around him. He teaches them to fly and, in so doing, to reject their consumerist lifestyles in favour of a journey into an ultimate realm where they will celebrate 'the last marriage of the animate and inanimate, of the living and the dead'.

I remembered when Ballard had first returned to me, during that moment of reverie in the Netherlands as I contemplated the Delta Project. I recalled the quote about Shepperton and the reservoir and how its spectral traces had fed into *The Drowned World*, one body of water draining into another. I was desperate to reinhabit that feeling but this time in situ, and as soon as the plane landed I resolved to take the train to Shepperton, following the traces of Ballard's imagination that, like Blake's boundless seed, had spilled all over this quiet residential pocket. Everything had been decided for me.

It took forever to clear customs. Rivers of people were trapped in endless lines, wearing thoroughly miserable expressions. *Children of Men* was replaying in my head, the scene where illegal immigrants are herded into a refugee camp in dystopian England, meshing with the activity at Heathrow, and for one insane minute I thought I'd stepped inside the world of the film. My jetlagged brain was twenty-four hours behind, superimposed onto a steel-grey past. I was not given a chance to say goodbye to the woman. I was shunted along ahead of her and then she disappeared into the crowd. Our interaction seemed decades in the past and I began to doubt that it had happened at all. Yet I could still feel the touch of her hand on mine and the warmth I'd felt from the way she had spoken to me, and I became confused and sad.

Circadian rhythms—do not mess with them, ever.

At last, I was out of Heathrow and on the train to London. I remembered my last time in the capital and felt nostalgic about seeing Ballard on stage back then, despite the hideous embarrassment of my malfunctioning question to him. Now I was travelling to see multiple simulacra of Ballard projected into mindspace by a gaggle of academics.

All the women on the train wore big sunglasses and all the men wore boot-cut jeans and T-shirts patterned with mindless slogans. For some reason, the David Beckham fauxhawk was still a popular haircut. There was a huge, old bald man reading a leather-bound book called *How We Were: The Britain of Old*. He kept looking up at the passengers then darting back to the page as if seeking solace. He was in good shape for his age and looked like he wanted to bust some heads, but all the males on the train were huge, too, so he sat tight, silently directing the vigilante flick inside his head.

I arrived at Victoria Station and boarded the train to Shepperton. Two girls sat across from me. They spoke in Spanish. They were tall and their nails were pink. They were supremely confident and ate Big Macs, but their grooming smacked of cash. They just didn't care about eating Big Macs. I remembered visiting a McDonald's in Munich. I could buy beer there and there were Dali prints on the walls. Decapitated, vaginal Dalis. In Australia, the walls of McDonald's are covered with photos of racing cars and wholesome, sunkissed people on beaches, more horrific than any nightmare imagery the surrealists could conjure up.

I found a newspaper next to a discarded egg-and-salad sandwich. On the front page was a story about the installation of talking CCTV cameras across Britain. The cameras had loud-speakers that could shout at anyone engaging in anti-social behaviour, and competitions were being held at schools for kids to become the voice of CCTV, because the sound of a child's voice was thought less likely to encounter resistance. Aside from the obvious Orwellianism of surveillance that talks, the idea of children shaming adults, enabled by the Surveillance State, is purely Ballardian. In Ballard's novella *Running Wild*, CCTV enables children not only to shame adults but to slaughter them wholesale. In an exclusive gated community, the children that live there use surveillance to communicate with each other and evade detection by outsiders, prior to enacting their unmotivated plan to kill all the adults and disappear en masse off the face of the earth.

How did the saying go?

Our children are the future.

78

BALLARDIAN SEED

Despite his fame, Ballard was relatively unknown in Shepperton, even post-*Empire*. To locals, he was a peripheral figure. In the song 'Me and J.G. Ballard' by Shepperton singer Dan Melchior, the lyrics chart parallel lives that never quite intersect amid the town's everyday tedium. Melchior visits the local supermarket to buy frozen peas, only for Ballard to beat him to the last packet and disappear through the checkout line. They walk down separate streets and sit in their separate rooms; while Melchior watches TV, Ballard is 'contemplating doom'. Melchior takes a walk, heading for the park at the end of Ballard's street. He passes by Ballard's house, but Ballard is unaware he's out there and Melchior doesn't know Ballard is inside. The song captures the thorough ordinariness of Ballard's suburban life and the near-invisibility that belied his literary reputation. For locals, he existed in the background, caught in fleeting glimpses in the cracks between perception, working his magic behind his yellow front door with no more fanfare than a village cobbler.

When I arrived in Shepperton, I headed for the fields and water meadows surrounding the motorway, just past Ballard's street. I thought I'd be required to negotiate a concrete jungle in order to get there, but instead I was taken aback by the sight of a picturesque town with a village atmosphere, winding streets and quaint pubs. Shepperton was hardly the suburban wasteland Ballard made it out to be in interviews. I'd expected something like the concrete brutalism of the Thamesmead setting in the ultimate dystopia, *A Clockwork Orange*.

I passed his house, walking on the other side of the street, since I had no intention of intruding on his privacy. For some reason, perhaps due to my crushing inadequacies as a scholar and my inability to interpret his work in any meaningful fashion, I was drawn to the shadowy, peripheral 'Ballard', an authorial entity that could not be categorised, could not be contained and therefore meant everything and nothing. As I neared the end of his street, I saw a walking trail passing through verdant parks and meadows. The trail was unexpected, a portal to another dimension. In *The Unlimited Dream Company*, that same vegetation is transformed into a macabre landscape filled with 'strange predators' and snakes moving through the grass, as well as trees marked by the webs from a 'plague of spiders' and a halo of 'white flies' hovering above. Trickling water blended with the Doppler effect of speeding vehicles, and I could see a tiny creek cutting away under concrete slabs—a motorway footbridge intertwined with snaking, leafy vegetation. The structure was significant. Perhaps it was the model for the mysterious pedestrian bridge that recedes further away from Blake the closer he gets to it, signifying his descent into interdimensional weirdness and his inability to leave the boundaries of the town.

The entrance to the bridge began in a curve of concrete, flattening out to broach the motorway. Leaves and tree branches were entangled around this weather-worn spiral, recalling Blake's 'marriage of the animate and inanimate', the absolute state he craves in his transmogrification of the Shepperton landscape. As Blake's sexual appetite becomes polymorphously perverse, plant life springs up wherever he throws his semen. The novel's description of 'the tropical vegetation that had invaded this modest suburban town' was remarkably close to reality. As I stood in the middle of the bridge, I saw a bank of green on either side of the motorway. It was so high that the township vanished behind it, and the immense vegetation made the motorway seem like a river of tarmac slicing through an Amazonian jungle in the London edgelands. A car passed underneath, travelling so fast that it barely registered save for the high-pitched buzzing sound it made as it flew into the distance. Its speed and power were disorientating, a stark, alien contrast to the greenfields before me.

Across the bridge, I discovered a micro-world—an agricultural area complete with farms, fields, horses and cows. Just beyond were the reservoirs and film studios. In *The Unlimited Dream Company*, celluloid realities leak from the studios into the surrounding streets. The book suggests we are nothing but actors in a never-ending film, existing within the dreams of late capitalism, reading the lines we are given but never allowed to improvise the script, trapped in a three-act structure, our potential forever unrealised unless we wake up.

It is indeed remarkable how the studios rub up against the backstreets, juxtaposing otherworldly celebrity dreams with the drabness of the residential zone. Behind the studios, I discovered a row of backstreet houses adjoined to open-plan gardens and, in one of the gardens, three tiny wooden effigies. One had been struck down by unknown forces, its face flat to the ground. The other two were seated on a miniature swing and seesaw set, obviously designed to evoke the simple joy of childhood, although this minuscule furniture functioned as a sinister mirror of the children's playground appended to the studio's back wall just a few metres away.

After Blake helps the townspeople realise their innermost fantasies, he is left with the feeling that he is no longer their guardian but instead 'a brutal shepherd, copulating with his animals as he herded them into their slaughter-pens'. The killing fields are Shepperton's nondescript domestic gardens, 'the pens of a huge abattoir' where he imagines himself cutting the throats of the residents. Perhaps Blake had already visited the children in the playground at the back of the studios, leading them off to a sacrificial land where absorption into the next world is possible, leaving behind their physical bodies in that mysterious backyard—demented effigies, reverse-human images solidified as petrified wooden shells. Completing the ritual, I half expected to find a trio of abandoned prams around the corner.

Opposite the studios, the banks of the Queen Mary Reservoir loomed large, the vast body of water that had irrigated Ballard's fertile mind. It was fenced off and I was disappointed I couldn't explore it, although I remembered something he once said about his Shepperton novel, that it is about 'the writer's imagination ... transforming the humdrum reality that he occupies and turning it into an unlimited dream company'. For a man of his imaginative powers, the reservoir, despite its disappointing ordinariness, looms as a doorway into a richer reality: a marine world that envelops the suburbs and plunges its residents into a transcendental realm. It was not necessary to see everything. Just a hint of water would do—let the mind invent the rest.

I remembered a passage from Sinclair's *London Orbital*, the book that had inspired the film he'd made with Chris Petit. *London Orbital* records Sinclair's long and meandering walk around London's M25 motorway, including his observations on landscape, time and memory. As part of the journey, Sinclair had made his own pilgrimage to Shepperton, where he noted that the 'specifics of the geography that inspired a writer seem, in their turn, to be responding to that oeuvre'. He was referring to the peculiar affliction of the dedicated Ballardian, for whom places of rich Ballardian significance can only be experienced through the lens of Ballard's fiction, as if the fiction had dreamed the reality into existence—a phenomenon brought to bear by Ballard's highly imagistic style and surrealist influences, which render the everyday in vivid and memorable prose.

In Shepperton, I witnessed this effect for myself as the virtual and the actual merged down to the smallest detail. When Blake heads towards the pedestrian bridge over the motorway, he notes how 'poppies and yellow broom brushed my legs, hopefully leaving their pollen on me'. As I returned to town, passing through the parkland just before the bridge, I found yellow poppy pollen dusted on the legs of my jeans.

Suitably tagged with Ballardian seed, I walked back across the bridge and back into my mind.

79

FLYBLOWN

The next day I travelled to Ipswich, where I checked into a quaint B&B complete with floral toilet-seat covers. It was the kind of place that in my travel-writing days I would have reviewed with the usual snark, tossing off an insulting one-liner, something like 'a circle of hell is reserved for this approximation of a British classic, with its dim-bulb floral motifs'.

In the morning, Jack, the proprietor, greeted me in the hallway.

'What's your talk at the university about?'

'Micronations and the writer J.G. Ballard. Heard of him?'

'Sure. He's in the papers a lot. What's a micronation?''

'When people form their own nations.'

'Sealand's a micronation, then?'

'Yes, Sealand is a micronation. It's near here, right?'

'Just off the coast of Harwich. Not too far away. No one really talks about it, but everyone in Harwich knows Sealand. You can see it from the waterfront. By the way, I heard they've decided to take visitors again. But you have to apply for a visa, and I'm told they're very hard to get. Strange place, Sealand.'

I stared at him. Sealand has never embraced tourism or out-siders, and if what he'd said was true then here was the grail: a chance not only to visit the world's most notorious micronation but also to test the outer limits of Applied Ballardianism. After all, like Sealand's founders, Ballard's characters willingly remove themselves from civilisation, as the man himself concedes: 'My fiction is all about one person, one man coming to terms with various forms of isolation.'

'How often do trains go to Harwich?'

'On the hour.'

'Thanks. Would you keep my bags here for me? I'll pay for the room.'

That evening, I travelled to Harwich. When I arrived, I checked in to a hotel near the station. I sat alone in the dining room. One wall was covered by an enormous, badly executed painting of the Queen, her hands rendered so ineptly they looked like rubber dishwashing gloves. The other walls were filthy and yellow, like a flyblown animal carcass. The elderly man who served me could barely speak, and when he did release a word or two his breath whistled so much he was unintelligible.

Eventually, a younger man appeared. He said he was the manager. He took the elderly man by the elbow and led him from the dining room. The manager returned with my dinner of sausages and mash, stringy and blotchy meat as decrepit as the old man.

I asked him if he knew how to get to Sealand.

'You can't go there. They'll shoot at you.'

I took the warning seriously. Sealand had a certain reputation. For starters, its 'Royal Family' was notorious for firing at anything that moved, even British government boats. However, when the heir apparent, Prince Michael, was summoned to court for doing just that, he got off scot-free. Sealand is outside Britain's territorial limits so it was ruled outside of British law. All of this was no surprise, for the micronation was built on violence.

During WWII, Sealand was a Royal Navy gun platform known as HM Fort Roughs. One hundred and twenty naval personnel were stationed there, crammed twelve to a room, battling boredom, confinement and claustrophobia. Post-war, Britain abandoned the fort and it lay disused until 1967 when the pirate radio station Radio Caroline occupied it. Caroline planned to broadcast with impunity, since the platform was beyond Britain's reach, but Roy Bates, a rival broadcaster, had other ideas. With his son Michael and three other men, a feral gang he referred to as 'the hard bastards of the North Sea', he hustled on board and took the platform by force. Bates didn't do things by halves. During the struggle, one Carolinian was shot in the ear and another had his fingers severed. Having secured the fort, he declared it the 'Principality of Sealand' and himself 'Prince Roy', Sealand's ruling monarch.

Inevitably, given that brutal template, Sealand would itself be invaded. In 1978, a cartel of Dutch and German 'businessmen', armed with bombs and guns, overwhelmed the platform. They took Prince Michael hostage and threatened to hurl him overboard, and although he was eventually released, they continued to occupy Sealand. Prince Roy's response was as expected. Commanding a mob of tough mercenaries and a helicopter piloted by a former James Bond stuntman, he retook Sealand and locked the invaders in the brig. Beyond that, the fate of the cartel is unknown.

The hotel manager wanted company. He brought a bottle of whisky to the table and we shared it. He was in a bad way, lamenting the state of his father, the elderly man I'd seen earlier. Now that he had to care for his dad, he felt trapped in Harwich. After enough alcohol, I asked again about Sealand, mentioning that I'd co-written a book on micronations. When the manager heard this, he sobered up.

'Go to the marina at 6am. Ask for Brian. He can tell you what you want to know. You got that?'

'Yeah, I got it. Ask for Brian.'

The manager tapped the side of his nose, normally an innocuous gesture but in my drunken state freighted with significance. I thought of the Elvis fan who'd told me about the method for dumping dead bodies in Crown Casino. He'd tapped the side of his nose, prefacing my descent into madness that day. American Rob and the Man from Morioka had each tapped their temples, signalling that I was about to enter a new phase of Ballardian awareness. But most of all I thought of Ballard himself and the strange eye gesture he'd made in that *i-D* photo portrait from long ago. When I'd finally linked it to the bikers' war signal, it had shunted me into a different dimension, changing my life so completely that I never recovered. It seemed that in all of these actions, there was a secret awareness being transmitted, one that added a different meaning to the words being spoken but one I had to concentrate very hard to receive.

I stared at the man's nose. It was bulbous and veiny from alcohol and bore the faintest red spot from the pressure of his finger. I focused on the spot and tried to read his mind.

What was it the Man from Morioka had said about the Japanese concept of non-verbal communication?

To convey understanding without any voice.

Something like that.

Concentrate.

Tune into the signal.

The manager seemed galvanised by the mention of the book. Why?

This marina arrangement—is it a trap? Who is Brian? Tell me.

But it was no use. I was too inebriated. The only mental image I received was that of the manager's unsavoury nose.

Eventually he passed out, slumped over the table. I retired to my room but I was unable to sleep, my mind swamped with nonsensical thoughts. After an hour or so, I heard an argument on the street, right below my window. I looked outside. A young man with severe acne was arguing with none other than the manager, who had somehow roused himself from his drunken stupor to force one last confrontation with the world. The manager was slurring his words, but I could just make out his command.

'Would you move away from the entrance? You're disturbing the guests.'

The acne victim snarled, baring jagged teeth.

'You don't fucking own the road, cunt!'

Under the flickering street light, something glinted in the acne victim's hand. A knife? In the end, I cared little about the manager, other than what he could tell me about Sealand, and once I'd obtained that information I felt disengaged from his fate. I couldn't even muster ironic excitement at the street theatre down below, enacted seemingly for my benefit.

The pockmarked youth continued to threaten the manager, his voice rising higher and higher in volume. I heard a dull 'thud', like a watermelon dropped onto the ground. Then several more thuds—smaller, contained. The manager, who had been whimpering pathetically, went completely silent, but the percussive noise continued and I could hear the young man grunting from his exertions.

I refused to look out of the window and retired to bed, whereupon sleep came to me at last.

80

STASIS WITHOUT A CAUSE

I awoke the following morning, lost within a thick hangover. I left the hotel. Outside the entrance, a patch of dried blood was visible on the pavement. I stepped over it and made my way to the marina. The manager had instructed me to look for a yellow fishing boat. I found it. The man called Brian was inside the cabin, preparing to go to sea. I called out to him. He looked up at me with cold, angry eyes. He wore filthy blue overalls and a ratty beard, making him a dead ringer for Arthur, my guide to Nan Madol. Unnerved by the similarity, I turned heel to depart but he caught me in mid-stride. His unfriendly tone rooted me to the spot.

'What do you want?'

'The hotel manager said you could take me to Sealand.'

Brian looked me up and down.

'Get out of here.'

'Wait! I worked on a book about micronations. Sealand's in it.'

He clenched his jaw.

'Right, well you won't be needing a visa where you're going, pal—and it ain't Sealand.'

His hostile gaze bore into my skull, causing me to look away. On the horizon, Sealand was visible in the distance. I could see a flat platform spanning two concrete towers—a sawn-off 'H'. One tower contained living quarters. The other, supposedly, was a top-secret 'data haven' filled with computer gear and available to rent by anyone wanting to store uncrackable data beyond the law. I asked Brian about the mysterious tower.

'What's really in there?'

'Shut your hole. None of your fucking business.'

Silence.

'So you're a travel writer? You wrote that micronations book?'

'Used to be a travel writer. I co-wrote it.'

'Well, that book made Sealand out to be full of loonies.'

I tried to lighten the mood.

'But you have to be a little mad to start a micronation, right?'

Brian stared hard but didn't respond.

'Look, the book was just a bit of fun. I'm still researching micronations but trying to take it more seriously. I'm tying it into the writing of J.G. Ballard. You know him?'

'He's in the papers a lot.'

'Yes. Well, during my research, I came across stories of people forming micronations in their homes and declaring their land as sovereign territory. Sometimes it was done as a joke but sometimes purely because they hated the outside world.'

'Yeah, well we don't hate the outside world, mate. We just like it better when we can shut it out.'

'Yes, I know. That's the trend. But it doesn't have to be nation-building. When I was a travel writer, I visited Japan and learned about something called *hikikomori*, a mental illness that compels young males to lock themselves away in their bedrooms for months, sometimes years, with no contact with anyone outside the home. Some live in their rooms for decades.'

I barrelled on, convinced that what I was saying was of interest to the average person, committing the same dull mistake so many junior scholars make, with their blind resistance to the unimpeachable truth—that outside of academia, *no one cares*. Not only that, but in my ego-driven desire to impress upon Brian the absolute importance of my research, I was oblivious to the fact that what I was saying was deeply offensive to him—yet another tedious mistake made by a socially inept academic.

'Many *hikikomori* withdraw in response to the uncertainty of conditions in contemporary Japan. On the one hand, Japan is still a deeply traditional society, but on the other, *hikikomori* are confronted with the bewildering amount of choice and lifestyle opportunities available to them in Western media. Rather than face this confusion, they withdraw.'

'What are you suggesting?'

'Nothing. I'm just trying to tap into global currents, which I think you Sealanders might be a part of.'

'But how? And what's it got to do with this Ballard?'

'Well, in his story "The Enormous Space", withdrawal into a private world translates into overt micronationalism. The main character is Ballantyne, a man demoralised by a serious car crash, a painful divorce and a taxing job. He's had enough of the world and resolves to shut himself off by never leaving his house again. Sitting at his kitchen table, he types out a "declaration of independence". By the simple act of closing his front door, the declaration states, Ballantyne has formally "seceded" from society—from his friends, family and job. That's the link between the *hikikomori* phenomenon and micronations: withdrawal from the world, couched in secessionist terms. Now, as to where Sealand fits in...'

But Brian wasn't interested. His eyes had glazed over and he pushed me hard in the chest. I fell backwards onto the jetty.

'Fuck you, pal,' he barked. 'Game over.'

I remembered Arthur and how he'd shoved me onto the Kolonia beach, as if I were nothing more than effluent discharged from the boat. I picked myself up but Brian had sailed off. Did he have anything at all to do with Sealand? Maybe he and the hotel manager were in league, working a scam to fleece idiots like me of cash for non-existent visas. In that case, the manager deserved everything that had happened to him. I looked back across the water. The 'H' of Sealand was still visible on the horizon. Like Wake Island, I'd never get there, but perhaps it didn't matter.

I'd been terrified of Arthur but this time around I felt energised, for the encounter had made me realise something of profound significance. It was a mistake to locate Ballardian zones in the physical landscape. Micronationalism was a sham and Brian, if he really was a Sealander, didn't seem all that engaged with the implications of his 'zone of transition' out in the sea. For certain he was anti-authoritarian, but it seemed a stasis without a cause. I couldn't see how the 'radically new environment' Ballard describes in *The Drowned World* could be enacted there at all.

I remembered a line from *Super-Cannes*: 'In a totally sane society, madness is the only freedom. Our latent psychopathy is the last nature reserve, a place of refuge for the endangered mind.' In that light, perhaps the sovereignty of the imagination was the only valid 'micronationalism' in a world where everything has been mapped and commodified. Perhaps such a movement was already starting to emerge. In the early 2000s, a micronation, 'State in Time', was founded by the Slovenian art collective NSK. It 'claims no territory, but rather confers the status of a state not to territory but to mind, whose borders are in a state of flux, in accordance with the movements and changes of its symbolic and physical collective body'.

The micronation was influenced by the breakup of Yugoslavia, the subsequent reorganisation of geographical boundaries and the re-emergence of Slovenian independence. For NSK, the process of globalisation changed forever the role of the nation-state; physical space has become an empty commodity fought over for consumerist purposes. Time, they believe, as an aggregation of individual experiences, has become the only productive way to measure and inhabit space. Because movement—a nomadic existence—creates new experiences and therefore subjective time, the imagination evolves into a State in Time, indeed a *State of Mind*.

I considered Sealand. Without that third dimension of the imagination, physical micronations would invariably degenerate into a replication of pointless nationalism, defeating the impulse that led them to be created in the first place. In my mind, Brian's thuggish behaviour was clearly a result of that lack.

The connection I'd made seemed important. It seemed grounded in reality and purported to say something profound about the world, about the futility of mindless political action. I tried to remember it, tried to hold onto it until the moment came when I was due to give my talk and I could use it to stare down the ghost of my inexact, occult-obsessed younger self.

The mission is important.

As I waited on the deserted platform for the train back to Ipswich, I prepared for war. The conference was my last chance to find myself but first I was required to defeat the malevolent doppelganger that had always threatened to destroy me, that had once again forced its way into the world by walling me off from reality, inuring me to the manager's fate, a man who could be lying in a morgue now for all I knew.

I simply had to win the internal battle before my worst impulses stamped out the last vestiges of academic ambition forever, like radioactive snow snuffing out the embers of a campfire constructed by the last survivors of a nuclear winter.

81

KICK ME

I returned to Ipswich just in time for the conference. The program was filled with talks on Ballard and the Cold War, Ballard and evolutionary psychology, Ballard and schizophrenic urban space, Ballard and surrealism, Ballard and William Blake—even Ballard and Lovecraft. I attended the morning session and by lunch I was exhausted from parsing the brain power on display. In the foyer I conversed with a fellow who said that he was a Marxist but that his university department was all Derridean. As he described his institutional entrapment, he glanced furtively around the room like a desperate criminal on the run.

'What do you identify as?' he asked. I was stumped but eventually answered.

'A Ballardian.'

The Marxist looked concerned.

'Don't worry,' I said. 'I don't do Derrida.'

When the day ended, I went to the pub with some of the presenters and delegates. A middle-aged man attached himself to the group. No one knew who he was. He was short and wore thick black glasses and a brown cardigan. He'd overheard me telling someone I was interested in Baudrillard and Ballard, and asked me to explain myself. In the twenty-first century, it had become unfashionable to admit to an interest in Baudrillard and I felt as though the man was judging me for it.

'I'm just interested in the symbiosis,' I said. 'Years ago, Baudrillard wrote a controversial essay on Ballard's *Crash*, declaring it the greatest work of fiction in the age of hyperreality because it was as surfaceless as the new kind of consumer culture it describes. "Is it good or bad?" Baudrillard had asked. "We can't say." However, a mob of prominent academics had accused him of devaluing Ballard's quasi-cautionary tone, and a storm in a teacup erupted over how "irresponsible" he'd been in refusing to condemn the painful physical consequences outlined in the book.'

The man in the brown cardigan regarded me like I was a simpleton explaining how the Earth was not flying through space but carried on the back of a giant turtle.

'I'd never agreed with the academic mafia,' I said. 'After all, Baudrillard's line of questioning informed my decision to traverse the path of Ballardian ambivalence in the first place. Nor did Ballard agree, I might add. In his infamous rant against postmodern theory, in an issue of *Science-Fiction Studies* from the 90s, he named Baudrillard's *America* as among the greatest books he'd ever read. In *Super-Cannes*, the narrator even orders wine from a waitress who wears a vest printed with a Baudrillard quote. Baudrillard, the great philosopher of hyperreality, of depthless consumerism, had become a commodity in a Ballard novel, a fitting epitaph.'

When I'd finished, the man in the brown cardigan flew into a rage, slamming his pint glass onto the table. He hadn't been listening and was simply waiting for his turn to speak.

'Baudrillard and Ballard, eh? I suppose you believe nothing is real? Well, let me tell you something. Baudrillard is wrong and Ballard is wrong. They are irresponsible. The body *is* real, and if someone attacks you on the street then you will bleed, you may even die, and then you will know that your corporeal self is very real and not part of some fantasy virtual reality theory.'

It was as if I'd been returned to that academic war all over again. The man was just parroting the same arguments and insults that had been levelled at Baudrillard ever since the publication of his fateful essay on *Crash*.

'Take it easy. How can you be so offended? Whether you subscribe to his arguments or not, Baudrillard's ideas are so banal now. They're mainstream. Believe me, I know what it's like to be attacked on the street, and yes, I thought would die.'

At that point, I realised the exact depths of my hypocrisy. While I could recognise the threat of violence against my person, and even become appalled by it, when it happened to others, such as the hotel manager, I became desensitised, an affectless living corpse sleepwalking through reality. But I kept that insight to myself, not wanting to give Brown Cardigan any more ammunition.

'Is that the point, though?' I said. 'The idea of the mediated spectacle has become so accepted in popular culture it's now a marketing cliche. Surely you've seen *The Matrix*, with its spray-on "desert of the real" shtick. It explicitly references Baudrillard to provide a mirror on our current world of fake news.'

But he was having none of it.

'You people make me sick. Bloody academics. Get a real job.'

I tried to calm him down, tried to find common ground.

'Did you go to university?'

'Yeah.'

'What did you study?'

'Derrida. I'm a Derridean. *A realist.*'

The Marxist looked at me in terror, like a veteran who'd had a flashback to the war, although luckily Brown Cardigan rose from his seat and left us alone for the rest of the night. I thought of the brutality I'd experienced at the hands of Brian. It was but one in a long line of bizarre and unpredictable events that had dogged me for well over a decade. Invariably, they took the form of violence against my person, implied or otherwise, but they also manifested as nonsensical arguments that sucked me in, drained me of energy and gummed up the works of civilised interaction—like the idiotic exchange I'd just endured. I was a lightning rod for random chaos, big and small.

'Sorry about that,' I said to the quailing Marxist, empathy

flowing through me for his blighted condition, which somehow I felt responsible for.

'I must have a neon sign on my forehead: KICK ME.'

82

STATE OF MIND

On the last day of the conference, a veteran Ballard scholar gave a presentation arguing that Ballard was not a novelist but a philosopher. As such, Ballard supposedly presided over something called 'the Ballardosphere', which the scholar defined as a loose agglomeration of people who had begun to contextualise Ballard's work beyond the stifling constraints of the literary sphere and into the more expansive realms of music, film, visual art, fashion, cultural theory and architecture. Initially, I'd failed to recognise the scholar, having been off the scene for a long time, and also because I was late and had missed the introduction. But then, during his talk, he looked directly at me. He'd recognised me alright, and as I stared into his eyes I finally knew who he was: the superstar Ballard academic from the Liverpool conference, yet another wormhole to my former life. Clearly, after all that time, he still considered me unworthy to breathe the same rarefied air as himself. He broke my gaze, returning to his paper, and afterwards walked straight by me, as if he'd never seen me before, as if we'd never locked eyes.

Yet I was not deterred. Instead of allowing his lofty arrogance to corrode me, as it had done in Liverpool, this time I felt invincible, as if I could surpass him. His call to arms, presented as something new, was superficially exciting but really it was just a shallow echo of the same argument I'd been pushing for some time, for what was Applied Ballardianism if not an analysis of Ballard beyond the literary realm? My mission was to track what

I considered to be Ballard's transdisciplinary mutant word virus, a mysterious code that could not be readily distilled into
biography or literary theory. I wanted to analyse how that virus
absorbs other cultural forces and the way other cultural forces
absorb it and, in so doing, to arrive at a preliminary understanding of the dark forces that shape our lives. Or was it just *my* life?
I forcibly subdued the note of doubt, trying to maintain clarity
in order to steel myself for battle.

My talk was scheduled for the afternoon. I skipped the
preceding sessions in order to gather my thoughts and bask in
the knowledge that maybe, just maybe, I was ahead of the curve
for once. Then, before I knew it, I was on stage. My allotted
twenty minutes were almost up. I drew breath and headed for
the home straight.

'In "The Enormous Space",' I concluded, 'Ballantyne collaps-
es the outside world into a fatally narrow inner perspective. After seceding, he decides to exist only on the food available in the
house and beyond that to "rely on time and space to sustain me".
He becomes crazed with delusions of immortality, referring to
himself in the third person, and believes he can detach himself
from the physical plane. His hallucinatory narration describes
chronological and spatial dimensions expanding away from him
as he succumbs to hunger. He survives by trapping and eating
neighbourhood pets, and when animal stocks are exhausted he
kills and eats the TV repairman. Finally, when a colleague calls
on him he kills her too before planning to join her in a suicide
solution.

'The story frames a consistent theme in Ballard's work: the
concept of a neural freezone that is the last node of unspoiled
reality in a fictionalised, surveilled and controlled world. However, the story pushes it to the extreme, warning against total
immersion in the realm of the imaginary and against fatal disengagement from reality. In later works, Ballard explores the

obverse of this equation but charged with the same warning, as his characters drag their psychopathologies kicking and screaming into the outer world of reality, which they attempt to reshape in accordance with their degraded inner maps.'

I paused to survey the audience. Given my Liverpool ordeal, my last reference point, I expected to see a battery of coffee cups and water bottles arcing through the air towards the stage. Instead, a few people were nodding thoughtfully. Some were even taking notes.

I could get used to this.

I resumed, tricking myself into believing that I was a real scholar at long last.

'In these later works, we see the first stirrings of a sense of entrapment within late capitalism, an intuition that manifests in a harder, more defensive version of micronationalism. Ballard's fiction shifts from an obsession with time to a fascination with physical space, from defending inner space to protecting actual territory. *Cocaine Nights* and *Super-Cannes* supply examples of the professional middle classes retreating into fortified enclaves, disconnecting their senses from the rest of society and replacing them with a nervous system of CCTV, satellite dishes and industrial-strength security locks.'

Unbelievably, the audience was still attentive and it was around this point that I grew too cocky, forgetting the lesson of Barcelona: that there was nothing of any consequence worth smiling about in the world. Yet smile is exactly what I did, as I rambled towards the utopian conclusion I'd drafted previously in some godforsaken mood of sickening positivity.

'In Ballardian micronationalism, secession of the consumer state seems the logical solution, yet Ballard's failed secessionists cannot see that consumerism is already autonomous, that it is everywhere, limitless and relentless, redefining the world as itself—even the acts of transgression enacted in its name. However, in *Kingdom Come*, although the explicitly micronational elements in the narrative are easily recouped by consumer capitalism, what cannot be absorbed is Pearson's new sense of worth—the sense that he has found himself in a confrontation with the forces of consumerism and has summoned the nerve to walk away.

'Pearson broadcasts his creations—his mini-noirs starring the cypher Cruise—but when they reach peak capacity he disengages, refusing to follow the logic of transgression—the cycle of action-reaction-destruction—to its bitter conclusion, a trajectory that destroys Prentice in *Cocaine Nights* and Sinclair in *Super-Cannes*. Both men come to embrace their unconscious roles as switches in a perpetual relay of destruction, avenging the injustices inflicted on other characters, yet they are undermined by the knowledge that their rebellion will be nothing more than balm for violence-hungry consumers. In the end, it is Pearson alone who sees the folly of the Metro-Centre micro-republic and the soft fascism that lies in wait. "Unless the sane woke and rallied themselves," he reflects in the book's final sentence, "an even fiercer republic would open the doors and spin the turnstiles of its beckoning paradise."'

I stared at the audience. No one had left. They were all still listening. It was unbelievable. I blinked. It was not a dream.

'Ballard's characters have been claiming allegiance to their minds, to the sovereignty of their imaginations, since the start of his career. As he told an interviewer, "gathering ecological and other crises" compel us to realise that our imaginations are all we have, because everything we've invested in—our consumer goods and suburban homes—could be swept away in some sudden and startling catastrophe, whether climate driven or an act of terrorism. Therefore, the ultimate challenge, he says, is to "remake as much as we can of the world around us, because no one else will do it for us. We have to find a core within us and get to work."

'His final words from that interview are well worth remembering. Therein lies a genuine call to arms that puts his failed revolutionaries to shame—the likes of Ballantyne, Prentice, Sinclair. Instead of encouraging us to enact their fatal trajectories, Ballard points towards the future and to Pearson.

'"Don't worry about worldly rewards," he instructs. "Just get on with it!"'

And with that, the first paper I'd given in ten years was over.

There was applause, which I initially soaked up, although ultimately it felt unnatural to be basking in appreciation. Somehow, I knew I didn't deserve it. Everything I'd thought, everything I'd written, had been lifted from somewhere else. I'd become so good at appropriating quotes and lashing them together with a sleight of hand that it was as if I was writing fiction rather than objectively explaining the world.

I was fake news, an impostor.

Can't these people see?

I supplied stock answers to a few questions from the audience and then turned to leave, but the moderator grabbed my arm.

'Hold on. You're on a panel now with the two previous speakers.'

I looked towards the stage. Three chairs were lined up, two occupied. Wearily, I sat down, resigned to my fate, for I knew the facade was about to crack. I could only sustain it for so long.

After interrogating the others, the moderator turned to me.

'Thank you for your presentation. Now, you spoke about Ballardian microcommunities, but what do you consider to be the global exemplar of Ballardian spatial logic?'

I sat there under the stage lights, racking my brains for an answer.

'It's...'

I froze. I was doomed. I knew I was incapable of mixing it

with these super-smart Ballard scholars and their talk of 'urban semiotics', 'machinic vectors' and 'carceral logic'. Everyone waited patiently but the answer would not come. But many other things did come, both from the past and from the future, jammed into my brain in those micro-seconds of panic.

Rotterdam.

Charles.

Big Brother.

The Balaclava People.

Alenka/Lamb.

Alyssa.

Rob with the bowl haircut.

Liverpool.

Daniel.

Hollywood Dave.

Lovecraft.

Guam and Saipan.

The Man from Morioka.

The Woman in the Wheelchair.

Markerian and Kubrickian.

The Ghosts of Tohoku.

The orange orbs.

Street-light interference.

The Bearded Man.

The Acne Victim.

Brian.

Arthur.

Brown Cardigan.

Catherine, always...

And the stopover in Dubai that lay ahead of me, blocking my way home.

'It's Dubai.'

'Dubai?'

'Yes, Dubai. There are ghosts in the sky in Dubai.'

The audience fell silent. I had to go all the way, now.

'In Islamic lore, the Jinn are supernatural beings that live in a world parallel to ours. Dubai is a supercharged, hypercapitalised land and its masses of new buildings, perpetually under construction, inhabit that non-place. The Jinn watch us from the steel and girders of those undead cityscapes. They represent life pushing through into our world, our dimension. There are ghosts in Ballard's novels, too, but in reverse. They are found in his ruined urban landscapes and abandoned hotels, in the empty swimming pools that are his stylistic signature. They are a psychic mist, trace outlines of life once lived.'

'I see,' the moderator said. 'That's, uh, very interesting. Well, thank you. All the best with your research.'

There was a sprinkling of applause. The goodwill I'd attracted during my talk had dissipated.

I rose from my seat and left via the back door, avoiding further interrogation from those milling around the foyer. I went for a walk by the student ziggurat. I sat down on the grass as a swarm of rabbits darted between my legs and into hundreds of interconnected rabbit holes.

That was it. I'd self-destructed yet again.

Instead of sticking to the hard grounding of micronationalism and urban space, instead of locating Ballard in the physical world, I'd returned to my occult obsessions. I didn't know 'ghosts in the sky' was the answer I would give. It just welled up inside me. I'd remembered the lesson of Barcelona after all and had adjusted my trajectory.

And now my mind was empty.

There was nothing left to do.

There was nothing I *could* do.

I was inert, my natural state, waiting for something to break.

PART V
CLONES

83

TOWARDS A PHILOSOPHY OF JETLAG

Stopover in Dubai.

Between worlds.

A supercompacted blip in time.

I couldn't leave the airport. No one could. Dubai, like everywhere in the Gulf, had retreated indoors. No one could love nor live in the hot sun. The air was artificial and so were we. We made our own fun.

A woman brushed past. She reminded me of someone I'd once known. Someone long ago. I followed her from an electronics shop, to a cafe, to the departure lounge. She was all I had.

She sat down two rows ahead of me.

She hadn't seen me.

She couldn't see me.

Has she seen me?

I tried to remember the conference. I'd wanted to test my ideas there. I'd wanted to be tested. I tried to remember the details. The people I met, the paper I gave, the things I learned. But it was so long ago. Another person. If I thought I could, I'd be making it up. All I knew was Dubai. I would always be in Dubai. Dubai would always be in me. I would never leave the airport. I would forever walk the endless travelator that bisected the long terminal, staring at the gold leaf stamped on the ceiling and the plastic fronds of the omnipresent fake palm trees.

The stopover had been planned by the airline, which included it on its flight plan. I had been placed there, some kind of operative, picked up from England and deposited in the Gulf. The Gulf was Ballardian. The Gulf was a cliche. Dubai was a Ballardian cliche.

As soon as I left the plane, I was easy prey, a jetlagged zombie stalking the airport's gleaming chrome. I don't suffer jet lag well. I had endured it throughout the conference and it tripled in intensity as I hopped timezones home. Jet lag is worse flying west to east, when the body clock jumps forward in time. Biological rhythms follow a twenty-four-hour cycle and 'desynchronosis', jet lag, occurs when the body cannot adjust to a new chronological regime. Physical functions fail and mental faculties are impaired.

I'd once read a medical textbook that documented the condition. It contained amazing case studies, reading like treatments for Romero zombie films. Jetlagged people embarking on violent rampages, unaware of their actions, like disturbed sleepwalkers wandering from their beds. Jetlagged travellers walking into the paths of moving cars, oblivious to the speed and motion around them. Jetlagged motorists driving off cliffs and into lakes. Jetlagged construction workers falling off scaffolding hundreds of metres high. Jetlagged businessmen falling asleep in meetings, yet still closing important deals. Once, corporations banned executives from making major decisions within twenty-four hours of crossing an international time zone. Today, the organism has evolved. If you can sleep with your eyes open, especially during transatlantic meetings, you are an extremely valuable piece of meat.

In William Gibson's novel *Pattern Recognition*, jet lag is referred to as 'soul delay'. The protagonist believes that when you cross multiple time zones, there is a gap as your soul catches up with your body. My affliction was more Ballardian than Gibsonian. In *Cocaine Nights*, Prentice, the travel writer, is chastised by his brother Frank for endlessly travelling, for refusing to set down roots. Will he ever 'arrive' anywhere?

'It's hard to tell,' Prentice reflects. 'Sometimes I think I've made jet lag into a new philosophy. It's the nearest we can get to penitence.'

The flight from Australia to Europe took twenty-four hours and passed through five airports and five time zones. By the time my soul had caught up, my body had changed beyond all recognition. There was no reunion. The docking operation was aborted and my soul was left to drift alone in violation of my physiology.

A man blocked my way. He said that he was a taxi driver, that he could take me anywhere I wanted to go for very little money. I accepted. I was tired and my mind was dull. I have never been a fast thinker, even when fully rested, and have always yearned for a 'slow thinking' movement that could validate my kind, like the slow food and slow travel movements.

I followed him like an obedient puppy. I told him the name of my hotel and entered his car. We drove and the meter ticked over. He was no taxi driver. He knew what he was. He knew that I knew, so he dropped the small talk and we continued on in silence. I was resigned to it, my face Botoxed, my forehead stitched tight in perpetual ambivalence. I knew we would reach my hotel eventually, after he had taken me far out of my way and charged me the fare he intended to charge. That was okay. Dubai was his country.

Through the windscreen, dreaming architectural spires pierced the heat haze. The road was enclosed on all sides by enormous, variegated skyscrapers. I will never forget that sight. Previously, the most intense culture shock I'd experienced came when visiting Shinjuku in Tokyo for the first time, with its sea of cosplay youths flooding the streets and its onion-peel layers of neon-lit, cyberpunk buildings. But this was not that. Dubai transcended that. This was nameless, unknown. Unstoppable. This had no time for me.

In the film *The Man with X-Ray Eyes*, a scientist invents a serum that gives him X-ray vision, but he is tortured to madness when it allows him to access the fourth dimension. At first, he sees through everyday objects, including the facades of buildings, and is both amazed and repulsed.

'I see the city as if it were unborn,' he says, lapsing into a diseased reverie. 'Limbs without flesh, girders without stone, signs hanging without supports, wires dipping and swaying without poles. Flesh dissolved in an acid of light. A city of the dead.'

At the time, I'd never heard of the Burj Khalifa, today the world's tallest building, but that day I was looking through the window at its exoskeleton, a super-elongated edifice under construction, already halfway to the sky, its scaffolded frame like 'limbs without flesh', like R'lyeh's impossible geometries.

I remembered the film's shocking denouement. As the scientist's vision pierces through more and more layers of reality, he sees a monstrous, evil force at the heart of the universe, a terrifying alien eye watching us from the fourth dimension. Unable to handle the torment of seeing what no person has ever seen before, he gouges out his eyes.

He will dream of being blind.

In the taxi of that man, who might well have turned out to be something more threatening than a mere scam artist, I felt flattened under glass, observing the unborn dead city. I closed my eyes, desperately willing myself to retard the total visibility that I knew would eventually pitch me into the beyond. I opened them. There was nothing beyond the wall of skyscrapers. The X-effect had stalled. The desert, everything beyond, ceased to exist, blurred at the edges. Then the taxi moved on, the skyscrapers receded and the sky was revealed to me. White-blue, a porcelain rinse. The sand bleached of colour. A violent blast, a scorched palette. An alien eye beyond the next layer of reality.

We came to the hotel. The driver took all my money. I let him. When I left the hotel in the evening to visit the market, the concierge asked for my passport. I fumbled for it in my bag but it was gone. I went back to my room, scrambled under the bed, looked everywhere but nothing.

I told the concierge, strangely fearful of his reaction, but all he said was this: 'Go, go. Come back later to look for it.'

I was adrift for a moment, my inner tension failing to sync with the world, but as with the taxi driver the feeling passed.

The next day I found a new driver, a recommendation from the concierge, who had almost imperceptibly lured me into his confidence. I asked the driver to take me to the Palm Islands, the artificial islands of Palm Jumeirah and Palm Jebel Ali on Dubai's coast. Built on land reclaimed from the sea, they are constructed in the shape of palm trees, with self-contained leisure, residential and business sectors. The Palm Islands are a modern-day Nan Madol, a discrete kingdom in the shadows of reality.

I first heard about the Palm Islands from Paul, a friend I have never met. Paul was a Ballardian. That's how we became friends. I knew him from the net. We used to visit Second Life together. We had so much fun there. I remember every moment, every pixel. We danced in virtual clubs and wore different bodies every night. Paul was attracted to the Palm Islands because they are perfect Ballardian worlds, for what is 'community' in Ballard if not an artificial environment sealed off from the world—a gated community, a shopping mall, a high-rise, a motorway, a suburban home.

Paul told me that the Palm Islands use fractal geometries not only to determine the shape of their fronds but also to make the most of a coastline of finite length. He was developing a theory that tied economics to fractals and property development. I told the driver about Paul's ideas but he was not interested. He was angry. He wanted to rail against the world. He was Indian. He told me about his countrymen working on Dubai's super-sized construction projects and how they sleep ten to a room in filthy conditions for a few rupees per day. He advised me not to fall for the hype about Dubai, to purge myself of any thoughts about it being the promised land. For him, for his friends, Dubai was dystopia.

He said that the frond outlines of the Palm Islands can be seen from space, and that with this projection into space, Dubai is advertising to aliens how morally bankrupt it is—a decadent superstructure supported by a base of wage slavery. He said that when Michael Jackson died, there were plans to make a third island in the outline of a moonwalking Jackson. This would ensure Jackson could live forever. This, too, would broadcast to aliens that the human race was nothing, just pond scum.

'Only in Dubai,' he said, 'can such bullshit take shape.'

He took me back to the hotel, still complaining. The concierge was there to meet me, a curious look of disdain on his face. Something had happened while I'd been away. The concierge seemed to know some vital detail about me that he had no intention of ever revealing. As I walked upstairs to my room, I felt his eyes burning into me. I turned around and he held my stare. I could not read what was behind those eyes.

When I entered the room, my passport was on the bed. I opened it. It was intact. I didn't want to ask questions, didn't care.

I laid down on the bed and slept.

84

SENTIENT LAND

I awoke in the terminal, hours in the past, watching the woman, waiting to go home.

I know this feeling.

Dubai was in the way.

The woman is.

She was slim, with shoulder-length brown hair, high cheek-bones, long arms, long legs, large blue eyes.

She was real.

She was self-contained.

A micronation.

A mannequin.

I could not read her. I was soul-delayed. I couldn't take it, couldn't handle my condition. My watch had paused, the second hand taking forever to complete a single click. I was in purgatory, inhabiting multiple time zones, a reflex mechanism consuming breakfast at midnight, preparing for sleep at midday while daytime action buzzed all around me. The past coexisted with the present. The future was bleeding in.

I was sick with time.

On the way to the conference, travelling from Melbourne to London, I had experienced the strangest sensation, as if I was passing through a planet-sized geodesic dome that sealed off an irradiated outer world from Earth's depleted population. Time had folded in on itself. The physiological morning was encased in an environmental night. In Dubai, I listened to the leaden thud of the airport travelator and became possessed by a prickly sixth sense that a version of myself from four weeks ago would glide down it, passing through on its way from Australia to England. Perhaps I'd always been there.

The woman remained.

Soon, we will be together again.

I tried to look busy, tried to avoid suspicion. I opened my laptop and clicked on a link Paul had sent me. It took me to his Vimeo channel and a short film he'd made, part of a series he'd shot when he was living in Abu Dhabi a few years back. He was working on computer systems there, some kind of government contract. I never knew the details, never cared. He lived in a mega-hotel high above the clouds on the top floor. Micro-movement fascinated him. He filmed the Abu Dhabi city-scape at night, the million pinpricks of light across its multitude of construction sites and half-formed buildings. In the morning, he filmed the clouds from the top of the hotel as they slowly swathed the highest skyscrapers and again as they evaporated in the Gulf's nuclear heat. At ground level, he filmed the reddish orange sand blowing over the highway, which covered the road so completely that the tarmac was no longer visible. Then he filmed the sand drifting away, slowing down the footage as if the tarmac was being revealed in an archaeological dig thousands of years into the future, perhaps by aliens attracted to the Palm Islands space beacon.

It was that particular film, the vision of the red sands, that possessed me above all. Paul had recorded Abu Dhabi's sonic ambience, manipulating everyday Gulf sounds on his laptop, slowing them, stretching them, breaking them apart and reassembling them to become the soundtrack to the video, sound moving apart and reforming in the same way as the brilliant particles. With these simple tools, married to his extraordinary eye, he'd uncovered something I'd never seen before: a new spatial logic, a sentient, self-replicating landscape powered by hyper-capitalism, the strange stirrings of the future urbanism that was erasing the Gulf.

In his films Paul merged Ballardian landscapes with Islamic mythology. I'd learned about the Jinn from him, the supernatural beings that haunt the Gulf's new buildings. He told me another story. One day, he was relaxing on the artificial beach at his Abu Dhabi hotel, reading *Vermilion Sands*, Ballard's cycle of short stories about a leisure resort of the future, set somewhere in an unnamed desert. A woman appeared from nowhere. She saw the cover of the book.

'*Vermilion Sands* exists,' she said.

She told him about a sea of red sand that could be found out on the highway perimeter, a few hours from the hotel. She gave him directions and left. He never saw her again. Paul drove to the location and recorded the sand, producing the indelible micro-film that left its psychic imprimatur on my soul.

I couldn't let the terminal woman go—she held the key to escape that interdimensional maze.

I must not arouse suspicion, must look busy.

People are being followed.

Soon, they will die.

85

PURPLE LIGHT

'Stopover in Dubai' is the title of a short film by Chris Marker. It was published with no fanfare or advance notice, and for a long time no one knew if it was authentic or a hoax. Later, it was revealed that Marker had for years maintained his own YouTube channel under a pseudonym, 'Kosinski', where he'd been quietly releasing subversive micro-films including this one. The film purports to be CCTV footage released by the Dubai Department of State Security. The footage tracks a Mossad assassination squad. They stalk Hamas leader Mahmoud al-Mabhouh across Dubai's architectural interiors as they prepare to kill him in his hotel room. Al-Mabhouh meanders through Dubai's airport terminal. He traverses arid shopping centres and beige hotel lobbies. His stalkers follow. Because it is CCTV we never see the outside world, only Dubai's airlocked interiors. Intertitles and captions explain the story.

'2.39. Peter meets with a team member in a taxi before leaving for the airport.'

Marker overlays a haunting soundtrack by the Kronos Quartet. With its sudden stops and starts, the music moulds the found footage into a stifling narrative of inevitability.

When I first saw it, I knew the 'storyline' but did not know the context. I just knew it was a Marker film I'd never seen before. Were those people actors? If so, how did Marker gain access to the airport's secret recesses to film in stealth? How did he arrange for the actors to walk past the camera on cue in a live setting, with hundreds of people milling about, threatening to disrupt the filming? And if not actors, then who where they? Innocents caught on CCTV footage downloaded from the net? Yes, that must be it. Marker has invested these random people with agency, with a narrative, weaving an assassination plot around the crushing predictability of their quotidian environment.

At my lowest ebb, when I was given to trawling live surveillance feeds for hours on end, I would watch the people on the feeds, waiting for them to react against their dull prison, willing them to commit a crime, any crime, live on CCTV. But they never made a wrong move. And that's all Marker's 'characters' were to me: dreary people wandering around hotels and airports, emerging from lifts, passing through doorways, jumping into taxis. Everyday citizens manipulated by a bored Marker into a plastic passion play about mundane architecture, surveillance and murder.

I returned my attention to the woman. I had given her agency, life, a narrative. Who was she? She was my found footage, my interdimensional key. I replayed her. She rose and left. There was nothing I could do but follow her.

Submit to her.

Witness her.

Experience Dubai through her.

Go wherever she goes, no matter where she goes.

She would lead me away from there.

Chosen at random.

I noticed something about the airport light. It was purple. Purple lighting everywhere. And so many plastic palm trees. Plastic Palm Islands. My skin was purple under the light, as if a subcutaneous poison was resurfacing after years of lying dormant, the mauve haze afflicting my body like a long-delayed after-effect of the madness I'd suffered on that hellish slip road years ago when I'd photosynthesised electric light. Perhaps my skin was purple because I had aged. None of it mattered. Dubai would be gone, but I would be in Dubai forever.

Paul's video was set to 'private'. Unlike the rest of the series, it was for my eyes only. I entered the password. It was filmed in Dubai. His camera watches the city. The only movement is that of clouds behind skyscrapers as they drift across the bleached desert sky. There are no people. The soundtrack is an industrial assault, like razor wire scraping across a blackboard. It generates a mad, claustrophobic chaos, a tone unlike his other more contemplative desert films. It is full-on rage, a scream into the void.

Breaking the unbearable stillness, the first-person camera lurches toward the edge of an elevated walkway and then over the edge. The vision tumbles and twirls, end over end, a shudder of blurred vision. The last shot: Paul's bloodied face, his broken body lying on the ground below the walkway. He blinks slowly, his life expiring from his eyes.

Absorbed in the screen, I'd forgotten to keep watch on the woman and now she was gone, taking everything with her, taking the world.

I found an unread email from Paul and opened it.

'I never fully explained what I was working on in Abu Dhabi, but it's time you knew. It was an all-encompassing surveillance system for a government agency. Serious surveillance, designed to track every available signal coming into Abu Dhabi from every possible source. They wanted to link together airports, hotels, banks, taxis, shopping malls, restaurants. The lot. They wanted to connect *all* data, trying to find patterns of anomalous behaviour. It was a crazy project in a crazy place.'

Sensation of falling.

'Filming was my release. I'd walk around, wondering about everything I saw: *Is this real?* I filmed on Al Reem Island, when the whole place was under construction. That became my video, *Majlis al Jinn*, or "Meeting Place of the Jinn". Al Reem was between dream and reality. I shot worlds to come, empty structures in the process of becoming whole. Ruins of the future. I filmed a half-finished shopping mall, where the Reem Island Ghost would draw blood a few years later, when the mall was completed. Maybe that was my subconscious attempt at surveillance: recording crime before it happened.'

Al Reem Island is another land reclamation project, another artificial community embedded in the Gulf. The 'Reem Island Ghost' was what the media called a Yemeni woman who stabbed to death an American teacher on the island. CCTV captured the incident and the Abu Dhabi police uploaded the footage to its YouTube channel.

Paul had sent the link and I watched it. Everything was on film, except the murder. The 'ghost' was covered by a burka, dressed head to toe in black, a completely anonymous form that gave rise to her nickname.

The ghost glides into the mall, picks up a newspaper, enters the toilet.

Cut.

The ghost races from the toilet, trying to reach the lift.

Cut.

Panicked shoppers scatter away from the ghost.

Cut.

The camera records streams of blood smeared across the toilet floor.

Cut.

The ghost darts away from the mall.

Cut.

For some reason, the police had overdubbed the footage with the soundtrack to the Batman film *The Dark Knight*, in its own way as artful a choice as Marker's Kronos Quartet. The music's dramatic, swelling chords punctuate the action, turning the vicious attack into a thrilling cat-and-mouse game. It plunges the remote footage into a valley of deep surreality and places its violence squarely on show, throwing into stark relief the fact that violent crime in Abu Dhabi is rare. Perhaps the police, with their Batman fetish and dull day jobs, had enjoyed the entire spectacle. Possibly it was the most exciting thing that had ever happened to them.

Although covered by the burka, making her ostensibly immune to surveillance, the Reem Island Ghost was arrested within forty-eight hours.

Ghost in the vision machine.

Nowhere to run.

Where to hide when everything is visible?

She will dream of being blind.

The provenance of the soundtrack nagged at me, making me question the authenticity of the Marker film. What if it was Dubai State Security, not Marker, that had added the soundtrack and intertitles to the al-Mabhouh footage? What if all Marker had done was upload the film exactly as is to his own channel? Perhaps the production aesthetic was some weird, shared kink in the way Gulf security updated the community about crime. In the near future we will all star in someone else's psychodrama, whether we want to or not. Whether we are aware of it or not. The police are the real auteurs. Warhol's fifteen minutes of fame have become a judicial sentence.

As the thought formed I lost my bearings. I couldn't recognise myself, that place, that person. Lost between worlds, I couldn't find my way home, everything now an illusion.

The woman.

Marker.

The heat haze.

The concierge.

The taxi driver.

The architecture.

The police.

The Reem Island Ghost.

My own body.

Flesh dissolved in acid of light.

Paul's email...

'The Dubai video is my final statement. Project cancelled. My Gulf mission is over. By the way, I recommend you kill yourself. I mean, act it out. It's cathartic. It will change your life. You will return to the world, like a ghost. Your perspective will change. Because someone is watching you right now, without doubt. You think you're watching someone, and that's where it ends, but someone else is watching you. Always. The Gulf has eyes. That's how it is. Look around. Can't you see? The air is so still. There is no choice. Get off the grid. Knowledge comes with death's release.'

I was so tired I could see spots before my eyes, not the naturally occurring vitreous gel normally attached to the retina but grains of time dispersing like Paul's shifting red sands blown off the highway, and as time itself was swept away by the cosmic wind, Dubai's coastline was revealed beneath the grains and I zoomed into the Palm Islands' fractal fronds, becoming lost within them as I followed their contours.

The further out I went, the more the fractals replicated and the more I realised there was no beginning or end.

Until I understood.

There is no way home.
There never really was.

86

PHOTOREALITY

When I finally arrived in Melbourne two days later, my recall of Dubai was fuzzy round the edges, dregs of a half-forgotten dream. Paul's unnerving command sliced through the haze.

Kill yourself.

But I couldn't find the email. A system-wide search of the laptop drew a blank. It was nowhere to be found. It was possible I'd deleted it in a fit of paranoia, but the memory lapse disturbed me. I couldn't forget the woman. She was a dead ringer for Catherine. It was only now, on the Skybus taking me from the airport to the city, that I could admit it. Like the recurring dream I'd endured before we'd ever met, Catherine would not leave me and the proximity to her doppelganger cleaved my grieving mind in two. At the airport, I'd wanted to touch her, stroke her hair, caress her body. Stalking her through the terminal was bound to get me arrested (and in Dubai of all places; I'd never see daylight again), but I'd lost her inside the crowded departure lounge.

Her acid burned me from inside.

The Skybus negotiated an intense and interminable traffic jam and then I was home. While away, I'd rented my apartment to a friend of a friend—a notorious local junky, but I needed the cash. The place was trashed. Syringes, beer cans and pizza boxes were everywhere. The smell of bong water, vomit and shit hung heavy in the air. I entered my bedroom. The sheets were streaked with blood and semen. My books had been pulled from the bookcase, ripped and torn on the floor. My photo album was on the bed. It was open at a snap of myself and Catherine at a friend's wedding. I saw it and dropped to my knees, vomiting so intensely I couldn't breathe.

I had never wanted to die more than I did at that moment. But the longed-for state of nothingness would not come.

I was condemned to exist.

87

SCALAR

I returned to the sweatshop hell of sessional teaching, my per-hour wage slashed to the poverty line once the unpaid time spent marking countless essays and preparing for tutorials was factored in. I picked up scraps of extra work as a research assistant, envying tenured academics like a hungry shoeshine boy watching rich people stuffing their faces in a fancy restaurant. One job required me to format 250 footnotes for five papers written by an associate professor. I resented this person. I used to respect her. Why couldn't she format her own bloody footnotes? I hated myself for doing it, and when the semester ended, and with it the piecemeal work, I signed on for the dole to supplement my meagre scholarship.

One day, at the university library, a man approached me. He was a few years younger than me, familiar in a way I could not place.

'Hello,' he said. 'We've met before.'

'We have? Where?'

'At the airport.'

I tried to excavate my memories but his identity was elusive.

'We were watching the skies.'

Of course. The bearded man in the army jacket. But he no longer wore glasses and he'd shaved his beard off, which had shaved years, a decade, from his appearance. He'd lost a stack of weight and gained a lot of muscle. Disturbingly, two large scars plunged down each side of his face from ear to mouth, criss-crossing at the chin to form a large 'X'. I wasn't sure if the scars had been there before, covered by his beard. All I knew was that he now looked like an assassin, his martial-arts physique in stark contrast to my skinny cyclist's frame. I couldn't believe it was him.

'That was you?'

'Yes, of course it was me. Did you contact the airport about the sighting?'

'No. It was probably just space junk, or a contrail.'

I began to laugh.

'You know, at one point, I actually thought I'd hallucinated it—and you.'

He stared hard, killing the levity, an effect enhanced by his hideous scars, which hinted at some veiled threat of savage violence.

'It was real, alright. So am I.'

He told me his name: Philip.

He said he had some kind of funding from a 'government think tank' to shoot a documentary on Melbourne's roads. He was interested in Ballard, especially *Crash* and *Concrete Island*, which he believed were the only accurate documents of the psychosocial effects radiating from the modern road network. He never explained what he was doing at the university and I never bothered to ask. I assumed he was teaching or studying.

'I'm filming this weekend,' he said. 'Care to join me?'

I did, despite initial reservations (mainly to do with his now-bizarre appearance), for Philip exerted a pull over me that I found hard to resist.

It was the beginning of a partnership, of sorts. Over the next few months, we explored Melbourne's road system. Philip always drove, at the wheel of his battered black transit van, with me in the subordinate role of perpetual passenger. The back of the van was crammed with padlocked grooved-metal flight boxes covered in army-green tarpaulins. From under the tarpaulins, wires spooled out in all directions, covering the entire floor. I assumed the boxes contained camera gear, but the contents could have been anything. For Philip, Melbourne's sprawling road network was a scientific experiment to be observed. For me, it was like watching a petri dish to see what mutated lifeforms might emerge.

He took me to places I never knew existed. Abandoned underground car parks secreted away in the middle of outer suburbs—massive, labyrinthine structures like subterranean cities. Biker clubhouses in dead-end roads in industrial parks, fortified like prison compounds with razor wire and observation turrets. Truck stops the size of small airfields on the edge of town, where Philip would engage truckers in conversation, working his 'man of the people' charm to discover all kinds of outlandish detail about their life on the road, uncovering stories of prostitutes and drug orgies in the sleeper cabins and even UFO sightings out on the open highway.

I would sit on the kerb, listening to him as he laughed and joked with the truckers, sharing beers and joints with them. Occasionally, he would glance over his shoulder, fixing me with the type of stare one might give an obedient dog.

Stay. There's a good boy.

88

DELTA SIERRA JULIET

One day, Philip took me to the aircraft viewing area on Sunbury Road, just past Melbourne Airport. The place was infested with a convivial atmosphere. The cameras of sightseers and rubberneckers flashed non-stop and the air was punctuated by screaming jet engines every five minutes. The sights and sounds blurred into the ambience, adding excitement in continual doses. The constant anticipation of another jumbo jet passing low overhead, so low it seemed you could touch the undercarriage, gave everyone a buzz. The effect of being under so much metal, bathed in so much sound, was unreal. It couldn't be experienced anywhere else.

As families gathered around the ice cream truck, a gang of bikers thundered in on their custom choppers, menacing and unclean. They began to drink beer and push each other around. A fight broke out. The bikers were angered by a family man who wanted to park next to their machines. I thought I saw one biker expose the pink of his eye to the family man, a scarily familiar gesture, although I pushed it out of mind. All I cared about was Philip, now.

Another jet flew overhead, jolting me from the memory. In the cyclone-like wind, it appeared to wobble from side to side as it came in to land. It looked as if it was about to crash and everyone drew in breath. Even the bikers stopped fighting, for deep down we were all there for one reason only: to witness metallised death raining from the skies.

There's something about talking to people when you are under low-flying aircraft. It gets you high, puts you in an altered state. Philip and I both felt it. You can't relax, you've always got that *frisson* knowing that the next jet is about to emerge from the clouds. You see the landing lights in the distance long before you see the body. Then the nose and wings materialise and the jet swoops low, beginning the final descent. You instinctively stop what you're doing, forget who you're talking to as it thunders by, engines screaming at full power metres above your head.

We met an ex-pilot there. He used to fly from Essendon

Airport in the 80s and he was nostalgic about it. He said the airport had a disco called Cockpit where pilots could release their hedonistic side. He missed the social scene immensely.

Philip mentioned the ghost at Essendon Airport, the vanishing dwarf cyclist, and the ex-pilot looked forlorn.

'Hangar Three?'

'Yes, Hangar Three.'

The ex-pilot asked if we knew about Frederick Valentich.

'Of course we do.'

I told him that I used to live near Moorabbin Airport and that the spectre of Valentich haunted the area. He looked me squarely in the eyes.

'You're searching for something, aren't you boy? You always have been. I can see it in your face. Well, I can help you find out what you want to know. There's a support group. All us old pilots have had the experiences, like Fred, but somehow we survived, unlike him, God rest his soul. We meet every week and we talk and we help each other out, help each other to understand what we saw up there in the skies. Sometimes, we try to summon the entities, using the power of our minds—to ask them questions, to find out *what they want*. Now, you can come with us. We'll tell you our stories, show you our rituals, but I can't take you there. I mean, I can't be *seen* to be taking you there. You have to talk to the old man.'

'What old man?'

'The UFO hunter, Ian Walker. He's got a desk at Moorabbin Airport, in one of the hangars. They let him sit there and write. They think he's harmless but he knows things. Just go to the Aero Bar, near the control tower, on a Friday night, and ask for Ian. Ian's always there, drinking with the pilots. Ian will help you, okay? You got that? Ask for Ian.'

Philip, who'd been silent for a while, suddenly broke into the conversation.

'Yeah, we got it,' he snapped. 'Ask for Ian.'

I looked at the ex-pilot's fingers. They were scabbed, bleeding and raw—hamburger meat. He was always biting them, I mean, really *tearing* the flesh from his fingers with his teeth. It was the worst external manifestation of anxiety I had ever seen.

A man and a woman arrived. They started waving at the planes, as if they were in one of those little road parties the country folk hold in *Close Encounters* when they're waiting for the UFOs to arrive. In the paddock behind the viewing area, a mountain of detritus had accumulated. Plastic plates, beer bottles, plastic forks, cellophane wrappers. The waste glinted in the sun like a metallic film of scum on a polluted post-apocalyptic lake. In its own special way, it was utterly beautiful.

Next to us, the man and woman began to kiss and with each landing jet they grew hotter and heavier, turned on by the thundering metal, the thrust of the engines and the public audience. By the fourth jet they were semi-naked and a ring of bikers had encircled them, egging them on with filthy remarks and lewd gestures. One biker unzipped his fly. I could see his semi-erect penis.

Philip turned to me. He spoke with pre-emptive jealousy in his voice, as if the sight of the low-rent sexual decadence might cause me to desert him.

A 747 came in to land, directly above our heads.

'Time to go,' Philip said.

I clasped my ears to block out the noise of the jet.

'What did you say? Time to *what*?'

He said something else, which I couldn't hear at all. Then he walked away, disappearing into the crowd.

When I caught sight of him again, he was behind the wheel of the van. He crooked a finger through the window. I couldn't hear him but I could read his lips.

Come here.

89

EMERGENCE

Philip and I shared a deep admiration for Melbourne's roads, for how well Melbourne *builds* roads. We thrilled to these networks as others do to football teams or bands. We were fans of the Eastlink freeway, especially the eastbound tunnel called Mullum Mullum. The interior was covered in orange cladding inset with multicoloured strip lights. When we first drove through it, the cladding lights blurred into a continuous visual display, one long strip of variable colour, as if we'd plunged through the psychedelic Star Gate in *2001*.

On the other side, we were pushed out into a different plane of existence. A few kilometres past the tunnel, in a slip road next to an open field, we encountered a structure that defied time and space: a roadside artwork called *Hotel*, created by the artist Callum Morton. This large-scale model of a high-rise hotel is twelve metres long, twenty metres high and five metres wide, but when I first saw it from a distance I could not judge its scale. It was positioned disconcertingly in the middle of nowhere, as if it had fallen from the sky according to random coordinates. Philip said there had been reports of drivers pulling up to it, fooled by its uncanny appearance, expecting a real hotel only to find a descaled shell inhabited not by people but thousands of redback spiders.

'Morton designed *Hotel* so that it looks like many places at once,' Philip informed me, in the stentorian tone he adopted when he wished to emphasise how little I knew of the world. 'Its identity is shifting and unstable, distanced from our reality. *Hotel* is part of Morton's longstanding project to construct what he calls a "parallel built universe", a world that is the same as ours but just out of focus, where strangely familiar objects appear in the urban environment in unusual circumstances, their form subliminally altered.'

I leaned back in the passenger seat, exhilarated. I could listen to Philip talking about parallel worlds and the road networks forever. He had a habit of shifting my perception by introducing me to people, places and theories I had never heard of but which would come to have a profound effect on my thinking. Morton was one example, bringing a deeper meaning to my Ballardian obsessions. Another was Marion Shoard, the environmentalist who coined the term 'edgelands' to describe the interfacial inter-zone between urban and rural, the mysterious zone that rings all cities, which she describes as an 'apparently unplanned, certain-ly uncelebrated and largely incomprehensible territory'.

'We are all her disciples,' Philip said. 'Marion taught me that the edgelands bear the same relation to the built environment as the unconscious does to the human mind—as a repository of fear, desire and repression. She is an environmentalist but also works in elder care. Marion is a radical. She takes senior citizens on walking tours throughout the edgelands because she wants to expose them to a terrain that she reckons has a therapeutic effect on the human psyche—a terrain where, in her words, "the normal rules governing human behaviour cannot be altogether relied upon".

'For Marion, the edgelands are the fulcrum of modern life, where past, present and future collide, offering a privileged glimpse at "history as in the stratified layers of an archaeologi-cal site". For example, electricity pylons, perhaps the edgelands' most recognisable symbol, were not conceived of when most settlements were founded. They were only dumped on the edge much later, as close as possible to the city, where they mingled with the essential services that grew with the settlement itself, like mills and excavation sites.

'In their purest state, the edgelands are unburdened by strict planning laws or design controls. This laxness attracts industry and commerce to them but also explains why the normal notions of taste, aesthetics and good judgement that shape the gentrified inner city ring are absent. Put simply, the edgelands are where the future waits to happen.'

For most of the day, we'd been driving up and down the Hume Highway—an intense four-lane blacktop crawling with trucks and cars, plugged like a mainline cable into the city's flagging heart. Out on the fringe, we'd discovered an entire ecosystem of sex-toy superstores, faux-Roman brothels and billboards promising longer-lasting sexual intercourse.

'*Where the future waits to happen*,' I said. 'Yes, that rings true, at least in Ballardian terms. In "Myths of the Near Future", Ballard writes: "A widespread taste for pornography means that nature is alerting us to some threat of extinction." On the evidence of what we've seen out here, perhaps the human race is breathing its last.'

'Oh, you're good,' Philip purred. 'Now let me show you something really interesting.'

We drove to an enormous Sikh temple way out on the Hume. It was an amazing sight on that barren strip, its bleached white towers setting into stark relief the junkyards and smoke-stained factories surrounding it. At the time, there was uproar in overseas media about the treatment of Indian students in Melbourne. Some of these students had been subjected to racial violence and Melbourne was subsequently portrayed as an unsafe city for Indian people. In a nearby truck stop, over stale sandwiches and dirty coffee, we discussed the temple's significance.

Philip spoke first, as always.

'The edgelands are the runoff of a centre shunting out to the fringe that which it does not understand, or that which threatens it. The Sikh community, similarly dumped at the edge, either through fear or ignorance, represents a potentially vital

320

contributor to the new Australian economy. The temple services the needs of a community currently unable to find a niche in Australia's stratified social order, condemned instead to serve time in the edgelands, waiting for acceptance and admittance into the centre.'

I looked outside. Behind the temple, a truck breaker yard recycled the vehicular runoff from the Hume. Around the yard, land and equipment were also reused. Shipping containers doubled as advertising hoardings and immigrants maintained a warren of sovereign businesses, trading out of containers retrofitted as kebab shops and grafted onto the sides of warehouses.

I waved my hand in a 180-degree arc, airily signalling the landscape.

'Behold the interfacial jungle, teeming with industry, animals, emergent wildlife and itinerant humans. But soon all of it will disappear and there will be no interface, just rampant development—an endless monoculture. The lax planning controls that initially attract business to the fringe ensure that the edgelands become a dumping ground for more construction as the private sector extends its rule. It is this development, not the edgelands, that is detrimental to the environment. It is the interface that must be preserved.'

Philip looked at me approvingly, like a father whose toddler has just uttered its first words.

'Very good. Now, let's test your theory.'

90

ANIMAL KINGDOM

We drove further down the Hume, a terrain of supreme mythological violence. The Hume is the main route between Melbourne and Sydney, hosting an endless stream of road trains and truck convoys, and I grew up hearing endless tales of cars being swiped aside or crushed under their wheels. The Hume's vehicular violence was even an inspiration for the original *Mad Max*.

Twenty kilometres from the Central Business District, we discovered a kangaroo colony boxed in by exurban development. The colony was scrabbling for food on a patch of denuded ground, trapped between rapidly expanding industrial estates on one side and ceaselessly flowing freeways on the other. With no signage warning motorists to slow down, the hapless creatures were destined to become roadkill. Indeed, a number of their brethren were already splattered on the tarmac.

'Shed no tears for these creatures,' Philip said, as we watched the sad and bedraggled marsupials, beguiled by the baking sun, sheltering under the slight shade of a threadbare tree.

'This is an inevitable process. As industry is sucked out to the edgelands, the roads reform to accommodate access to them and the fringe gradually disappears or is pushed further afield. Melbourne, among the world's largest conurbations, is built around the car, not animal colonies. The arterial freeway is king.'

I replied, more confident, having done my own research.

'Yet the roads initially adhered to the natural order. The original township of Melbourne was aligned with the Yarra River, while its two main thoroughfares, Flinders Street and Spencer Street, were sited alongside a river and swamp respectively. When the town grew into a city, the power grid followed the line of creeks and natural water bodies. What is inevitable is this: when the emergent, the anarchic, rears its head, the organic symbiosis is ritually shunned by government planning and development, which imposes urban growth boundaries to shunt the edgelands back and forth, forever mindful of the chaos embodied in the interzone that threatens to overwhelm order, reason and structure.'

In essence, I was a conservationist, keenly protective of the strange, hidden environment we'd discovered, and the more time we spent in the edgelands the more I became possessed by the thought that there was deep evolutionary potential beneath the surface of that bizarre terrain. In 2004, the artist Richard Box created an installation in a field under electricity pylons in the edgelands of Bristol, England. In the field he planted an array of 1,301 fluorescent light tubes. The waste emission from the pylons' electromagnetic field powered the tubes, which lit up at night to reveal a secret world of hidden energy and powerful currents beyond the limits of perception. When asked if the installation was supposed to highlight the harmful effects of pylons, Box said 'no'—his motivation was simply the wonder that came from making the invisible visible.

That potential was confirmed by Shoard, a radical theorist who kicks against the default position of environmentalists when discussing the effects of industry on the environment. Instead of condemning this rubbish-strewn landscape, she strives to expose and celebrate how the chaotic, neglected nature of the edgelands allows it to play host to new life that would previously have been impossible, such as hybrid flora that thrive in the mixed-use soil—recombinant industrial lifeforms that cannot occur in nature.

If residential development was to take hold, she observes, the clutter of the edgelands would be cleared and removed from sight in order to create a 'normal' landscape. Yet this shambolic infrastructure supports wildlife by creating new habitats, such as the empty milk crates dumped in lakes that become spaces of play for the fish that dart in and out of them, or the holes and ledges in the brickwork of abandoned buildings that form ideal nesting grounds for birds. For Shoard, even the much-maligned electricity pylon reveals a richer relationship to the land, belying its public image as an eyesore.

Pylons, she explains, are a visual reminder that plants in the edgelands thrive not on natural soil but on the fly ash deposited from local power stations.

As I worked my way through my attraction to her vivid re-imagining of the city's blurred zones, I suggested to Philip that if such mutations could occur in nature then surely prolonged exposure to the same technological/organic interface could provoke an evolutionary step change in humans. In positing this, I was returning, albeit unwittingly, to my initial attraction to *Crash* and the fascination I'd always felt at the novel's proto-posthuman thesis.

'It is only a matter of perception,' I said, fully aware that my reading of Shoard was fundamentally different to Philip's, being more concerned with emergent life than technological systems. That schism finally turned him against me, and he regarded me with murderous intent, as though he wanted to tear my throat apart. I realised we'd been acting out a peculiar version of an iconic Ballardian relationship. Vaughan, *Crash*'s 'hoodlum scientist', actually makes his first appearance in *The Atrocity Exhibition*, luring T- into his car, escorting him on a death trip across the urban edgelands, possessing the tortured psychiatrist with the non-human potential of the terrain.

'Deliberately he had allowed Vaughan to take command ... Together, they set off on a grotesque itinerary: a radio-observatory, stock car races, war graves, multi-storey car parks.'

I was seduced by Philip in exactly the same way, in thrall to his toxic charisma, and had signed up to his demented mission without a second thought. I would always be enslaved to his dark energy. As in the union between T- and Vaughan (and indeed between Vaughan and 'Ballard'), I knew how the relationship would end. It was written in my genetic code. I was the submissive partner, he was the dominant. We were fundamentally at odds. When I grew too cocky in my assertions about the cyborg nature of the industrial/natural wonderland we'd been exploring, Philip perceived that as a challenge to his philosophy of the roads as an evolution in machine learning.

Involuntarily, I covered my throat with my hand, exposing my belly to him like a frightened animal signalling its lowly status to a predator.

Back off.
Please don't hurt me.
I'm no threat to you.

91

DIGITAL TATTOO

Despite the electric hate that had arced between us, we continued to traverse the road networks, although the atmosphere inside Philip's van became exceedingly tense. He had invented some kind of heads-up display that translated images from Google Maps and Google Street View onto the van's windscreen, where they appeared as digital outlines. One night, as we drove at high speed, he selected a map of Greater Melbourne. Strangely three-dimensional, it unfolded onto the windscreen like a hologram, the map's topographies, gridlines and reference points appearing as purple-and-gold virtual LED displays.

Along the city's metropolitan grid, Philip had rendered a dotted-line boundary that followed the major roads: EastLink, Nepean Highway, Western Ring Road, West Gate Freeway, Tullamarine Freeway, Calder Freeway. The twists and turns of the boundary formed a brain-shaped halo around the city, which he intended to film from a custom dashboard camera, another weird invention of his, cobbled together from existing camera parts yet somehow producing an image definition of startlingly high resolution.

I studied the map. It appeared to be suspended inside the windscreen, and with the black of night behind it, the variegated dots and dashes looked like a formation of UFOs hovering in the sky, an ominous sigil that once again I chose to purge from my mind. Along the dotted line, and sometimes kilometres inwards, but never too far from the imagined boundary, Philip had flagged key spots of psychic resonance. Somehow, these corresponded with the imaginative touchstones I had always carried around with me. Rendered as flashing gold dots, the locations formed a necklace of madness that threatened to strangle the life from me.

Moorabbin Airport, where Valentich was last seen.

Cape Otway, the site of Valentich's last transmission.

The area around Lara and Little River where *Mad Max* was filmed.

Callum Morton's *Hotel*.

The Sikh temple.

The You Yangs mountain range, where I'd witnessed the orbs, a terrain of spiritual significance for indigenous people (Philip's ostensible reason for including it).

Diggers Rest, the location of Houdini's flight, a flutter of recognition that sent shivers down my spine as I recalled Arthur, my savage guide at the gates of Nan Madol.

I looked in the rearview mirror. The purple glow from the cartographical grid was reflected across my face, a digital tattoo marking my disordered psyche, and I could not shake the sense that somehow, by scanning that brain-shaped road network, Philip could read my mind.

He turned to me and smiled, yet far from reassuring, the gesture filled me with dread. The sparkling gold dots reflected off the side of his skull, covering his face from the deep valley of his scar downwards, as though his cheek had burned away to reveal a malfunctioning control panel.

WIRE MUSIC

Over the course of a month, we visited all the designated points on the map. To kill time on the long drives, we developed a treatment for a film about a man who desires nothing more than to fall off the grid, to escape from CCTV and surveillance—from a world in which everything is visible. The man escapes into the edgelands where he survives in the cracks between urban spaces. He carries *Concrete Island* everywhere he goes, the book functioning as his edgelands survival manual, capturing Maitland's routine in the wasteland and the methods he uses to survive. Our hero scavenges car parts and sells them at truck stops along the perimeter. He camps beneath bridges and underpasses. Hot on his trail, police interview freeway prostitutes who report having sexual congress with a male of his description. Long after his disappearance, he broadcasts his spectral presence on social media, leaving enigmatic photos, videos and epigrams on Facebook, Instagram and Twitter. He is last seen alive at the Portsea surf beach, the most southwesterly point of Philip's dotted boundary, where Australian Prime Minister Harold Holt disappeared in the 60s while swimming in rough waters.

We really thought the idea had legs, but the more we collaborated the more we drifted apart. Philip, like all the rest, had grown tired of my lack of academic rigour. After all, he took his own research seriously, and my flights of fancy into the occult and theories about the posthuman evolutionary potential of the edgelands held no truck with him. Oh, he would listen indulgently but deep down I knew he couldn't wait to return to his van, maps and cameras, to continue filming those endless unspooling roads as he'd been doing long before we met.

It came to the point where I wanted to explore the edgelands more than he did, or at least more than he did with me. He would answer my calls only sporadically, and on the odd occasion I bumped into him at university he claimed he was too busy with other projects to join me on the road, whereas I yearned to be out there every day and would do anything to satisfy that desire. I did not have a car, so with Philip out of the picture I had to walk.

I moved out from my East Melbourne apartment to be nearer the terrain, finding a cheap place in Reservoir in the northern suburbs. My new apartment was under a row of electricity pylons in the brownfields near Newlands Road, a circular strip of tarmac snaking through Reservoir's industrial back end, a zone full of junkyards, panel beaters, porno superstores and cement works. The location was perfect for the kind of Shoardian rebirth I sought, bathed in the subliminal electrical hum of mysterious pylons, which, I was convinced, had become imbued with a mystical power following my discovery of Box's experiment in hidden worlds.

I could not help but compare the landscape with my experience of Dubai. Here, there was nothing but a degraded accumulation of junk, while Dubai's cityscape was a supercapitalised emergence of a totally new landscape. Yet both environments were cursed, built on ghost soil. Pentridge, the fearsome former prison complex, was near the edgelands, now converted into an upmarket housing estate. I knew a man who had been incarcerated in Pentridge in the 80s. He said people were mad for *choosing* to live there today. They would be living with the ghosts of the eternally damned, he said. He knew. He'd seen these apparitions in the cells, in the dark, when the guards had locked everyone in for the night. I took his word for it. All I really knew about Australian prisons was drawn from films, especially *Chopper*, which documented the old-school, caged-animal brutality of Pentridge, and *Ghosts... of the Civil Dead*, among the most shocking films I've ever seen, a near-future dystopia set entirely within Central Industrial, a high-tech prison in the middle of the desert.

Central Industrial is a panopticon controlled by computers, designed to make prisoners worse than when they entered. This state of psychological warfare is achieved through its architecture, leaving everyone and everything exposed (there is nowhere to hide in this flat, 360-degree space), and in the way it is run, which combines perpetual lockdowns, beatings and the mixing of psychotic, mentally disturbed inmates with the general prison population. This program of surveillance and terror is designed so that prisoners will be brutalised inside and then released to run amok on the streets, instilling perpetual fear in the citizenry and leaving the door open for more government control and surveillance of the masses. Yes, there were ghosts in the edgelands, in more ways than one.

I began to visit the terrain at night, backsliding into self-destructive behaviour as I stalked the dark perimeter, drunk and alone, passing empty industrial areas, crackling power sub-stations and huge breaker yards, a stark landscape that reminded me of nothing so much as my old suburb, with its sacrificial chickens and occult prams. Back then I was desperate to escape, but now I was voluntarily immersing myself in a carbon copy of the place.

As if my mind had been warped towards an attraction once considered repugnant.

Walking Newlands Road was an electrifying experience. On those nocturnal drifts, I would listen to the works of the sound artist Alan Lamb. His soundscapes were created when he attached contact microphones to an array of abandoned telegraph wires in the Australian outback, recording a hidden dimension of sound that boasted incredible complexity, frequency and range. The soundscapes are at once industrial and otherworldly yet also organic in some strange way, capturing the whiplash of wires as they're buffeted by the harsh outback wind. In the liner notes to his album *Primal Image*, Lamb, a biological scientist by trade, draws connections between the human body and the music of the wires. Why do these soundscapes evoke such emotional connections in the listener, he wonders? Such feelings of awe, mystery and deep cosmic harmony? For Lamb, the principles of harmonic resonance in wire music are similar to certain biological patterns, such as the way a human embryo develops or the way the brain functions. Since these principles are found in other natural systems, he concludes that wire music is an 'aural embodiment of some of the most fundamental dynamic laws of the universe'.

Fuelled by this merger of the organic and the manmade, I considered wire music the authentic soundtrack to the edgelands, to my own alternate universe. It blended seamlessly with the hum from the generators in the council substations, merging interior and exterior worlds. However, with this soundtrack turned up full on my headphones, my ambient hearing was impaired and I was in constant danger from predators. I became burdened with an apocalyptic, fearful mindset, constantly on edge as the music's terrifying peaks and troughs generated a sensory overload, amplified by the experience of traversing a terrain where I was violating the unspoken rules of engagement merely by the act of walking.

No one walks Newlands Road at night. Barely anyone walks it during the day. I never saw another person except in the hotted-up cars that sped by, their occupants hurling bottles and abuse, making me their target. I was also required to negotiate the junkyard dogs that nearly leaped high barbed-wire fences in their bloodlust to reach me. I have never seen such vicious dogs. They looked as if they'd been grown in a laboratory for maximum devastation, all razor-sharp teeth, murderous eyes and rippling bodies.

I was forever looking over my shoulder, past the concrete plants, car workshops and sex-toy warehouses, always checking to see who was behind me as the taut vibe of the wire music tipped me over the edge into total paranoia. There were no surveillance cameras out there and that was part of the perverse appeal, for it represented a chance to fall off the grid, but it also laid me wide open. If a car stopped and I was attacked or murdered, no one would ever know.

Yet I continued to visit, night after night, walking an eight-kilometre round trip that took two hours to complete, because I felt I could change myself. I believed that I could expose myself to something revolutionary, something that could induce a physiological change in my body and mind as I bathed in the wire music and the hum of the generators, in the constant noise of the hoons in their killing machines, in the genetically altered wails of the junkyard dogs.

Lost and alone in this edgeland otherworld.

93

DOUBLE EXPOSURE

Meanwhile, my thesis, my intellectual life, had drained to nothing. Online, I'd found a photo of Ballard that came to possess me and my attempts to theorise it supplanted all other paths of enquiry. Alien Earth was destroyed. Affirmative dystopias were on the scrap heap. Micronations were forgotten. Applied Ballardianism was in tatters. I'd rejoined the theatre of the unwell and the end of my PhD was nowhere in sight.

Ballard took the photo in 1950, when he was 19. It is a self-portrait, a double exposure—a photo of not one but two Ballards. In this mirror world, they sit across from each other on a sofa. The Ballards are immaculately groomed, wearing freshly pressed suits and ties, their modish hair slicked and parted to the side. The Ballard to the left sits high on the sofa, radiating a supercilious air. It rests one hand upon its knee. The other hand is closed, the arm bent at the elbow, poised as if to snap the fingers. Or perhaps the fingers are in mid-snap, the gesture having already summoned the clone, the Ballard to the right, which appears in quizzical repose, contemplative yet possessed of dynamic agency. This second Ballard rests its chin in one hand, eyes lowered, deep in thought. Its other hand is poised over the armrest, as if ready to spring into action upon receipt of orders.

Between them is a fuzzy white orb, an artefact of the contrived photographic technique. It stains the right side of the emulsion paper, partially obscuring Ballard 2's reverse profile, blurring its face into the void. But perhaps it is more than just an accident of emulsion. Perhaps it signifies the clone *already* on its way, having received its orders. Perhaps the photograph captures not the summons but the clone in mid-travel, the orb signifying that the teleportation process has been initiated, since the blur makes it seem like the doppelganger is fading from view. Perhaps the clone is already halfway to the future, destined to become the rough copy 'James Ballard' in *Crash*. Or perhaps it is travelling sideways in time to inhabit the body of 'Jim Graham' in *Empire*. Ballard 1's snap of the fingers would not be a summons, then, but a dismissal, a downward flick of the switch, a coded bon voyage to the author's self-replicating cosmonaut of inner space.

Hello, Mr Ballard. I'm you.

Then again, maybe Ballard 2 is the original and is wary of the clone, the haughty Ballard, who somehow has seized the upper hand. It is impossible to tell which came first, for the double exposure is superbly executed, but whatever the provenance what is certain is this: one Ballard moved to Shepperton, living the rest of its life there, while the other returned to Shanghai, revisiting the trauma of its childhood.

In my more incoherent moments, I deluded myself that time and space had collapsed due to the cosmic strain of the teleportation process and that one place had become superimposed over the other. One might assume that Shanghai was overlaid with Shepperton, given the order of settlement in the Ballardian biography, but in fact no one can ever be sure which town was which or even which came first. Once, an interviewer asked Ballard if he had 'remembered the future' when writing *Empire*, only to be met with the equivalent of a nudge and a wink. 'I know what you mean,' Ballard admitted, although he never answered the question. How could he? How could this process ever be explained? Even he had to succumb to its uncanny force.

When he moved to Shepperton, he incorporated specifics of the town into his writing but in ruined suburban settings that recalled Shanghai, his internal map of the world folding in on itself like an Escher building. During my lowest ebb, when I was unable to piece together my theory of Applied Ballardianism and became filled with desolation and feelings of crushing inadequacy, I imagined I could see a flaring wormhole between the two Ballard residences: his modest, semi-detached house in Shepperton with its distinctive yellow door, and the former Ballard family home in Shanghai, once a grand old colonial mansion, now a chain restaurant with all traces of its former owners erased.

In 'The Enormous Space', Ballard describes the house's mysterious architecture. Ballantyne, deep within his insanity, decides to exist solely on 'a far richer realm formed from the elements of light, time and space', and when he becomes feverish from hunger, he imagines the walls of the house closing in on him before receding into infinity, forming 'the enormous space' that gives the story its title. In *Empire*, after Jim has become separated from his parents, he returns to his neighbourhood, which has been abandoned following the outbreak of war. Hungry and alone, he scrabbles for food in the deserted family home. Like Ballantyne, he too fantasises that the architecture is a portal to another dimension, another enormous space: 'Even the house seemed sombre, as if it was withdrawing from him in a series of small and unfriendly acts.'

I was back on the pills, since my anxiety levels had recently shot through the roof, and in that hallucinatory state I suffered my own erroneous perception of reality. Somewhere, deep within mindspace, I could see a white-hot axis, a molten core like an imploding star, and inside the core, instead of the walls of my apartment crumbling around me—the familiar side effect from the doves—the walls of the two Ballard houses disintegrated, collapsing into one another and generating an antimatter explosion that ruptured the fabric of space-time. Forged within that Ballardian Big Bang, worlds collided—Shanghai and Shepperton—forming infinite forking pathways, generating the many Ballards that inhabited the wild and speculative tomes of secondary literature, those auctorial phantasms uncovered in the review I'd performed upon my return, the buzzing cornucopia of Ballardiana that had so perplexed me and stopped me dead in my tracks.

Within that fever dream, however, there was a glimmer of hope. Even in my most delusional states, I was always able to find at least one tenuous hook upon which I could hang yet another halfbaked theory. This time, the photo was the key. The double exposure was my long-sought doorway into the Ballardian multiverse, where many Ballards co-exist but none are more truthful than others, and at long last I knew how to open it. I made an appointment with Anthony to test the theory.

To blow his mind.

94

DEFORMED MACHINE

I sat in Anthony's office, hopping about on the chair with nervous energy, trying to explain the significance of the double exposure.

'Please listen,' I instructed. 'This is complex. The photo reveals how anything can be connected in the Ballardian universe, but it also demonstrates why such a concept cannot be clearly articulated or explained within the standard academic format.'

'Well, you're going to have to try,' Anthony replied, 'if you want to submit your PhD any time soon. Anyway, I don't understand your fixation. It's just a photo.'

'No, it's not just a photo! There's something to this.'

I opened a heavy volume: *The Collected Short Stories of J.G. Ballard.*

'Ballard is renowned for his similes, detonating them constantly, carpet-bombing the text to add layers of unreality. Let's take a typical sentence.'

I turned to a dogeared page, its corner creased for easy reference. I transcribed words from the story 'Studio 5, the Stars' onto a notepad.

'*I stood up and walked softly across to her, looked down at her strange face, its skin smooth and grey, like some pharaonic bride in a basalt dream.*'

'Now, let's dissect it.'

I drew cryptic diagrams linking the dominant narrative (the text before the hinge point, preceding the 'like') with the subordinate narrative.

'See how it's compacted with layers of meaning? The text builds a secondary mental image that gradually overwhelms the primary structure.'

I produced a photocopy of an obscure Ballard story, 'Journey Across a Crater', published in *New Worlds* magazine in 1970 but never reprinted or anthologised. I copied a few lines from it onto the pad.

'He began to approach, face hidden behind the camera, feet moving in oblique passage across the concrete like the stylised dance of a deformed machine.'

I drew more diagrams underneath the sentence and also under the subordinate section from 'Studio 5, the Stars'. I illustrated geometric shapes that linked the two passages, anchoring my rant in some kind of internal logic.

'Connections can arise at any point, wormholes into subordinate universes. Anthony, I have learned how to *see*—everything is connected to everything else. Watch, OK? I'll explain. Let's suture the two sentences. What is revealed? *A pharaonic bride in a basalt dream performs the stylised dance of a deformed machine.*'

I looked up from the page, my mind racing with excitement, remembering how I'd once been defeated by the *Atrocity* chapter 'Why I Want to Fuck Ronald Reagan', with its layers of coded realities. Although I'd excavated its subversive substratum back then, I'd felt powerless with the knowledge, as though I was entering an infinite hall of mirrors, lost within a daze of ill-formed connections. But now all that had changed. I was intellectually alive, maybe for the first time ever.

'See? A new narrative becomes clear. Who is this "bride"? Why is she being transported from ancient associations with minerals, with the earth, to a broken technological future?'

I copied a few sentences from *Crash* onto the page, scaffolding them with more insane diagrams: spirals, parallelograms, rhombus angles.

'In *Crash*, Ballard describes how the angular surface of a car's interior forces the human body to contort itself in unfamiliar and unnatural positions, "like the first act of homosexual intercourse inside an Apollo capsule". Vaughan collects photos of crash injuries, which "hung in the gallery of his mind like exhibits in the museum of a slaughterhouse". When he fantasises about crashing his car into Elizabeth Taylor, he imagines her face breaking the windshield, the shattered glass frosting her features "like a death-born Aphrodite".'

I began to revise my parallel narrative.

'*In the museum of a slaughterhouse, a death-born Aphrodite invades the basalt dream of a pharaonic bride, replicating the first act of homosexual intercourse in an Apollo capsule—the stylised dance of a deformed machine.*'

Anthony buried his face in his hands but I paid him no mind.

'Like a scientist scanning the galaxy for evidence of wormholes to other galaxies, I have been searching for this gateway for a long time, although I realise it has been hiding in plain sight. The Ballardian simile is the doorway to the mirror-world. It is the guiding principle for how everything is connected in the Ballardian universe. And now that I've found it, I know what I must do. I must strip the simile of its anchor to the real. I must destroy the "like" and liberate the simile from its subordinate role so that it becomes the dominant narrative. Only then will I be able to escape to the other side.'

At length, Anthony raised his head.

'You know, I don't think you're well. Forgive me for saying so. I've been in touch with a colleague in psychology. She thinks you've developed clinically significant apophenic-schizophrenic behaviour.'

'*Apophenic?* What's that?'

'It refers to apophenia, which, broadly speaking, describes a schizotypal cognitive condition—the mental state of perceiving patterns in meaningless, random and unrelated data.'

'Ah. Like in the Gibson novel, *Pattern Recognition.*'

'I haven't read it.'

'In *Pattern Recognition*, apophenia is widespread. It's linked to the aftermath of 9/11, rationalised as a by-product of living in a nihilistic era where all the certainties of the immediate past and all the utopian promises of the future have been swallowed whole by an apocalyptic event.'

Anthony sighed.

'Sounds like you're describing a Ballard novel. Maybe you need to broaden your critical vocabulary.'

I ignored him.

'A cult develops around seemingly random pieces of film footage dispersed across the internet. No one knows who uploaded the footage. So-called "footage heads" spend their days trying to interpret them, fuelled by a desperate drive to make connections between the film fragments, which Gibson pitches as a kind of survival tactic—overlaying meaning and substance onto a flat, confusing and valueless world.'

'The survivalist aspect rings true,' Anthony said. 'When the term "apophenia" was coined by Klaus Conrad in 1958, it was used to describe a condition rooted in psychosis. Today, it's recognised increasingly in normatively healthy people.'

'So, is that what you're driving at? That somehow I've developed apophenic tendencies to make sense of the world?'

'I'm not driving at anything. I'm just relaying what my colleague told me: a combination of apophenia and confirmation bias can produce highly unusual results.'

He produced a sheaf of annotated papers and pointed to a highlighted passage.

'According to Jeffrey Mishlove and Brendan C. Engen, paranormal events, in a general sense, are a direct result of apophenia: "the mistaken attribution of intent or meaning to events that in fact are meaningless or purely chance occurrences".'

'Again, I refer you to *Pattern Recognition*. When the protagonist's father dies in the September 11 attacks, her mother develops an interest in EVP. She thinks she can use it to locate his ghost.'

'What's EVP?'

'Electronic Voice Phenomenon. It's when people supposedly hear the voices of the dead on audio recordings. Typically, they emerge from random noise generations, such as radio static. I guess, if you don't believe in the paranormal, experiencing EVP would be a form of apophenia.'

'Maybe. In your case, I think that apophenia, filtered through the Ballardian lens, has coloured your worldview so completely that you have begun to perceive a paranormal element to Ballard's work: the sense that it is a conduit to other dimensions. I think that you have entered the peculiar prison of the self-aware paranoiac, simultaneously within and without your inverted reality. You once said that conspiracy theory is the "people's novel".'

'Yes. It's a chance for ordinary citizens to construct a fiction that opposes the dominant narratives of media, culture and politics—to reconstruct reality.'

'But for the immersive conspiracist there is no return to reality. Everything becomes fiction and everything can be rewritten and connected with anything else—including the self. Reality itself becomes malleable, shaped according to whatever fantasy is generated. What's frustrating is that I know you have it in you to do well, but you write as though you're living in a dream world. You say you've been in contact with UFOs and telepathic entities, and you claim you've experienced lucid dreaming and out-of-body experiences, and all of it you seem to think is a methodology by which to interpret Ballard. But I assure you, it's all apophenic by-product.'

He returned to his sheaf of papers.

'For Peter Brugger and Christine Mohr, the concept of apophenia serves to explain the "motor hallucinations" endured by people undergoing out-of-body experiences, that is, "the sensation of a separation between body and observing self".

That separation becomes necessary in order for the immersive conspiracist to step outside of reality and perceive a different meaning or intent to social functions and norms. Do you understand what I'm saying? Does any of this ring true?'

I wasn't sure how to react. Should I be insulted? He was clearly insinuating that I had lost my mind. Should I be thankful that he was trying to help? In the end, I felt only pity. How could he be so blind as to not see what I could, to not feel what I could feel?

'I think you're tired and burnt out,' he said, 'and I think you need to rest. Go away for a while and recharge your batteries. Take a holiday. Let's discuss this when you come back.'

'Anthony, I will prove you wrong. You'll see.'

I left without another word and returned home, emboldened by the mission I knew I had to complete and the utter certainty that I was most definitely the man for the job.

95

PROJECT CANCELLED

My methods were primitive, marbled with madness. First, I assembled my Ballard library: nineteen novels, the mammoth collected short stories volume and assorted photocopies of uncollected curios and experiments. Then I took a razor and carefully sliced each page from each book's spine, resulting in a haul of 5951 debooked pages. I scanned and digitised every word until I had at my disposal an archive of 2,015,085 words written by the master. Finally, I embarked on a laborious search-and-destroy mission, painstakingly locating and recording every simile—5,875 in total. I pasted them into a bank of 100 spreadsheets, thematically ordered. In the spreadsheets, I recorded connective tissue—tunnels and pathways from one simile to another—annotating each with observations and comments about the strength or weakness of that tissue. Once I'd found the strongest connections, I printed the top-ranked similes onto colour-coded filing cards, annotating and combining them with tentacles of biro and highlighter-pen markings.

I filled hundreds of pages in notebooks and pasted hundreds of similes all over the walls of my apartment, trying to make sense of it all with homemade diagrams and symbols. The project took a month, during which I barely left the apartment, surviving on fast food that turned my skin yellow and swollen. I thought of Ballantyne's fatal trajectory in 'The Enormous Space'. Where would it all end? I pitied anyone attempting to knock on my door at that point, given what I might do to them, although of course no one did, for I'd completely alienated and pushed away every friend I had, cutting them off like limbs.

I wanted a new metanarrative to emerge, one that could shed light on Ballard's secret intent, a metanarrative taking place within a fake space capsule that becomes a human slaughterhouse filled with sexually advanced astronauts and presided over by a suicidal goddess figure. But I could not find the glue that would link it all together, having tried every available technique. I even attempted the notoriously difficult-to-master cut-up method deployed by the master magician William S. Burroughs, who rearranged found texts to fold time and space in on itself.

'I take page one,' Burroughs explains, 'and fold it into page one hundred—I insert the resulting composite as page ten. When the reader reads page ten he is flashing forwards in time to page one hundred and back in time to page one.'

Naturally, the concept of time travel appealed to me, however the Burroughsian, despite some similarities, was a very different universe to the Ballardian. I did not need to travel to the past or to the future but *sideways* in time.

The task was rendered even more difficult given that I had

forgotten the dynamic of inner space—the logic of ambivalence that had first allowed me to excavate the secrets of *Crash* many moons ago. Per Ballard's formula of inner space, no narrative is subordinate to another: 'dream and reality become fused together, each retaining its own distinctive quality and yet in some way assuming the role of its opposite'. Given that I had lost sight of that principle I was doomed never to unpick the Ballardian simile, since I was too focused on privileging one dimension over another, liberating one by destroying the other, rather than allowing each to retain its unique characteristics while absorbing the function of the opposite. Inevitably, the sub-narrative collapsed in on itself and my project imploded as the hinges broke under the strain—as all my attempts to decode his work had done.

As I sat in my apartment among the detritus of my insanity, overwhelmed by the debris of torn paper and discarded similes covering the floor, which resembled nothing so much as the accumulated junkspace from the edgelands I'd spent so much time in, I realised that all I'd managed to print out was a broken encephalogram of my decaying self.

96

SHADOWPLAY

Two months later, the Comparative Media Studies department held a symposium for postgraduate students to present their work. I was scheduled to give a paper on Applied Ballardianism but I could no longer see the point. Faced with the hypercomplex Ballardian matrix that I had falteringly probed, it had become impossible to land on any kind of surface meaning or to untangle a start point from which one could launch an analysis. The more I explored, the further I disappeared down the rabbit hole, like the characters in the film *eXistenZ*, who emerge from one virtual reality simulation into another, then another, propelled through so many wormholes that they forget how to return to reality. Applied Ballardianism was not a theory that could lend itself to rigorous academic scrutiny but then again that was never my style, so I decided to admit my situation and present my failure as the very point of the exercise. I could see no other way to escape the labyrinth of incomplete thought in which I had imprisoned myself.

I arrived at the auditorium and waited for my turn to speak. When I walked to the lectern, I saw a smattering of friends and colleagues in the audience, including Anthony, who'd turned up out of ongoing concern for my sanity. Charles was also present. I hadn't seen him for months. He'd met a woman and subsequently disappeared from the scene but deep down I knew he had escaped me, for our relationship had become decidedly unhealthy as we dragged each other into the abyss of academic psychosis.

In the row behind them was Philip. I was surprised to see him and couldn't shake the sense that he'd shown up purely to watch me fail.

Alright. Give the people what they want.

I drew breath, steeling myself. I would spare no detail, that much I knew. Eventually, my voice took shape around me.

'After a painful bout of self-examination, I have come to an uncomfortable realisation: I am finished as an academic before my damnable career has even begun. For over a decade, I have been consumed with the task of composing a dissertation on the author J.G. Ballard, whose life has cast a benign shadow over my own, although I never knew why or even how I came to arrive at that point. I am reminded of a curious phenomenon: if you pick up a dog and carry it down an escalator, its legs will move as if it is walking. There is a disjunct between what it can see, the movement of the escalator, and what it can feel, its limbs thrashing about, never touching the ground—but it will perambulate in mid-air nonetheless, hoping the two actions will synchronise. Likewise, I went through the motions, surviving on instinct, attempting to weave a critical narrative around random elements, trying to convince others, principally my supervisor, of the validity of my argument even though I could not convince myself. I became mired in mental white noise, like a satellite dish with broken receptors erratically scanning the sky, tuned in to 10,000 signals at once.'

At the mere mention of his role, Anthony furrowed his brow and began fiddling with his phone. Doubtless, he knew I was about to deliver the academic equivalent of suicide and was embarrassed that he hadn't been able to arrest the slide. I sensed he was texting the details of the train wreck that was me, live on stage, to someone we both knew—but who?

I glanced at Philip. He was intently studying his phone.

'The conceit of literary theory is that it can produce a legible interpretation of the text under examination—even works of highly speculative and fantastical literature. Nevertheless, I, a so-called critical theorist studying speculative fiction, have become hobbled by the deadly belief that the critic, the interpreter, can only fly blind, mangling connections between discrete elements where previously there were none, inventing a cosmology for texts so mysterious, so elusive, they confuse the mind with their ineluctable antimatter and therefore must be categorised and explained in order to be shorn of their uncanny power. In my case, career-ending power.

'For a dilettante scholar such as myself, with schoolboy powers of deduction, the task of decoding Ballard's work has become insurmountable. Asking me to complete my thesis is akin to commanding a mouse to tile a roof. I have tried to be clever, tried to invoke a battery of French theory gods, but truth be told I am not well-read enough to pull it off. I am just a reaction, a random discharge. I consult books; I don't *read* them. I lack the patience to dive deep into theory, instead scanning for surface-level, tic-tac-toe quotes that I can misappropriate and lash together to back my weak-as-water analysis. Make no mistake, I am an idiot paddling in the neurological shallows but even so I have managed to drown myself.'

I caught Charles smirking to himself, enjoying the painful spectacle. Perhaps he thought my stage death was for his benefit alone. Doubtless, my self-destruction made him feel better about his own on-stage malfunction, when he'd abandoned his Houellebecq presentation without warning.

I waved a sheaf of papers above my head.

'My thesis notes are a mess, a total abomination. There is no plan, no structure. Reading them is like tracking the contents of a diseased brain, like surveilling a madman metastasising into a serial killer. Within the porous parameters of my sprawling, incoherent argument, I have sown the seeds of my annihilation. Whenever I think I've nailed the argument, it disappears into thin air and I am flying blind again. Nothing coheres because I am too stupid to understand that in the Ballardian universe fiction doesn't just predict reality, it doesn't even *shape* it. It invents it.'

Philip's face was devoid of emotion, although he took notes throughout.

'What is Ballard?' I continued. 'A serious novelist? A cult writer? A serial autobiographer? A con artist? A master fabulist weaving fake life stories into his fiction? What is he, if not his *Empire*-driven public image? I have no idea, but what I do know is that my narrative about Ballard will be just as fake as those he told the world about himself, since the meaning of Ballard, of his work, is as vaporous as the contrails of a wraith, and as soon as one attempts to fix a referent to it, even a biographical reality, it forks off into a million sub-paths, a million overlapping passageways.'

As I barrelled on, I felt as though I was acknowledging something to myself. In that moment, stepping outside the rules that governed my constricted situation, I was finally speaking for myself, effectively presenting my thesis for the very first time, more articulate than ever before, the words tumbling from me without needing to be forced or circumspectly manipulated.

'I have tried to make sense of my failure, tried to talk myself into believing that it is not my fault, that it is because any meaning or substance attributed to Ballard can only be experienced indirectly, in peripheral vision, like a trick of the light responding to an individual's unique mental bias. Thus provoked by the peculiar mechanics of his fiction, with its essential layers of undecidability, each reader is forced to interpret the text differently, resulting in as many Ballard clones, as many Ballardian worlds, as there are readers.

'I have come to view this phenomenon as a peculiar type of aftereffect, or more exactly a kind of hallucination born from over-interpretation of an unplaceable phenomenon, like a ghost story forged from the forced entry of "reality" material into a person's awareness. Sometimes, when people think they see ghosts or UFOs, what they really see are subliminal shards from the real world: a slim crack of light from a door ajar or the dull sodium glow of distant street lights. When glimpsed in peripheral vision, these shards form the shape of an entity, a ghost no less, with the power to trick the paranoiac's mind so that what they have seen assumes human or alien form. Yet when the witness looks at the phantasm head on it melts back into shadow and is re-absorbed into the noir-shade of everyday life. Ballard's writing is like that. It cannot be categorised, captured or explained and is so nebulous, so unstable and so undecidable it becomes everything and nothing.

'For years, I have lived with this shadowplay, this "ghost" effect, woven into my cortical grid in a kind of backbrain awareness. Once the pain and confusion of my earliest academic failures had subsided, the effect matured into a permanent overlay, acting like snug-fitting contact lenses that give natural vision to the short-sighted, a device for perceiving the world in a particular way—a *Ballardian* way—that brings certain detail into focus. It made sense of what Ballard has defined, via the proxy of his fiction, as the goal of his work: the exploration of "a far richer realm formed from the elements of light, time and space". But ever since I first attempted my blighted dissertation, I have not been able to articulate precisely why this obsession should have gripped me so. So snug was the lens I had forgotten its existence and this places me in an invidious position today, when, ten years after withdrawing my candidature, I find myself here before you now, forced to confront anew the spectre of Ballard, and the tormented ghost of my younger self, with the charge of explaining my self-imposed academic remit: no less the study of Ballard's work.

'Yet today, a decade on from that first moment of torment, I must admit something to myself: I cannot play the game of insincere objectivity the academy demands. Either I am unwilling or unable to, in which case the personal nature of my addiction must necessarily power the spiral grooves of the circular argument that has forced me to arrive at this point, which is rendered, in part, as a self-fulfilling attempt to explain Ballardian philosophy by examining the nature of fixation. But this obsession no longer derives solely from fandom, hagiography or auctorial aspiration—shamefully, when it comes to Ballard, I have inhabited all three—but from a renewed mania to solve the mystery of the internal dynamic of the man's work. Even the mental fug that led to this state advances the argument.'

I sat down on the edge of the stage, waves of ecstasy passing through me. I had been honest if nothing else.

The moderator spoke.

'Is that it?'

'That's it.'

'Aren't you going to explain this "circular argument"?'

'No, I don't think so. I've had it with you people.'

The moderator looked at me like I was something he'd dug out of his ear and walked away, muttering ominously under his breath. Anthony was on his phone, talking in low tones. He glanced up at me and stared hard, as if fixing my coordinates in time and space, before resuming his conversation.

Charles approached, shaking his head and laughing.

'Now I've heard everything. Well, good luck. You'll need it.'

As he left the auditorium, he bumped into Philip, who did not appreciate the intrusion. Philip stared Charles down until my former friend scurried away like a startled cockroach. Everyone else had left. It was just the two of us. Philip remained at the rear of the auditorium, staring at me with the shotgun intensity of a loan shark waiting to collect.

At length, he crooked his finger.

'Come here.'

I froze.

We've been through this before.

He walked slowly towards me. I ran off the stage, escaping through the back door.

I never set foot in Hartwell University again.

97

JAMES AND JIM

That night, I had a dream. I watched a photo come to life. It was taken in the early 70s. It exists. It is real. I found it online. I found everything online. Ballard and the great writer Jorge Luis Borges are sitting on a sofa, deep in conversation, their poses almost identical to the Ballard clones from the double exposure. On the left, elderly, half-blind Borges dispenses wisdom to the younger, portlier Ballard on the right, who relaxes with a glass of wine. With a flourish, Borges snaps his fingers, intending to send Ballard on his way, but instead it is Borges that fades from view, and as he does so he says, more in resignation than anything: 'Every writer creates his own predecessors. His work modifies our conception of the past, as it will modify the future.'

Despite Ballard's ascendancy, he knows Borges is right. After all, it was Borges, not Ballard, who first used the term 'condensed novels', describing his own super-compacted stories that had been stripped of padding and discursion (Borges argued that the heart of most novels should take only a few minutes to articulate, so why not reduce them to their essence?).

Ballard is deferential.

'The greatest short stories, by Borges,' he admits, 'are nuggets of pure gold that never lose their lustre.'

Eventually, Borges fades from view and a second Ballard replaces him. This is the Ballard that attracts all the attention. Now there are two. The first Ballard, the static one, remains behind in Shepperton, never moving beyond the town's boundaries, rooted to the spot at the wooden desk in the study in his house upon which a typewriter is perched, next to the window overlooking the overgrown, lush greenery of the back garden, across the way from the reproduction Delvaux painting hanging over the fireplace in the lounge room.

The static Ballard, Jim, knows of the other Ballard, James, and sees his name in reviews. When the day's work is done, Jim walks toward the end of his street, pausing to admire the arch of the motorway pedestrian bridge as it reaches for the green parkland below and the fog-shrouded haze of the reservoirs beyond. James, the dynamic Ballard, shares the other's taste for surrealism, fine Parker Pens, whisky and the work of Burroughs, although he assimilates them in a mechanical way, as if learning by rote.

Theirs is a benign, though odd relationship. James exists, and continues to exist, for the other to go free. Occasionally there is outright hostility, as when James recounts the story of their life and is believed above all. Jim's temper flares and then ebbs, for he knows that James justifies him, even after death, because, through James, Jim lives and will go on living, although the war over words and autobiographies is futile, and the life, finally, belongs to no one but language and the books in their jackets.

Dali knew that, spiritually, all art wastes away once its appearance is perfected, leaving behind only an intellectual process incapable of apprehending reality. Eventually, Jim surrenders to James, residing in him, not himself (if indeed he ever did exist independently), although he recognises himself less and less in the books and more in the telling or the act of construction.

Once, Jim tried to extricate himself, moving away from the early stories about time and memory to the existential horror of the suburbs, but all stories are the property of James now, leaving Jim free to conjure up whatever it is the dead can see. His life is a line of flight in which the spoils belong to James, or to a state of forgetting.

This dream belongs to neither, and never will it.

98

NEGATIVE SPACE

Consumed with the fatal pressure induced by my devalued academic standing and my all-consuming attraction to the edgelands, I accepted the inevitable and discontinued my candidature for the final time. The PhD would never be complete, and I knew I'd spend the rest of my life chasing its memory. Perversely, remaining incomplete and unfulfilled was the only way I knew how to define myself.

With no sessional teaching to fall back on, I commenced employment as a storeman at the Buyco wholesale warehouse in the Melbourne Docklands. Everything had come full circle, for the job was merely a continuation of the dull months I'd spent many years ago, heat-sealing ballpoint pens into plastic blister packs, back in the cavernous warehouses and suburban warzones of my early adult life. It was as if the intervening years—the stalled academic ambition, the disastrous romance, the failed travel writing career—belonged to a protracted and endlessly frustrating dream. There was no past, no future, just the frozen present.

Having said that, in some ways I was better off at Buyco. Not only did it pay more than sessional teaching, the employees didn't whisper in the corridors about stabbing each other in the back. Mostly, I couldn't see any difference at all between the two worlds. Both were symptoms of a fast-food culture, peddling pre-packaged goods and services. University students were like Buyco's 'revolving stock', where items on sale one day are replaced by others a few months later. You never see the earlier products again. They are never to be repeated. They exist purely to make money in the moment. But at least Buyco was honest about it.

At work, I kept to myself. My colleagues knew I'd started a

PhD because someone had found my Ballard blog. They called me 'Doc', teased me about *Crash*.

'Fucked any good cars lately?'

I think they suspected I thought I was better than them.

I did. I was.

I never ate lunch with them, never asked them about their kids or their football teams. I wasn't interested in human interaction until I started fighting with the customers. Physical stuff. Punches. I would always try to provoke the customers. I guess I was still waiting for reality to crumble. The Buyco environment had given me licence to finally release my most violent impulses.

I tried to turn the staff onto Ballard but they didn't get it. I told them *Kingdom Come* was the Buyco bible, but I may as well have been peddling Scientology for all they cared. There was serious trolley rage among the Buyco customers, precisely the kind of behaviour predicted by *Kingdom Come*. In any place pushing discount goods, you're going to see action. People jumping queues, shoving and pushing, getting right in each other's faces. At Buyco, it was worse than most and my barbaric attitude did absolutely nothing to help.

The architecture of the building was a negative space. There was no ornamentation in the design, which made customers paranoid and on edge because there was no escape from the surveillance cameras and the security guards. It was like the malevolent, fully exposed prison architecture in *Ghosts... of the Civil Dead*. No mystery or emotion in the building. Nowhere to hide. The naked functionalism of this consumerist shed was the true architecture of the age.

I never checked membership cards. Every day, people who weren't members would walk in and grab goods off the shelves, eating and drinking without paying before walking out. Then the security guards would step in, a disaster waiting to happen. I was always in the thick of it. One time, there was an all-in fight and ten guards had to sort it out. There was a big mob of customers all fighting in the Number 8 line. I jammed an elbow into one man's ribs when he wasn't looking. He was well built, and he just turned around and flattened someone else next to him who had nothing to do with it. Then it was *really* on: wives, husbands, children, dogs. Everyone fighting everyone else. It was hilarious. We had to call the cops, declare a warzone. There was blood on the concrete floors, the young man from the cafe had the webbing of his finger split to the tendon and a woman copped a broken nose from a full soup can to the face.

I started at Buyco while they were dismantling the 'Observation Wheel' next door, a shoddy, oversized Ferris wheel copied from the London Eye. It had structural cracks that made it unsafe, and I watched on my lunch breaks as it came down bit by bit. It was a cracked industrial totem and the shopping centre that sprang up around it was a failed consumerist utopia. Soon after they dismantled it, they rebuilt it, even though it hadn't worked the first time—not only did the metal crack, it had failed to attract the expected crowds even when it was briefly operational. But it just kept coming back. The wheel was zombie architecture: you couldn't kill it. Instead of building a grassroots community to attract people to the Docklands, they'd invested in an undead clone of a tourist attraction from the other side of the planet.

There was a forest of high-rise blocks in the area and I could sense all the people in all the residential cubes waiting for something to happen, facing off like warring tribes. What else was there to do? The old, vintage docks were dead. Long live the urban-regenerated Shocklands. Never mind zombie architecture, this was 'zombie urbanism', where urban life is killed off and reanimated under external control—a dead history woken from the grave and manipulated by witch doctors. The qualities that made the area vibrant in the past had been sucked out, formalised and re-injected into a distortion of its former self until the old way of life was remaindered. The old buildings that could have been salvaged were gutted, surviving in traces as a grotesquery. The vintage maritime culture was reduced to a row of high-rises designed to look like the prows of ships. The facades of plastic cafes and restaurants were decorated with fibreglass anchors, rope and sailor caps. The names of restaurants provided the final touches to copies of originals that never existed. Cap'n's Cafe. Steam Packet Restaurant. Mariners Tavern.

The new buildings were designed so close to each other, they formed hyperactive wind tunnels that repelled all street-level activity with constant motion and noise. The buildings faced away from the sun and the 'instant city' effect created cold, empty streets that went nowhere, with no organic relationship to the infrastructure, new or old.

The main human functions were spending and excretion. No one visited the area for anything but shopping, sleeping, abluting and copulating in airlocked apartments after work. It was pure Ballardian terrain, such as you might find in *Super-Cannes*, where 'a lack of intimacy and neighbourliness' is enabled by an 'invisible infrastructure that takes the place of traditional civic virtues'.

One day, the local councillor visited to address the workers and praise Buyco's economic miracle. I wanted to throw up. People were genuinely excited when Buyco opened, as if a new economic dawn had broken over the land. What we needed, though, was a version of London's infamous IKEA riot, when a new store was completely trashed on its opening as rabid consumers fought over the bargains. That would blow the cobwebs away. All it needed was a discount sale and a little provocation.

Then the inevitable happened: I mauled a customer. He was buying American rubbish over the better-made Australian versions and that bothered me, so I took a bag of coins from the till and smashed it in his face. The boss ran up, puffing his chest out as the customer spasmed on the floor in pain.

'You maniac!' the boss screamed. 'You can't do that. You just can't. That guy will sue! You can't fight with the customers. Absolutely out of line. Nobody fights customers in my place of business except me. If people want to buy American pens, well then that's democracy. Who cares? They're good pens, too! End of story!'

'Well, you don't have to worry about that. I've had it with you people. I'm quitting before someone gets killed.'

What I meant was: *I'm quitting before I kill you.*

I threw my apron to the ground, spat on it and walked out the door. For once in my life, the tough-guy act worked.

No one tried to stop me.

99

MOEBIUS STRIP

Soon after, I was convicted for the assault (obviously, since it was all on CCTV), although I managed to emerge with a suspended sentence (no doubt the prisons were full that day). Meanwhile, Philip, the idea of Philip, would not leave my mind. I could still picture him, the beautiful bastard, standing at the back of the auditorium, commanding me to follow. I had been too scared to do so then but with the passing of time, and since I'd become jobless, lost between worlds, I desperately wanted to see him again. Besides, with the sentence looming over me I had to keep moving, had to keep my mind busy and active before the walls closed in on me again. I wanted Philip to give me one more chance, for I knew I had something to prove. I couldn't let him go, not like I did Catherine and all the others who came before him—a parade of lost friends and lovers, their absences felt keenly with the intensity of death.

I phoned him and he answered casually, as if expecting my call.
'It's you.'

I spoke an incantation.

'Doncaster.'

Doncaster is the Melbourne suburb most enslaved to the car, with more vehicles per capita than any other, and I hoped the idea of travelling there would turn Philip on. It was the first time we'd been in contact for months and he acquiesced, although, true to form, he needed to put me in my place before we could begin. He summoned me to his apartment. When I arrived he gave me a lecture about how I should never have left his program of automotive therapy. I emerged twenty minutes later, remembering little else of his diatribe but clutching a marked-up map of where we were to meet: around the corner from my place, at a little-used children's playground. I wasn't sure why he'd chosen that location and didn't bother asking, for I was giddy with excitement. I was fulfilling my innate purpose after all, since my own deviant charisma was strong and Philip would be unable to resist exerting further control over me. My submissiveness was the only gift I had to offer.

Our assignation was scheduled for the following day, but in the morning he called to say he was running late. I didn't receive the call. My battery was dead. He tried a few more times before giving up and driving to Doncaster alone, where he proceeded to film the freeways solo, as well as the suburban McMansions and service stations that festooned the area like weeds.

When my battery recharged, I called him. He told me what had happened but I didn't believe him. I was furious and lost my temper, accusing him of 'hijacking the project'.

'What project?'

In his usual calm fashion, he ignored my outburst and said he would return to pick me up, but I'd overstepped the mark. I'd gone above my station and the consequences would be dire.

After completing what we had to do that day, I knew we would go our separate ways forever. Philip had set some kind of test for me, perhaps even a 'deep assignment', and I had fallen at the first hurdle.

The mission is important. It must be completed.

I walked to the children's playground. Behind the swing set, I noticed three tiny wooden effigies nestled among the tan bark and beyond them three shredded prams. One of the effigies had been struck down, its face flat to the ground. The other two were seated on a miniature swing and seesaw set, minuscule furniture that seemed a sinister mirror of the playground before me. My blood froze and the weird and dislocating deja vu that often came to me in dreams swamped my mind.

I knew I'd seen the figurines before, but where? I was on the verge of remembering when the association melted away into nothing, as all dream resonances eventually do, leaving me frustrated and alone, my memories hanging in a white void.

I felt hot breath on the back of my neck.

I turned around.

Philip.

His mouth was so close to my neck, it was if he wanted to bite my jugular vein. The proximity of his hard body to mine was intensely erotic, an electric residue of the power dynamic that had always bonded us. He pressed up against me, but I summoned every inch of my willpower to back away, pointing at the effigies.

'Where did you get these? What the devil are you playing at?'

He stared at me with cold, angry eyes. Without warning, he swiped my jaw with the back of his hand. I felt my teeth wobble. Then he did it again, across my ears and eyes, as hard as possible, almost breaking my nose. I spat out blood and a tooth. My eardrums reverberated as if a bomb had gone off.

'Shut your fucking hole,' he said. 'You talk too much, always have. Now, get in the van.'

I obeyed, scared out of my mind yet reluctantly aroused. We drove down the Eastern Freeway towards Doncaster. Philip's temperament was balanced on a knife's edge the entire journey, waiting for something to break. As we approached Ringwood, I was struck by the tall light cowlings embedded in the nature strip that bisected the dual carriageway. I blurted out a command, my raw excitement overriding my animal fear. I'd forgotten my place once again.

'Stop! Over there. Look.'

'I can't stop. We're on the freeway.'

'Then turn back. Pull in over *there*.'

I pointed to the lower-tier slip road on the side of the freeway, visible through wire mesh.

'Down there.'

Philip did as I asked but he was angry, unused to me giving the orders. He checked his phone as if waiting for instructions about whether to let me have my way or not. At the next exit we doubled back, left the freeway and parked on the slip road below. We emerged from the car and I could see the high embankment we'd driven past minutes before. The sound of constant traffic created a continuous din, a wall of sound as massive as the embankment itself.

Philip grew increasingly irritated.

'What now?' he said.

'Come with me.'

We scrambled up the embankment. There was a hole in the wire mesh. Through the hole, I pointed to the grass median strip dividing the inbound and outbound lanes.

'Over there. I need to get over there. I want to break the frame, to get outside of time. That patch of ground—it exists between worlds. It's a micronation. Something will happen over there.'

'No, I'm not following you. We'll be killed trying to get across.'

358

I saw a break in the traffic.

'Fine. See you later.'

As I darted across the outbound lane, I looked back to see Philip following, as I knew he would, his camera bag slung over his shoulder, for he could never resist a chance to film an unusual perspective on Melbourne's freeways.

We made it to the middle and stared at the endless ribbons of cars looping back and forth from the eastern suburbs into the city. I was exhilarated by a line of tall metal posts snaking into the heat-hazed background, each topped with high-powered sodium lamps. The street-light interference that had once plagued me was long forgotten. I was interested only in the symbolism of the lights now and felt excitement at the thought of being exposed to the limitless energy of the endless freeway—a massive feat of construction in an indeterminate zone where, I knew, in true Shoardian fashion, the rules governing human behaviour would cease to apply.

A white car peeled away from the ceaseless traffic. It drew closer, pulling onto the strip. A man emerged, dressed in a white nurse's uniform. He was massive, bulging with muscles, and seemed immensely angry with me. He looked right past Philip, pointing his finger at my forehead as if he wanted to pierce my brain.

'What the hell are you doing here?' he said. 'You know you're not allowed outside.'

I could've sworn that he and Philip exchanged a brief, mysterious look, freighted with mutual understanding yet so intimate I almost missed it. An unspoken communication had passed between them, but what? I put it out of mind. Obviously, I'd imagined it.

The man lowered his voice, still staring at me.

'*Get in the car. NOW.*'

Who was he? A roadside authority? But why was he dressed

like a *nurse*, and why so threatening? As he marched towards us, Philip whispered.

'See that hatch over there?'

He pointed to a hole in the middle of the median strip, which led to the parkland below. I could see the greenery beneath. It beckoned like an oasis.

'I'm leaving,' he said.

As the 'nurse' came nearer, Philip slid down the hatch on his back. Stunned into action, I jumped after him. I lost my balance and went flying, tumbling end over end and banging my head on the concrete drainage slab at the bottom. I heard Philip's voice way off in the distance, and I could just make out the out-line of his body as he moved towards me. He looked blurry and indistinct and I blacked out from the effort of trying to bring him into focus.

When I came to, he was gone.

100

EXPULSION

It was dusk. I tried to remember what had happened but drew a blank. I couldn't remember where we'd been. Somehow I stag-gered home to my apartment, just a few blocks down the road, although, judging by the freeway's location, I was sure that we had been in Collingwood, a full fifteen kilometres from where I lived in Reservoir. I crawled to the bathroom and looked in the mirror. I was appalled. My face was a bloody mess. My nose was smashed to the side like a Picasso painting, my left ear sliced almost in two, most of my upper front teeth sheared away.

Why did Philip leave me?

I entered the living room and collapsed onto the couch. The photo album was on the floor. I picked it up and sought solace in a photograph of Catherine that always left me short of breath. She looked so beautiful, her head tilted slightly to the side, a faint smile on her lips, wearing a look of startling intelligence that always thrilled me to the bone.

A newspaper clipping was affixed to the opposite page.

Man acquitted of manslaughter after horror smash
An East Melbourne man has been acquitted of dangerous driving causing the death of his former girlfriend after the defence counsel admitted he was intoxicated but denied he was culpable.

Inset into the story was a reproduction of the beautiful portrait I'd just been looking at. I was stunned, unbelieving. I'd never seen the clipping before. What sort of joke was this? A Photoshop prank hatched by Philip, placed in the album when I wasn't looking? It would be just his style, firing yet another shot in his endless psychic war.

I blinked and shook my head, attempting to swim back to reality's shore.

This can't be. Catherine flew back to Osaka after her family visit.

With great effort, I rose from the couch, my head throbbing from my injuries. I stumbled down the hallway to my bedroom. Was I dead? Dreaming? But I could detect none of the usual dream residues. I did not feel vertiginous, did not have the sense that I was inhabiting a fake reality. It all felt natural and normal, except that I could remember none of the backstory.

I dabbed at my wounds with a cloth. I felt sharp pain, my nerve endings screaming in agony as a flash of purple light overwhelmed my vision, flaring like a sun-spot expulsion.

This is familiar.

I've been here before.

The flash ebbed away, replaced by a strange scene, as if I was glimpsing a frame from a movie played at rapid speed. For a microsecond, I could see an empty medical bed in a doctor's surgery. I did not know where this 'memory', if that is what it was, had originated, any more than I did the newspaper clipping.

I collapsed onto the floor. I closed my eyelids slowly and felt the lids twitching, a maddening sensation more irritating than the extreme pain crawling across my broken face. I lapsed into sleep and a scene stitched into place, interlaced like video codecs resolving into coherency.

The medical bed, now occupied.

Catherine, reclining patiently, her face partially obscured by shadow.

Her body naked.

Me (an image of me) kneeling by the bed, shirtless, a large stainless steel needle in my hand.

Tenderly holding back the folds of her labia.

Lovingly pushing the needle in.

Piercing the skin.

Watching the blood flow.

101

BROKEN CIRCLE

I awoke the next morning, bewildered yet intensely eroticised by Catherine's long-delayed return to my dreamworld. I went to the bathroom and looked in the mirror. There was not a single scratch on my face. I kneaded it, testing for cracks and bruises. Nothing. I looked for the newspaper clipping but couldn't find it anywhere. Now what? Was I awake or in another dream nested within the first? Were there now three versions of me: the man awake, the man in the dream and the man in the nested dream? Three identical bodies moving in and out of phase, never in sync, a nebulous entity shifting at the edges.

I dragged myself back into the waking world by focusing on what I needed to do for the day, like an injured rock climber pulling up a sheer rock face, inch by painful inch, handhold by agonising handhold.

I have to teach.

I have to be at the university.

I have to start the car to get to the university.

Once at the university, I can look for the classroom.

Once inside the classroom, I can teach.

Once I've taught, I can go home.

Once I'm home, I can rest.

Once I've rested, I can forget everything.

That was enough for now, enough of a mental roadmap to keep me sane for the next few hours. All I had to do was follow each step in turn and wait for further instructions once the sequence was complete.

I pulled the car out of the driveway, still numb from the previous night's confusing mix of raw terror and carnal electricity.

What happened to Philip? Call him when you get the chance.

As I drove through Mullum Mullum, I caught a glimpse of my face in the rear-view mirror. The tunnel's interior lights bathed my face in alien hues, the shadows performing a trick of the light, somehow morphing my face into another man's. I was horrified to remember I'd suffered this phenomenon before, back in Kolonia. The recall triggered a series of painful memories. The airport UFO. The orange orbs. The street-light fugues. The phantom concussions and injuries. It was time to face facts. I had slipped irretrievably into madness and I knew I would never return to sanity if I didn't commit myself to treatment soon. Perhaps I'd already done so. I could have been anywhere at that point in time, anywhere dreaming that nasty dream. In a padded cell. In prison. In a fresh grave, buried alive, breathing my last.

As I drove, I cried hot tears, wondering if I would ever feel normal again. I needed help. A lobotomy. Death. A suicide solution. Anything to release me from the living hell that was my interior life.

Just remember the sequence.

Follow the map.

Find the university.

Look for the classroom.

Teach.

Go home.

Wake up.

Overpasses and concrete pylons flew by and feeder roads flowered into spaghetti junctions and intersections. High above, the semi-spherical cowlings of light fixtures skimmed the sky like flying saucers. After some time—days, weeks, months?—I merged with traffic at the Bolte Bridge and drove towards the southeastern suburbs. Cars were banked up towards the city. As the traffic moved forward, I pressed the accelerator and took off. The song 'Peacekeeper' came on the radio, returning me to the moment of my virtual death in Second Life. I snapped it off, horrified at the memory, taking my eyes from the road for a few seconds, just enough to break my concentration. The steering wheel juddered and I felt the car swerve towards the emergency apron as if it were autonomous. Ahead, a woman was walking along the apron towards the car. In those micro-seconds of fear and desperation, as I tried to avoid hitting her, I saw who it was.

Catherine.

She didn't conform to the image I carried around in my mind. Somehow, this was an older, middle-aged version—her hair was grey and short, her face fuller, worn and wise. I swung the steering wheel to miss her, forcing the car into the crash barrier. The vehicle came to a jarring halt, propelling me forward. My head smacked onto the steering wheel and the familiar purple flash engulfed my vision like a long-forgotten enemy. As I staggered from the car, I was stunned to find the road now utterly devoid of traffic, as if a metallic lake had been drained. I sank to my knees beside the vehicle, opening the passenger-side door to retrieve my phone. My briefcase and wallet fell to the ground in slow motion. I stroked a rip in my jacket, half expecting my fingers to probe further, right through my flesh. I touched the blood trickling down my forehead and looked around for Catherine, but I was alone.

I picked myself up and leaned against the crash barrier, fascinated by the frosted glass strewn about my feet from the car's smashed headlamp.

Death-born Aphrodite.

102

SLEEPY BRAIN

Woozy and lightheaded, I leaned backwards and lost my balance, toppling head first over the barrier. I somersaulted and landed on my stomach, sliding backwards down a steep grass incline. I came to rest in a parkland of some kind, terrain far removed from the concrete jungle I'd exited. The parkland was empty, preternaturally silent. It was perplexing. Was I remembering the first incident, when Philip and I were on the run from the male nurse? Or was that first incident a premonition of the moment I now found myself in?

I suffered a buzzing in my head, how I'd always imagined tinnitus would sound. It crackled and faded, like a radio being tuned in stormy weather. I could hear many overlapping, garbled voices, faint and slowed to a guttural growl, like degraded memory-tapes of inner space reused over and over for new recordings. Like EVP.

Gradually, one voice overwhelmed the rest until it became clear, coherent and pitched at a normal tempo.

'You have had an accident. You've suffered a blow to your head.'

The voice was Philip's. At least, I thought it was. I looked around for him.

'You have what we call a "sleepy brain". In other words, you've lost consciousness.'

The voice confounded me. The enunciation was more formal than Philip's, yet it was clearly him. I couldn't remember how I'd met him. I couldn't remember my own name, how old I was, where I came from. Fragmented memories surfaced, splinters in the mind, but they were too diffuse to hold much meaning.

A raucous party scene.

Disembodied, unformed faces.

My younger self taking a self-portrait in a mirror. Catherine in the reflection behind me, her hand stroking my cheek.

I remembered Ballard's mental Polaroids: 'A ghostly and alternative version of our own past.'

These dispatches from my subconscious were disturbing and unwanted, condemning me to inhabit a terrifying half-life, and I closed my eyes, trying to dislodge the satanic images from my brain. When I opened them, the woman from the freeway stood before me.

Old Catherine, my beloved visitor from the future.

I heard Philip's strangely clipped voice, narrating the movie playing in the cinema of my mind.

'Consciousness is like waking in a dream. We carry our mirrors around us, our filters, both on the outside and the inside. The ego, or consciousness, is like a film, and dreams are the playground of our existence, traumatic re-enactments of the primal seed.'

'Philip! Where are you? Stop this!'

The air suddenly became very cold, my breath forming condensation clouds. As Catherine walked towards me, she seemed to fade from view, as if she was superimposed onto the scenery, blurred around the edges.

I brushed the outline of her arm, reassured to be met with the sensation of touch. As with my own body just a few moments before, I'd expected my hand to pass right through the flesh.

'The brain likes recurrences,' the voice continued. 'It is drawn to mirrors. A survival mechanism: the brain anticipates patterns, and it projects anxieties and expectations onto our actions and perceptions.'

Another mental Polaroid: Catherine smiling, from long ago. *Young Catherine.*

'We are facing a catastrophe in our times, brought on by the multiplication of images, of mirrors. It is overload. Our society demands this of us. Images not only reflect, they become an all-encompassing world. You have stepped through the mirror and watched your double multiply.'

Catherine walked behind me. She stroked my face, echoing the self-portrait in the mirror from long ago, mimicking the image dredged up from my long-buried memory tapes.

'Because you are still concussed, you are not fully awake. Your brain has lost energy. It has lost power. Think of headlights dimming as a car battery drains. Until you are fully awake, until your brain is completely charged, normal activities and regular interactions will be hard to negotiate. Your sense of time may elongate or even stall. You may find you cannot fully recall key moments from your past.'

I placed my hand on Catherine's shoulder to steady her, to fix her in a state of permanence. The action of extending my arm seemed to take hours so I withdrew it. I stared at the lines in her face. As an older woman, she was more beautiful than ever.

Or rather, I watched myself do it. I was someone else. I was

the narrator, the voice, watching a pathetic lovelorn creature
trying to win back an indifferent lover.

EXT. PARKLAND—DAY.

Gentle drizzle pierces a film of autumn mist.
The man closes his eyes.
Focus pull as he opens them.
The woman is gone.
He panics.
Close on his agitated face as he lies on the ground.

A montage of anxiety.
He smokes a cigarette.
Bangs the ground.
Pulls his hair, slaps his face.
Sleeps.
Awakes.
Screams soundlessly.

Dissolve to another part of the landscape.
Wider: the man looking towards a creek.
The woman is there. She waits.
Pan beside him as he runs towards her.
Slow motion, then still frame.
The fabric of time vitrifies, freezing him in mid-stride.

And then the voice returned, external to me, as I knew it must.
  'You may lose balance and find yourself more uncoordinated
than before. If your vision is blurred, it may be that your brain
is having trouble processing sensory inputs. Give your brain a
break—help it do its job. Go slowly so that your brain can properly process everything it needs to, so that it can send the right

messages to the right parts of your body.'

I took a nervous, halting step towards her.

When I arrived by her side, she used the water from the creek to wipe the dried blood from my forehead, then she put her arm around my waist, drawing me close. She cradled my head and laid me down on the grass. I watched the sky, drifting into the world of sleep.

The voice varied its tone, trying a different tack, becoming more soft-spoken.

'*We are our psychic wounds. Take away the wounds and you take away the self.*'

My body was rigid, and I grew exhausted from the effort of focusing on secondary images of myself, from watching myself watching myself.

I yearned to rejoin my physical self, to stop drifting in and out of phase, and once I'd made that resolution the mental Polaroids stopped.

103

THE HUM

I awoke with a start. I was alone.

Where is she?

I looked at the embankment. I thought I could hear something, a buzz, a hum. It grew louder. I clasped my hands to my ears, crippled by the piercing sound.

The monologue returned in strong, low tones.

'When concussed, you may hear voices in your head. Don't worry about this. You're not crazy. The voices provide a safe haven until you are ready to emerge into full consciousness. But be warned. You may continue to hear them for a time after you have woken.'

I reached into my jacket pocket, locating the clipping.

'For example, you might be talking to your partner about an uncomfortable personal matter that is coming between you. Your internal voices may provide commentary on what your partner is saying. The commentary may even be unflattering about her. It may even give you guidance on how to deal with the situation. Think of the voices as your special friends, nursing you back to health during this dead time.'

As I reread the newsprint, absorbing what I'd supposedly done to the woman I loved, tears streamed down my face. I glimpsed Catherine further ahead. I was always playing catch-up to her. She had even reached middle age ahead of me, leaving me to wallow in the shallows of perpetual immaturity.

She looked over her shoulder, extending her hand. I caught up to her and clasped it in mine. We walked side by side to the freeway overpass, which was partially obscured by a hill. As more of the overpass was revealed the nearer we came, I backed away in fear, terrified at the looming sight.

'You may suffer from panic attacks. When you finally awaken, you will be moody and emotional. Your temper will be frayed and you will be on edge. But you can deal with this. Try using up all that excess energy you've stored by meditating or going for a long run.'

Catherine disengaged from me and ran towards the overpass. I followed her with trepidation, but then I picked up speed, terrified to see her pulling further away. She reached the grass incline and scrambled up, heading towards the freeway. At the summit, she ran towards the car and climbed into the front seat.

I moved gingerly towards her.

'But I can see I'm losing you,' the voice said. 'Let me play you some music. Let me try to bring your old self back to the surface. Tune into the signal. *You might recognise this.*'

The soundtrack faded in and out, ebbing and flowing with

the freeway's ambient sounds. When it became clearly audible, I realised it was the wire music of Alan Lamb. I looked towards the freeway. It was no longer empty but had restocked itself with peak-hour traffic, although the line of cars had slowed almost to a halt. Staring at the vehicles, I could have sworn I was looking at a still image, a 'freeway scene', if it wasn't for the almost imperceptible movement of fumes emanating from the exhaust pipe of a large truck. My heart had slowed down, too, synced to the traffic flow. If the traffic slowed any more, I'd drop dead on the spot.

'In normal circumstances, what you see and what you feel is transformed into memories instantaneously, if only on the subconscious level. However, after concussion, your short-term recall will suffer for a while because your sleepy brain is low on power. It needs more time to store your experiences as memories.'

Slowly, as more wire music could be heard, the motion of the cars sped up and bled into the frame, like a still shot giving way to moving film, leaving behind superimpositions, ghostly after-images and double-screen effects—until there was a clear, flowing stream of traffic once more.

I opened the door and leaned in, sweeping Catherine's hair from her face.

'Be prepared to forget intimate details, such as where you work, the whereabouts of your keys, your partner's phone number, even her name. Details will be incomplete. Memories will be half-formed or blank. But if you are prepared for this, the sensation should pass quickly with few side effects.'

We lingered in a kiss, the moment shattered when a car pulled up and a woman disembarked. She looked me up and down, her face contorted with concern. I wondered what the problem was, and then I understood. My head had been split wide open. I was losing a lot of blood.

The woman panicked.

'Oh my god! Are you okay?'

I looked towards the car, expecting to see Catherine, but the vehicle was empty. I knelt on the concrete verge. My credit card had fallen to the ground. I picked it up and stroked it gingerly. I saw my name on the card and touched the raised letters as if they were Braille.

I turned towards the woman, carefully mouthing the syllables of my name.

'...'

104

MEMORY HACKER

I awoke on a bed in a doctor's surgery, huddled in the corner, gripping a sheet tightly around my naked body. In the mirror beside the bed, I could see a tangle of wires trailing from pads arranged around my head wound. My back ached intensely and I rubbed my spine. The familiar trio of scars had become three fresh wounds covered with bloodied gauze. Four bright orange lights were inset into the ceiling, arranged in a quarter circle. The air was coated with a weird medley of stenches, a rotting-egg smell mixed with human sweat and a type of burnt-electrical odour. I wanted to vomit but could only dry retch, and I stared at the quarter circle of lights for so hard and so long that they seemed to move around and form different shapes. Crosses, triangles, squares.

I have been here before. I have always been here.

A man entered, wearing green surgical scrubs and carrying a set of bizarre scalpels and implements. They looked like a hybrid of human knuckle and metal, and the sight of them plunged me into a paroxysm of fear. I backed away even further, pressing up tight against the wall.

The surgeon spoke.

'Can you hear me? Don't be alarmed. You're awake now. Take your time. I've given you a sedative.'

The voice.

'Philip. Is that you?'

The faintest smile formed behind the surgeon's mask, rippling the fabric. He stroked my cheek with surprising tenderness, but I flinched and he took his hand away. I couldn't see his face, but I could sense his palpable disappointment at my rejection of his touch.

'We had to arrest the slide,' he said. 'You know how that works. You remember from the other times. The simulated concussion allows us to check your habit of contaminating your new reality. I know this is traumatic for you, but think of it as a way to slow you down. It's like rebooting the system. But we have to crash the system first. It's complicated. Every time we build something nice for you, you tear it down with your paranoia and lack of self-esteem and we have to shut down and begin again. Of course, your loved ones have brought you here. Like the vast majority of our patients, you yearn to escape from yourself. Nonetheless, I am going to go over the fundamentals again, since doubtless you will have forgotten and I want to put your mind completely at ease about the process.'

I sat up, clutching the sheet, trying to regain a shred of dignity. The surgeon was too talkative, as if his continual overexplaining was just a way of soothing me, yet it had the opposite effect. His merciless attempts to remap my scattered fragments onto the coordinates of a reasoned monologue induced only panic.

'Human memory is a vast continent that we are yet to explore in full, although we know a little more about how it works than yesterday. We used to think memory was like a tape recorder that accurately recorded sensory inputs. Now we know memory is in fact much more plastic, much more malleable, and can be erased and rewritten over and over by anyone with access to the neural circuits. Given your unhealthy penchant for viewing your life only in terms of movie references, I can guess what you're thinking. *Eternal Sunshine of the Spotless Mind*, right? But that is just a science fiction film, nothing more. This is reality.'

I could see an unmarked box on the desk behind him. Spilling from it was a blister pack of doves. The surgeon removed one and held it to the light.

'The technique is simple. Much of it is to do with the drugs we give you. They alter the plasticity in the hippocampus, the part of the brain that generates spatial awareness and long-term memory functions. Once that occurs, we can delete unwanted memories, change existing memories, invent brand new ones. If it helps, you can think of me as a "memory hacker".

'Now, when people imagine the past or future, they participate in a type of mental time travel. Humans are the only species that can do this. Mental time travel, or "chronesthesia", is located in the sensorimotor systems that allow humans to move about in time and space. We've found that our conceptions of space and time are interlocked. Each is dependent on the other. Movement is created by time.'

Even in my sedated state, a sliver of my old life managed to rise to the surface. Ballard and micronations. The sovereignty of the imagination. NSK and the State in Time.

Movement creates time.

'The contents of mental time travel unfold like the elements in a film. Our tests show that when people think about the past, present and future, specific areas in the brain are activated in different ways, playing out like narrative action on a movie screen. Once we could track this process, it made the past, in neurological terms, easier to edit and the future easier to manipulate. For example, when people experience severe trauma, their brains are imprinted with indelible, fearful memories that can ruin the rest of their lives. But by isolating the memory through chronesthetic analysis, we can locate specific activity—the moment of mental time travel, when the person reinhabits the memory—and effectively "pause" the memory, just like freeze-framing a film.

'We can then remove certain proteins from the part of the brain responsible for remembering fear, deleting painful memories forever. We can also implant a new, artificial memory by a combination of subliminal projection of the desired scenario and the injecting of an artificial protein that allows the projection to set. Of course, the way you subsequently imagine the future will be vastly different, because your past has been altered. We must therefore use the same technique to alter the chronesthetic future so that it conforms to your new reality.'

The surgeon selected a serrated scalpel from his leather pouch, placing it on the metal trolley next to the bed. A stubby antenna protruded from the knuckle-bone handle. A type of LED display was inset into the handle but I couldn't read it. It was not in any language I could recognise.

'Okay, are you happy with all that? Shall we try again? I will have to put you under, but please remember, when you wake up the process may not have stabilised and you may find you inhabit two realities at once. Really, two "memories" at once. That's because either a deleted memory is taking its time to fade from your mind or a new artificial memory is taking longer than expected to graft into place. Although we apologise for the imperfections of the technique, we can't control the side effects or even predict when they will happen. Sometimes it's over quickly, sometimes not. It all depends on the original memory being deleted or overwritten and how entrenched it is. It's like having a tattoo removed with laser surgery. You need multiple attempts to remove the unwanted image, there will be trace outlines of the image until the treatment is complete, and your skin will burn intensely until the image is erased—sometimes well after.'

The surgeon reached for a rubber hose, attached to some type of gleaming silver machine. He pressed a button and the hose discharged a fine mist that filled the room. My chest felt tight and I couldn't breathe. In the mirror I caught my wild eyes. They carried the unswerving resolve of a caged animal trying to avoid being experimented on. The surgeon continued, apparently unaware that his interminable monologue was impossible for me to absorb in my current state.

'Something else to note. With implanted memories, we have observed that in some patients there is such resistance to the graft that elements from the real world can bleed in and blend with the implant. For example, I myself might appear briefly in a new memory, in place of someone you were hoping to see, such as a close friend, or even as an entirely new "actor". We're not sure why this occurs. It could be a way for the mind to cushion the shock of waking into a new reality by recycling the reality materials closest to hand at that particular moment, such as the operating theatre and the people in it. You have not coped well with this aspect in past attempts, which is why we have to continually start over, but I want to again reassure you that it will eventually pass and everything will sync in phase.'

As he turned to gather the scalpel, I sprang from the bed and made a break for the door. He grabbed my arm, pulling me back into the room.

'Wait!'

He looked intensely annoyed.

'What are you doing? You know you're not allowed outside.'

I hesitated, chastened by his words. He drew nearer. His hot breath on my neck sent me into a delirium and I almost gave in, but I gathered my senses and punched him full in the stomach. He doubled over in pain, dropping the scalpel onto the floor.

I mimicked his patronising voice.

'You told me to use up energy.'

My hand hurt from the punch. I flexed it, trying to work off the pain, and could see every bone and vein under the skin, my hand glowing as if it'd been passed under an X-ray. I picked up the scalpel. The surgeon was on his knees. He raised his arm in surrender.

'Try not to exert yourself. You're in shock. Put down the blade. Can't you see none of this is real? *Look at your hand.*'

'That's not what you said before. *That is science fiction*, you said. *This is reality*. Remember? You did say that.'

I pretended to hand the instrument to him. He smiled gratefully, and as he motioned to take it I slashed the scalpel diagonally across one side of his face, then the other, writing an 'X' that tore his features apart like overripe fruit. He raised his hands to his face, blood spurting through his fingers. His mask fell away. Although his face was mangled, one eye hanging from its socket, I could just make out his identity.

Philip.

I stabbed him in the stomach and for the first time in years felt content, my mind clear and uncontaminated at last. Again, I imitated his avuncular tones.

'Hush. Don't be alarmed. There's nothing to fear.'

'Philip' toppled over in front of me, face down on the floor. He made an odd gurgling noise as I sat astride his back, jerking his hair towards me. Acting on primal instinct, I pounced on his exposed throat, its pure whiteness tripping me into an animal frenzy as I sawed away at it with the scalpel. I decapitated him after a good five minutes' hard labour. The scalpel's serrated edge made the job less smooth than I'd hoped, and the rough hacking motion dislodged the sheet from me. Naked and covered in blood, I cradled Philip's severed head in my hands, playfully ruffling his hair, half expecting the headless torso between my thighs to roll over and pull me to it in a loving embrace, for I had to admit, despite the atrocity I'd just committed, that I really missed him. Stalking the edgelands alone was never quite the same.

Something caught my eye. A photo on the wall: the surgeon posing with a colleague, both in scrubs. Underneath was an inscription:

PHILIP SANDERSON AND ROBERT COONEY. JOINT WINNERS: WALTER E. ALEXANDER 'SURGERY OF THE MIND' PRIZE. FACULTY OF NEUROINVASIVE PROCEDURES, CENTRE FOR CRYOGENICS, PLASTIC AND RECONSTRUCTIVE SURGERY, HARTWELL UNIVERSITY.

Incredibly, the colleague was that repulsive creature, Rob. There was no doubt about it. I could see his stupid bowl haircut poking out from under his cap like a mushroom cloud. The animal fear returned. My loathing for Rob returned. I sprang up and hustled down the surgery's white corridor, dropping Philip's head instinctively. The head made a 'thud' on the floor like a discarded watermelon. Meanwhile, the retinal imprint of the quarter-circle ceiling lights would not fade. I could still see the four blobs darting about my blurred vision as I bashed open the front door and tumbled outside.

Inevitably, the street was deserted.

'Help, please help. I'm in trouble.'

I sat down on the kerb, despondent. I gripped my head, a welcome change from holding Philip's, and felt the slimy imprint of his viscera on my fingers. I began to sob, then became aware of a presence before me. I looked up. It was Catherine. The middle-aged marque. She was wearing a crisp white nurse's uniform. In the dark night air, her outfit imparted a glow as shimmering as polar ice.

I stared into her eyes.

'Help me, please. I'm in trouble.'

She extended her hand. I took it and she pulled me to my feet. She wiped the surgeon's muck from my face and hands and we kissed lovingly and long. We returned to the surgery. As we passed through the doorway, we looked back out. Catherine snaked her arm around my waist and pointed to a flickering street light.

'Something will happen over there.'

As soon as the words left her mouth, the street light extinguished. Then she closed the door and locked it, sealing us from the outside world forever.

CODING SEQUENCE

In memoriam J.G. Ballard.

Vale Leonie Naughton, Claire Walsh and Mark Fisher.

Thank you to Christopher Brown, who named the theory and provided the sparks.

Thank you to Robin Mackay, who knew the mission was important and where to find the tripwires.

Thank you for ideas, inspiration and encouragement: Sophia Al-Maria, Mike Bonsall, Brendan C. Byrne, Melanie Chilianis, John Coulthart, Andrezj Gasiorek, Mike Holliday, Ken Hollings, Rory Hyde, Roger Luckhurst, Andrew Milner, Reza Negarestani, Anne Hilde Neset, Daniel New, Ashley Perry, Andy Sharp, David Southwell, Martin Thurnheer, Andrés Vaccari and Paul Williams.

Michael Anderson. *Logan's Run*, United Artists, 1976.

Marc Augé. *Non-places: Introduction to an Anthropology of Supermodernity* (*Non-Lieux, introduction à une anthropologie de la surmodernité*), Seuil, 1992.

Anonymous. 'J.G. Ballard: Live in London', *Sub Dee* 5, Summer 1997.

——'Ask J.G. Ballard transcript', BBC Live Chat, www.bbc.co.uk, 2002.

——'Australia's un-doing', *The Sydney Morning Herald*, 15 March 2005.

——'Cube Project Helmond', Mimoa, www.mimoa.eu, 2010.

——'Man "made gesture" before fatal brawl', *The Sydney Morning Herald*, 13 July 2010.

——'Ballardian', *Collins English Dictionary*, HarperCollins, 2012.

Peter C. Baker. 'Eric's world', *The National*, 1 May 2008.

J.G. Ballard. *The Drowned World*, Berkley Books, 1962.

——*The Crystal World*, Farrar, Straus and Giroux, 1966.

——*The Atrocity Exhibition*, RE/Search Publications, 1990 (1969).

——'Journey Across a Crater', *New Worlds* 198, February 1970.

——*Vermilion Sands*, Berkley Books, 1971.

——*Crash*, Jonathan Cape, 1973.

——'Introduction to the French edition of *Crash!*' (1974), *Foundation: The Review of Science Fiction* 9, November 1975.

——*Concrete Island*, Vintage, 1994 (1974).

——*High-Rise*, Jonathan Cape, 1975.

——*The Unlimited Dream Company*, Jonathan Cape, 1979.

——*Hello America*, Jonathan Cape, 1981.

——*Empire of the Sun*, Gollancz, 1984.

——*Running Wild*, Hutchinson, 1988.

——'Jane Fonda's Augmentation Mammoplasty', in Rudy Rucker, Peter Lamborn Wilson and Robert Anton Wilson (eds), *Semiotext(e) SF*, Autonomedia, 1989.

——*The Kindness of Women*, HarperCollins, 1991.

——'A Response to the Invitation to Respond', *Science Fiction Studies* 18:55, November 1991.

——*Rushing to Paradise*, Flamingo, 1994.

——*Cocaine Nights*, Flamingo, 1996.

——*A User's Guide to the Millennium: Essays and Reviews*, Flamingo, 1996.

——'J.G. Ballard's comments on his own fiction', *Interzone*, April 1996.

——'Airports', *The Observer*, 14 September 1997.

——*Super-Cannes*, Flamingo, 2000.

——*The Complete Short Stories*, Flamingo, 2001.

——*Millennium People*, Flamingo, 2003.

——'Look back at *Empire*', *The Guardian*, 4 March 2006.

——'A handful of dust', *The Guardian*, 20 March 2006.

——*Kingdom Come*, Fourth Estate, 2006.

——*Miracles of Life*, Fourth Estate, 2008.

Lynn Barber. 'Sci-Fi Seer', *Penthouse* 5:5, 1970.

John Perry Barlow. 'A Declaration for the Independence of Cyberspace', Electronic Frontier Foundation, 1996.

Lukas Barr. 'Don't Crash: Psychosis, Euthanasia, Apocalypse and Other Fun Ideas: An Interview with J.G. Ballard', *KGB*, 1995.

Jean Baudrillard. 'Ballard's *Crash*', *Science-Fiction Studies* 18:55, November 1991 (1976).

——*Seduction* (*De la séduction*), Éditions Galilée, 1979.

Jeannette Baxter. 'Age of unreason', *The Guardian*, 22 June 2004.

Kathryn Bigelow. *Strange Days*, 20th Century Fox, 1995.

John Birmingham. 'Peddling commuter anger', *The Sydney Morning Herald*, 25 October 2007.

Jorge Luis Borges. 'Kafka and His Precursors' ('Kafka y sus precursores'), *La Nación*, 19 August 1951.

Richard Box. *Field*, installation, 2004.

Claire Boylan. 'Provocative Pen: Clare Boylan on the strange world of J.G. Ballard', *The Guardian*, 5 September 1991.

Fiona Broome (ed.). *Mandela Effect: Alternate Memories, Alternate Realities*, mandelaeffect.com, 2010–current.

Mick Brown. 'Cult Classics Part Two: J.G. Ballard', BBC Radio 4, 1993.

Peter Brugger and Christine Mohr. 'Out of the body, but of mind', *Cortex* 45, 2009.

Alan Burns. 'The Imagination on Trial: J.G. Ballard' (1974), in Alan Burns and Charles Sugnet (eds), *The Imagination on Trial*, Allison and Busby, 1981.

William S. Burroughs. *Naked Lunch*, Olympia Press, 1959.
—— and Brion Gysin. *The Third Mind*. Viking Press, 1977.

James Cameron. *The Terminator*, Orion Pictures, 1984.

Ted Carnell. Introduction, 'The Waiting Grounds' (by J.G. Ballard), *New Worlds* 30:88, November 1959.

John Carpenter. *The Thing*, Universal Pictures, 1982.
—— *They Live*, Universal Pictures, 1988.

Harley Cokliss. *Crash!*, BBC, 1971.

Francis Ford Coppola. *Apocalypse Now*, United Artists, 1979.

Sofia Coppola. *Lost in Translation*, Focus Features, 2003.

Roger Corman. *X: The Man with the X-Ray Eyes*, American International Pictures, 1963.

David Cronenberg. *Crash*, Alliance Communications, 1996.
—— *eXistenZ*, Miramax Films, 1999.

Alfonso Cuarón. *Children of Men*, Universal Pictures, 2006.

Albert Camus. *The Stranger* (*L'Étranger*), Gallimard, 1942.

Jean-Paul Coillard. 'J.G. Ballard: Theatre of Cruelty', *Disturb*, 1996.

Jonathan Cott. 'The Strange Visions of J.G. Ballard', *Rolling Stone*, 19 November 1987.

Eda Cufer and Irwin. 'NSK State in Time', nskstate.com, 1993.

Salvador Dali. *The Persistence of Memory*, oil on canvas, 1931.

Dan Melchior's Broke Revue. 'Me and J.G. Ballard', *Bitterness, Rage, Spite and Scorn*, In the Red, 2002.

Graeme Davison. *The Unforgiving Minute: How Australians Learned to Tell the Time,* Oxford University Press, 1993.

——*Car Wars*, Allen & Unwin, 2004.

Sam de Brito. 'When pushie comes to shove', *The Age*, 11 September 2011.

Don DeLillo. *White Noise*, Viking Press, 1985.

Jonathan Demme. *Silence of the Lambs*, Orion Pictures, 1991.

John de Mol Jr. *Big Brother*, Endemol, 1999–2006.

James Der Derian. 'Future War: A Discussion with Paul Virilio', *virtually2k*, 1995.

Miranda Devine. 'When will they stop pedalling nonsense?', *The Daily Telegraph*, 18 January 2012.

Paul Di Filippo. 'Ballard's Anatomy: An Interview', *SF Eye*, 1991.

Doctor Champagne. 'Britain at Occult War: Folk Songs of the Near Future', English Heretic, http://englishheretic.blogspot.com.au, 18 August 2007.

Phillip Dodd. 'Marinaded in war and violence: Philip Dodd interviews J.G. Ballard', *Nightwaves*, BBC Radio 3, 2008.

Andrew Dominik. *Chopper*, First Look Pictures, 2000.

M.C. Escher. *Belevedere*, lithograph, 1958.

Fleetwood Mac. 'Peacekeeper', *Say You Will*, Reprise, 2003.

Thomas Frick. 'J.G. Ballard: The Art of Fiction', *The Paris Review* 94, Winter 1984.

Adam Gearey. 'The materiality of symbols: J.G. Ballard and jurisprudence: law, image, reproduction', in Michael Freeman (ed.), *Law and Popular Culture*, Oxford University Press, 2005.

William Gibson. *Pattern Recognition*, G.P. Putnam's Sons, 2003.

Michel Gondry. *Eternal Sunshine of the Spotless Mind*, Focus Features, 2004.

Kenneth Grant. 'Dreaming Out of Space', *Man, Myth and Magic* 84, 1970.

John Gray. 'Interview with J.G. Ballard', BBC Radio Four, 2000.

Val Guest. *When Dinosaurs Ruled the Earth*, Warner Bros, 1970.

Brendan Hennessy. 'J.G. Ballard Interviewed by Brendan Hennessy', *Transatlantic Review* 39, 1971.

John Hillcoat. *Ghosts... of the Civil Dead*, Outlaw Values, 1988.

Tobe Hooper. *The Texas Chainsaw Massacre*, Vortex, 1974.

Michel Houellebecq. *Atomised (Les Particules élémentaires)*, Flammarion, 1998.

——*Platform (Plateforme)*, Flammarion, 2001.

Andrew Hultkrans. 'Body Work: Andrew Hultkrans talks with J.G. Ballard and Director David Cronenberg', *Artforum*, March 1997.

Billy Idol. *Cyberpunk*, Chrysalis, 1993.

Mick Jackson. *Threads*, BBC, 1984.

Kraftwerk. 'Showroom Dummies', *Trans-Europe Express*, Kling Klang, 1977.

Stanley Kubrick. *2001: A Space Odyssey*, Metro-Goldwyn-Mayer, 1968.

——*A Clockwork Orange*, Warner Bros, 1971.

——*Eyes Wide Shut*, Warner Bros, 1999.

Alan Lamb. *Primal Image*, Dorobo, 1995.

Peter Linnett. 'J.G. Ballard: The *Corridor* Interview', *Corridor* 5, 1973.

Toby Litt. 'J.G. Ballard: Unedited Transcript', www.tobylitt.com, 10 July 2006.

Robert Longo. *Johnny Mnemonic*, TriStar Pictures, 1995.

Robert Louit. 'Crash & learn: J.G. Ballard on the auto-erotic', *Foundation: The Review of Science Fiction* 9, November 1975.

H.P. Lovecraft. 'Imprisoned with the Pharaohs', *Weird Tales*, May 1924.

——'The Call of Cthulhu', *Weird Tales*, February 1928.

Adrian Lowe. 'Rex Hunt found guilty of cyclist attack charge', *The Sydney Morning Herald*, 8 May 2009.

George MacBeth. 'The New Science Fiction', in Langdon Jones (ed.), *The New S.F.*, London, 1969.

Jim McLellan and Steve Beard. 'J.G. Ballard: Traveller in Hyper-Reality', *i-D* 53, 1987.

John McTiernan. *Predator*, 20th Century Fox, 1987.

Thomas Mann. *Death in Venice (Der Tod in Venedig)*, S. Fischer Verlag, 1912.

Chris Marker. *La Jetée*, Argos Films, 1962.

——*Sans Soleil*, Argos Films, 1983.

——*Stopover in Dubai*, gorgomancy.net, 2011.

Hendrik Willem Mesdag. *Panorama Mesdag*, oil on canvas, 1881.

Nicolas Meyer. *The Day After*, ABC Motion Pictures, 1983.

George Miller. *Mad Max*, Roadshow Entertainment, 1979.

Jeffery Mishlove and Brendan C. Engen. 'Archetypal Synchronistic Resonance: A New Theory of Paranormal Experience', *Journal of Humanistic Psychology* 47:2, April 2007.

D.M. Mitchell (ed.). *The Starry Wisdom: A Tribute to H.P. Lovecraft*, Creation Books, 1994.

Callum Morton. *Hotel*, installation, 2007.

——'About *Hotel*', *Eastlink Hotel: No Vacancies*, www.eastlinkhotel.com.au, 2007.

Scott Murray and Peter Beilby. 'George Miller: Director', *Cinema Papers*, May–June 1979.

Hans-Ulrich Obrist. 'Nothing is real, everything is fake: an interview with J.G. Ballard', *Beck's Futures*, Institute of Contemporary Arts, 2003.

Chris Petit and Iain Sinclair. *London Orbital*, FilmFour, 2002.

David Pringle. 'Memoirs for a Space Age', *Fear*, 1990.

——'The SFX Interview: J.G. Ballard', *SFX* 9, February 1996.

David Pringle and James Goddard. 'An Interview with JG Ballard', in James Goddard and David Pringle (eds), *J.G. Ballard: The First Twenty Years*, Bran's Head Books Ltd, 1976.

Natalie Puchalski. 'Magda Szubanski's anti-cyclist rant', *The Sydney Morning Herald*, 1 October 2009.

Anita Quigley. 'This disturbing cycle is just a critical mess', *The Daily Telegraph*, 24 November 2006.

Rembrandt. *The Anatomy Lesson of Dr Nicolaes Tulp*, oil on canvas, 1632.

Reuters Limited. 'Dying for Information? An Investigation into the Effects of Information Overload in Hong Kong and Worldwide', Reuters, 1996.

George A. Romero. *Dawn of the Dead*, United Film Distribution Company, 1978.

Peter Rønnov-Jessen. 'Against Entropy: Peter Rønnov-Jessen talks to J.G. Ballard', *The Literary Review*, August 1984.

Boris Sagal. *The Omega Man*, Warner Bros, 1971.

Ridley Scott. *Blade Runner*, Warner Bros, 1982.

W.G. Sebald. *The Rings of Saturn* (*Die Ringe des Saturn*), Eichborn, 1995.

Will Self. 'Conversations: J.G. Ballard', in *Junk Mail*, Bloomsbury Press, 1995.

Simon Sellars. '*The yes or no of the borderzone': J.G. Ballard's Affirmative Dystopias*, unpublished thesis, Monash University, 2008.

James Sey. 'Psychopathology, Inner Space and the Automotive Death Drive: J.G. Ballard', *South African Journal of Psychology* 32:2, June 2002.

Sebastian Shakespeare. 'JG Ballard Talks With Sebastian Shakespeare', *The Literary Review*, 2001.

Marion Shoard. 'Edgelands', in Jennifer Jenkins (ed.), *Remaking the Landscape*, Profile Books, 2002.

——'A Call to Arms', in Anna Jorgensen (ed.), *Urban Wildscapes*, University of Sheffield, 2008.

Alex Simon. 'Paul Verhoeven: Back in Black', *Venice Magazine*, April 2007.

Iain Sinclair. *Crash: David Cronenberg's Post-mortem on J.G. Ballard's 'Trajectory of Fate'*, British Film Institute, 1999.

——*London Orbital*, Granta, 2002.

Steven Spielberg. *Close Encounters of the Third Kind*, Columbia Pictures, 1977.

——*Empire of the Sun*, Warner Bros, 1987.

Jannick Storm. 'An Interview with JG Ballard', *Speculation* 21, February 1969.

Andrei Tarkovsky. *Solaris*, Mosfilm, 1972.

——*Stalker*, Mosfilm, 1979.

——*Time Within Time: The Diaries 1970–1986*, Seagull Books, 1991.

V. Vale (ed.). *J.G. Ballard: Conversations*, RE/Search Publications, 2005.
——and Andrea Juno (eds). *RE/Search #8/9: J.G. Ballard*, RE/
   Search Publications, 1984.
——and Mike Ryan (eds). *J.G. Ballard: Quotes*, RE/Search Publications, 2004.

The Velvet Underground. 'Venus in Furs', *The Velvet Underground &
   Nico*, Verve, 1967.

Paul Verhoeven. *Robocop*, Orion Pictures, 1987.
——*Total Recall*, TriStar Pictures, 1990.
——*Starship Troopers*, Buena Vista Pictures, 1997.

Johannes Vermeer. *Girl with a Pearl Earring*, oil on canvas, 1665.

Paul Virilio. *Bunker Archaeology (Bunker archéologie)*, Centre Georges
   Pompidou, 1975.
——*The Vision Machine*, Indiana University Press, 1994.
——*The Virilio Reader* (James Der Derian, ed.), Blackwell, 1998.
——*Politics of the Very Worst*, Semiotext(e), 1999.

Leopold Von Sacher Masoch. *Venus in Furs (Venus im Pelz)*, 1870.

The Wachowskis. *The Matrix*, Warner Bros, 1999.

Martin Wainwright. 'Major Roy Bates obituary', *The Guardian*, 12
   October 2012.

Alexander Walker. 'A movie beyond the bounds of depravity', *Evening
   Standard*, 3 June 1996.

Peter Watkins. *The War Game*, BBC, 1965.

Paul Williams. *Majlis al Jinn (Meeting Place of the Jinn)*, vimeo.com,
   2010.

Louise Wilson. 'Cyberwar, God and Television: Interview with Paul
   Virilio', *CTheory*, ctheory.net, 1 December 1994.

Simon Winchester. *The Pacific*, Hutchinson, 1991.

David Winner. *Brilliant Orange: The Neurotic Genius of Dutch Football*,
   Bloomsbury, 2000.

Zinovy Zinik. 'Russia On My Mind' (1998), *The London Magazine: A
   Review of Literature and the Arts*, February/March 2003.